Death Seeks You Out

Death Seeks You Out
(A Mike Cannon jumps racing mystery)

Eric Horridge

Death Seeks You Out

Copyright © 2024 by Eric Horridge

All rights reserved.

Front Cover Design: Michael Horridge

Book design by Eric Horridge

No part of this book may be reproduced in any form or by any electronic or mechanical means including information storage and retrieval systems, without permission in writing from the author. The only exception is by a reviewer, who may quote short excerpts in a review.

This book is a work of fiction. Names, characters, places, and incidents either are products of the author's imagination or are used fictitiously. Any resemblance to actual persons, living or dead, events, or locales is entirely coincidental.

Eric Horridge

DEDICATION

This book is dedicated to all my friends wherever you are in the world.

Death Seeks You Out

Death Seeks You Out

Prologue

It had been a long day. The kids had enjoyed catching up with cousins and friends, while the adults had taken full advantage of the family get together. With the exception of Uncle Frank, who always seemed to be obnoxious at such events, most of those over voting age had been well behaved. Nathan took a quick look into the mirror, glancing to check on the children who were fast asleep on the back seat of the car. The drive through the Peak District, the southern end of the Pennines was always a challenge, especially at night and more so with the strong winds and slashing rain that they were currently negotiating. The trip back to Hasland just south of Chesterfield from Warrington would normally take a few minutes short of two hours, but travelling at the speed they were, it would take them much longer. Tracy let out a hiss, leaning forward to rub her hand against the windscreen, trying and failing to improve her view of the road. The headlights of the car illuminated the twisted serpent ahead of them. Water rushed across the road from their right, falling away down the embankment and swishing against the underside of the car as it was swept away into the dark of the night. She had begged him to slow down some time ago and thankfully he had complied.

"We should have stayed until tomorrow," she said, knowing that it was a sensible statement but one that was of little use now. Nathan didn't reply immediately, he was concentrating on where the eyes of the car were pointing their beams. Having left behind civilization at Chapel-en-le-Frith they had been diverted, due to an accident that had closed the A623, their usual route, and onto the Castleton road which would take them over Winnats Pass, just south of the Blue John Mines. Fortunately, the road was quiet, but that was of little comfort. The long narrow straights hemmed in by the stone walls were followed by sudden sharp twists and turns along Rushup Edge that sucked the light from the headlights. This made Tracy more uncomfortable. She held onto the seat belt that rested across her chest with her right hand, her left gripping the hand rest on her door. Occasionally the light of a desolate farmhouse could be spotted in the distance. A glimpse of life in an inhospitable landscape. Nathan tried to lighten the mood, despite feeling somewhat uncomfortable himself.

"We should be passing the turn off to the Blue John cavern shortly," he said. "It's only forty-five minutes from there to home."

Tracy tried to smile. She remained nervous, silently praying that the next three quarters of an hour would pass quickly. Twenty-five miles didn't seem far but in the conditions time seemed to stand still and the distance to go seemed infinite. Nathan peered through the gloom, noticing a mist rise up from his left, slowly creeping across the road ahead of them, engulfing everything in its path, a tsunami of moisture. He began to slow the car even further, reducing his speed to twenty miles per hour. "I can't see a bloody thing," he complained, "this mist is…."

As he spoke, he felt the car jump as his right front wheel hit something in the road, then his back wheel did the same. The car skidded slightly as the tyres bit the bitumen again, the wheels slamming down after riding over the obstacle that had been lying unseen in their path. Tracy screamed as Nathan fought the elements, the rain and mist, the slippery road and the twisting, sliding car.

"Hang on," he shouted as he stood on the brake and the clutch, wrestling with the steering wheel as it bucked in his hands, before he finally brought the car to a stop, inches from a stone wall that seemed to appear out of nowhere, ready to smash against Tracy's side of the vehicle.

"Are you okay?" Nathan asked, reaching across to his wife, who seemed almost catatonic. He noticed that she was shaking. The light from the car's headlights reflected back from the mist that covered the road. It speared through the windscreen and the drizzle that dripped and fell in long rivers from the top of the glass to the bottom, disappearing into the tray beneath the car's bonnet.

Tracy nodded, her head barely moving, her eyes closed and her face set in a mixed state of fear and relief. Nathan turned to look at the children in the back seat. Both seemed to have barely flinched. Samuel, the eldest at eight, moved slightly, his eyes flickering as if he was dreaming. His chest rose gently which sent a spasm of comfort throughout his father. Gillian, two years younger lay with her head against the back seat arm rest. She seemed to be curled up, the seat belt around her body slightly twisted, but again she was unharmed and sleeping soundly.

"I'd better see what we hit," Nathan said, looking back at his wife. "It could be a sheep or something."

Tracy stared at him, then pointed at the rain that continued to find its way through the curtain of mist. She tried to see through the car's beam of light that was supposed to pierce the gloom ahead of them but was failing miserably.

"You'll get soaked if you go out there," she said.

"I know, but I have no choice. Besides, I need to check if there is any damage to the car. Whatever we hit was big enough to take out the exhaust pipe, not to mention damage the bodywork."

Tracy knew that he was right. As Nathan opened his door, struggling to climb out as the wind whipped against his side of the car, pushing hard against the door panel, his foot landed in a pool of water that had formed in a small pothole on the road. "Shit!" he said, as the cold water covered his shoe and invaded his sock. The sensation sent a shiver up Nathan's spine. With the help of the breeze, he slammed the car door and tried to pull his jacket over his head in an attempt to keep his face dry. As he did so he noticed through the window that Tracy had her mobile phone in her hand. What he found out later was that she had no signal despite them being just a few miles from the village of Castleton. Nathan looked at the side of his car. There was no damage that he could see. He bent down briefly to check underneath the car and was pleased to see that the exhaust of his Honda Civic was still intact. At least it seemed that way. There was nothing dragging on the ground or obviously out of place. Happy that the car was none the worse for wear, he peered back along the road. The red taillights of his car offered an eerie view. He peered into the darkness and through the mist and rain was able to make out a bulk that was lying in shadow on the road. It was about twenty yards or so away from where he was standing. He couldn't make out what it was, it was just a mass. His first thought was that it was likely to be a sheep, given the farmlands that crisscrossed the area, and the number of animals he had seen each time they had driven across the Pennines. He also knew that it was unlikely to be a cow as the impact would have been much worse. He had once seen on TV the damage a cow had done to a car that had hit it head-on. No one in the car had survived the crash and the car itself had crumpled as if it had run into a brick wall. Looking up the road to check if anything was coming and seeing nothing but mist, he slowly made his way in the opposite direction toward the bulk lying in the road. As he got closer he heard Tracy open her door and call to him. With his back to her as he approached the bulk on the ground, he waved an acknowledgement, but his focus was on the carcass of a horse that lay in the middle of the road. At least that is what he thought it was. The body of the animal lay on its side with its back to him. All four legs stood out from the trunk like cramping fingers on a hand, straight as dies. There were tyre tracks over the rump of the carcass. Nathan guessed that they were where his own car had bumped over the poor animal. He heard Tracy call him again but despite a quick glance back to his car, he couldn't see her, noticing something that disturbed him, something that he hadn't seen originally due to the shadow in which the animal lay. The head of the horse was missing. It had been severed from the rest of the body halfway along the neck, about eighteen inches above the shoulder. Nathan looked around. Was it possible that his car had created so much damage? He didn't believe it was likely. He walked to the other side of the body and into the shadows, the car's red lights unable to penetrate the darkness. Nathan's eyes were adjusting to the poor light and as he stepped around the animal he noticed its stomach had been torn open, and the entrails and other internal organs were splashed across the road. Nathan gagged slightly. He had seen roadkill many times, particularly of cats and dogs, but never anything of this size. He stared for a second unable to comprehend what could have caused such a sight, then he heard Tracy call his name in a panic. He looked up to see where she was. He couldn't see her near the car, then noticed the torchlight from her phone a few yards to the right, on the opposite side of the road from where the beams of the car headlights still shone. She called his name again, this time with more urgency. His face now dripping with rain and his clothes soaked, he ran towards where she was standing. As he got within five yards of her, he saw where she was pointing her torch. A spot just off the road, at the base of the stonewall, partially hidden in the weeds that grew and flourished in the dampness of the hills. There pressed down in a small and narrow ditch was a smallish man. It was difficult to guess the man's age but he certainly didn't seem more than in his thirties. The eyes were open as was his mouth but it was obvious that he was dead. The face was set in a grotesque mask of agony. Dressed in casual clothes of jeans, and a checked shirt yet barefoot, with hands and feet bound with wire it seemed to Nathan that the poor man had been tortured. Blisters on the face and feet, still puffy with fluid suggested that they were recent. Nathan grabbed the phone from Tracy, encouraging her back to the car. Once they were both inside he slammed the car into gear and drove as quickly as he could until they found mobile reception and dialled '999'.

CHAPTER 1

"I never thought I'd be praying for rain," Rich Telside said, "but with the drought during the summer and the few showers we've had over recent weeks, it's really playing havoc with the grass. These low clouds are doing nothing to put moisture back into the ground. If things don't improve soon, we may have a few issues."

Mike Cannon turned to look at his friend, his assistant, slowly lowering the binoculars that he held to his face, releasing them and letting their weight be carried by the strap that was slung around the back of his neck. The two men stood beside each other, their backs against the side of the Land Rover Defender that Cannon had purchased just over a year prior. The vehicle had been a workhorse already, clocking up nearly twenty thousand miles in such a short period of time. It had been used to transport Mike and his partner, now wife, Michelle, all the way up to Scotland for their honeymoon in May; to get Rich to hospital when he suddenly became ill and needed an urgent heart bypass operation a month later, through to Cannon collecting his vet in the middle of the night when the latter had broken down on his way to Cannon's stables to treat a horse suffering from severe colic. The constant chalking up of miles added to all the travelling they had done during the previous season whenever Cannon had runners at the many racecourses throughout the country.

Standing as they were in the early morning chill of late October, the rolling downs stretched out before them. They were a short distance away from Cannon's stables located just outside the small town of Stonesfield, in rural Oxfordshire. The two men had been watching the second lot of horses in Cannon's care, eight of them, go through their paces. The sun was watery, having risen above the horizon an hour ago, but its rays seemed unable to penetrate the low mist that blocked out the sky. The grey cloud higher up seemed to hang around like a cold sheet, stopping what little warmth that could be drawn from the sun from reaching the ground. The mist, called Radiation Fog by the Meteorological office gurus wasn't thick but it was a nuisance to the two men. The swirls of grey limited their ability at times to follow the progress of some of their horses as they and their riders charged through the gloom, each undertaking specific exercises mapped out for them by Cannon and relayed in turn by Telside to the riders.

"You're right," Cannon said, "the ground is a bit too hard for my liking, Rich. We need to be careful with a few of these." He nodded towards the left from where the sound of thudding hooves could be heard. A ghostly silhouette gradually took on its real shape as it slipped out of the grip of invisibility that the mist caused. The two men could not see anything unless it was within a hundred yards of them. To the casual observer the animal that came into view appeared to be riderless. The jockey on its back was tucked in, hands holding the reins tightly and heels remaining hard against the horse's flanks. The rider's body was bent low to maintain the best aerodynamic posture, their head almost lying on the long, graceful neck of the equine athlete. Cannon and Telside watched as the horse passed them, before disappearing once more into the mist, the sound of the animal snorting and hooves thundering slowly softening as the horse and rider slipped away to their right.

"I'm not sure how she does it," Cannon said, "but she's a natural if ever I saw one."

Telside smiled, "Aye, we were very lucky to find her, Mike."

He was referring to Cannon's first ever apprentice, known as a 'Conditional' jockey in jumps racing. Her name was Angela Fryer, the rider on the horse that had just been engulfed by the swirling mist. Cannon turned in the direction of the retreating sound his thoughts tinged with sadness. He had made a commitment to himself to help a young person who wanted to get into the racing game, and specifically jumps racing. He had done so in memory of another young rider who had been killed very close to the spot where they were now standing. A horse being skilled that fateful day fell at one the four 'chase fences currently lost in the mist. Thank God that today they were only exercising the horses, not schooling them over the jumps. With the poor visibility it would be foolish and way too dangerous to even attempt to clear them. Cannon had been devastated at the tragic accident that had ended a young jockey's life and had vowed that the boy's life would not be forgotten. He had established a foundation and with it a small stipend that the eventual candidate they chose would receive, in addition to their apprentice wages and any prize money that they won during a season. The latter, the prize money, was to be placed into a trust on behalf of the relevant individual who would receive it once their apprenticeship was completed. The amounts earned through winning races were not particularly large but anyone who got involved in wanting to ride racehorses did it predominantly for the love of the sport, not the money. Very few jump jockeys became wealthy from riding, likewise horse trainers. In time a successful jockey could climb the ladder, getting better rides and winning bigger races, but apprentices at the start of their career were only learning the ropes, and for that they were basically paid a pittance. Cannon knew that it must be tough for anyone starting in the game and he did what he could to help those that worked for him. Sometimes he lost staff to other trainers in the region and at other times those that had left him would return. The problem he had was the same as the bigger stables like those situated in the Lambourn area where so many horses were being schooled. The local stock of staff moved around frequently. Some seeking change, some leaving the sport altogether and others on a merry-go-round of work options. Fortunately, Angela was indentured to him for some time yet. She had been with him for just over 18 months now and had ridden a number of winners in her first year which had been a blessing for Cannon. Keeping up the number of successes and placings per runner for the stable had ensured that his owners had predominantly stood by him, even throughout the Covid-19 pandemic. During the busiest period of the previous season, from October through to April, Cannon and his team had won forty-six races, thirteen of which had been under the hands of Angela. She had also ridden winners for other trainers during the 'off-season' taking her total for her first full year to 24, and already losing her 7lb claim. She was now only able to offer a 5lb weight reduction on her mounts, until she reached the milestone of 50 career wins. Given she was only nineteen years old, she would very likely lose her claim as a conditional jockey entirely, well before the cut-off age of twenty-six. If she carried on the way she had started she would become a sought-after Professional jockey in just a few years' time. Cannon sighed, taking a few seconds to gather his thoughts. He had a few other matters on his mind and several hard questions he needed to ask, but now was not the time. He would talk with Rich when he was better placed and had thought through all the implications.

"Are you alright, Mike?" Telside said, hearing his boss' exhalation as another of their horses galloped by before retreating once more into the mist that was beginning to show promising signs of dissipating. Cannon turned towards his friend. Telside noted that his boss' face seemed pained, worsened by being blotched blue and red from the cold. Despite the stubble still on the chin his cheeks seemed to glow like the skins of a polished apple. Cannon had always been able to live with the cold but was conscious that it did affect him at times, especially when on the heath for extended periods. In his former life as a Detective Inspector, he had spent many an hour on stakeouts. Sometimes sitting in a car or a van, and other times standing out in the weather, hopping from one foot to another, waiting for something to happen. At least that problem was long gone now and so would his need to stay out in the morning gloom for much longer. He could hear the last of the string of horses heading in their direction, finally passing them just thirty feet away, before again, like the others, merging into the lingering but slowly lifting fog.

"Oh, it's nothing, Rich," Cannon responded eventually, his mind unsettled with the subject he needed to address as soon as he possibly could.

"Are you sure? You seem to be a little distracted. Didn't you see the action of Cabin Fever? She seemed to be favouring something," Telside stated. Despite his advancing years he was still extremely observant of most things when it came to the horses under their care. Their moods, the way they walked, jogged, ran, ate, slept, and particularly their courage.

"Yes, yes, I'm okay," Cannon lied, "I just remembered a couple of things that I need to check when I get back to the stables. Some unfinished paperwork that I left on my desk."

Telside stared at Cannon, his eyes narrowing slightly, but he said nothing. He knew how meticulous Cannon was when it came to nominations and acceptances for races, and how well the stables were run. To an outsider the place would have seemed like a military operation, such was the routine. Training times, feed times, feed type per horse, normal vet appointments, the tackle used, and even owner visits were regular and well organized. Things generally ran like clockwork, though it had not always been the case. Cannon and Telside had worked hard and despite a few errors made along the way they had built up a mutual respect over the years such that their relationship was now an extremely close friendship. Cannon had relied on his assistant far more than one would usually expect of a colleague or an employee; the two of them acting like family members at times, almost father and son. Sometimes they knew the other's thoughts before a word was ever spoken between them. Cannon being vague in his response was particularly unusual. Telside wondered if there was anything on a personal level that could be pointed to that may have been occupying Cannon's mind. There was nothing obvious, and anyway, he was sure that Cannon would have mentioned it to him if there was. He briefly considered if there had been any recent signs of financial stress that the business may be under, before again discounting the notion as unlikely. When it came to managing the financial affairs of the stables, that was also extremely well organized. That area of the business was managed by a local firm, Plumberry Accounting, in Sanders Gate, just a few minutes' drive away from where they were standing. Telside had not seen anything obvious in recent times that one would have garnered suspicion from. Staff wages, suppliers, equipment and tack purchased recently had all been paid for without interruption, even during the challenges of Covid-19. So, whatever was on Cannon's mind must be something very different from the norm, Telside concluded, deciding to keep his thoughts to himself.

The sound of horses neighing, whinnying and sneezing, broke the silence that surrounded the two men just as a brief hole was torn in the whiteness that seemed to swirl like angry wraiths around them before suddenly lifting skywards as if the ghosts had decided to find another place to haunt. Cannon pushed himself away from the side of the vehicle, sauntering slowly towards the first set of four thoroughbreds that walked abreast of each other, twenty yards to the right of the Land Rover, halting before him in a perfect line. Telside just a few steps behind looked at the scene in front of him. The horses and riders were silhouetted against a backdrop of the residual and lingering mist from which they had appeared; an image similar to those from a spaghetti western of the 1970's.

Stopping a few feet in front of the quartet, Cannon waited, the sound of the other four horses in the lot getting closer and louder as they also emerged from the mist to stand in another perfect line, twenty feet behind the first group. Cannon wanted to hear from each rider, asking how they felt their individual mounts had worked, specifically the view of the rider of Cabin Fever. If Rich was correct, then the plans for the horse that he had already mapped out for the coming few months would need to be put on hold at best and scrapped at worst. Any horse with an injury, be it simple lameness or something more significant was of concern. The welfare of the animals was paramount, and it was a trait that Cannon was known for by his peers and by his owners; a trait that Telside had instilled in Cannon when the ex-policeman first began learning the ropes and had sought out his now best friend, for guidance, mentorship and ongoing support. Any owner that wanted their injured or unsound horse to race for gain only, was quickly told by Cannon to move on; to take their business elsewhere. Cannon believed in the sport, but not at any cost, even to his own financial detriment at times. He would rather lose a client than lose a horse to a permanent injury or worse, a death, just because of a greedy or uncaring owner. Fortunately, the issue had not been a significant one over the journey, however on the odd occasion that it did happen, he tried to ensure that whoever was going to carry on training that animal had all the facts about the horse's welfare and any treatments used or undertaken while in his stables. The British Horseracing Authority (BHA) and other stakeholders in the industry had protocols about animal welfare and whole of life care. However, despite these measures and the ongoing work to ensure a racehorse was able to live its 'best life' not all trainers were as diligent nor as caring as others. Some saw owners as a bank and the horse as the key to the vault. It was those trainers that allowed horses to race while injured that gave the sport an unsavoury reputation in some quarters. Fortunately, since the introduction and oversight of a whole of life horse welfare strategy some years prior, the industry had lost many of the miscreants who had sullied the sports name, and despite what some protesters said, animal health and wellbeing had improved substantially.

"How did he go?" Cannon said, pointing to a rider with thin red edging around his riding cap?

"He went super, boss," the jockey replied, slowly tapping the horse's midriff with his size 6 boots to keep the horse still. Steam surrounded the animal as it jig-jogged occasionally where it stood, the effects of its exertions merging with the remaining whiteness of the day. Having enjoyed the workout, the horse was ready for further feeding and some good grooming. Cannon liked to ensure that his charges had something small to eat before taking them out for exercise but was also very careful not to over feed them. Horses' guts were sensitive and the last thing one needed was an animal with ulcers or colic. Despite being careful it did happen, but fortunately for the stable, only infrequently. Each horse was different, and Cannon was particularly hopeful that this one would remain healthy during the coming winter months. "He's in for a good season, Sir," the rider continued. Cannon smiled for the first time that morning, walking up to the horse, a six-year-old, pure grey, aptly named White Noise, and he patted the animal's neck. His plan was to aim the horse at the Champion Hurdle the following March, at Cheltenham. The race, a Grade 1 event run just over 2 miles and eight hurdles, was the last leg of the hurdling Triple Crown. There was no expectation of White Noise winning the race, but it was a prestigious event, and the prize money was good even down to the lower placings. In addition, it would continue to help grow Cannon's brand. By the end of the Covid pandemic a number of trainers had shut-up shop and moved on. Accordingly with a few good horses, and some luck, there was the potential for his stable to re-establish itself as a small but respected operation that produced great athletes and punched above its weight when compared to the giants of the business, those who had multi-millionaire backers and were regularly sent the best horses.

"Good boy," Cannon repeated several times, before dropping onto his haunches and feeling the horse's legs. There was no heat in them; everything felt as it should. Cannon stood, looked at the horse's rider, Samuel Simmons, and nodded. "Good work, Sam," he said, making a mental note of the confidence the jockey felt about the horse. Cannon, like most other trainers, relied on the feedback of the work riders who did the hard yards of taking a horse to exercise, day in and day out, irrespective of the weather, come hail, rain or shine! They were the backbone of the industry. Without them there would be no racing. Repeating the process with each of the other seven jockeys, Cannon eventually had all the information he needed, concluding that Telside was right in his observations about Cabin Fever and that the horse would need to be put onto a rehab program. The stable vet, Peter Lightman, would be able to determine the best course of action along with Cannon, and once concluded they would discuss it with the horse's owners. It was a pity as the gelding had a talent for steeplechasing but unfortunately seemed to be injury prone. As an eleven-year-old former flat racing horse, he had won six races during his career under NH rules, but that had been during a very truncated period, often interrupted by injury. A career of thirteen starts in just less than four years over 'chase fences during which time he didn't race for almost twenty-two months.

"I'll see you back at the house Rich," Cannon said finally, as he jumped into the warmth of his vehicle, quickly starting the engine. "Pop in when you're able. There are a couple of things I need to talk with you about," he added.

Telside responded with a thin smile. He would make his own way back down to the stables with the exercise riders. It was part of the routine that he always enjoyed. Despite his age he was still very fit and healthy for someone who had reached and passed retirement age. He preferred to walk alongside the young people who rode out each day and observe how they discussed their respective mounts workout or how well things were going on a personal level. This ensured that he could provide Cannon with information about any issue with a horse that had merit to it, rather than relying on the simple answers they received to the questions Cannon regularly posed after each exercise session. Over the years many riders had come and gone, some were very good, those who relayed the truth about their mounts. Others were not, offering comments that they thought Cannon and Telside wanted to hear rather than the truth. It was for this reason that Telside took more interest in their personalities, trying to understand their goals, ambitions and their futures.

Walking alongside Angela Fryer's mount, a bay mare with a teardrop mark on her forehead named Summer Kisses, he looked up at the young girl sitting confidently in the saddle. "Are you going to watch her race next week?" he asked, tapping the horse gently on the shoulder. Angela looked down at the old man, who was now facing forwards. She stared at the top of his head which was covered by a flat cap with a chequered pattern. She didn't respond immediately, noting that they were now only a few hundred yards from the stables. After the slight hesitation, she answered him. "I don't think so Mr. Telside. I've got an appointment on that day, which I can't miss. And anyway, to go all the way to Wincanton for only one race for me and have Giles Mainwaring ride her for the stable doesn't make any sense."

Telside continued staring ahead of him. He understood her position. A young jockey with great potential, limited in some ways by being indentured to a small stable, was obviously going to be upset at times when not getting sufficient rides. Sometimes the stable had to make hard decisions about who to have ride their horses. Sometimes the race conditions made the job easier. With regards to Summer Kisses, the weight she was expected to carry in her forthcoming event meant that a senior jockey would be a better bet than a young apprentice who was so much lighter than the handicapper had set. To have the horse carrying dead-weight in the saddle would be detrimental to the horse's chances. Even with the 5lb claim that Angela still had as a conditional jockey, Summer Kisses would be carrying nearly a stone (seven kilograms) of lead in her saddle..

"I understand," Telside replied, "but I think Mike will be disappointed that you won't be riding Brightside Manor for him down there either."

"I know, but I did inform Mr. Cannon that I'd have loved to ride him on the day if I didn't have to see the doctor. In any event no other rides have come up so I think it makes sense….and Mr. Cannon agreed."

"Anything serious?" Telside asked nonchalantly, as they walked through the stable gates. The rest of the lot began forming into a circle in front of the stable block. Some of the first lot of horses from the morning poked their heads above their half-stable barn doors, as if welcoming the second group back home. As the newcomers continued with their warm-down those ensconced in their boxes from earlier turned away as if losing interest and headed back to their feedbags or to have a roll in the hay before enjoying a well-earned rest. Joining the group, Angela let her mount take the initiative and slot into the routine that all racehorses seemed to need, a regular pattern of activity. As the horses continued to circle, their hooves collectively clip-clopped on the cement of the yard. It seemed at times like an ancient song that only the horses could understand Telside watched as Cabin Fever was taken directly to his box, his rider having dismounted before leading the horse away from the rest of the lot. As Telside walked into the middle of the circle and observed each remaining horse and rider, watching to see if anything appeared amiss, he realized that Angela had not responded to his question. He shrugged his shoulders, thinking as he did so that what she was seeing a doctor about was none of his business. He put the matter out of his mind and continued his observations. Sometimes a horse could be found lame only after the exercise process was complete and the animal, like all athletes, had cooled down to a restful state. Telside had seen plenty of horses with injuries over the years, many of them caused by the simplest of things, not necessarily through the jumping of fences. The standing on a loose stone, knocking a knee or a head against a box wall, or receiving a kick from a stable mate. The legs of a racehorse are both strong and fragile, carrying the weight of the animal, but are also the subject of extraordinary forces that can often end a career without notice. Injuries and debilitating conditions like Joint ankylosis, Osteoarthritis, Myositis, Osteochondrosis, Tendinitis and Demystis affecting joints and tendons are commonplace and keeping horses sound and healthy required the necessary amount of time to be taken to watch out for any signs of these conditions developing. After ten minutes, with the sky slowly showing its face as the mist eventually evaporated Telside whistled through his teeth and the circle broke up, each animal almost without asking, went towards their respective stable block and its own box. He turned to enter his office which was an area at the back of the tack room, a place built many years ago when Cannon and he first got together. It was a place that held many memories, a lot having happened there over nearly twenty years. Sitting down, Telside sighed, his face ruddy from the cold, his grey hair still plastered on his head under his cap. He had an odd feeling, but he wasn't sure about what. His conversation with Angela seemed unusually stilted. He would mention it to Cannon when they got together shortly. Rubbing his hands, he decided it was cold enough to make himself some tea. His office was small, but it was well equipped with a kettle, a small fridge and a laptop computer (rarely used) that sat on his desk. As he went to stand, he heard a voice at the door asking if they could enter. He nodded without delay, offering a chair that had been secreted away to a corner of the room. His visitor picked up, then placed the chair opposite him, and sat down. "I need to tell you something," she said.

CHAPTER 2

It had been a difficult morning with nothing but interruptions and by the time Telside walked into the house, Cannon was on his fourth phone call.
"Get yourself something to drink," Cannon whispered as he removed the phone briefly away from his ear indicating that someone was speaking on the line.
Telside left the room allowing Cannon to carry on with the conversation. Upon his return with two mugs of tea, placing one on Cannon's desk, Telside sensed a level of frustration surrounding his boss. "Those bloody idiots at the tax office have just sent me this notice," Cannon said, pointing to his computer screen. "They say I have an unpaid amount totalling nearly seventy-two grand! Can you believe it?!"
"Was that who you were talking too…just now?" Telside asked.
"No, that was Cyril Horowitz down at Plumberry. I know it's a bit early in the morning, but I messaged him earlier and he said he would look into it and call me back. If he didn't, then I was to call him, which I just did. Obviously the tax office is supposed to deal with him as my accountant, but somehow they came directly to me."
"Asking for money," Telside noted cynically.
"Yes, and I'll occur a penalty if the amount is not paid by the end of January."
Taking a sip of tea, the older man raised an eyebrow. He hadn't seen Cannon as stressed for quite some time. Reflecting on the morning's discussion, Telside was concerned that his boss had gone from being somewhat removed and distracted to now being quite frazzled. It was most unlike Cannon, and Telside was afraid that he was about to make matters worse.
"And another thing," Cannon went on, "this wedding that Michelle is planning for Cassie, it's taking way too much of my time. To be honest I wish they would just get on with it rather than keep asking my opinion on things."
Telside smiled inwardly, understanding where Cannon was coming from on this one. Perhaps it explained his mood and agitation? Daughters and weddings! He had been through that process himself

but fortunately, that was many years ago now. Today he was a grandfather six times over. His son and two daughters having expanded the family quite rapidly. Turning his mind to Cannons' comment, he knew that on top of keeping the owners, the staff and the horses in the stables happy, the last thing Cannon needed at this point in time was the distraction of a wedding, even that of his own daughter. Coupled with the added 'bonus' of a demand for unpaid taxes, no wonder his boss was annoyed. It was funny how things often seemed to conspire against one, all at the same time. Was this the reason why Cannon had suggested they needed to talk or was there something else behind it? Telside had often taken over the running of the yard when Cannon had needed time to sort out an issue or had to focus his energies elsewhere. Was this another such time? Cannon's legacy as a cop never seemed to leave him alone. It was as if something could never let go and was always seeking him out. Fortunately, during the Covid-19 pandemic the past had stayed away, remaining locked down like much of the country. Perhaps that was a good thing in a way? It had allowed the stables to get on with life as much as humanly possible under the circumstances, without having to worry about matters that were unrelated to racing….except weddings!

"I suppose it's to be expected, Mike. After all, this is about your daughter," Telside replied eventually. "I suspect Michelle just wants your input as an affirmation."

"Affirmation? Of what?"

"That your money is being well spent. That she hasn't gone overboard."

Cannon considered what Telside had said for a few seconds, before finally nodding in agreement. "I guess you are right, Rich. But as I told Michelle, Cassie is old enough and wise enough to know what I think about her and Taylor and their wedding plans. She doesn't need me to get in the way."

"I'm sure you're not in the way, Mike, and I doubt that Cassie or Michelle think that either. It's a wedding, the most important day of a woman's life. If you let Cassie share the planning with you, I'm sure she'll appreciate it."

"I know you are right, Rich, but when Michelle and I got married early last year, it was a breeze compared to what I am being asked to be involved with now."

"Yes, but that was your second remember; a much smaller wedding, just you and Michelle and a small number of guests exactly as you both wanted it. But…do you recall the first?" Telside asked, questioning then suggesting that Cannon be more accommodating of his daughter's wishes.

Cannon's mind briefly turned to Sally, Cassie's mother. She had died of breast cancer nearly 15 years ago, diagnosed six years earlier. Cassie was too young to understand the diagnosis at the time and was only just able to understand why her mother had left them when the actual time came. Now she was a grown woman, a qualified lawyer, twenty-four with a bright future ahead of her. Despite his protestations about how much of his time it was taking, and how much of his mind space the planning occupied, when the wedding date was nearly a year away, he was secretly pleased to be asked for his opinion. He would however have preferred that once a specific matter had been discussed and agreed upon that it wasn't re-opened later for further discussion. Things like the wedding location, the number of guests, the colours, the invitation process itself were always changing. There just seemed to be so many variables that needed to be dissected over and over again and then be amended despite consensus having been reached. He wasn't sexist or misogynistic in any way, but he did think it a woman thing. He recalled Sally's excitement nearly three decades ago and concluded that nothing had really changed over the years. She had been the same as Cassie; like mother like daughter.

Michelle, however, was different to his late wife. He loved her, just as he had loved Sally. By the time they finally formalized their relationship, things were different between them compared to how he and Sally were when they had decided to marry. They were both wiser, more mature. Middle age for him, she not yet forty. He recalled their wedding day, not even a year ago, with fondness and noted that while the generations moved on, the human spirit always seemed to create a sense of excitement and positivity at such an event. Thoughts of how the future would unfold and what adventures lay ahead of them had made the day magical and for that he was eternally grateful. The wedding was made even better with the acceptance of Michelle, by Cassie, as his soulmate. That, in itself, felt like a race victory, like any he had experienced over the years. A proxy for his life that he could relate to even now. It was a new start, just like a new racing season. Whenever a new horse arrived into the yard the owners had dreams of success, their excitement often tangible, palpable. They had hope for the future and he knew that those who owned a horse that won even the lowest grade event were just as excited as those who owned a horse that won a Derby, a Grand National or a Gold Cup. Cassie's wedding was no different. With that consideration Cannon realized that Telside was right, that he needed to be more pragmatic about his daughter's plans. He answered him. "Yes, I do remember, Rich. Sally was so beautiful, so young and vibrant. I'd just forgotten how much I was affected by it until now."

Putting his cup down, Telside put a hand on his boss' shoulder. Appreciating the gesture, a smile creased Cannon's face. Telside gave out a supportive cough as if he was slightly embarrassed by the experience. Taking a small step back, he rubbed his chin before picking up his cup and hid his face behind the porcelain, while he drank another mouthful. Cannon said, "There's something I want to talk to you about Rich, so take a seat if you wouldn't mind." He pointed to the only other chair in the room which stood in the corner to the right of the door. Telside noted that Cannon's demeanour had suddenly reverted to his earlier state of agitation. It was obvious that his boss had something serious on his mind.

"Sure Mike," he answered positively. "The yard is under control, and I've got a few minutes break, but before you carry on, I have something I need to talk to you about as well."

Cannon nodded, suggesting Telside go first with what he wanted to say, then sat back in his chair and crossed his legs. "The floor's yours," he said.

"It's about…."

Suddenly the phone on the desk, the landline, began to ring, interrupting Telside before he had even got mid-sentence. Both men knew that the call was unlikely to be a personal one as the majority of calls Cannon took from his family or friends were on his mobile phone. "Probably a spam call," he said, noting the incoming number on the base station was one he did not recognize and deciding to ignore the continuing shrill of the receiver. He had more important things on his mind than answering a call from India or the Philippines that probably wanted to tell him that his bank account had shown an unauthorized transaction or something similarly false.

"Hopefully it will stop after a few rings," he sighed, "and they can leave a message, which I know they won't."

Telside's face indicated what he was thinking. He was in full agreement with Cannons' comment. They waited for the ringing to stop. After what seemed an age, it eventually did.

"Okay, sorry about that Rich. Please carry on," Cannon suggested.

"I.."

Almost immediately the phone began to ring again. The sound caused both men to sigh outwardly. It was going to be one of those days. Cannon looked at the base station noting that the incoming call was the same number as previously. Irritated at the second interruption, he vacillated before deciding to answer it. The incessant ringing added to his annoyance with how the morning had already unfolded. His regular routine was being impacted by what seemed to be continuous distractions. His planning for the start of the season and how he was to place his horses during the next couple of months seemed to be getting further out of reach. He had hoped to finalize a number of things during the morning, amongst which included having a heart to heart with Telside, his friend, his 2IC. Now he was doubting if he would ever get the chance. Irritated at the persistent ringing, he grabbed the receiver from its base and without giving the caller a chance to deliver the expected pitch, shouted into the phone.

"No, I don't want to change my gas and electricity supplier and no I don't have any parcels due today nor am I in the market for a new credit card, so …"

"Excuse me?" the caller replied, sounding quite surprised at the mouthful being served up to them. "Can I speak to Mr. Ca…..?"

"You heard me," Cannon answered, cutting off the caller in mid-sentence. His tone indicating the level of irritation he was feeling at the caller who was making a second attempt to contact him. He was about to tell the person at the other end of the line to "fuck off," when his brain suddenly engaged his tongue. Something in the caller's request made him realize that this wasn't an individual from some far away call centre. This was somebody much more cultured. He took a deep breath, trying to calm himself down. He realized his mistake of assuming one thing when in fact the reason for the call was possibly something else.

Telside watched Cannon's facial expression change. He hadn't seen his boss so pugnacious in a long time and sensed that his combativeness had initially got the better of him. However, something had clicked in a few milliseconds and the anger seemed to dissipate like the morning's mist. Cannon turned on his chair and faced his computer screen, a hand at his temples as if he was suffering from a headache. While his back was turned, Telside slipped quietly out of the room. He would try and make another time to talk through the subject he wanted to raise with his boss. Whatever Cannon had on his mind, could be discussed then too.

With his shoulders slumped Cannon closed his eyes as if in defeat. He resigned himself to the interruption and accepted that he would need to apologize for his outburst.

"I'm sorry," he said, contritely. "Can I help you?"

"I'd like to speak with Mr. Cannon, please. Is he about?"

"Whose speaking?" Cannon asked. He was still slightly suspicious of the caller's motives so decided to remain vague in his responses. He had already ruled out a potential owner being behind the voice as most contact nowadays for his services was usually conducted via email. A request to move horses into or out of the stables was much more impersonal now, post Covid, and he met the majority of owners at the racetrack or at the occasional stable visit. Owners very rarely contacted him telephonically but if they did it would be via his mobile, in which he had their names and numbers. They were more like friends now and by setting up communication in this way he could see who was trying to contact him at any time. The world had changed a lot in recent years, the pandemic having left its legacy on many aspects of life, including remotely engaging with each other. Being at arm's length meant that one could be anywhere in the world, not just around the corner or in the same country. One could easily get in contact as long as your arm could stretch to the use of a mobile phone. Cannon waited for the man to speak.

"My name is John Silvers," the man said eventually, "Detective Chief Inspector, John Silvers." The addition of Silvers' full rank made Cannon sit up a little. A DCI calling him out of the blue brought back so many memories from his own past. He had made many a cold call himself during his time in the 'force and they generally only meant one thing: Trouble.

Cannon sighed audibly. It had been several years since he had needed to face his ghosts. If there was one positive thing to come out of the pandemic, it was that he had been able to concentrate on his horses, his stables, his family and nothing else. It was as if the world outside of racing had disappeared into the malaise that took away two years of people's lives and in some cases, life itself. During Covid the numbers of those who died or were in hospital, and the number of jabs people needed in order to protect themselves from the virus were splashed across newspapers, the TV stations and social media continuously. At times it was as if the country was unable to focus on anything else. Murders, disasters (natural or otherwise), and most crime seemed to move to the back pages. Only the shenanigans of politicians filled the headlines alongside the Covid statistics. With society back to normal Cannon had been spared the resurrection of his past. He hoped it would stay that way. He and Michelle, along with Cassie and Taylor had moved on with their lives, Cannon didn't need Silvers to drag him back to a place he had tried to forget. Reluctantly, Cannon asked the question that he had hoped never to say again. "DCI Silvers, how can I help you?"

CHAPTER 3

It was always a difficult procedure, made all the more problematic by the man sitting in the corner smoking his third cigarette in less than thirty minutes.

Amar Hyseni watched as the surgeon placed the scalpel on the impression in the skin that he had made moments earlier. The line stretched across the neck of the prostrate figure lying immobile on the operating table. The bright lights that had been placed above the table lit up the immediate area, and beads of sweat glistened on the surgeon's forehead as he carefully began the incision.

Hyseni was impatient, almost immediately interrupting the process, speaking in his native Albanian. "What the fuck is taking so long? I thought this would be over by now."

The surgeon did not respond, continuing to concentrate on what he was expected to do. He had conducted the operation many times over the past couple of years, but each time there was always a variation of sorts and he needed to be careful so as not to leave too much of a scar. He had been chosen to do the job as he had a steady hand and was extremely skillful with a knife. In addition, being the partner of Hyseni's sister, he was family. When he had first met Ardita at university in his very first year, he had no idea that her family was part of a group that were linked to a number of overseas Albanian crime gangs; the Rudaj Organization in New York, the Hellbanianz in London and the Xhakja clan, amongst others, who operated locally. By the time he had lost his heart and his naivety to her, and she her virginity to him, it was too late. Family honour meant that he had no choice but to marry her. He wasn't unhappy with the situation as she was extremely beautiful. A slim body, long dark hair, a teasing smile that lit up her olive skin and a good brain. The attraction had been mutual. He was taller than her, just over one hundred and seventy-eight centimetres tall with brown curly hair and an almost persistent two-day growth on his chin that never seemed to change no matter how often he took a razor to it. His eyes had been the telling factor for her, however. Green and piercing, complemented by heavy 'brows made him seem intense and focused, which indeed he was, but he had a fun side too. Having come from the historic town of Kruja, fifteen miles northwest of Tirana, the nation's capital, he was the only son of a couple who produced him as they reached middle age. His father had run a small shop, a tobacconist, and his mother was a cleaner. She had suffered from multiple health issues which meant that she had limited scope to work, eventually being unable to continue the two days a week she had managed to hold down for six years at the Panorama and Mervin hotels in the city. With limited support from his own family the surgeon had struggled to fund even the modest fees (by international standards) of his course, and he had taken out a personal loan in order to do so. When he first met Ardita, he had been embarrassed about being unable to date her properly. No nice restaurants, just long walks in the parks, picnics of cheap wine and homemade sandwiches. Fortunately for him she didn't seem to care. It was his charm, his reasonably good looks and his view on life that attracted her to him. His determination to succeed was more enticing to her than anything else. She had hoped to get away from the family and he seemed like the vehicle on which she could ride. She was a year younger than him, a student liaison officer, when they first met on the campus of the *Universiteti Bujqësor i Tiranës*.

She hadn't told him of her family background, being deliberately vague, not wanting to scare him off. Eventually, however, the truth came out, as it needed too. She had hidden behind a wall of silence until she could hide things no longer. Almost a year after they had first met, and six months since they began sleeping together, the inevitable happened. Fortunately, he had stood by her, willing to accept the consequences of her pregnancy. It was then, however, that her family background was revealed. He wasn't angry when she told him, as he believed her story and that she had a genuine desire to get away from their clutches. The family octopus had long tentacles and it soon became obvious that it would be difficult for them no matter how hard they tried. He had nothing but his future to offer her and that in itself was subject to their mercy. The only bargaining chip he had was her commitment to him. Despite an initial attempt to negotiate a solution allowing them to marry and move away from Tirana, it soon became clear that without money, they had no option other than to accept what the family proposed. It was a compromise of sorts made to protect the family honour but stacked heavily in their favour. Time and money would be given which would allow him to finish his studies. They would leave him and Ardita alone, providing them with everything they needed until the debt he owed them was to be called in. They paid for the rest of his education and subsequent training, and they arranged for her abortion, even though she had originally wanted to keep the child. It was only when they both realized the enormity and responsibility it would require of them to be parents at such a young age that it was decided to terminate the pregnancy. It had been an extremely hard decision but his commitment to her had strengthened their relationship into an unbreakable bond. That was fourteen years ago. Today they had a child, a son nearly eight; Dardan. Dardan Abazi, his boy, who carried his surname. It was such a pity that they had been forced to leave their homeland. Dardan was growing up Dutch now and speaking less and less of his mother tongue. The family had ordered it as part of the debt. Erjon Abazi knew now that the debt he owed would never be paid back in full as far as the family were concerned. He was tied to them forever. Inwardly he had never accepted it but he did what was asked because of his love for Ardita. He resented how she was manipulated and told her so, letting her know that at some point in the future he would find a way to break the chains that they held him by.

"I ask you again, Erjon. What is the hold up?" Hyseni enquired angrily, "I need to leave soon and I can't sit around all day!"

Taking his time to turn around and face his questioner, the surgeon slowly placed the scalpel onto the steel table. His hands were covered with blue latex gloves and his torso enveloped in a green gown. He was the epitome of someone who was in the process of conducting an operation. Erjon Abazi walked the six steps to where his brother-in-law was sitting. As he did so Hyseni stood, took a drag on his cigarette then dropped the remains onto the floor and crunched it with the ball of his shoe. At full height Hyseni was at least eight centimetres taller than Abazi and much stockier. He was a big man in every sense consisting mostly of muscle. A man who ironically worked out in his private gym every day despite the amount of smoke he regularly poured into his lungs. He pulled at his belt to tighten it and highlight his trimmed waist. Then he straightened his jacket sleeves while Erjon's eyes bored into him. The two men stood toe to toe. A smirk traversed the bigger man's face, revealing a small gap in his front teeth where a bridge had once been, lost in a fight a few months prior.

"If you want to do it yourself Amar, you are welcome to," Abazi said. "So…be my guest," he added, beginning to remove his gloves and nodding towards the operating table.

"What?" replied Hyseni.

"You heard me. If you don't like my work then I'm happy for you to get someone else to do it for you!"

"Don't be fucking stupid, Erjon. You of all people know that's not possible," retorted Hyseni, a fleck of spittle on the bigger man's chin, his face flushed red with anger. Abazi ignored the comment and continued to stare into his brother-in-law's eyes, the pupils of which were slightly narrowed in the bright light, the man's irises however were dark and cold. It was almost like looking into the man's soul. He could tell that there was little compassion or care regarding what he was trying to do with the patient, just a single-minded pre-occupation by Hyseni to get the job done. The two men stared at each other, engaging in a battle of wills, both waiting for the other to blink. In the immediate silence the patient suddenly began to stir, the anaesthetic given earlier slowly beginning to wear off. Abazi turned away concerned that he hadn't yet started to make the deeper cuts he needed to as part of the procedure. Interruptions had eaten into the thirty minutes he had available to do what was required, and he hadn't been helped by Hyseni's bitching.

"Look," he said, turning his back to his brother-in-law, as he began to focus on the increasingly restless patient, "just get the hell out of here and take your filthy habit with you! Leave this to me," he added angrily. "I need to sedate my patient again so that I can complete my work, so piss off!"

With a grunt Hyseni took a step forward, his body language threatening, his large hands opening and closing as if he was thinking about throwing a punch. He knew that it would be a stupid thing to do, but he wasn't thinking about self-control, it was more about his pride. After a few seconds of silence, as he stared at the back of the now anxious surgeon, a smile of disdain spread across his face. He always knew that he had little time for the man. If it wasn't for his sister, he would have killed him a long time ago. As it was, perhaps that time would come one day? Hyseni made his way towards the exit of the operating theatre, brushing against some of the equipment that beeped and pipped as they registered some of the vital signs of the patient that seemed to be settling back into an unconscious state. As he reached the door, he turned around, pointed at the patient and said with a touch of malevolence, "Just finish the job, Erjon… and by the way," he added, indicating the operating table. "If she dies. She dies. There is always another one."

CHAPTER 4

She had been occupied all evening marking papers at the dining room table, and he had been busy in his office. They hadn't had a chance to talk over dinner other than the normal pleasantries about their respective days. Michelle had been late getting home from school. It was already dark by the time she had driven into the yard, parking her car as usual directly in front of his office. The headlights had shone directly through the windows and illuminated the interior. The few drops of rain that fell, sparkled in the brightness before she turned off the engine and ran quickly into the house. What Telside had complained about, nature had considered answering. Cannon hadn't been seated at his desk (which was where she had expected him to be) as she entered through the door, he was already in the kitchen preparing a meal. He wasn't much of a cook, but he took the job seriously whenever he needed to. Earlier he had set the oven at 180C and placed three salmon pieces that he had defrosted earlier, onto a tray; adding some fresh vegetables meticulously cut into bite size pieces and dropping them into a roasting dish. Along with the fish he had baked them for twenty minutes. He was happy with his efforts.

The meal had gone down well, and she had been complimentary to him about it. Not specifically a summer or winter dish, it was appropriate for the time of year. At least that was his view.

She began packing away the documents she had been working on into a folder, just as Cannon walked towards her, coming down the passage from his office. She looked up with a tired smile.

"Tea?" she enquired, tapping her watch.

"I was going to ask you the same question," he replied, giving her a gentle kiss on the cheek. Standing up, she stretched her arms towards the ceiling and briefly rubbed the back of her neck. Then, she proceeded to turn her head alternately left, then right, before hunching her neck a few times as if to soften the stiffness she was feeling between her shoulders.

She yawned an acknowledgement. "I'll make it," she said.

He smiled in agreement then followed her into the kitchen as she picked up the kettle and moved to the sink in a well-practiced dance she had done many times before. She turned on the tap letting the water fill up to the required mark.

"Is this going to continue for a while?" he asked, referring to the work she had been busy with.

"Probably until the end of the year."

"What, December? That's nearly two more months," he said, expressing surprise.

"No, until the end of the school year."

"What?!" he repeated, incredulously.

She grinned as she placed the kettle onto its stand, the sound of bubbling water almost instantly beginning to emanate from the vessel.

"That's the joy of being a Head of Department," she answered. "Sometimes you have to jump in and help some of your team when there are problems."

Cannon sucked his lips in response. He knew how much she enjoyed her job and her career. Everyone had ups and downs at times. It reminded him of his own situation; the job he had now, which he loved and had worked so hard to develop over the years, and the one he had fortunately left behind a long time ago. Two careers, both with challenges, at times some days were better than others.

Whenever he thought of his past life, he reflected mostly on the good days when even a Detective could be content with his lot. However there were always those 'other' days when the job could be murder…quite literally. He briefly recalled some of the good people he had worked with during that time. The teams he had around him and those he had been a part of. Good times! Unfortunately he also remembered the Ying to the Yang. The other side of the fence. The bad cops. Those who went rogue, those that took bribes, those that looked the other way, those that killed. He was glad that he had left that shit behind him years ago, but despite the passage of time he knew that even if he wasn't looking, sometimes the past sought him out, never wanting to let him go. He pushed the thought out of his mind concentrating on the here and now, watching as the kettle boiled considering what Michelle had just told him. The school she taught at was located halfway between Charlbury and the village of Shipton-under-Wychwood and was positioned on a small hill overlooking the northern Cotswolds. It was a small private school and one that had a good name, both for students and educators. A name didn't always prevent issues arising however, and there had

been several problems that the school had needed to address over the years. The current one was a hangover from the Covid era. Several of the teachers had caught the virus and one had sadly passed away. The current problem was that two of those who had been infected had long-term complications and both were specialist teachers; one in Mathematics and Physics and the other in Languages. The latter, Rosemary Brindle, was a member of Michelle's staff, who was also Head of English herself. Rosemary was expected to be away from work due to heart problems for at least six months, a period which began during the latter part of the previous school year. Cannon had assumed that the problem of staffing would have been resolved by now. Clearly he was wrong. He recalled that Michelle had previously mentioned that being a smallish school and in the locale that it was, meant that it was difficult to find short-term support post the Covid pandemic let alone find any long-term replacements. As they waited for the kettle, Michelle told him that even after they had advertised for staff, it was taking months of searching, interviewing, reference checking, deciding on a candidate and waiting for notice periods to be served before anyone was likely to be in a position to start at the school. That proposition itself was also a concern. The reality was that they could not replace an incumbent teacher who was likely to return to work at some point, without approval from the relevant authorities. The rules in relation to the job required that the role be kept open for a reasonable period ultimately allowing the original occupant of that position (should they wish) to return to it post their recovery from the virus. The position could be filled if the teacher decided not to take up the role again and they formally resigned. This had not happened to date and Rosemary Brindle was not expected to. Accordingly, in the interim, the gap in resourcing was required to be filled by the Department Head. In this case, Michelle.
"I understand," he said, once she had finished. He began to pour boiling water into the cups she had laid out on the bench top.
"Changing the subject slightly," she said, "have you had chance to speak with Rich?"
"No, I was going to this morning, but was interrupted. I received an odd phone call and after I'd finished with it, Rich had already left the office."
"And you didn't see him subsequently?"
"No, I was hoping to during evening stables, but I've been a little

sidetracked today. What with the nominations for upcoming races, some emails from Cassie and a quote from a wedding photographer to look at....not to mention a few queries from a couple of owners about their horses, I just didn't have time. It's just been hectic."
"The horses. Coming in or going out?" she enquired.
"Both to be honest. Two from separate owners who are wanting to give me a go, and a couple of owners who want to move their horses out because they want them to run asap."
"Even though they are not ready?" she inquired.
"Yes," he answered, surprised that she was aware which horses he was referring to.
"Rich told me the other day," she answered, noticing his reaction then adding. "While you were still on the heath and he was getting the second lot ready. I was just leaving for work when we ran into each other," she explained, slightly embarrassed. "He mentioned that you and he had discussed a couple of the horses that you thought needed more work put into them but with the hard ground you wanted to protect their legs. Are those the horses you are talking about?"
"Basically yes." He passed her the now ready tea, suggesting that they take their drinks through to the lounge. "I think he also wanted to talk to me about something that was on his mind, but I'm not sure what it was about," he continued, as he settled onto the couch next to her.
"Rich, you mean?"
"Yes."
"Perhaps the same thing that you want to discuss with him? Maybe he's got wind of it?"
"Maybe."
After pausing for a second to take a sip of her drink, she asked him about the phone call that he had received earlier in the day. "The odd call?" she reminded him.
"Oh, sorry I forgot about that. It was from a DCI Silvers, from the Ayrshire Police."
"Up in Scotland?"
"Yes."
"What did he want?"
"He was trying to find out about a horse I once trained, Noble Goblet. I'm not sure if you remember him. A nine-year-old bay

gelding, with three white socks and a single image on his face, a bit like the map of Japan. The lads and girls in the yard nicknamed him the Samurai. He was quite fearless at the jumps, but he wasn't particularly disciplined or had much stamina beyond two miles."

"Is that why you let him go?"

"That and the owner was insistent that I wasn't doing enough with him. I mentioned at the time that the horse needed more schooling. He had only been with us for less than a season, and I told the owner that if we rushed things the horse or whoever rode him in a race was likely to get hurt."

Michelle frowned slightly before asking, "So how long ago did the horse leave us?"

Cannon smiled inwardly at the use of the term 'us'. For a long time Michelle had never referred to the yard or stables as 'ours' but since they had married, it seemed that she was much more in-tune with the business. Cannon liked that. "Nearly two years ago now," he continued, "just as we were getting back on our feet after Covid. I didn't follow what happened to the horse after that."

"Until now, you mean?"

"That's right. I think he went through a few trainers, before finally being retired. I found him on the BHA website, which as you know is not 100% foolproof, and which the BHA themselves readily accept. It seems that the horse has been retired but the site didn't indicate as to where. So I'm not sure if it was being used for showing, dressage, eventing or even just as a hack in a riding school. I have no idea what the owner had intended to do with him."

"So, what did the police want with you then?" she enquired.

"Just that. Some background into the owner, the horse. Various bits and pieces."

"Why? Isn't it unusual for a DCI to be asking you about a long-forgotten animal that you've had nothing to do with for ages?"

"Yes, it is, and it's not something I'd expect such a senior cop to be concerned with either."

"Well, what was he enquiring about?"

"Something to do with the horses ID. He asked if I had any details about the horse's markings."

"Why?"

Cannon hesitated slightly. He felt that what he was about to say may upset her. "The horse's head and neck were found in a field just south of Kilmarnock a few weeks ago."

"My God," she replied, "the poor animal."

"Exactly. But that's not the only thing," he continued. "Apparently, it's not the first one. There have been a few more found up there recently."

"What, heads and necks?"

"Yes. Gruesome don't you think? Discovered by kids mostly, as they were walking through some farmer's fields."

"I'll bet. Not something I'd like to come across on a dark night or even during the day," she replied. All thoughts of her own issues they had discussed earlier had now vanished from her mind. She sighed as she considered what he had told her. After a few seconds she asked, "So what were you able to tell him?"

"Nothing really. The markings Silvers described that were found on the head, the shape of Japan, made it obvious that it was the right horse. I was able to verify it with a photo I had in my own records. That seemed to satisfy him. So that was that. Quite simple really."

"But why you?" she queried. "Why didn't the police ask any of the other trainers? Or even the owner?"

"It seems like the last owner wasn't the same person who owned him when I trained the horse, and whoever it was had recently passed away. The family hadn't wanted to keep the animal in work any longer, so they had retired him from racing."

"And then…?"

"I don't know, and Silvers didn't elaborate. He just thanked me for the information and that was that."

Relieved at the thought that there was nothing else likely to come from the conversation with the police, Michelle changed tack and despite it nearly their bedtime questioned him about Cassie's wedding plans. Cannon had little to say on the subject other than that he was happy to be asked but didn't want to be seen as a roadblock. He gave Michelle carte blanche to do whatever she and Cassie decided to do, but to keep him informed about the cost. At the time of their own wedding and months in advance of Cassie's big day, they had agreed a budget with her for the entire event. The invitations, the venue, the dresses, everything! However, from what Michelle told him it seemed that the figures were running away from what was expected. "A bit like a horse that can't settle in a race", Cannon said. "It bolts away with the jockey and before you know it, crash! It hits a fence and the

whole partnership goes its separate ways."
Michelle smiled at the analogy, countering with the observation that Cassie's husband to be, Edward Taylor, a Haemotologist at the Chesterfield Royal Hospital, and his family, were more than happy to share the cost of the wedding.
"Probably just as well," Cannon continued. "I think both of them have some grandiose ideas about the big day."
Michelle punched him gently in the arm, a kind of love tap but with a small amount of venom. She smiled at him knowing that while he was serious in one way about the whole process and the ever-increasing cost, she understood that he only wanted the best for his daughter; as most fathers would.
"Hey," he said, rubbing his arm in mock indignation, "what was that for?"
"You know," she countered, "you, we, have had our day, now it's Cassie's and Ed's. So let them do what they want…"
"Within reason," he interrupted.
"Yes, within reason…and if we go ahead on that basis it will be much easier."
"I agree. As I keep telling Cassie, stick to the course and jump the hurdles when you come to them, but don't expect the prize money to get any bigger at the end of the race…once it's set, it's set."
"Very philosophical of you, Mike," she laughed, beginning to stand and reaching for her now empty cup.
He touched her briefly on the arm. "Thank you," he said.
"For what?"
"For keeping me grounded. I've got a number of things on my plate that I need to….oh shit!" He stopped mid-sentence. Michelle looked at him quizzically, waiting for him to continue.
"Sorry," he sighed, "I just realized something."
"Go on."
"I didn't hear back from Cyril down at Plumberry's and I was supposed to call him back."
"Well, I'm sure it will wait until the morning. He's not likely to be in his office at this time of night, is he?" she sensibly pointed out.
"No," he answered, annoyed at himself for leaving a loose strand from the day now flapping around in his mind. He liked to keep things orderly, to be on top of matters, to pre-empt rather than be reactive. Despite his best efforts in recent weeks, things seemed to be

unravelling from the norm and he didn't like it. When he considered all the other issues on his plate, life had suddenly become unnecessarily complicated.

"Let's go to bed," he said eventually, "I've got to be up soon."

CHAPTER 5

The rain that had been absent for weeks had returned with a vengeance; its intensity having increased over the past few hours. The day had changed dramatically. Earlier in the morning there had been a mist that seemed to creep along the ground having risen from beneath the streets, the fields and the nearby streams. Then without warning the heavy clouds had rolled in, which brought the downpour and finally burst the bubble of drought. The precipitation was good for the gardens and would keep the overnight frost at bay, but with the ground currently harder than it usually would be at this time of year, the runoff was quite significant. Fields had huge puddles lying within them, ditches filled rapidly, and the roads had become ever more treacherous, made worse by the scudding low cloud that continued to leak torrents of water. The rain missed some parts of the country, but where it did hit, those caught in its intensity were made to feel extremely uncomfortable.

The jogger had been trying to get home as quickly as possible, but her training regime meant that she needed to push through to achieve the goal she had set for that day. Ten miles was her target and she only had three to go. When the weather had changed, she realized that she wasn't properly dressed for it, but she decided to make do with what she had on. She would have liked to be wearing her yellow reflective vest but without it she hoped that the three white stripes along the sides of the tracksuit would be sufficient to give others the ability to see her. She knew that she could be exposed, especially when she found herself outside the limited span of the few streetlamps that lit the way. She had passed the George and Dragon pub in Long Hanborough a short while ago and was heading back to North Leigh along the A4095. The light from the surrounding estates had diminished dramatically as she passed Cuckoo Lane on her left, reducing even further as she continued to jog along the slippery bitumen. The lack of road markings made the run hazardous, and she felt a little uneasy as the rain and darkness tried to envelop her, grasping at her with unseen hands. The high trees on both sides hid the farmland beyond. The only break in the darkness other than the small glow from a headband torch plastered against her dripping forehead, was a small glint of light that grew ever larger on her right as she came level with Boddington Lane. She could tell that it was a car of sorts, its headlights on high beam the arc of which followed the winding road. The vehicle pierced the gloom as it traversed the coiled wet serpent and she noticed it was slowing down as it came to the intersection, an indicator suggesting that it would turn towards the way she had come. As the driver began a slow crawl readying to turn left, she was illuminated for a second, the driver and passenger both noticing her as she jogged away from them. Suddenly, without warning, a motorbike travelling at speed, so fast in fact that she had not heard it approach from behind her, came careening along the road. The headlights of the car that was moving away, driving in the opposite direction, briefly lit up the bike and rider, as they screamed past, black leathers and a dark helmet glistening in the rain. Within less than a second the motorbike was upon her, the blackness and the heavy weather having hidden her from view. The rider on the bike caught a brief glimpse of a figure attempting to get out of the way, but it was too late. Shifting their weight and pulling handlebars swiftly to the right the rider fought for control. As the bike went into a skid, the rider bucked briefly from the seat, just as the rear of the bike smashed into the jogger sending her somersaulting into the trees that stood like statues alongside the road. The runner's torso slammed against a low tree branch which pierced her chest, impaling her, while the back of her head smashed into the trunk of the tree. She was dead before the sound of the impact had been lost in the silent emptiness of the evening. The rider of the bike meanwhile had regained control, accelerating out of the skid and was already a hundred yards away from the collision, still travelling at speed. Despite the obvious impact the rider had decided without hesitation to accelerate away from the scene, fully aware of what had happened. It had been impossible not to know that someone had been hit. With the merest of glances into a rear-view mirror the rider rode on, noticing a car's red tail-lights that had once been receding, now changed to white as the vehicle behind began to turn around and head back to where the accident had occurred. The rider felt the slight shudder of the back wheel as it vibrated against the damaged mudguard. It would need to be removed and replaced before anyone started asking questions.

CHAPTER 6

He put the phone down. At least the conversation had been a positive one. Cyril Horowitz had told him not to worry about the HMRC notice.
"It's obviously a mistake," Horowitz had opined.
"I'll say."
"Yes, Mr. Cannon, I'll say so too," the accountant had responded. "I can assure you that you have nothing to worry about. I'll get this sorted for you as soon as I can," he went on, his voice clipped, and affected by a slight lisp. It reminded Cannon of the way the old film star Terry Thomas used to speak. "The information we have on file shows that you are up to date with your affairs, so I'll try to find out the cause of this query and I'll advise you in due course."
Cannon heard the smile in the man's voice. In his minds' eye he saw the gap in the man's front teeth, just like that of the late actor.
Feeling a little better about the situation, the subject of which having caused him a disturbed sleep, Cannon eventually relaxed and terminated the call. As he sat back ready to commence work on nominating a number of his horses for upcoming races, Telside knocked on his office door.
"I know you're busy Mike, but I just wondered if you had a minute?"
"Yes, yes, come in, Rich," Cannon replied, waving his friend towards the ubiquitous spare chair. "I was just about to do some noms and a couple of acceptances, including White Noise in a Class 2 Hurdle over two miles at Chepstow next week."
"That would be a perfect start to his campaign," Telside replied, "the horse is jumping out of his skin and couldn't be in better shape. This morning he just flew, and Sam Simmons struggled to keep the horse from doing too much such was the enthusiasm for his work. I think the softer ground helped too."
Cannon nodded. He hadn't been able to get up to see his horses exercise due to him wanting to speak with Horowitz. Having such a restless night meant that he was up and about as normal but he had used the early hours of the day to review his own financial records. Something was bothering him and whatever was niggling away inside was refusing to show itself. It was as if he had an itch that he couldn't

scratch, and it gnawed away at him. After a fruitless hour of searching, he had to let it go for now and move on. He needed to concentrate on the upcoming season and having mapped out a number of campaigns, he had begun the process of completing the formalities. After studying the racing calendar online, he had started to add the details of each of his horses that he wanted entered into specific race(s). This was done directly into the BHA website. The process was relatively simple but also quite laborious and could take some time, particularly when events ended up being cancelled or rearranged at the last minute. An example was when a change in the weather caused flooding or tracks were impacted by ice, snow or dense fog. Fortunately with the change that happened overnight, the forecast for the immediate short term suggested that some of the country's racecourses would be lucky and receive enough rain to allow the going to soften after the recent dry weather. This would help those tracks to have some 'give' in them. A few locations however, would miss out and only receive light rain thereby leaving their tracks harder than Cannon would like. It was a trainer's job to work with the vagaries of the elements and to evaluate how and where best to place his runners.
"So, what's on your mind, Rich?" Cannon asked, remembering that he had his own questions to put to his friend.
Telside hesitated slightly. "It's Angela."
"What about her?" Cannon asked, noting the tone in Telside's voice. It was obvious from it that there was something bothering him.
"She's pregnant."
"What?!" Cannon replied, shocked. His immediate concern was for the girl's wellbeing and mental state. She was still so young. Too young to be a mother. In the short amount of time he had known her, from the initial series of interviews they had had, through to their discussions about her career ambitions as a jockey, she had always been clear about what she wanted from life, a baby so early on wasn't one of them.
"How…how far is she?" Cannon queried, not wanting to get into too much personal detail at this stage, but he needed to know so that he understood the implication. Under National Hunt rules, a pregnancy would require a specialist's opinion as to whether an individual's license to ride should be revoked immediately or not. The usual decision in the first instance, Cannon knew, was a deferment of a

license, allowing the individual concerned to return to racing after the birth of the baby. This was subject to meeting certain medical and mental health requirements at the time. The immediate problem for Cannon was how soon his apprentice would have to stop riding? While he would have to consider that scenario in the short term, he parked it for now and without waiting for Telside to reply, raised the obvious question. As did so he was unsure whether he really wanted to know the answer.
"Does she know who the father is?"
"Yes."
"Nick?"
"Yes."
Nick Van der Linden was Angela's Dutch boyfriend. Cannon disliked him immensely. The man was nearly ten years older than her. Almost thirty, he was known as a party animal who enjoyed a night out and a good drink. He owned and ran a tattoo parlour in Witney, a town roughly seven miles south-west of Cannon's yard. He was often the subject of complaints by some of his neighbours for arriving home late at night on his high-powered motorbike. When Cannon had chosen Angela as his first conditional jockey, she had been unattached at the time. The relationship started a few months after she was indentured, having met Nick when one of her friends had suggested she get a tattoo to celebrate her very first winner under National Hunt rules. Things had developed from there. Shortly after their first meeting, they had become a couple, moved in together and now....
"Fuck!" Cannon swore, annoyed at the circumstances and the implications for his yard. If it wasn't one thing, it was another, and in this case another thing he didn't need right now. Noting that Telside had remained silent, Cannon apologized for his reaction, parking for the moment the conversation that he had intended to have with Telside.
"Sorry, Rich," he said.
"That's okay, Mike. It's understandable. It was just as big a shock to me when she let me know."
"Did she say what she intends to do?"
"Yes. She wants to keep the baby, even if it affects her career in the short term. She said she sees it as a blip on the road rather than a bump, which is admirable I suppose."

"I suppose," Cannon echoed, still disappointed at the news.
"Apparently, she's already discussed it with her family, and they are happy to support her in whatever decision she makes," Telside continued
"And what about Nick? Did she say what his reaction was?"
"Yes, and it's surprised me no end."
"Which is?"
"He told her to have the baby."
"And he would support them, bring up child with her…together?" Cannon queried.
"Apparently so."
Cannon rubbed his chin. Like Telside, he was stunned by the apparent attitude of Van der Linden. It seemed impossible to believe, based on their experience to date. That the father of Angela's baby would be so accommodating and willing to be part of the its future, was totally unexpected given his exploits in recent times. While it was not impossible for individuals to change as their life circumstances changed, there were certain indicators, perhaps pre-conceived notions, that were hard to displace. Cannon had seen this so many times before in his former life as a cop. Promises made by one individual to another, especially in domestic situations, were often scattered like leaves in a dusty wind when reality hit home. When a lifestyle was compromised with the arrival of a baby into the comfortable space of what was a couple, three made a crowd and not everyone appreciated or understood the impact of the interloper. For now, that reality for Angela and Nick was still in the future. The problem they needed to understand was that time would fly and things had a habit of turning out differently to what was expected. Cannon decided to withhold judgement on what he had heard and to keep his thoughts on the subject to himself. He would deal in facts only and not speculate about other people's motives.
"I suppose I'd better talk with her?" he said.
As soon as he opened his mouth, he realized with irritation that the rest of the day would require reorganizing from what he had expected to be doing. The work he had done that morning and the plans he had developed for his runners over the coming months may need to be changed. This was particularly so for those runners that Angela was scheduled to ride. His idea had been to get the benefit of her obvious skill, her knowledge of his horses and her weight claim.

Now, given the situation, he had a few questions that he needed to get answers to. The first was whether Angela could ride at all. The second was, for how long?
"By the way, Mike," Telside added, interrupting Cannon's thoughts, "do you want to know how far gone she is?"
"Uh-uh."
"About eight or nine weeks."
"So still six to seven months to go."
Cannon's thoughts briefly turned to the birth of Cassie and all the drama he and Sally had gone through during his late wife's pregnancy. He hadn't expected that his life would change as much as it ultimately did, however he now looked back at that early time with fondness. As a young Detective making his way through the ranks, he was acutely aware of what he needed to deliver while on the job and how to act in order to meet that expectation. He was hard when he needed to be when out in the field, or in an interview room, but when he was required to play an expectant father, he did it wholeheartedly. He doted on Sally, making her feel special, making her feel wanted and loved, despite her own admission during her pregnancy of "feeling ugly and fat". He remembered how much Sally thanked him once Cassie was born, subsequently realizing that without his support she may well have gone over the edge as she tried to weather the storm of her first baby. The post-partum depression took its toll and it took a significant amount of time for her to get over it. It was tough during that period but eventually they got through it together. That was a long time ago now and support related to the condition had improved considerably since then. Society was much more understanding of depression. Mental health was now better understood. The treatment of pre-birthing fear, alongside concerns by first time parents about the future, was as much in focus now as the physical health of mother and baby. Unfortunately, the position of a pregnant jumps jockey had not improved much over time, indeed the thinking surrounding such a situation was still one of limitation. Limitation of risk, of harm, of decision making. Cannon himself was in favour of the rules as they stood, but also realized that they would be restrictive to someone who he believed had the potential to be a star of the game. Accepting the need to have the necessary conversation, he indicated that he would make a point of having a chat with Angela the following

morning. Telside smiled sadly. He understood that Cannon was very disappointed.

"I'll leave you to it then, Mike," he said making his way towards the office door. As he reached the threshold Cannon made to thank him for letting him know about Angela, but as he did so his mobile phone began to shrill. It broke the quiet silence that had swiftly surrounded them as the depth of understanding about Angela's situation had sunk in with both of them.

"Bloody hell!" Cannon said, reaching for the handset, watching Telside continue on his way out of the office. Once again the phone had interrupted another opportunity to talk one on one about a subject that was beginning to eat away at him.

"Yes, love?" he questioned, noting from his screen that it was Michelle calling.

"Hi Mike, it's me. Sorry to disturb you," she apologized, her voice sounding somewhat strained.

"What is it, love?" he replied, sensing her concern. She rarely called him during the day as they were both usually busy, she in the classroom or on other duties, and he attending race meetings or working through the many stable issues he was continuously juggling. It was a routine they had built up over the years and it seemed to work for them. For Michelle to call him before lunchtime was very strange.

"Did you hear the news?"

"No, should I have?" he enquired, wondering whether there was some significant event that he should have been aware of. He rarely concerned himself with the politics of the day or what was reported on the news nowadays, having lost interest in the minutiae that was considered important by some people. The thirty second sound bite and the constant social media posts that seemed to be the story of the day had deadened his enthusiasm for the news a long time ago. He focused his attention on what was important to him and the things that he could influence, not on something that others wanted to push down his throat. He would much rather pay particular notice to his staff and what they said about his horses, than listen to some idle Hollywood gossip about some stupid reality show.

"Unfortunately, I've been busy in the office since you left for school this morning," he continued. "I haven't even had a chance to do stables as yet, and as I told you on your way out, I wasn't able to get up to the gallops either. What's worse, I've only just been able to speak with Cyril a short while ago and even that took more time than it should have," he moaned. Before she was able to respond to his complaint, Cannon wondered if what she was asking was to do with Angela. The staff around the yard knew most of what was going on in each other's personal lives. It wouldn't be too long a bow to draw and conclude that Michelle had heard a rumour from someone in the local village, or at the school, about the situation. It was after all a reasonably small community and Angela was a local girl, born and bred.

"Do you mean regarding Angela?" he quizzed.

For a second there was a pause on the other end of the line. It was as if time stood still just long enough for his question to register.

"What? No," Michelle answered, "it's about Sue Gladstone, my colleague, my equivalent in the Physics department."

"What about her?"

"She was killed last night. Knocked down it seems by a car or something. The Head was contacted a short while ago after one of her extended family members had identified the body. We've just come out of meeting of teachers, and I thought I'd let you know, especially as she used to own a share in one of the horses we had in the stable. 'Candlelightnight' I think it was."

Cannon tried to recall the various faces associated with the horse Michelle was referring to. He remembered that it was a large syndicate of twenty individuals but couldn't place the teacher's face specifically.

"I'm so sorry to hear," he said. "Where did it happen?"

Michelle shared with him what she and the rest of the staff had been advised. He was curious when she mentioned where the accident had apparently taken place.

"Did anyone see it happen?" he asked. "Any witnesses?"

"I'm not sure," she replied. "We don't have any more detail other than what I've told you, but it's absolutely awful," she continued, her voice now at breaking point. "Sue was such a wonderful woman, for something like this to happen to her...well it's just so sad."

He could hear her quietly sobbing, the incident having an effect on her much greater than Cannon would have expected. He tried to calm her down, suggesting that the police would be able to get to the bottom of what happened.

"You're probably right," she countered, "but it's been such a shock."
"I can imagine," he replied sympathetically, before adding, "does the school intend to close early then?"
"No, in fact quite the contrary, at least for the teaching staff. The kids may get sent home early, but we have a lot of work to do now. We need to rearrange classes, work out which of the kids are impacted directly and indirectly and then provide counselling where we can to those that want it."
And to those teachers similarly impacted as well, Cannon thought.
"So, I suppose I'll see you when I see you?" he said.
"Yes, I'm sorry about that. I should be home before dinner though…at least I hope so. I believe the police will be on their way shortly to ask us a few questions."
Cannon briefly considered her comment. From experience he knew that statements would be taken from any number of people either directly or indirectly associated with the victim. Questions such as where certain people were around the time of the incident? Whether anyone knew of any issues between the deceased and a colleague, friend or partner? Was there any beneficiary from the individual's death and if the matter was a simple and tragic accident, then who was involved and how did it happen? The police needed to be thorough and when a brief was given to the coroner to make a determination as to the cause of death, the matter would be scrutinized and evidence led for an appropriate conclusion to be drawn. Foul play or pure accident? To get to the result, the process needed to be followed, and it always took longer than expected.
After saying their brief goodbyes, Cannon disconnected the call and placed the phone back on his desk. He wondered if the day could get any worse. What he had hoped for that morning was a simple phone call to Plumberry's and a necessary chat with Telside, leaving him the rest of the day to concentrate on racing. It had been nothing of the sort and the day had been completely turned on its head. So far he had achieved very little. He decided to take a walk into the stables and see whether the temporary change of scenery and a quick look at how the horses had eaten up after exercise would improve his mood.

CHAPTER 7

Detective Inspector Sam Walker wasn't considered a local. He had lived in the area for the past nine years but would always be considered a Geordie. Originally a native of Tyneside who had moved around the country during his career, he had never lost his accent despite spending sixty percent of his forty years away from his birthplace in Denton, a short drive from Newcastle's city centre. Most people struggled to understand him at first, but within a short period of time, either through listening more closely or getting used to his pronunciation, were able to converse with him without too much of an issue. At six feet four inches (one hundred and ninety-three centimetres) and just shy of a hundred kilograms he was the ideal build for a traditional 'bobby' or perhaps a lock-forward for the Newcastle Falcons. He was renowned for being quick to jump to conclusions and it had got him into trouble at times with his superiors. Despite this flaw in his character, his errors in judgement had been tolerated as he had solved a significant number of crimes over his career. He was quite a handsome man who always wore a crew cut hairstyle in line with his original police training. Deep blue eyes offset his slightly fleshy nose (broken several times) while undefined cupid's bow lips gave the impression of a deep thinker, reliable, responsible and trustworthy. He wasn't quite the caricature of a policeman but whenever he walked into a room or a supermarket it was obvious to most what his profession was. Stationed at Abingdon but living in Witney, he had the unfortunate requirement to travel to the city and visit the mortuary run by the Oxfordshire County Council He never enjoyed the experience. He was standing in a dark green garb alongside one of his team, Sergeant Chris Conte, and listened to the forensic pathologist, Dr. Jenny Cribb, as she explained her findings.

"As you can see from the puncture wound in the chest the victim would have died almost instantly," she said. "The branch pierced the rib cage, sliced through the heart and protruded through the left side of the body."

Neither man made a sound. Listening intently, their eyes alternated between Cribbs' face and that of the late Susan Gladstone. The body was resting on a steel slab having earlier been covered with a new white sheet after the postmortem had been completed. The pathologist partially removed the sheet to show the policemen the wound to which she was referring.

"We have removed fragments of wood from the entry and exit wound, as well as material from the tracksuit and a running vest that she was wearing underneath at the time of death. Apart from that there was nothing much of interest."

"Nothing? Was she....?" Walker asked, leaving the question hanging but knowing that Cribbs knew to what he was referring.

"As I said, nothing of interest and no, she wasn't pregnant. There was no sign of any disease or illness other than a slight calcification of the lower pelvic area. She may have suffered a little pain in her hip, but other than that she seemed particularly healthy."

"Any sign of drug use?"

"Not that one can see, but toxicology will confirm that. I expect to get the report back sometime tomorrow."

"What about externally?" Walker asked. "Any sign of whatever it was that caused this?" He pointed at the lifeless corpse just as Cribbs' assistant who had been standing to the side pulled the sheet to re-cover the body and give some dignity back to the deceased. Walker hadn't even noticed the subtle glance and gentle nod that Cribbs had given to the assistant, thereby initiating such a request. Removing a pair of latex gloves and starting to undo her laboratory coat Cribbs indicated that the two men should follow her into a small office. Once inside she offered them both a seat on the opposite side of an old wooden desk that had seen much better days. "The only thing that we could extract from the apparent point of impact were some tiny fragments of what appears to be blue paint that had embedded into the fibre of her tracksuit bottoms. I don't know if they are relevant as yet as they may have been there before the incident but my guess is that they come from a vehicle that struck the poor woman. I should have also mentioned that whatever it was that collided with her, broke her right leg and smashed the knee to pieces."

"Any guess as to the direction of impact?"

"Not a guess, Inspector, I can tell you exactly."

"Go on," Walker asked, intrigued to hear what she had to say and encouraged to find out any more information.

"She was struck from behind, or at the very least on the right side."

"You mean deliberately?"

Cribbs looked at both men, a glance that said a lot, but she kept her thoughts to herself. "That's not for me to say or even speculate. That would be your responsibility Inspector. But what I can say is that however this incident occurred, an accident or not, the driver involved would have been aware of hitting the poor woman. Of that I have no doubt."

"Because?"

"The force, Inspector, the force of impact."

Walker turned to Conte. "I think Sergeant we need to take a look at the scene again while we wait for the report from 'traffic'. In the meantime, I want to meet with the guy who called 999 to report the accident on the night. Can you get hold of him and set up a time to have a chat?"

Returning to Cribbs he asked, "The fragments you found, will you be able to find out where they came from? A car, a truck, the type of vehicle?"

"I've already requested the analysis to be done, Inspector. It will take a while unfortunately as we only have a couple of technicians available. With luck we should be able to narrow it down, but to what, I don't know as yet. However when you first arrived here you confirmed that the incident was originally being considered an accident, right?

"That's correct."

"Which meant that the Constables who interviewed the driver at the scene, only raised their concerns about the matter being a hit-and-run when they discovered that he wasn't involved but was just a witness, yes? That those who caused the accident weren't there on site, right?

"Right," Walker repeated.

"Which meant that by the time the police got to the site of the accident, the scene had been disturbed?"

"That's right, it was a mess. That's why we are here, to see what additional information you may be able to provide us after your examination. Not staying at the scene to render assistance is a crime and the person or persons involved in this seemingly drove off leaving an innocent person lying on the side of the road to die. Unfortunately however, at this stage we don't know if this *was* an accident or if there was something else behind it."

"So, with everything going on that night you would be lucky to get anything from the scene that was useable?" she questioned.

"It looks that way. Unfortunately, the immediate area was significantly compromised due to the actions taken by the paramedics, the witness and the Constables who responded to the call. From what I have been able to establish, there were no clues to indicate what had happened. That included on the road or in the immediate surrounds. It seems the rain made light work of anything that may have fallen off the vehicle involved and there were no skid marks or tread impressions to be able to check the type of tyre used on the vehicle either. Which is why we are here." Walker stated again, nodding at his colleague. "It may well be an accident but as I said there was somebody else involved and we need to find out who."

"And why they didn't stop."

"Exactly."

As she jotted down a thought on a small pad of post-it notes that sat to one side of the desk just below a computer screen, Cribbs remarked, "Well, we will do our very best to help Inspector, but unfortunately you will just need to be patient with us. As I mentioned earlier we have a staff shortage currently."

Realising the conversation was at an end, Walker climbed out of the chair, holding out his large hand. "Thank you again, Doctor," he said, knowing that for now, there was little else for them to discuss. He had other avenues of enquiry to follow, even if they were tenuous, and he wanted to pursue them as quickly as possible, otherwise he would need to move on to other cases. With some older matters before the courts and requests to investigate other incidents crossing his desk every day, the volume of work required prioritizing. Without evidence or firm lines of enquiry, some matters were put on the shelf. Sometimes for days, sometimes for weeks, some for even longer or even permanently. With the immediacy of what had been discussed, Walker hoped that they would have something more substantial to work with within days. In the meantime, he would task Sergeant Conte and a Constable from Abingdon to look into Sue Gladstones' background. Hopefully their enquiries would lead to something of use while they waited for Cribbs' report.

"Don't get up," he insisted as he shook her hand, allowing Conte to do the same. "We'll see ourselves out."

When the two policemen had left her office and had vacated the laboratory completely, Cribbs smiled to herself. She was of a similar age to Walker. Born and bred in the area and educated locally before attending the Sir William School of Pathology at Oxford University. She liked the man and enjoyed what appeared to be harmless flirting with him. Being married to her job meant that she had little time for a long-term relationship but when the opportunity arose, well....?

CHAPTER 8

She had tried to hide the marks on her face and the bruises on her leg, but Cannon had noticed how she limped before being legged up onto her first mount of the morning, 'Diogenes the Cynic'. She was scheduled to school another horse later, but Cannon was wary given what he had already observed. For now however, she had a horse under her that was appropriately named and Cannon hoped that she was able to manage him. He was known by those who looked after him in the yard as the Doc, but often called the Dog when he got into a mood. He wasn't aggressive, any more than any other horse could be, but occasionally he could be stubborn, with a mind of his own. This morning however, he was on his best behaviour. Scheduled to run the following week in a three-mile novice chase at Chepstow, Cannon wanted to keep the horse ticking over. Knowing of Angela's condition, he realized that his mindset about her had changed from that of twenty-four hours earlier. Now he had a duty of care. She had been in his thoughts, front and centre, since Telside had given him the news. So much so that he became concerned about putting her on any horse from now on, especially in a race. He wanted to protect her but given they hadn't yet spoken he needed to be circumspect in how he approached the issue. As the six horses walked around in their well-practiced circle, their breathing and snorts were lit up by the spotlights that illuminated the yard as each clip-clopped around in front of the stables. The sounds of hooves on cement mixed with the still quiet air and the silence of the dawning day that was still an hour or so away. Cannon studied each pair, each horse and rider, as they circled in front of him. He was looking for any signs of lameness, illness or fatigue, which could easily have applied to either man/woman or beast. He called out to each of the riders in turn giving them specific instructions that he read out from his prepared notes. This told them what he wanted to see and how to do it. Then he asked each of the riders for a response. Did they understand what he had asked? Did their mounts feel comfortable in their walking action? Were there any questions? Once he was satisfied with the answers, he let Telside take over, agreeing to meet him on the gallops in ten minutes. As he walked away, he looked at Angela again, noticing her wince as she briefly touched her face while adjusting her riding helmet then checking her stirrup lengths and settling herself into the saddle.

"How are you feeling?" he asked.
They were sitting in his office. The cup of tea he had offered her was still warm and barely touched. She held it between her cold hands. He finished his own drink while he waited for her to answer. A third cup, empty, sat on the side of his desk where Telside had left it.
"I'm okay, Mr. Cannon," she replied eventually, her eyes looking down at the floor. She remained still, staring at her feet and at the blue and black lines of the carpet's pattern that delicately squiggled across the room, ultimately disappearing under his feet and chair, before hiding under the desk.
"Are you sure?"
"Yes, I'm sure," she answered weakly, refusing to look at him.
Cannon sighed. He knew where the conversation was going. The scenario he was facing reminded him of the number of times he had needed similar chats with Cassie. A father/daughter bond was said to be extra special, but it was always fraught with danger. Talking to such a young woman like Angela, an employee not a relative, was going to be even more difficult. And did he really expect to understand what she was going through? He drew comfort from the fact that he had had many similar conversations over the years. He believed that his experience as a Detective in asking pertinent questions of suspects, witnesses, the guilty, the stupid, the vain and the evil would hold him in good stead, but that was conjecture. He wanted to be sensitive to her feelings, compassionate to her plight, but he also needed her to be honest with him about her situation. After all, this was someone who he believed in, had high hopes for. He waited for her to continue. The silence stretched until she realized he was waiting.
"Why do you ask? Are you unhappy with me? Is there something I'm not doing?" she blurted, her words exploding like a demented machine gun that had locked itself on automatic fire. "Have I done something wrong?" she continued. "Is it because I won't be watching Summer Kisses run this week? Because…"
"Whoa! Whoa! Angela," Cannon pleaded, his hands in the air in a surrender-like pose. "Take it easy will you? I just want to help," he

added compassionately. "It's why I asked you to come and see me after morning stables. I wanted to be discreet as I'm not sure if the others in the yard know, so…"

"Know what, Mr. Cannon?" she asked, interrupting him. "Know what?"

Sighing inwardly, Cannon took a few seconds to let the tension drift out of the room. He had noticed her body language demonstrating a level of defiance to his questions, as she continuously crossed her arms and legs. However it was her eyes that showed that she was desperately trying to hide her feelings. Occasionally looking up, then down, he could sense her nervousness.

Speaking as gently as he could, he said. "Rich told me that you'd had a chat with him. He filled me in on what's been going on." He let the words hang between them for a second, then added, "I hope you understand that he did so in order to help you, Angela?"

There was no immediate response. She remained mute, gingerly touching her face and moving her hair to hide the marks he had seen earlier. In the light of day and sitting so close to her, he could see the damage to her face. Without a riding helmet, it was much easier to spot. Cannon also noticed the scab from a cut and the remains of the 'egg' that had swollen just below the right eye. She had tried to hide them during the morning exercises, but now they were much easier for anyone to see. That, despite her ongoing efforts to conceal them. He pointed to her face. "What happened?" he asked.

"Nothing."

"Nothing?" he questioned. "Come off it, Angela. You don't get a cut and a bruise to the face like that without *something* happening."

Again, there was no response other than a tightening of the arms that she had wrapped around herself.

"Did you fall?"

"Yes," she answered, too quickly for his liking.

"Where? When?"

"At home. I tripped. Fell down some stairs."

"How?"

She raised her face to look at him. The carpet was no longer her safety net. "I tripped over the cat," she replied. "I wasn't looking where I was going and…" Her voice trailed off which convinced Cannon that she was lying, protecting something….or someone.

"Have you seen a doctor?"

"Why would I do that? It's only a cut and a bruise, nothing serious."
He had anticipated her answer and had prepared himself for what he was about to say. "To check if your baby is okay," he declared.

It was the first time that he had been able to get to the point of the conversation and the words were barely uttered when she began to wail. Tears poured down her cheeks and she let out a savage cry that reverberated around the room. He reached over to try and comfort her, but she pulled away from him, burying herself in the chair. She curled up into a small ball leaving Cannon unsettled, embarrassed. He offered her his handkerchief but she refused to take it. He waited for her to calm down, using all the patience he could muster. As he did so his office phone began ringing. 'Not now,' he thought, letting the ringing continue its own shriek. He looked across at Angela who had begun unravelling herself from the chair. She pointed at the phone, "Aren't you going to answer that, Mr. Cannon?" she sniffed.

"No, I'll let them leave a message."

"Okay," she answered above the noise of the ringing, while rubbing a hand over her face. A sad brief smile crossed her face.

While the phone continued to interrupt them, Cannon indicated to her that he wanted to continue the conversation once the caller had got the message that the phone would remain unanswered. Unfortunately they didn't and eventually his patience having worn thin, necessitated him picking up the receiver. He indicated to Angela with a wave of his hand that she should remain seated while he took the call.

"Yes?" he said brusquely, before he had even put the phone to his ear.

"Mr. Cannon?"

"Yes, what is it?"

"John Silvers again, Ayrshire Police, sorry to bother you. Can we talk?"

"What about?"

"Well something has come up and I need your help."

"My help? Why?"

There was a slight hesitation before Cannon received an answer to his questions. It wasn't what he expected.

"Let's just say, your….experience," Silvers said.

It was a coy answer, somewhat unsettling and Cannon responded accordingly.

"I need more than that DCI Silvers," he answered, noticing Angela react to the mention of Silvers' rank.

"Okay, can we get together somewhere? Have a chat, discuss a few more…details shall we say? Given the nature of it, I think it needs to be a face-to-face meeting."

Cannon found the cloak and dagger approach to whatever Silvers wanted to discuss rather annoying. He preferred some straight talking and when added to the current conversation he was having with his only conditional jockey and her ongoing obfuscation he was beginning to become more than a little pissed off.

"Look, Inspector. I've got a business and a stable to run, I can't just drop everything just like that without any context. If it helps and you want to come here to my yard, then…."

"No, no, not at this stage, Mr. Cannon," Silvers countered.

"Well in that case, I have an obligation to be at Chepstow in a few days how about meeting me there? It's a long way from Ayrshire I know but at least it's closer than Wincanton, which is the meeting I'll be at after that. What do you think?"

There was a pause and a cough while Silvers considered Cannon's proposal. Chuckling slightly to himself, the DCI responded with a smile in his voice.

"I suppose the drive might be pleasant," he said. "Can you send me the details?"

After requesting Silvers' email and mobile number, Cannon wrote down the details on a small notepad that he extracted from a drawer in the desk. Promising to relay the necessary information later he finished the call, turning his gaze back to Angela who had composed herself again. He looked at her tear-stained face which was streaked with small black lines, an accumulation of mud and grime after riding out and her morning stable duties. He gave her the previously offered handkerchief. This time she took it.

"I'm sorry about that," he apologized, referring to the interruption.

"Is there a problem, Mr. Cannon….with the police?"

He watched her closely, remembering how she reacted when he answered the phone.

"No, they were just seeking some information from me, about a horse I once trained. It's nothing," he lied, sensing that there was more to Silvers' request than he had been told to date.

"Oh, and I noticed that you mentioned Chepstow where…"

"You are down to ride the Doc and White Noise too."
"Yes."
"Do you think it wise?"
"What do mean?" she enquired.
Cannon turned his head askance, his action clearly letting her know what he meant. There were no words necessary.
"I'll be alright, Mr. Cannon. I can still ride for a while."
"Maybe."
"Please Mr. Cannon," she pleaded, "please let me ride. I won't let you down, please!" She began to cry again, sobbing, and words fell out of her that were incomprehensible. Cannon reached over and cradled her in his arms. Her sobs continued as he tried to calm her down. With his arms around her, she hugged him tightly, her body shaking, the top of her head just reaching the middle of his chest. He spoke quietly, slowly, reassuring her.
"I'll need to seek permission," he said, gently moving her away from him, holding her at arm's length, checking to see if she was aware of what he was saying. He was sensitive to her request but still not overly happy. "Do you understand, Angela? It may be out of my hands. There are protocols to follow."
Angela nodded, "I know, Mr. Cannon. I know."
"And you understand that they are there to protect you *and* the baby?"
He pointed towards her still flat stomach.
"Yes."
"Good."
She smiled at him, a smile of resignation, acceptance and gratitude. He took the opportunity to get the answers he wanted.
"So, did you really fall? Trip?"
"What do you m...?"
"The face, the limp you have been trying to hide all morning, was it really due to a fall?"
She looked straight into his eyes. Cannon knew the answer straight away.
"Was it Nick?" he asked. "Did he do this?"
There was no reply, her eyes reverting downwards was a dead giveaway.
Cannon was outraged. He had seen many a woman beaten up by a partner or husband in his time in the force, but to see such a young

woman like Angela, so small and petit, being abused and while pregnant, incensed him.

"The bastard!" he said, caught up in his own emotions. "Why? Why did he do this to you? Tell me what happened?"

She tried to tell him that it was none of his business, that he should stay out of it, but he seemed deaf to the idea.

"Please Mr. Cannon, just leave it alone. It was nothing, it was my own fault."

Cannon thought that if he had been given a penny for every time he had heard those same words from a woman who had been beaten up in a domestic, he would have been a very rich man. He knew that it was a nonsense, a way that the defenseless tried to keep the peace. *Don't react or make a fuss and things will get better,* that seemed to be the formula many women had unfortunately subscribed to. He guessed it was the same the world over and he hated it.

"Look," he said. "I think you need to go to the police. I think you need to let them know what happened."

"No!"

"Yes!" he retorted. "If you don't then it will only happen again. Maybe not today or tomorrow, but it will happen."

"No."

Sighing again, he asked, "And what about the baby?"

"What about it?"

"Are you sure it's okay? That what happened to you hasn't resulted in any harm to….?" As he watched her face, Cannon realized he might have gone too far and ceased his questioning.

"I'm sure it's okay," she answered, naïvely. "I'm not even three months."

"Perhaps, but I suggest you go and see your doctor."

"No. I'm okay. The baby's okay."

"Angela," he stated firmly. "If you want to ride, then I insist you get checked out. If you don't, then I'm sorry, I won't seek an exemption from the BHA for you."

As soon as she realized that he was serious, her eyes opened wide. A feeling of dread coursed through her veins. Riding racehorses was her dream, her passion. She had a future, a career ahead of her. The baby was only a blip on that path, a short period of time when she would be away from racing. If Cannon carried out his threat then who knew what the implication could be long term. And, in the immediate future, would he also consider terminating her indenture? She wasn't sure if he could, but the very thought disturbed her the most. Reluctantly she agreed to do what he asked.

"I'll go to the doctor first," she said. "After that I'll talk with the police, but I don't want Nick charged with anything. As I told you, it was my fault."

Accepting her change of heart, Cannon was satisfied that she had taken on board what he had said to her, and he acknowledged it. A soft smile creased her face and she silently thanked him. She turned to leave the room suddenly realizing that she still had his handkerchief.

"Keep it," he said, as she offered it back to him.

"I'll wash it for you," she replied.

"Okay, thanks, but it's not necessary," he answered, softly.

"It's not a problem Mr. Cannon…and…thank you."

With that, she turned and walked out of the room, still limping slightly. Cannon sat in his chair for a while. Being alone gave him time to think. He reviewed what had transpired during the morning and contemplated a number of scenarios. One of them was to pay Nick Van der Linden a quiet visit.

CHAPTER 9

The shipment had been ready for a while. Amar Hyseni was getting quite nervous at the slow pace. The transaction should have been completed already. He needed the money but wouldn't be paid until the delivery had been made. In the meantime, his supplier was pushing for payment. Business was business and Hyseni was reneging on his part of the deal. The easy part had been obtaining the drugs, the difficult piece was procuring the right vessel to ensure they arrived safely. This had proven much more difficult than usual. Two attempts had been tried already but due to circumstances both had to be torpedoed at the last minute. Neither had been total failures, the backup plan would provide some return on his investment, but it was marginal compared to what could have been.

The two men busy with the third attempt worked under his instructions. If things went as they should, the packages would be in Leeds via Hull the next morning. From there the contact would arrange distribution to Middlesbrough in the north, Manchester in the west and Coventry in the midlands. The route had been used many times already but was not exclusive. Ever since he and his family had moved to Holland, Hyseni had managed to avoid the failings of so many others who tried to expand their business. They had ultimately been caught or had to escape back to the safety of their own countries, when their true business dealings had been revealed. Falling into the trap of laziness and routine, many had made the mistake of forgetting that Interpol never slept and that any error was quickly pounced upon. One simple mistake could alert the police in one country, to pursue a line of inquiry that could lead to the police in other countries combining with it into a joint task force. The specific intent of that collective team; the conducting of an operation against such individual or gang. Hyseni was aware of this risk and had researched the way that the authorities in multiple countries operated to counter his method of conducting business. He had looked at the best routes to use, tested the mettle of the authorities by using decoys and travelled to and from the continent, sometimes alone or sometimes with others to legitimize himself as a bonafide businessman who needed to cross borders regularly. All the while he was getting to understand the procedures that the various police forces followed and methods they used. Such knowledge allowed him to eliminate the errors that could have exposed him. An example was his uncontrollable temper, whereby he was quick to ire and to express his anger with others, especially when there were delays which cost him money or red tape that cost him time. Getting a shipment to one of his markets, when they were held up at a border for some reason, would often result in him becoming extremely agitated. At one stage, he would have made an example of one or even a group of his men. His rage would have resulted in them losing an eye, a hand or even their life, yet when it came to dealing with the border authorities anywhere in the world, he was a picture of innocence. He never argued when they queried anything with him, and he always maintained a posture of compliance and acquiescence whenever he was questioned. He had built up a convincing story about himself and was always ready with an answer which he was able to back up 'legitimately'. By keeping a relatively low profile in Holland, he hadn't brought any attention on himself or on the business and that was the way he wanted to keep it. He had even made sure that Brexit had not impacted how his dealings with the UK were seen. By doing the right thing *prima facie* and pretending to follow the rules of trade, it meant that those in authority who he came into contact with, at the various ports including Rotterdam, Felixstowe, Calais, Dover and others, had no reason to suspect his business was anything but lawful. It had taken some time and now he was reaping the rewards of his investment, however days like today and during the last week had pushed him close to the limit of his patience. The Crack Cocaine, Heroin and Ice had been sold already. The customer had the money, Hyseni had the product, he just needed to deliver it. If it hadn't been for Erjon and his bullshit, he thought, he wouldn't have been in this position. He wondered if his brother-in-law had been deliberately slow. Resolution of that problem however was for another day. Today, he needed to focus on the shipment, as the ferry to Hull was due to leave at 8:30 pm and the parcels needed to be ready for boarding several hours before that.

He was about to seek an answer to the delay when one of the two men indicated that they had managed to resolve the problem.

"Are you sure?" Hyseni asked. "We don't a repeat of what happened last time."

"Yes," the man said, "we've given them what we were asked to."
"Good," Hyseni replied. "Let's get this show on the road then. We've got a boat to catch."
The two workers began loading the cargo into the van that was situated inside the garage beneath the building. When he had acquired the warehouse on a long-term lease, it was the basement parking that had sealed the deal. Location and secure access made it a no-brainer. While his front company upstairs dealt with legitimate import and export activities, the real business was conducted out of site in a hidden part of the building that had been secreted behind false walls and hidden doors. Wireless remote cameras hidden inside light fittings throughout the building and linked to a base station recorded all internal movements and a silent alarm provided additional protection from anyone snooping around the perimeter.
Hyseni watched the men as they worked, knowing that the journey from *Nieuw-Zeelandweg* in the city to the Europoort in Rotterdam would take at least an hour. He would be glad when the shipment was on board the vessel but was aware that things could still go wrong at any time. There were procedures to be followed once the ship arrived in the UK and the was a need for others to do their piece to ensure that there were no mistakes. That was one part of the process that Hyseni detested as he was relying on others. It was always risky and it always made him nervous. He continued to hover around the men, issuing instructions, and checking again the details of the shipment before he was satisfied. He looked at his watch. The ship would leave in just over three hours. Outside, darkness had fallen adding an additional layer of security over the activities. It was these types of measures that had ensured his success in expanding the business. He made a phone call to his supplier assuring him of payment within the next seventy-two hours. The call had been deliberately short and through an app that provided him the necessary protection. Security was paramount. Even when he needed to use email, which was seldom, it was always via a VPN.
"You had better get going," he said, as the two men locked the back of the van pulling down large levers that slid thick round bolts into place. Two large locks completed the process.
Hyseni pressed his thumb on a small remote control, and the door to the garage opened with a quiet efficiency, allowing the van to creep from the garage and out into the cold of the early evening. Dew was

already beginning to form on some of the cars parked along the roadside as the van made its way towards the coast. Hyseni closed the garage door and then texted his customer. His deals were always cash-on-delivery, payment received via several banks in Ireland, Spain and Austria. It had worked so far and he had no reason to doubt that it would continue to do so. He had checked the paperwork himself.

It had been a difficult forty-eight hours. Michelle had struggled with the effects of her colleagues death like most of the school community. A sombre mood, one uninvited, appeared to have inveigled its way onto the premises taking hold of the school room by room. From the administration teams through to the Headmaster, there were signs of stress and collective sadness. Sue Gladstone had been liked, indeed loved by everyone, and her death had shaken them all.
"I still can't believe it. Who would do such a thing?" Michelle asked, as she lay next to him. It was almost 11pm and she couldn't sleep. Light from a small bedside table lamp on her side of the bed softly illuminated the room. She had her head against his chest and her arm across his stomach. Cannon had his eyes closed and his mind was playing tricks on him. He was only half listening to what she was saying, being conflicted himself. The conversations with Horowitz, the query from Silvers and now the way Michelle was feeling about Sue Gladstone's death all added to his confusion. He drifted in and out of consciousness, his brain reviewing the day's events. He still hadn't had the chance to catch up with Rich again, which had been one of his main priorities, and now he was battling with what to do about Angela. After their conversation he had decided to wait twenty-four hours before going to see Van der Linden. In the interim he had contacted Angela's doctor having received permission from her to do so. He wanted get a view from the professionals on the dangers of her continuing to ride and the potential impact on the baby's development.
"There is always a risk," he had been told, "and my advice is to be as practical as possible. I would be extremely concerned if she ever had a fall."
"So that means no riding at all?"

"Ideally, yes. However, I've known Angela almost all her life and as you would be aware, she can be extremely stubborn."

"Indeed, though that can be a good thing at times," he had responded, aware that it was one such trait that had got her the position as his Conditional jockey in the first place. Her determination and focus to the job at hand.

"Well it can be, but being headstrong can also lead to…"

"Say no more Dr. Philips, I get the picture," he had interrupted. He had then thanked her for her insight and recommendation that another four weeks was the maximum amount of time she would sign off on, should he decide to apply for approval from the BHA for Angela to continue riding. With that in mind, he had completed the necessary forms during the day and submitted them on-line after Philips had signed them.

Michelle lay silent for a while and he thought that she had fallen asleep at last. He turned to face her, intending to check. She stared back at him, her face questioning.

"So what do you think?"

"About what?"

"About what I just asked you?"

Carefully trying to recall what she had said, he eventually gave up.

"Sorry, I didn't hear you."

"Were you sleeping?"

"No, well perhaps I did for a few seconds," he admitted, sheepishly, "but, in my defence I was thinking about something else."

"Which is?"

"Chepstow…and Angela," he said, deciding not to mention the call with DCI Silvers and complicating matters any further. "I'm not sure I want her to ride for me until she's had the baby, but…"

"But she's insisting?"

"Yes, and so I've decided to give her another month and that's it."

"That sounds reasonable."

"Umm," he answered, touching her face gently with his hand, "I'm worried though. If something ever happened then…" He let the thought drift off into the cool night, aware that she still wanted an answer to her question, but he had forgotten what it was.

"So what is it you wanted to ask me?"

"Wanted to?"

"Yes."

"Asked you, more like it."

"Yes. So what was it?" he teased, suggesting to her that they should get some sleep and perhaps his answer could wait until morning.

Her eyebrows raised, she tutted softly. "I was asking if you thought the person who ran Sue down, would be easy to find?"

Cannon considered the question. He knew from experience that hit and run accidents were never easy to resolve unless there was plenty of residual evidence at the scene that could be used to piece together the type of vehicle involved. What was always helpful was if there was any CCTV or dashcam evidence available. From what Michelle had told him as to where the incident had taken place, and the lack of any witnesses on scene, it was likely that the police would have their job cut out on this one.

Trying to be positive he said, "If it was a local involved then maybe they'll get lucky."

"And if it wasn't?"

"Then....I'm not sure. Unfortunately with so few resources at the police's disposal now, there are more and more crimes that are going unsolved. It's such a.."

"Travesty!" she interrupted. "A bloody travesty!"

He stared into her eyes, not having seen her so upset in such a long time. It was obvious that she was still shaken by what had happened. "That could have been me," she continued. "I could have been walking down that lane. Imagine if my car had broken down on the way home from school and I had needed to walk to the nearest house to call you. In that area, the phone reception is pretty poor so it's a possibility."

He realized that she was starting to get worked up and imagining scenarios that may never happen. "Hey," he said quietly. "I think you may be upsetting yourself unnecessarily."

She began to shake, tears slowly leaked from her eyes, running in single rivulets down her cheeks and along her nose. Cannon reached for her, holding her tight. With her face pressed deep into his chest, he let her sob while trying to reassure her that he understood how she felt. He let her know that it was okay to feel the way she did. In time her tears slowed until she finally drifted off to sleep. Cannon decided to leave the light on rather move her away from him. With his own thoughts still swirling around in his head, he noticed that it was just after midnight. Planting a soft kiss on Michelle's head he closed his eyes. Within minutes he was asleep. Two hours later he was wide awake. A vision of Cassie flying through the air, thrown from the back of a jumping racehorse and landing on the side of a dark and damp road before being surrounded by angry tax officials startled him into a cold sweat. He instantly sat bolt upright, his heart pounding in his chest. Realizing that the nightmare was nothing more than his jumbled thoughts taking him on a terrible trip through the dark hours of a cold late Autumn night, he fell back onto the sheets. He looked at Michelle who was lying quietly, her back to him, her breathing steady and soft. He briefly wondered whether she was dreaming and whether the answers he had given to her questions before she fell asleep had removed any of her fears? He was hopeful. Realising that he needed to be out of bed in just a few short hours, he tried to settle himself down. When he awoke, the alarm on his watch sending a vibration through his wrist, he sensed that had been able to sleep again albeit fitfully. For that he was grateful.

CHAPTER 10

DI Sam Walker sat back in his chair ready to take a bite. The Abingdon police station was usually hidden away behind the trees that lined Colwell Drive. However with winter fast approaching, the leaves had fallen and lay along the footpath in piles, brown and crinkled, blown around by the breeze now whipping through the village. As part of the Abingdon business park, the Thames Valley police had made sure that the staff had been catered for by having a McDonalds restaurant directly opposite on Marcham Road. Walker was a regular.

He had just finished reading the report from Jenny Cribb when Chris Conte had stuck his head into his office and asked whether there was anything he wanted. Conte had then arranged for a junior constable to collect the wider teams' food order.

Sitting together while they ate, they discussed the Pathologists' findings along with the report from 'Traffic', those who had attended the scene on the evening of the accident. Walker and Conte had been to the crash site the previous afternoon, but it had revealed nothing of use to them. They concluded that the investigation was likely to be more arduous than they would have hoped.

"We need the results from the examination of the paint fragments Sergeant," Walker said, between mouthfuls of his burger. "It's the only thing that we have to go on at this stage."

"And the witness statement, Sir," Conte reminded him.

"Well, that's true, but all that tells us, is that a motorbike was possibly involved. It's not definitive."

Walker picked up the statement from his desk that had been taken by one of the junior officers who had been first on site.

"It says here that the witness, a Mr. Ted Fanchurch, and his daughter Wendy were travelling home to Chesterton along the Witney Road, the A4095 and that they had been visiting the daughter's horse at livery stables at Fish Hill farm. That's about a mile away from where the incident occurred."

"That's right,"

"And shortly after they turned onto the Witney Road, a motorbike came towards them heading in the opposite direction, at speed."

"Yep."

"But they didn't see the rider or riders, they didn't notice the colour of the bike nor did they see the incident itself."

Conte nodded, as he devoured another quarter of his own burger. Walker put what was left of his own lunch onto the paper bag that it came in and wiped his hands, then mouth, with the small white napkin that accompanied it.

"So what we don't know," he went on, "is whether there was another vehicle involved, perhaps one that wasn't using any running lights. It's possible something may have turned onto Witney Road from…where was it?"

"Boddington Lane."

"Or indeed Cuckoo Lane, just 300 yards away."

"Yes, that's true, Sir. And it *is* possible given where the accident occurred, just a short distance away from either intersection. Unfortunately both those roads are quite long and there is nothing down there, no estates, single houses or even farmhouses. So there is no one we can question that would have heard or seen another vehicle speeding along either road."

"So why did the witness turn around? What made them do that?" Walker queried, licking some of the burger sauce stuck between his fingers.

"Well, Sir, as the statement suggests. After the motorbike passed their own vehicle at speed, Mr. Fanchurch said he was looking in the rear-view mirror and cursing the bike rider for giving him a fright, when he saw the tail-light of the bike suddenly veer then brighten before quickly disappearing from view. As he indicated," Conte continued, pointing at the document still in Walker's hand, "he thought the bike had gone off the road, so he turned around to check it out."

Walker sighed. What they were facing appeared to be pretty obvious in terms of what had occurred that night. However what they still needed to understand was whether there was an ulterior motive behind the incident or whether it was just an accident. If the former then they needed to establish a motive and find a suspect. If the latter, they needed to find the culprit. At this stage they had nothing. They couldn't even begin to speculate.

"While we wait for the report on the paint fragments I think we should take a quick visit to see Mr. Fanchurch," Walker said. "In the meantime get Constable Timmly to see if he can find out if any of the local repair shops have been requested to fix a blue motorbike over the last day or so. If that was involved in the incident and a local owns it then it's likely to be fixed by someone in the area."

"Will do, Sir," Conte replied.

Walker placed his hands together and looked down at his desk. It was as if he was contemplating something. Conte waited in silence until Walker said, "We also need to check with any of our people working the streets to see if they have heard anything on the grapevine. It's possible the person or persons involved may have dumped the vehicle or tried to have it repaired by someone running a backyard operation."

"I guess that's always possible, Sir," Conte replied. "I'll put the word out."

"Good, and we also need to look deeper into Sue Gladstone's background."

"I've already begun that process. From what I've been able to establish so far, there is nothing that raises any concerns, but I'll keep digging. The poor woman seems to have been a dedicated teacher. Honest, kind, quiet, well liked and apparently with no money worries either."

"That's good to hear, Sergeant, but I can guarantee it's not the full story. Everyone has another side to them. What about boyfriends, ex-lovers, ex-colleagues, neighbours? There is always a possibility that someone from her past had some form of grudge against her."

"And decided to kill her?" Conte queried, feeling a little uncomfortable at Walker's quick assessment of the facts as they knew them.

"As I said, anything is possible and it's our job to find out who was involved. It still may be an accident, but if it was it would have been far easier for whoever hit her to stop and call it in. The fact that they didn't opens up a whole series of questions."

Conte shrugged his shoulders in response to Walkers' view of the case.

Was it really murder, he thought, or just a terrible accident?

"I'll get the car," he said.

The parlour was situated on Witney High Street, a few shops away from the roundabout where the A4095 became Bridge Street. The road was usually busy but Cannon had been able to find a parking spot just a hundred yards away. Locking his car he walked along the footpath, passing Boots, Fone World, the Co-op, and several smaller shops before stopping at the door to the tattoo parlour. He could see very little of what was happening inside as the front windows was plastered with brightly designed decals and posters with the name of the shop, *W'ink and Pierce*.

Cannon shuddered at the very thought of people being pierced for fun, and even worse paying someone to do it for them. He had seen enough stabbings while in the police, and he didn't see the difference between the two. A cut or a slit made by any form of instrument was still a cut and it still drew blood.

Pushing the door open, he could smell a sweetness in the air. The attempt to hide the all-pervasive aroma of marijuana with burning joss sticks failed miserably. Inside there were three steel tables, each covered with what looked to Cannon like a fake tiger pelt. On each, lay a customer propped up in different positions. One had both legs exposed, another their back and a third, their left arm. Spotlights above the tables lit the immediate area, while stainless steel bare bulb fittings illuminated the rest of the shop. Sitting beside every table was an individual wearing a mask over their nose and mouth. Each had a tattoo machine, a type of handheld metal gun used to penetrate a couple of millimetres below the skin and insert the required ink as the tattoo was applied. The sharp buzzing sound of the devices was partially drowned out by the offensive lyrics emanating from some piped rap music which reverberated through the confined space of the shop. Mid-size speakers had been placed above the door to the High Street. The beat thudded into the back of Cannon's head.

On the walls were multiple pictures showing various designs that the customers could choose from. Dragons, Animals, Cartoon characters, Football players, and a multitude of others. In addition, a banner on one of the walls stated that the artist would do anything the customer wanted. It was labelled; D-I-Y - D'Ink Yourself.

Having stopped a few feet into the parlour to take in his surroundings and to check if Van der Linden was inside, Cannon noticed that each of the tattooists were busy staring at him, their focus having changed from customer to interloper.

"Can I help you?" one of them asked, removing the mask from his face. Cannon guessed that the man was around forty. Medium height (if he stood), a little overweight, a lean face with brown eyes, and a Zapata moustache. He had long dark hair and wore a black t-shirt to go with his black jeans and new white running shoes. Cannon considered that the man was too old for the kind of work he was conducting but kept the thought to himself. By not replying immediately Zapata asked him again about his business.

"I'm looking for the owner," he said. "Nick."

The man smirked. "Are you a cop?"

The comment made the others smile, one customer laughing louder than he should have. Cannon looked down at himself. His clothes, his shoes. He made a show of opening his coat and pretending to search inside his pockets. While he did so, the other two tattooists turned back to their clients, carrying on with their work.

"No," he said, answering Zapata, who seemed satisfied with the reply until Cannon added an afterthought, "not anymore."

Within seconds the room fell silent, one of the other two artists had turned off the music using a remote control. Cannon's display of sarcasm had left its mark. Apologizing to his customer and asking for patience, Zapata put down his gun and took a step towards Cannon, while the others watched.

"So what do you want with Nick then?" he asked, with obvious malice in his voice.

"That's between me and him," Cannon replied.

"Really?" Zapata replied, his hands flexing. He was standing just a few feet in front of Cannon who could smell the man's breath. Elements of weed and alcohol mixed together. Certainly no toothpaste, Cannon thought, remaining aware but not reacting to the provocation. He waited for Zapata to make the next move.

"I don't think you are welcome here."

"Because I'm not a customer?" Cannon replied, pointing to the various tables. "And anyway, how do you know I'm not?"

"Because I can smell a pig anywhere and the stench of bacon is overpowering right now."

Cannon smiled at the old cliché. Looking around at the various sticks of incense burning on a couple of shelves high up above a counter at the far end of the shop, he responded to the comment. "I'm surprised you can smell anything with that lot." He pointed towards the light smoke that wafted towards them. Zapata looked to where Cannon was pointing. As he turned back to face him, Cannon hit him with a punch to the stomach and then another to the man's chin. Zapata crumpled to the floor gasping for breath. The others in the shop looked shocked, seemingly unable to move. Like statutes they watched as Zapata retched, trying to get air into his lungs. Cannon turned towards the shop door, and as he did so a shout came from the back of the parlour. From behind a black curtain roughly two metres beyond the furthest table a man appeared. He was dressed in a grey singlet top despite the cold outside, and light blue jeans which were stained red, black and green across the thighs from being in contact with too much ink. His arms were covered in sleeve tattoos and he had a similar amount of ink around his throat and chest. On his chin was a small red goatee which made him seem all the more menacing. Just shy of six feet tall (around 178 cm) he was muscular around the chest and his body was obviously bulked up through the use of protein powders. With a slim waist and cocky attitude Cannon had seen the likes of the man many times before. He had heard a lot about Nick Van der Linden through various sources, including complaints by neighbours from his repeated indiscretions that regularly got him into the local press.

Van der Linden looked at his staff member still feeling the effects of Cannon's fists. He tutted and suggested to the man that he go into the back room and get some water.

"That wasn't a very nice thing to do, Mr. Cannon," he said, noting his visitor raise an eyebrow at the use of his name. "Yes I know who you are. Angela has told me all about you."

"Umm, well she's said nothing much about you," Cannon answered, "and from what I can see, it's just as well."

The sarcasm wasn't lost on the tattooist. He looked around at the others in the shop, indicating that they should continue with their work. As he did so, Zapata returned from the back room, giving Cannon a dirty look before sitting down again next to his client.

"So what can I do for you, Mr. Cannon? Are you looking to have some work done?" Van der Linden smirked, pointing at the various pictures on the walls. Cannon noted the cynicism in the question. It was supposed to be a low-key visit but it had already gone further than he had planned and the Dutchman was getting under his skin. The subtle baiting was annoying and Cannon lost his temper. He walked right up to the man, his face a few inches from the goatee and through gritted teeth whispered, "You hurt Angela again and I'll be back here with more than a warning."

"What do you mean?" Van der Linden asked, professing his innocence, "I've never raised a finger to her."

"No?"

"No!"

"So she fell down the stairs on her own did she? Her cuts, the bruises, the limp, that's all from that are they?"

"Yes," she told me she tripped.

"I don't believe you," Cannon replied. "I think she's protecting you. I think you have been in enough trouble recently and she's hoping to stop the police from getting involved again."

"What? What are you talking about?"

"You know. The late-night drinking, the motorbike rides around the street at all hours, your excessive partying. If there was a domestic violence charge levelled against you now, then it's very possible that you may end up being arrested, charged and jailed, and all this," he pointed around the room, "could all soon disappear, couldn't it?"

"Look mate," Van der Linden said, "I think you'd better leave. What goes on between Angela and me, is none of your business."

Cannon looked down at the floor before answering. "Well that's where you are wrong, mate! Angela is an employee of mine and I take what happens to her very seriously. The fact that she is pregnant with *your* child and was beaten up by you, increasing the risk of damage to her baby and herself, *is* my business."

"I told you…"

"You told me nothing, you piece of shit," Cannon interrupted, his anger barely under control. "But I'm telling you this. If you touch her again, I'll be around here before you know it, and.."

"And what?"

Taking a deep breath, knowing that the others in the shop were listening, Cannon pointed a finger into Van der Linden's face and said, "What you'll get from me will be ten times what you do to her, and let me tell you this, I won't hesitate to do it," he warned.

"Is that a threat, Mr. Cannon?"

"No, no threat, just a statement of fact."

Van der Linden turned around to look at the others in the shop. The silence was deep, almost tangible. It seemed that everyone had stopped breathing and he noticed that the tattoo guns had been turned off as the sparring between Cannon and himself had

continued. Trying to save face he said, "Well thank you for the visit, Mr. Cannon, it's been enlightening, but as you can see I have a business to run, so if you would kindly…"
"And is this it?" Cannon asked.
"What?"
"Is this all you do?"
"What do you mean by that?"
"Oh, I'm just asking," Cannon said, cynically. "It's just that I'm wondering where all the money comes from for your various motorbikes, the partying….this!" He spread his hands outwards indicating the shop and its contents. "After all," he continued, "Angela's money is mostly tied up in trust, so how are you able to do all that here in Witney? It's not as if you are run off your feet every day of the week is it?"
"We do well enough," Van der Linden countered. "You may have noticed *old man*, that tattoos have become very popular."
Ignoring the jibe about their age differences, Cannon said, "Well, I hope you do, because with a baby and a partner to look after soon, you'll need to be a bit more circumspect than you are currently."
"What I do with my money, how I make it, and how I chose to spend it, has nothing to do with you, Mr. Cannon!" Van der Linden replied angrily.
Cannon smiled. He had a suspicion that there was more to Van der Linden's business interests than met the eye. His experiences during his time in the police, his antennae, came to the fore whenever he encountered the type of person he believed Van der Linden to be. He guessed that there were other things going on, and that the parlour was both a front, a place where 'other' business was conducted. The whole environment was one which reeked of drugs, the smell of marijuana being a dead giveaway.
Unfortunately that was no longer his domain and he assumed the authorities were across it. He repeated his position regarding any more violence against Angela, informing Van der Linden that he would advise her to contact the police immediately should anything happen, but Cannon himself would be back to carry out his promise when it did. With hands in mock surrender the tattooist professed to be scared. Cannon smiled again, unsettling the man even more. Then without saying another word, he turned and walked out of the shop leaving the door wide open allowing the cold air from outside to

infiltrate and mix with the aroma of the joss sticks and the marijuana. He was hopeful that it would send a chill down the spine of the partially dressed Dutchman.

CHAPTER 11

Chepstow was bathed in a milky grey light. The morning had been cloudy and a few drops of rain had fallen on the course overnight. This in addition to the downpour it had received during the two days prior to the meeting. Small puddles still littered the grounds and the punters who had braved the cool wind that blew up the Bristol Channel and the River Severn were pleased, though not optimistic, to see the sun trying to make a valiant attempt to break through. The recent stretch of dry weather had now been well and truly broken and the going on the racetrack was deemed to be soft. This was what Cannon preferred for the majority of his horses. Not too hard a surface and certainly not too heavy or gluggy. When horses needed to wade through heavy ground and run and jump over several miles, it was a slog that many took an extended period of time to recover from. Obviously there were those that preferred to get their toe into the ground, but heavy going and big weights could stop a tank at times, and racehorses were not tanks.

The Doc had travelled down without incident and appeared to be in good spirits. He had shown none of his cantankerous side and Cannon was pleased to hear it when he caught up with his groom Jack Radcliffe.

They were standing together in the stables where the horse would be saddled for his race, the second of the day. Cannon watched as Radcliffe rubbed the horse down after giving him a spray of water to settle him after the two-hour drive from Stonesfield. In the next box along was White Noise and he would get the same treatment from Radcliffe shortly. The grey would be racing in a two-mile handicap hurdle, race four on the six-race card. He was to carry a relatively light weight so Angela had been declared to ride the horse, however Cannon had advised her that he would be watching how well she was coping during the running of the Doc's race. If he saw that she was struggling, then he wouldn't hesitate to take her off White Noise. There were provisions in the rules to do so, and he would use them if he felt it best for Angela and her mount's interest. White Noise was ticking over nicely during training. His form was good and Cannon's plan was to get him to qualify for the Champion Hurdle which was just under four months away in March. A win today would be the start of his campaign. If things continued that way, he would get the opportunity to take on some of the best two milers in the country over hurdles. The big stables had plenty of firepower and while White Noise was likely to be a long shot for such a big race, the owner of the horse was keen to be involved in the journey. Just getting to the start would be a win, so the plan Cannon had prepared for the horse needed to go off without a hitch. A pregnant jockey and a conditional one at that, no matter how focused and skilled she was, could easily put a spanner in the works. So while he had faith in her, Cannon was nervous. He thanked Radcliffe for getting the Doc ready for his race and went off to find Angela who he expected to be in the jockey's rooms. She had made her own way to the course, a friend Jackie Wilkie had driven her down which allowed her to sleep in the car and to rest up for the three mounts she had at the meeting. Cannon had the two and there was a third for a local trainer, Noel Hardaker, in the fifth race. Cannon wasn't sure if she had told Hardaker about her condition, but he guessed the man would be aware by now anyway. The Stewards would have likely contacted him referencing Cannon seeking permission for her to ride at the meet. As he walked towards the main stands and the owners and trainers bar, he heard his name being called over the course tannoy. He was asked to contact the racecourse office and that required him to turn back the way he had come. As he stepped through the door of the building and into the office, a number of people were exiting, talking animatedly. He recognized one the trainers who had a runner in race four which was likely to be a serious competitor to White Noise.

"How are you doing, Alf?" he asked, of the man in his late sixties being hurried along by two excited owners keen to get to the bar in advance of the first race which was still over an hour away. Alfred Proud had been a feature of the sport for nearly forty-five years. He had achieved success both in flat racing and in National Hunt races and once was quoted as saying that he would never retire but rather be found dead in a horse's stable than in his own bed. Acknowledging Cannon, Proud apologized to his owners, asking them to go ahead of him to the bar where he would meet up them shortly. The two men then had a quick chat before each wished the other well with their runners. Cannon offering safe jumping for Proud's runner, Simply Splendid, and Proud reciprocating with the best of luck with White Noise.

As they two men parted, Cannon heard his name mentioned again, this time not over the course tannoy but from over his shoulder. Cannon turned to see a man, whose strong Scottish accent he'd only heard previously over the phone, from Ayrshire. He was standing a couple of yards away. DCI John Silvers was quite an imposing man in the flesh. Standing well over six feet four (one hundred and ninety-four centimetres) and around seventeen stone (one hundred and ten kilograms) he was the size of man that the police forces used to recruit. Very much a long John Silvers. His hands were huge and seemed to fit snugly around Cannon's own when they shook an introduction. In his early fifties with a ruddy complexion and a nose that seemed to be crusting with pockmarks, perhaps indicating that the man enjoyed a drink as well as a similar enjoyment of food. His short dull red hair was augmented by dark green eyes. The entire package was wrapped within a beige raincoat that seemed to struggle to stay closed across the man's girth.

"I was standing at the counter inside the building when the receptionist pointed you out," he said, referring to the short conversation Cannon had just concluded with Alfred Proud. "She saw you coming towards the door, which I assume you did because I asked her to page for you."

"No doubt Inspector," Cannon replied, non-committedly. Though Cannon had Silvers' mobile phone number he had not shared his own with the policeman. He wanted to know more from the Detective before he was willing to go that far. He didn't have a clue about Silvers' motives or reason to meet with him, so while he was curious, he still wanted to be cautious. What they had discussed to date had been vague though Cannon realized that the subject must be serious enough for Silvers to willingly drive all the way down from Ayrshire to meet with him in Wales.

"I stayed overnight in Birmingham," the policemen said quietly. "I had expected to stop in Manchester but that was a bit too far away from here," he continued, "so by driving a bit further I was able to get to the course earlier than expected this morning."

"I've been here just over an hour or so myself. So timing wise you did well," Cannon replied, suggesting that they take a walk to the Owners and Trainers bar. Cannon had previously made arrangements for Silvers to get a pass allowing him access to various areas of the course and he was pleased to see it wrapped around the second top button of Silvers' raincoat. The badge flapped in the wind as they walked out from the building together, silently slipping between the crowd that was starting to build for the first race. Drops of rain began to fall. The sun had failed, clouds began to roll in, blown by the gusty wind.

"What are you drinking?" Cannon asked, once the two men had found a quiet spot in the bar.
"If they have a whisky I'll take a wee dram with a dash of water, if that's okay? Plus some crisps if you wouldn't mind. I haven't eaten since I bought a donut at a BP petrol station on the way?" Acknowledging the request and without any thought as to why his visitor was drinking while on the job, Cannon went off to fill the order. He decided that tea to keep him warm would work best for himself.
Once settled back at the table and mindful of the time, Cannon sought some answers from the Detective.
Silvers took his glass of whisky and in a single mouthful drained it completely. Then he opened his bag of crisps before theatrically extracting a handkerchief from one of the pockets in his raincoat and wiped his mouth before returning it from whence it came.
"On the phone, we discussed a horse you once trained," he said, crunching a handful of the cheese and onion snack.
"Noble Goblet."
"Yes."
"And the fact that his head and neck were found in a field somewhere,"
"Yes."
"So now that you are here perhaps you can tell me what you want from me," Cannon asked. "You mentioned my experience, but I'm buggered if I know what you mean by that."
"Okay let me get straight to the point," Silvers said, moving his head closer to Cannon and lowering his voice slightly. Cannon thought the action laughable. They were in an O & T bar in Chepstow, not in an MI5 office worried about listening devices or bugs of some sort. "When we spoke on the phone I told you about Noble Goblet and I mentioned there were a few other incidents of a similar nature."
"Okay."

"Well it's more than a few incidents and there is more to this than meets the eye."

"I'm still not sure what you mean," Cannon replied, having no idea where the conversation was leading, "nor what you need me for."

"I need your help," Silvers said.

Sitting back in his chair Cannon laughed then sipped his tea. Silvers looked confused.

"I think you have got the wrong man, DCI Silvers," Cannon replied, "I'm no longer in the force and I've been out of that game for years now."

"Is that so?"

"Yes, it is. I'm a racehorse trainer, not a cop. Do you want my business card?" he added, facetiously.

Picking up, then holding the whisky glass in his hand, Silvers looked at a tiny sliver of alcohol at the bottom. The liquid shone in the overhead light. He lifted his eyes to face Cannon.

"I did some digging before I called you," he advised. "Prior to the pandemic there were a couple of incidents that you got involved in, that…let's say, were beyond a trainer's remit."

"What do you mean?"

"Exactly that."

"If you are referring to what happened during the Titan's Hand syndication, then I got involved because my family and I were at risk."

"Really?"

"Yes, Inspector, really."

Reverting his eyes back to the glass, Silvers said, "DI Tim Cummings sends his regards."

Cannon sat up in his chair, the comment seemed to have something behind it. Cummings was in charge of the Titan's Hand case, which was ultimately solved with Cannons' help.

"Cummings gave me your name. He said that without your experience he and his team would have struggled to solve what was a very complex matter."

"And it very nearly got my fiancé killed."

"I understand, but I…"

"But you what?" Cannon interjected, getting more annoyed at Silvers' vague inferences. He needed to bring the conversation to a head having a horse to saddle up shortly. The runners for the first race were already making their way to the start. He made to stand when Silvers put a hand on his arm. It was a gesture of contrition, of apology. Cannon recognized it as such, and sat down again, asking the Detective to say his piece.

"We may have got off on the wrong foot, Mr. Cannon…Mike, but please hear me out. I desperately need your help with this case, so let me explain."

The Doc ran a creditable third, staying on to come in about twelve lengths behind the winner. It was clear that the horse was on his best behaviour, and Angela suggested to Cannon that with a bit more fitness and a little more give in the ground, the horse would likely do better next time. "Provided his mind stayed on the job," she added.

"Talking about that, how are you feeling?" Cannon asked, as she dismounted the horse in the unsaddling enclosure. Alongside them, a couple of owners with the winning horse posed as they had their photographs taken. The steam coming off the Doc lifted briskly into the air as the breeze swirling across the course began to strengthen. The possibility of rain was increasing and the sun had now given up trying to break through. It appeared to have finally surrendered to some heavy dark nimbus clouds that were rolling in from the west.

"I'm fine, Mr. Cannon," she said, trying to switch the conversation to her mount. "He gave me a good feel and I had no problems at all in the run. The only thing he did wrong was finding an extra stride at the second last which cost him his rhythm and slowed his momentum."

"I appreciate the feedback about the horse Angela, but I'm really talking about you," he said, noting how easily she had tried to deflect his question.

Having finished his chat with Silvers, his focus of attention had shifted to his runners and particularly to Angela. While his head was filled with the detail that the policeman had shared with him and what it meant, he knew that it was important not be distracted with the implications at this stage. Angela, however, was trying to do exactly that.

"I'm feeling good," she said finally, as they both walked off towards the weighing room. Cannon noticed that she still limped slightly but decided not to comment. They had left Jack Radcliffe to lead away the Doc and wash him down, before giving the horse a good rub and getting him ready for the drive back to Stonesfield. White Noise would join him once the meeting was over. As they reached the door to the Stewards building readying for her to weigh-out, she turned to him sensing his increased concern.

"Look, Mr. Cannon, there is nothing to worry about. Please believe me. I'm fine and feeling really good," she pleaded, trying to convince him not to think otherwise.

While Cannon knew that she had a good head on her shoulders for such a young woman, he still believed that she had made a bad decision by getting involved with Van der Linden. It was a bit late now, he thought, but guessed that the previous day's events between him and Nick at the parlour, would have been discussed. He was concerned that Van der Linden may have started to take things further with her. There were no outwardly physical signs that he could see, but what about her mental condition?

"Okay," Cannon conceded, realizing that she was not willing to talk. "Let's have a chat later after you've ridden Noel's horse in the fifth. In fact why don't you ride home with me, and Jackie can go home whenever she feels like it? It will be better for her particularly now that the weather is about to change."

He pointed to the ever-darkening clouds. The course management had checked the radar and had advised all trainers about the impending deluge. This had caused a number of them to consider whether to scratch some of their runners. Declaring a non-runner so late in the day was possible under the rules and the going could be used as a reason if applicable. However, until the rain came it was unlikely that the Stewards would allow any of them to be taken out of their races. Angela considered the offer of the lift before smiling an acceptance. She understood that Cannon was trying to help and she was beginning to see how rapidly her life was changing as a consequence of her circumstances. All the things she had hoped to be doing at this stage of her life were being curtailed, put on ice. It was possible, she thought, that she would never achieve what she had originally hoped to. It was a dilemma that she was struggling with. The baby versus the career!

Could she have both?

"I'll let Jackie know," she said, reluctantly, sadly. "I think she was going to the lounge, but I'll find her."

"Okay, I'll see you in the parade ring for the fourth race. Hopefully it won't get too wet before the off."

Frowning at the changing sky, Angela brushed aside any concerns he had and indicated that she was okay to ride White Noise over his ideal distance despite the potential change in the weather. Cannon had expected her response, but he had an uncomfortable feeling about the race itself. It was an ideal event for the horse, but he was still concerned about Angela. Something was bothering him. With luck, he would be able to get her to open up a little more while on the ride home. Leaving her to complete the formalities of weighing-out, he made his way to the Members Lounge to meet with White Noise's owner, Joel Seeton. Seeton was a middle-aged businessman from the North of England who had made a small fortune with his packaging business and who had come down from York to watch is horse run. Making his way through the small crowd that milled around the course looking to avoid the few drops of rain now falling, Cannon took out his mobile and made a call.

The rain was steady but persistent and two of the nine runners in the race had been withdrawn. Cannon was quite happy with the situation as one of the horses concerned was expected to give White Noise a bit of a race. As it was, at least four of the other six runners were going to be relatively competitive as well, according to the bookmakers. White Noise was somehow favourite at eighteen to ten. The second line of betting suggested a horse called Silent Wink would be the main danger at five to two. The next two horses were at three's and four's.

Standing in the middle of the parade ring with the rain pouring down, Cannon felt the cold liquid seep into his bones as drops of water found their way under his raincoat's collar before running down his spine. He shivered, letting Seeton know that he need not endure the weather unnecessarily and that he should rather be in the bar or restaurant, staying out of the elements. The businessman watched as his horse slowly and professionally walked around the parade ring. Angela was wearing Seeton's racing colours of blue and grey halves, yellow sleeves and a red cap and if the rain was a distraction to the horse, whose coat seemed to gleam in the flood lights turned on by the course officials, he did not show it. The sheets of water that fell had scared the small number of punters still on the course into the bars and restaurants, leaving only those connections brave enough to withstand the elements watch their hopes parade.

Looking down at his sodden shoes, Seeton concluded that Cannon had made a sensible suggestion and agreed to meet him in the famous '1926' bar where they would watch the race together. Trudging off, he left Cannon to run a final eye over his runner as the field made their way out of the parade ring heading onto the course proper. Cannon smiled as he watched Seeton fight his umbrella as the wind tried hard to pull it from his grasp.

The drive back north was being made worse, and was taking so much longer, due to the inclement weather. DCI Silvers had made the decision to stop in Cheltenham and have a listen to what was happening in Chepstow after leaving the course. It had taken him just over an hour into his journey to find a William Hill betting shop on Tewkesbury Road. After what he had discussed with Cannon, he was keen to hear if anything unusual would show itself during the upcoming race. Standing with his shoulder against the counter which ran along two sides of the shop, he and two other men, both well past retirement age, stared at the TV screens.

The rain had continued to get heavier. The riders sat on their mounts waiting to be called into line. Those on course struggled to see the runners through the driving rain and the low mist that had now descended on the track, obscuring even the closest fence to the grandstand. Those using binoculars or even relying on long range TV camera lenses were finding things very difficult to identify the participants. The course commentator cursed into his silent microphone. All the work he had done to memorize the names of the horses and their colours was effectively wasted. He would need to rely on the on-course monitor until he could see any of the seven runners himself, using his own binoculars. Cannon stood next to Seeton who hopped nervously on the balls of his wet feet. The bar had gone silent. Those lucky enough to be inside looked towards the two television sets or tried to peer through the gloom that seemed to attach itself to the glass windows that faced the track. The rain continued to fall, getting heavier still, causing rivulets of water to spill over from the drains attached to the roof of the grandstand. Mini waterfalls that splashed onto the cement concourse.

"Shouldn't they call it off? Abandon the meet?" Seeton asked, as they waited for the 'off'. "With all this water it's likely to get treacherous out there."

Cannon was not entirely convinced, and he knew that abandonment would be at the behest of the Stewards on course. So far there was no indication that they would take such a decision. It was likely that they would make a determination after speaking with the jockeys from the current race, obtaining feedback as to the racing conditions underfoot.

"There off," Seeton said, pointing at one of the screens in the bar. Cannon squinted at the picture as he tried to follow the images on the TV. Above them, the inbuilt speakers relayed a stuttering commentary.

The senior riders had complained about the worsening conditions however Angela had remained quiet. The rain didn't bother her. Whether it was naiveté or over-confidence, her view was that she was on the best horse in the race and she was determined to win if she could. As the field was called up to the tape by the starter, she was still wondering about her conversation with Cannon, still unsure if she had made the right decision to travel back with him.

Lining up with the other runners, she waited to push White Noise forward once the tape rose. Alongside, Jim Franklin, riding a horse called Tinderbox, moved his mount ever closer towards them, trying to anticipate the start. The second favourite, Silent Wink, was on the outside of the seven runners keeping out of trouble. The old trick of Franklin and his mount trying to intimidate Angela worked. She had taken her eyes off the starter just as he pushed the button, and before she knew it, she was four lengths behind the rest of the field which had already bounded away towards the first flight. Angela knew she need not panic but was mindful that she was now at the rear of the field and was going to be chasing a group of horses that were digging their hooves into the ground and sending huge chunks of turf and mud in her direction. Visibility was bad enough without her googles becoming caked with flying debris.

The field reached the first flight, that suddenly appeared like a ghost before them. Two of the runners crashed through the top of the flights knocking parts of it down, flat onto the ground. This left a gap in the hurdle for White Noise to run through, which would have been a reasonable route for Angela to take, however, when he reached the flight the horse's instinct took over and he soared over the hurdle majestically. The leap was so quick and uninterrupted that Angela found that they had passed three of their rivals in flight and White Noise was almost on the heels of the other three. They raced towards the second fence, the rain and mud was already obscuring her vision but Angela sensed where her rivals were, even though she was less than 3 metres (10 feet) behind the triumvirate ahead. The second flight appeared to the front runners. The jockey at the head of the field misjudged his leap and his horse slipped just as it was about to jump the 1.1-metre (three foot six) high obstacle. Trying to make an adjustment in that split second, the jockey twisted himself in his saddle attempting to bring his weight onto one side of his mount, pulling in the reins as he did so, hoping to keep the horse upright. The move worked and the horse somehow scrambled over but was now in fourth spot in the race, the others including White Noise having cleared the fence without incident.

Angela let White Noise relax, and the horse settled into a steady rhythm as they tracked the two leaders racing as a pair ahead of them. She took a quick look behind her as they entered the straight for the first time, checking to see where the other runners were but she could only see mist and very little else.

"She's doing well," Seeton said, pointing upwards as the TV screen picked up White Noise passing the winning post in third position with still a circuit to run.

"She is," agreed Cannon, feeling a little better about the race and noticing Angela's confident riding despite the terrible conditions. He was almost in awe of her racing nouse and her ability to change race tactics on the fly. Rich had been right the first time they saw her ride. She definitely was a natural.

The field turned into the back straight and with only three flights to go, Angela made her move. The remaining runners behind her had pulled up or were running multiple lengths back but there were still the two runners ahead. She gave White Noise a kick in the belly and within seconds he had accelerated and was past the second horse which was now starting to flag and weaken its stride. As she drew alongside the leader, Tinderbox, the third flight from home appeared out of the mist like a dark black barrier which stretched across half of the racetrack. Both horses jumped it together and landed in unison. There was nothing to separate them as they ran neck and neck towards the penultimate hurdle.

Jim Franklin was the first to use the whip, giving his mount a whack on the rump, encouraging his horse for more effort. Angela continued pushing White Noise forward, her hands pumping backwards and forwards along the horse's neck encouraging him to remain on the bit.

Twenty metres (sixty feet) from the fence, the horses were still alongside, the gap between them so close that both jockey's boots touched several times and the flanks of their mounts bounced against each other. Angela and White Noise were on the outside, their rivals on the inside. No one was able to see what happened next but as they reached the fence Angela's boot slipped out of her left stirrup which resulted in her becoming unbalanced. White Noise took off slightly ahead of his rival but as he landed Angela flew off his back falling spectacularly like a rag doll onto the sodden turf. On the TV the disappearing jockey seemed to have been swallowed up by the weather as she fell from her mount. Cannon and Seeton were shocked by what they saw and it seemed incongruous for something like that to have happened. It was clear from what they could make out just before the fall that White Noise and Angela were in control of the race and that the Tinderbox was beginning to flag. So what happened, Cannon questioned?

The race finished thirty seconds later with only two runners ultimately crossing the line in once piece. Cannon told Seeton to meet him later at the O&T bar once Cannon had found out how Angela was doing. He told his owner that he could tell that White Noise would be fine, the horse had been mentioned in the on-course commentary as having pulled itself up after losing his jockey. Seeton expressed his concern for Angela as the trainer ran from the comfort of the bar and out into the rain.

Cannon watched as they loaded the stretcher into the ambulance. He was soaked through as were most of the paramedics. Angela was still unconscious but was breathing on her own. Due to a brief enquiry by the Stewards into the course conditions that he had needed to be present at, it had taken him way too long to get to where she had fallen. By the time he had squelched his way along the racecourse straight and reached the bend where the second last fence was set, the ambulance crew had been at work for twenty-five minutes. They had been assessing her condition when he told them that she was pregnant. Taking the information on board the medics had worked methodically and diligently. They had checked for signs of bleeding, broken bones and any significant head trauma before gently placing her onto a gurney. Thereafter they wrapped her in silver foil blanket to prevent her going into shock and to keep her warm.

The door to the ambulance closed and the blue and red flashing lights were turned on as the vehicle began to make its way to the Chepstow Community Hospital just a three-minute drive away.

Cannon watched the vehicle slowly make its way towards the course exit. He needed to get back to the stables and Jack Radcliffe before preparing himself to get home. It would be a lonely trip. Joel Seeton had also texted him, letting him know that he needed to get back to York after he realized that Cannon was to be held up in the meeting with the Stewards and was unlikely to be able to meet again as planned. He has also let Cannon know that he had spoken with Radcliffe himself and was happy to hear that White Noise was uninjured. He hoped that Angela was likewise going to be okay.

With his head bowed and his mind torn, Cannon made his way back up the straight. The rain was easing slightly but the rest of the meeting had already been abandoned. He found himself thinking about what had happened. As he reached the now empty stands and the racecourse concourse he wondered if he should call Van der Linden or not, but before he had decided to do so, his mobile rang. It was Silvers.

"I'm on the M6 just past Stoke-on-Trent and I'll be stopping overnight in Lancaster."

"And?" Cannon asked, his thoughts still jumbled, unsure why Silvers had called him again.

"I saw the race, well sort of."

"You watched it on TV?"

"Yes. In Cheltenham. Though it was almost impossible to see what was going on. How is she?"

"She's on her way to hospital. Still unconscious. I'll be going to the hospital later, before I leave for home."

There was a pause for a few seconds. Cannon stepped onto the first row of the Grandstand steps, the lights of which shone onto the wet concourse cement behind him. The rain continued falling in slightly softer sheets which glistened as the drops of water crossed the beams of light then disappeared into the darkness that was now beginning to creep across the racecourse. He suddenly felt alone.

"I'm sorry for what happened," Silvers said, breaking the silence. "I hope she'll be okay."

"So do I," Cannon replied, a far-away glance in his eye. "So do I."

"Does it change anything?" the Detective asked?

Cannon considered the question carefully. Their earlier conversation had required him to think about a number of things. Did he need to get involved? Why? Why would he want to? For what benefit?

For a few transient seconds he almost changed his mind then he thought of Angela, of Van der Linden, of the detail that Silvers had shared with him.

"No," he said, "nothing's changed."

"Thank you," Silvers replied, pleased with Cannon's answer. "I'll leave you to it then."

Terminating the call, Cannon stared out at the emptiness in front of him. The racetrack was now in almost total darkness. He shivered. He wanted to get home, but before he could leave he needed to speak to someone. He knew where to find him.

CHAPTER 12

The shipment had arrived without detection, it was now up to others to recover it. Three men, who always worked the night shift, had introduced a system that they had now used successfully for a couple of years. The factory was situated twenty miles southwest of Leeds just outside the small village of Holywell Green. It had been chosen primarily because of its remote location and was an ideal place for them. Hyseni's family had been able to secure its use after they made the owner an offer he could not refuse, along with a little bit of coercion along the way to 'sweeten' the deal. The opportunity had come after the owner's daughter had almost bankrupted the business. She had used her privileged lifestyle to get herself into serious trouble with the police and had needed good legal advice and expensive solicitors to get her out of the mess. The family had provided the funds to the owner and in return a blind eye was turned allowing the three men to do what was required of them every night. The method they used in their work was one that had been copied from a similar factory situated north of the border. It had been highly successful to date. Occasionally though something would go wrong with the process, which the three men accepted was just part of the job. When it did happen, they usually kept such mistakes between themselves, having made a unilateral decision to handle any resolution in their own way. There was no need to advise anyone in the family about a fuck-up. The men knew that they would be safe if they were able to demonstrate that what was supplied to them, was the same as that they made available for collection by the customer. No one knew exactly what came in due to the complexities involved, but as long as what went out could be reconciled, then everybody was happy. As far as the men were concerned, they took nothing that wasn't due to them. What was lost through mistakes or failures, was lost forever. It would mean certain death if they were found to be skimming anything off the top and they knew it. What arrived each night needed to be weighed, photographed and distributed accordingly. The three men always made sure that the quantities were adjusted for, citing losses during shipment when they had to. Those waiting for the deliveries always checked the product to ensure that everything they were expecting to receive, they did. If they were satisfied that it was,

then they would make the necessary calls and Hyseni would receive his money.
The three men got to work. It would be a long and bloody night.

CHAPTER 13

DI Sam Walker was frustrated. The investigation into Sue Gladstone had found nothing that would indicate that she had any enemies, nor indeed anyone who would have held a grudge against her that led to her being murdered. There was nothing in her background other than the fact that she was a well-loved teacher, a member of her local church, was active in the community and a regular jogger.

"She seems to have been a bit of a saint," Walker said, sitting next to Conte at the bar in the Three Horseshoes Pub in Long Hanborough.

He hadn't been hungry so had suggested that they have a drink instead. The warm fire in the hearth kept the few patrons safe from the damp chill outside. The lights of the building contrasting with the low-slung cloud that scudded across the early evening sky.

"So what do we do now?" Conte asked. "We only have Fanchurch's statement, but it's not much to go on is it, Sir?"

"No, and Timmly hasn't found anything either," Walker replied, his accent always more prominent when he was annoyed and under pressure. He took another sip of his pint of local ale. They were both on their second glass.

"So maybe whoever was involved wasn't a local?" Conte suggested.

Walker considered the question before dismissing it. "No, I think they must have been. The A4095 is not a main thoroughfare for the casual visitor. Anyone travelling to or from Oxford, Cheltenham, Gloucester or even Cirencester would likely use the A roads, like the A44 or A40, especially if they don't know the area and given what the weather was like that day."

"Is that just a theory, Sir, or is it based on your local knowledge?" Conte asked, aware of his boss's view of still being thought of as an outsider to the local area.

Staring at his Sergeant, Walker hardened his accent pretending to be hurt by Conte's comment.

"It's a theory based on a bit of logic, Sergeant. Unfortunately with little else to go on, we need to keep our minds open to all possibilities."

"Such as…Sir?" Conte quizzed, draining the last of his beer and placing his glass down just as his boss started to answer.

"What we need is to find….damn!" Walker stopped in mid-sentence

as his mobile phone began to buzz. Having placed it in silent mode and leaving it on the bar counter next to him, he noted that the caller was Jenny Cribb. Touching a finger to his lips to indicate to Conte to remain quiet, he answered the call then stepped away from the bar. He found a quiet seat at the rear of the pub. Conte watched him from his vantage point, his bar stool, noting how Walker listened intently to what was being said, occasionally nodding or raising an eyebrow. Eventually Walker concluded the call and put the phone back into his inside jacket pocket, traversing the fifteen metres back to where his Sergeant was sitting. Conte in the interim had procured himself a packet of crisps and a pork pie. He was about to take a bite of the latter when sitting down beside him, Walker said, "The toxicology report that Cribbs had been waiting for arrived at her desk a short while ago."
"And?"
"And nothing!"
"Nothing?"
"Not a thing. The woman didn't have anything of note in her body. No residual alcohol, no sign of any drugs, not even aspirin, paracetamol or cough medicines, nothing."
"So, she *was* a saint," Conte reflected.
With a shake of the head, Walker looked crestfallen.
"Anything else then, Sir?"
"Well, there was some good news. That paint they were looking into."
"What about it?"
"It's been identified as belonging to a motorbike."
"So not a car or a van?"
"No, it's definitely a motorbike. Specifically a Kawasaki Ninja. Apparently the 'bike has a unique paint on it that no other motorbike has, something called Silver Mirror."
Conte waited for his boss to continue. He noted a smile of sorts cross Walkers' face. It was the first time since they had started their investigation that they had something positive to work with.
"Cribb said that she will send me the report shortly," Walker advised, "but it seems that this Silver Mirror paint has flakes of silver in it that creates a glass-like metallic finish. Most other paint used on motorbikes contains aluminum."
"Technology hey, Sir?" Conte replied. "I thought all metallic paints

were the same, just the colours were different."

"Clearly not, Sergeant, and thank God that those who can have been able to provide us with a lead that we can use."

Conte agreed. It was the breakthrough they needed.

"We need to get back to the office and get the team together. I want a complete list from the DVLA of anyone who has registered a Kawasaki Ninja motorbike; metallic blue or otherwise," Walker stated.

"Since when, Sir? How far back do we need to go? There must be hundreds or even thousands of such bikes."

"Your quite right," Walker said. "According to Jenny Cribb, it was 2015 when the paint was introduced…"

"Bloody hell, that's years ago," interrupted Conte, suddenly realizing the extent of the follow up that would be required to Walker's request. He was worried about the manpower needed, and the time it would take to chase down everyone who had ever owned a Kawasaki motorbike since then. Talk about a needle in a haystack. "There must be any number of models as well, right, Sir?" he added, sounding deflated at the very thought. The police always had limited resources at their disposal and a never-ending workload. To get any job done it was often a case, ironically, of robbing Peter to pay Paul. The politics involved to source the resources required he would leave for Walker to address. It would be a bloody long process!

Walker finished what was left of his drink. "We're in luck actually, Sergeant," he said, putting on his coat and heading for the pub's exit, leaving Conte in his wake, feeling somewhat perplexed at the curious comment. Climbing into the driver's seat of their unmarked car, Conte turned to his boss seeking to clarify the nuanced statement that had been left dangling in the air. "What did you mean, Sir, about being in luck?"

"The paint, Sergeant, the paint."

"I'm not with you, Sir. You said….."

"I know what I said, but I haven't told you the rest."

"Go on."

"It seems that during any production process, motorbikes like any other vehicle, are spray painted using batched paints. That means the paint used in that batch is unique to that specific production run."

"And?"

"Ahh well, here's the rub. It seems that they may all look the same to the naked eye, but by using fluorescent microscopy and other techniques, which are beyond me, the path-lab have been able to check the particles they found with a data base of known paint compositions and bingo, they have narrowed it down to the specific model of bike."

Conte smiled at Walkers' enthusiasm and was about to ask the obvious question but was beaten to it.

"It's this year's model, Sergeant!" Walker said.

CHAPTER 14

"Look Mike, as I have already told you, I just kept my line and she shifted in on me," Jim Franklin said. They were sitting in his house on Kings Mill Lane in Painswick, about an hour's drive from the racecourse. Having left Chepstow, Cannon had called Michelle and told her that he was going to be late, letting her know what he was intending to do. He had tried to see Angela before departing for home but had been refused access to her room. The doctors had advised him that despite him being her employer, they were prevented from giving him any details about her condition due to 'privacy' reasons. He had tried to argue with them but had been ignored. So, with a lengthy drive ahead of him, he had wanted some answers.

Franklin had taken Cannons' call, while he was on his own way back home. He had ridden for Cannon a number of times over the years, and on the odd occasion they had dined together, especially when a track or racing club had held a festival of racing over a period of consecutive days. With the jockeys address in his mobile phone contacts list it had been easy for him to find the man's home again. He had been to the house some years before. It was a large four-bedroom home that sat behind high privet hedges and large yew and sycamore trees that protected the home from curious onlookers.

"Did you both touch at any time?" Cannon asked.

"Yes, briefly, a few yards before the flight, but it wasn't enough to stop either of us riding."

Cannon considered this for a moment. "You know I'm not trying to suggest anything, Jim, but I just want to know from you whether anything happened that shouldn't have."

"What are you insinuating, Mike? You know this is most unusual don't you? You asking me questions like this. If there were any issues from the race, then the Stewards would call them out. Call me out."

"I'm not suggesting anything, Jim. I'm just trying to piece something together and was hoping you could help me."

Franklin took a sip from a cup that he was holding on his knee. He had made them both tea. The house was too big for him now but it held many memories from the twenty-eight years he had lived there. At fifty-three years of age and a widower of several years, he had two grown-up children. One who had moved to live in London, the other to Canada. He enjoyed his own company and the peace and quiet of his surroundings. The semi-rural setting was an ideal place for his lifestyle. He could relax and study the racing form for the meetings that he was riding at, but he was always happy to have visitors. His housekeeper had long since gone by the time he had arrived home, but she had left him dinner which he had eaten long before Cannon had arrived. Chicken and a side salad was enough protein to sustain a jockey after a day's racing. Sitting back in his chair, Franklin replied to Cannons' assertion, "If you think I lifted her boot out of the irons, you are completely wrong, Mike."

It wasn't something that happened regularly given the way races were filmed and reviewed by the racing authorities today, but there had been many incidents in the past where a jockey on one of two horses that were fighting out a finish would lift the stirrup of a competitor, when out of sight of spectators or racing officials, which then caused the other rider to become unbalanced and fall off their mount. The act needed to be done swiftly, but when it was done with skill, it was almost impossible to see the offending jockey's hands noticeably taken off the reins of their own horse. That's all it took. One simple action. With the weather as it was during the race, there was no way anyone would have seen such a split-second move.

Cannon took a sip of his drink; the warmth of the hot liquid began to thaw him out. He accepted that his host was telling the truth.

"How is she anyway?" Franklin asked.

"I wasn't allowed to see her, but I believe she was still unconscious."

"Poor kid."

"Yes, and that's why I'm here."

"Because you thought I was responsible?" Franklin stated, unhappily.

"Look Mike, you know I'd never do anything like that just to win a race. You know me better than that."

"You're right Jim," Cannon conceded, "I apologize. I guess she must have just became unbalanced and fell."

Given the grace of Cannon's apology, Franklin said, "I want to help if I can Mike. Is there anything else I can do for you?"

Cannon thought about the offer and the conversation he and Silvers had shared earlier. "Before I answer that, I'm going to tell you something in confidence and in good faith. Something Angela specifically asked me to keep secret, for another month or two at least. I think she'll be okay with me sharing it with you now, particularly given the circumstances. And anyway, I think I may need your help with something."

"About?" Franklin asked, intrigued.

"Before we get to that, I wanted to check that you will be willing to do so."

"I'm happy to, I think, but does any of this affect Angela?" he asked.

"I'm not sure if it does directly, but she is pregnant and that complicates matters," Cannon replied.

"Good God! How far?" Franklin asked, suddenly understanding Cannons' concern about his young jockey.

"We believe she may be between 10 or 11 weeks now."

"And how long did she expect to ride?"

"She wanted to go on as long as possible but I agreed on another few weeks from now, then that was to be it. I told her that I would review things again sometime after the birth."

"That sounds like a sensible approach to me," Franklin replied.

"And that's the extent I sought permission for. I was very concerned for her wellbeing and I told her several times that she needed to be careful."

"Well you can't blame yourself for what happened Mike, some things are out of your hands."

"Agreed, though I just wish that it hadn't happened," Cannon replied, dejectedly. He looked at his watch. It was later than he thought. It was time to ask for the favour.

Franklin listened intently to what he was requested to do and once Cannon had finished, the jockey sought answers to a couple of questions.

"Unfortunately, I can't answer some of them," Cannon said. "What I've told you is all I know. That's why I need your help."

Franklin accepted the situation, knowing that what Cannon had requested of him would not be too difficult a task to undertake. He gave his firm commitment. Cannon smiled in response, thanking him accordingly. Then, standing, suggested to his host that it was time for him to be on his way.

The two men walked towards the front door just as Cannon's phone began to ring. He didn't recognize the number so he ignored the call. "They can leave a message," he said, indifferently, as he shook Franklin's hand. "Thanks again for your help Jim," he said, "I'll be in touch. But please....be careful."

He sat in his car. Having started the engine and turned on the heater he stared at the black night through a windscreen littered with spots of rain and tiny slivers of ice. The wind had dropped since he had arrived at Franklin's house but so had the temperature. He decided to listen again to the message that had pinged onto his phone while he was saying his goodbyes to his host.
"You fucking bastard, Cannon," Nick Van der Linden's Dutch accented voice echoed from the cars' speakers. Apple CarPlay linked via Bluetooth to the vehicles media console, spat out the vitriol. "I told her not to ride for you anymore, and now...," there was a short pause as the Dutchman seemed to consider his words, "... if you have killed my Angela, then you are a fucking dead man!"
The message ended. It was simple, angry, and a clear threat. In some ways Cannon understood it, but at the same time it was something that he needed to deal with. It would be unwise to leave it hanging. He requested Siri to delete the message, close the message bank and play him some music. He put the car into gear and drove out of Franklin's driveway. The hour or so that it would take him to get home, meant that he had plenty of opportunity to think.

CHAPTER 15

The men had completed their work. The shipment had been exactly as expected and those collecting it had been thorough, efficient and well organized as they always were. The morning had still to break, but it was expected to start with a red glow on the far eastern horizon. Rain was forecast, no different to the past few days.
It was time for them to go home, but first they would take the incriminating pieces and dispose of them in the usual way. In the past they had made mistakes and at various times even careless. They had been lucky so far, believing that nothing had come from the errors. Hyseni had heard about a couple of incidents and had sent two of his men a few weeks back to ensure that no such issues ever happened again. The men at the factory knew who they worked for and what was required of them. If they had any doubts Hyseni had no problem in taking it up with them. There were some who had tried to take advantage of the distance between the north of England and Holland but they were quickly dealt with. Some of them befalling the same fate as the cargo he sent for processing at the factory.
Having loaded the van the men climbed in and set off, driving through the early morning towards their safe house twelve miles away. At six thirty the traffic in the countryside was light, most people still struggling to face the dark and cold of the advancing day. The journey back normally took them thirty to thirty-five minutes at the most, depending on how things went when they stopped at their usual place.
It took them less than ten minutes before they turned off Elland Road. They then made the short trip past Cromwell Bottom Drive and drove a few hundred metres down the lane towards the nature reserve that bore its name.
Stopping on the Crowther bridge above the canal, known as the Calder and Hebble navigation, they turned off the van's engine, leaving them surrounded in an empty darkness. Exiting the vehicle they listened for any signs of life on the two narrow boats that were moored on the left bank of the canal, thirty or forty metres away from the where they were standing. Confident that both crafts were

empty, the men took six sacks from the back of the van, depositing each in turn onto the road. The hessian though unmarked with any branding was stained ruby due to the inner plastic bags having failed, thereby allowing the blood that oozed from the contents within to escape and seep into the material. Carefully and with some effort the men heaved the sacks over the side of the bridge, watching as each splashed into the dark waters below. The stillness of the canal water rippled towards either bank as the sacks temporarily bobbed up from the disturbed water as if each was searching for air, and a way to escape the cold dark liquid. Slowly however, the weight of the water seemed to grasp at the sacks from underneath. Each of them appeared to be fighting against hope as they struggled to stay afloat. Inevitably they accepted their fate and sank beneath the surface. The men stood in silence for a few seconds, checking that their night vision had not failed them and that the sacks had not resurfaced. Once they were satisfied that the sacks were safe within their watery grave they were content that their labour had resulted in a job well done. Knowing the contents of the sacks they understood that in time the water would remove any trace of their origins. They had made this detour away from the main road many times before and they would do so again. It was a quicker and easier method of disposal than the old way….that of burying the contents.

The men jumped back into the van, reversed the vehicle until they could turn it around and then drove back the way they had come. Once they reached Elland Road they turned on the van's headlights. Making a right they headed towards Little Horton and their bed.

CHAPTER 16

He hadn't told her about the call from Van der Linden. When he arrived home she had been in bed waiting for him. Having parked his car he had made his way into the stables and checked on White Noise and the Doc. Jack Radcliffe had done a great job, ensuring that both horses had settled in for the night. The groom had brought them back all the way from the racecourse and with help from another member of the team, arranged by Rich, they had provided a feed and given water to both horses. Rich had also arranged fresh straw and this was in place in their boxes by the time Radcliffe had driven into the yard.

Cannon had taken his time looking over White Noise for any signs of injury. The horse hadn't fallen during the race and had been jumping well. The slip which resulted in Angela falling off was unfortunate, and seemingly had no effect on the horse itself. For that he was grateful. His thoughts turned to Angela as he sat on the bed, readying himself to join Michelle under the sheets. He repeated what he had told her earlier detailing the circumstances surrounding the fall and his visit to the hospital.

"I was told they couldn't or wouldn't give me an update on her condition until a next of kin had been informed," he said, his body language suggesting to her that he was racked with guilt.

Leaning over to touch him on the shoulder, she reassured him that he had nothing to be sorry for. "I'm sure she'll be alright," Michelle said. "What happened was an accident and she's getting the best of care now. You can't beat yourself up about it Mike. If you continue that way then it's going to eat you up inside. Remember what happened after Ray died?"

Ray Brollo was a young jockey who was killed on the heath when exercising one of Cannons' horses. His death was the catalyst to him setting up a trust in Brollos' name. That result from that process was him taking on his first conditional jockey, Angela Fryer.

"Something good came from that, Mike," Michelle continued, "something you can be proud of, an opportunity for a young girl to follow her dream."

He looked into her face, his eyes moist. He had seen many shocking things in his lifetime and had wanted nothing more than to make something good come from such a shocking incident as Ray Brollos' death. With Angela in hospital he wondered if what he had done had been worth it. He knew that accidents happened in jumps racing. He knew that death was part of the game sometimes, but was death actually seeking him out?

"But what happens if she dies?" he asked. "Would it be worth it then?"

Michelle wrapped her arms around his shoulders and kissed him in on the neck. "Look Mike, when people do what they love, be it a mountain climber, an accountant or a jockey, they do it knowing what their chosen path is. Each one knows the good and the bad. Some take risks, others don't, but whatever a person decides to do, it is *their* choice, and you need to accept that."

He knew that she was right, but it didn't make it any easier for him, particularly when he realized what he had agreed to, by getting involved in with DCI Silvers. He decided that he would leave that subject until the morning, along with the threat from Van der Linden. He doubted the man would actually carry out his threat but he was wary of it nonetheless. Cannon didn't want to alarm Michelle but when he put his head on his pillow it dawned on him that what he was about to do was exactly what she had said. People make choices and he had made one for himself...willingly.

While Cannon slept, the dreams began. He had experienced many of them before; nightmares of long forgotten faces, places and events that continued to haunt him over the years. Somehow they merged with the people of today, including Michelle, Cassie, Angela, all were bound up in the horrors of his past. Screams, blood, murder! He woke up in a cold sweat. He tried to focus on the clock that stood on the bedside table in order to check the time. It was two seventeen am. He turned on the lamp, suddenly realizing that Michelle wasn't lying next to him. The bed was warm but the duvet was disturbed. He called out just as she walked back into the bedroom.

"What's going on?" she asked.

"Where were you?' he snapped, regretting the words the moment he said them.

"I was just getting a drink, I was thirsty," she said, slipping back into bed. "Are you okay?"

Falling back onto his pillow he told her that he had been dreaming again. She kissed him on the cheek, rolled onto her side and asked him to turn out the light. Lying in the dark he found that he was unable to sleep. His mind was reeling, thinking about Chepstow. As his thoughts continued to keep sleep at bay, he remembered that he still hadn't spoken with Rich. Given his discussion with Silvers it was too late now. He would need to park the matter for a while, knowing that without Rich he wouldn't have been able to agree to help Silvers. The realization reaffirmed the point that Michelle had made about people's choices. How ironic, he thought. He had planned to address one issue but decided on another.

He closed his eyes just as his phone lit up with a silent ping. Reaching across to retrieve it, he saw it was a message from a number he had seen before. Opening it up he read it several times trying to take in the implication, the anger was palpable in the words.

"ANGELA HAS LOST THE BABY," wrote Nick Van der Linden.

CHAPTER 17

From the information they had received from the DVLA, they had narrowed the list down to one hundred and sixty-two Kawasaki Ninja motorbikes sold and registered during the calendar year to date. This was across the whole of Oxfordshire and the surrounding counties, all six of them. Of that number, twenty-six were the right colour. Only four were registered to addresses in Oxfordshire itself. The rest were in Warwickshire, Northants, Berkshire and Gloucestershire, with none in either Buckinghamshire or Wiltshire. They were sitting in Walker's office within the police station in Abingdon, readying themselves to leave in a few minutes.

"If my theory is right, Sergeant, it would make our life so much easier."

"True Sir," Conte replied, as he and Constable Timmly sat on the opposite side of Walker's desk. "But wouldn't we be wasting time if we only concentrated on the four?"

"I'm not suggesting that. I'm just prioritizing. I still think we need to look into the others which is why I'd like PC Timmly here to get on the blower and contact all those outside of Oxfordshire that on the list. I want a statement from each of the owners as to where they were and where their bikes were on the day/night in question."

Timmly was in his third year on the force. Progression to the next rank of Sergeant would come in time. He was a good operator, still in his early twenties and only of average height, which was no longer issue to join the force anymore. He had short dark hair which curled at the fringe above green eyes. A dark skin from his Sri Lankan mother and a narrow nose from his English father, he always seemed to attract favourable glances from his female colleagues whenever he showed his perfectly white teeth which lit up his slightly narrowed face. He was prepared to work hard and was a good talker, able to charm when he needed to and push for answers when others tried to be evasive. He had done all the analysis of the data received from the DVLA and had presented Walker with the addresses of the four registered owners of Kawasaki's that lived in the county. Walker had praised him accordingly. "Great work," he had said.

With the four names and addresses noted on a printed A4 sheet, Walker rose from his seat, grabbing his jacket from a fake free standing nineteenth century coat stand that stood to his left and encouraged his Sergeant to make tracks. "Let's go," he said.

Nick Van der Linden had received his supply very early in the morning. As usual there was an *urgent* sticker attached to the box. It was still dark when the courier had arrived, totally unaware that the parcel he was bringing was not one that had originated from the on-line retailer he thought it was. The parcel had the same appearance as a legitimate purchase but had been embedded into the truck driver's route, by a 'friendly' resource. One that Hyseni had arranged to be secreted at a distribution centre in Warwickshire. Inside the parcel was a note warning him that payment for the previous two deliveries was overdue and needed to be settled within two days. The current delivery was to be the last until all monies had been paid or restitution would be sort.

He knew what the latter meant and he had been looking for a way out of his predicament for quite a while now. Not even letting Angela know of his plans. When she fell pregnant it had annoyed him. He was meant to be single, footloose and fancy free, not tied down to any one girl. However, until all the arrangements had been finalized and put into place he needed to give the appearance of being happy with her. When he heard that she had fallen from the horse it had given him an idea. By pretending to be outraged, he wanted to warn Cannon off, trying keep the man's nose completely out of his business. With the tattoo parlour only due to open around midday, he had used the early hours of the morning to meet with his major customer, and monies had changed hands.

"What about the rest?" he had queried, as he counted the notes he had received.

"That's going to take some time," the customer said, touching the backpack where he had hidden the parcel that Van der Linden had given him. "I've got to turn this into cash first."

Though each member of the chain was making money and each knew that while cash was once king, with the wider societal move to a digital currency, washing dirty money was becoming more difficult. Electronic money movement was fine for those at the top of the tree, they had the resources like accountants and lawyers able to hide transactions by using multiple bank accounts, trusts and tax havens.

Death Seeks You Out

The old business model relied on cash, with no taxes to pay and high margins…however cashflow at the street level was beginning to become a problem. Van der Linden had a third of his business going through his tattoo parlour customers, who all paid in bank notes. That money was being stashed away. He needed it in order to get back to Liege, in Belgium, and to set himself up again. It was where he had lived before moving to the UK.

Van der Linden and his customer had been standing two hundred metres along the entrance road into the Windrush cemetery grounds, an old sodium streetlamp providing just enough light for them to conduct their business. The trees along Oxford Hill Road protected them from any passing cars. The lights of the occasional vehicle flashed through the dark branches like the eyes of searching monsters. The customer looked away, trying to avoid looking at his supplier, readying himself to leave when the Dutchman grabbed him by the throat, knocking him backwards so that he was off his feet, half lying on his car's bonnet.

"I want that fucking money," Van der Linden shrieked.

The customer could feel the pressure on his larynx. He found breathing difficult and had pain in his back as the ridges on the car bonnet dug into him while he was pinned down. He thought of kicking out, but from experience he knew that Van der Linden had the strength and a big enough temper to inflict significant damage.

Through gritted teeth and supplicant demeanour, he managed to choke out a commitment that resulted in the pressure on his throat being eased and precious oxygen flow into his lungs.

Grabbing the front of his customer's coat, Van der Linden pulled him up allowing the man's feet to touch the ground. As he did so, the customer doubled over, retching and gasping. While he was prone, a boot was aimed into his stomach making him collapse onto the gravelled road, a whimper escaping from him in response.

"Tomorrow morning, here, the same time," the customer was told, as the Dutchman walked away. He had made his point, now he had another matter to resolve.

Cannon had told Rich about the text he had received from Van der Linden regarding Angela but decided to ignore telling him about the threat that the Dutchman had left on his voice mail.

"I'm not able to verify it yet as the hospital won't talk to me," he said, "but I'm going to take a trip to Witney to see what news Nick has about her condition," he added casually.

They were heading back from the heath to the stables, having decided that despite the cold and the fact that the rain had stopped for now allowing things to dry out somewhat, the walk would allow them to talk privately. Telside had made arrangements for the second lot to be taken back to the yard once they had finished their work. Sam Simmons and Jack Radcliffe were given the responsibility. Between them, they knew exactly what they were required to do. With some of the horses about to race again in the coming weeks it was important that they continue with their work. Being creatures of habit, racehorses achieve their best results when they have a good routine, good care and good schooling. Cannon had always been able rely on Rich to continue with the program that he had put together for each horse. No matter the problem or whenever something had gotten in the way, either the past coming to call or the future needing to be changed. It seemed incongruous to suggest the latter, but Angela's future would be irrevocably changed if she had lost her unborn baby.

For a fleeting moment Cannon was about to change subjects and talk about Rich's future but given his discussion with Silvers and the implication, he needed his friend to support him once more. Taking the next ten minutes Cannon filled him in on the situation as he knew it.

"Bloody hell, Mike," Telside exclaimed jokingly, once Cannon had finished. "I think we are both getting at bit old for this caper, aren't we?" A smile creased his face as he put his hand on Cannons' shoulder.

"Maybe," Cannon replied. It was a non-committal answer. He sensed that there was an underlying element of truth, an acceptance, of Telside's comment and he would have liked to pursue the discussion further but knew that it wasn't something easily debated at this time of the morning. It needed the correct time and place and this wasn't it.

"So Franklin is going to help too?" Telside asked, cutting into Cannon's thoughts.

"Yes."

"How much does he know about this?"

"Just as much as he needs to; at least as much as I was able to tell him."

"Right," replied Telside, stretching out the word as if he didn't fully accept Cannon's answer.

"And nobody else, other than you and I know," Cannon added.

"And the police."

"Yes."

"What about Michelle?"

"No, not yet. I want to keep her out of it. Remember what happened last time?" Cannon was referring to an incident a few years prior when Michelle was attacked inside their house while he was miles away in Liverpool. She was only saved by the intervention of Cannons' daughter.

"I do remember, Mike. So I guess you are not letting Cassie know either."

Cannon looked askance at his friend. With a sardonic smile he replied in the negative. "She has enough to worry about with the wedding," he said, suddenly aware that neither Cassie nor Michelle had spoken to him about the arrangements over the past week. To him that was good news.

They had reached the yard just as the second lot arrived back from their workouts. Briefly Cannon and Telside discussed the work they had observed while on the heath and the various programs already set in place for each animal. Due to the upcoming meetings at Aintree, Wincanton, Huntingdon and Cheltenham being scheduled very close to each other in addition to racing at Warwick, Exeter and Sandown's season opener shortly thereafter, the placement of his horses was paramount in order to get the best for the stable and the owners. It was going to be a busy period as long as the weather held and the stable occupants stayed fit and healthy. With the ground becoming a little softer after the recent rains, Cannon was much happier. Not every horse in his stables was a mud-lark but most enjoyed the sting out of the ground.

"Hopefully, I'll be on course to see ours run," he said, pointing towards the circle of horses conducting their warm down. "But I hope you'll be alright with all that's going on, Rich."

Telside smiled knowingly. Cannon had learned most of what he knew from his friend, and while his comment was not meant to be heard as condescending, it had come out that way.

"I'm sorry Rich, I didn't mean…," Cannon apologized

"I know Mike, forget it."

"It's just that I don't know exactly what I may be getting into Rich, and I don't want to over burden you."

"We'll be alright, Mike," Telside replied with another cheeky grin. "We've done this before," he added.

Cannon thanked him for his support. Yes, *he* had done *this* before, and not without danger to himself and his family. For the first time he doubted himself as to why he had agreed to work with Silvers.

"I've got to go," he said suddenly, "there is something I need to do."

Finding a place to dump the motorbike had been difficult, but the day after the incident it had been taken care of. Initially the intent was to burn it, but setting something like that alight was fraught with danger. Firstly, at night, it was possible that the flames could be seen and investigated or remembered should anyone come asking. Secondly a fire didn't always destroy everything, there was always something left to pick through.

The answer was Ducklington Lake, only two miles away, easily accessible at night and deep enough to lose it.

If anybody asked where it was, there was an easy answer.

CHAPTER 18

Cannon opened the door to the tattoo parlour. The street outside was relatively quiet as most shoppers were keeping out of the cold and the strong breeze that had started to blow across the west coast of the country. The forecast was for more rain in the next couple of days. The usual British discussion about the weather was heightened by the recent changes. Just a few short weeks ago, people were complaining about the lack of rain. Soon the TV weather men and women would be telling their audience about potential floods in some parts of the country. The current lull always seemed to make things worse when the rains did eventually arrive. The only concern Cannon had was whether any downpours like that which occurred down at Chepstow, would again put his horses and jockeys at risk. Some rain was okay, waterlogged courses were not.
The shop was empty of customers. There was no music playing and at first it appeared to be totally vacant.
"Can I help you?" a voice called. A man who Cannon recognized instantly from his previous visit rose from his chair that was tucked away in one corner of the room. He had been smoking a spliff and tried to hide it by grinding it into a half full ashtray. Trying to ignore the pins in the man's ears and a ring in his nose, which made the man's face seem bovine, Cannon queried whether Van der Linden was in the shop.
A quick glance towards the dark curtain at the back of the shop told Cannon all he needed to know. Ignoring any protestations, Cannon pushed past the man and hurried towards the curtain. He was a yard away when Van der Linden pulled it aside and catching Cannon by surprise, punched him on the jaw. Cannon fell backwards, landing on his left shoulder which took the brunt of the fall. As he attempted to get up he received a kick to abdomen which winded him.
"I told you that I'd kill you Cannon if Angela dies!" he screamed, spitting out the vitriol through an angry mouth and pointing an accusatory finger at the prostrate visitor. "As it is, I've lost my baby and all because of you, you bastard!"
Climbing to his feet, an arm held across his stomach and with a wince

from the pain in his shoulder, Cannon suddenly felt sympathy for the Dutchman. He understood how the man must be feeling having lost an unborn. Though he had not received any confirmation that it was actually true, he doubted the man would be so insensitive and to act so aggressively, if it wasn't. Cannon looked into his eyes noticing nothing but hate, saying, "I know you want to blame me for what's happened to Angela and that's your call, but I did tell her not to ride. It was due to her insisting on it, that she was on that horse."

"I don't care. Your responsible and you will pay for this!"

It was obvious to Cannon that Van der Linden was beyond reason. The implicit retribution was something Cannon had heard many times before in his former life. Mostly it was just a bluff. Often a reaction to the role he had played in arresting people. In this case he wasn't so sure.

"I'm not sure what you mean by paying," he said, "but if…"

"If what?!" countered Van der Linden, his voice rising, scaring his employee who moved to the front of the shop near the door. As he did so, someone began to open it, coming in off the street.

"Let me put it this way," Cannon said. "If you try to harm any of my family or come anywhere near my stables, I'll beat the crap out of you, you little shit! So just remember that."

He made to turn and walk towards the door, when he heard one of the two men who had just entered the shop say, "Gentleman, gentleman, what's going on here?"

"Fuck off," the Dutchman said. "Who are you two anyway, and what do you want?" He could see that the two men were not customers. Dressed as they were, they seemed quite official, possibly from the local council.

Cannon made a quick assessment. His instinct told him what they were.

"DI Sam Walker," the older of the two men said, flashing a badge from his inside jacket pocket. His Geordie accent was particularly prominent when he introduced Chris Conte. "We are here to have a chat with a Mr. Nick Van der Linden. Is that you?" he asked, pointing towards the Dutchman.

"Yes."

"And you are, Sir?" he asked Cannon, who was now almost at the door.

"Mike Cannon, ex DI."

Walker smiled. "Well Mr. Cannon, I don't know what was going on here, but I have no business with you, so unless you have anything further to say to Mr. Van der Linden, I'd suggest you leave."

With a brief glance towards where the Dutchman was standing, Cannon made his way out onto the street, slamming the front door as he did so.

Conte made brief eye contact with Walker. Whatever they had walked into was of interest but irrelevant to their specific inquiry.

Van der Linden noticed the exchange between the two policemen and suggested to his staff member that he should go for a walk. He also asked him to put a closed sign up on the shop's door. The man did as he was told. The Dutchman then apologized for his earlier outburst towards the men and the kerfuffle that they had experienced.

"So how can I help you Inspector?" he said, trying to divert their attention back to why the police wanted to speak with him. The attempt at distraction from what they had observed was futile, but Walker nodded in response as if the incident was irrelevant to them.

They had spent the previous afternoon, along with the first part of the morning chasing up the ownerships of two of the four Kawasaki Ninja motorbikes that were registered to people who lived locally. They had also checked the movements of those owners on the day that Sue Gladstone was killed. Statements had been taken and Walker's team had done the necessary checks and follow ups. The two motorbikes had been inspected and it was apparent that neither of them had been damaged recently, if ever. Garages and repair shops in the county and beyond had been contacted regarding the specific type of motorbike repairs that would be needed given that data that Jenny Cribbs had provided. Most of those contacted had responded, however some still needed to. To date there had been no information received that was of use. The third registered owner that had lived in the county had recently relocated to Canada and had apparently, according to neighbours, sold the motorbike to a dealer. At least that is what they understood. Walker was sceptical particularly because no V5C document, for change of ownership, had been submitted as far as they could ascertain from the DVLA records. It was an open matter still being investigated.

Looking around the quiet room and taking in the ambience and sweet smells, Walker and Conte looked at the same designs on the walls that Cannon had noticed. Walker then explained to Van der Linden why they wanted to speak with him.

"We are investigating an incident which you may have read about, Mr. Van der Linden."

"Nick, please, Inspector."

"Okay…Nick. The incident I'm referring to is the death of one, Sue Gladstone."

"So."

"Did you know her at all?" Walker asked.

"No. Should I?"

Noting the Dutchman's reply and aware that Conte was taking notes, Walker continued with his questions. "Mr.…err Nick, do you own a blue Kawasaki Ninja motorbike?"

"Yes, well I.." Van der Linden began.

Conte interrupted him by reading out the registration number that they had obtained from the DVLA database.

"Is that the registration of your motorbike, Nick?" Walker asked.

"Yes, well it is and it was."

"What do you mean? Is it or isn't it?"

"Look Inspector, I'm not sure what you are getting at, but for your information I have several motorbikes. I keep them in a garage I lease two streets away behind the shop."

"And you have the Kawasaki there now?"

"No."

"And the reason for that Mr. Van der Linden?"

The Dutchman noted the change in the tone of Walker's question and the use of his surname. It was now more official and obvious that he wanted an appropriate explanation.

"It was stolen, Inspector."

Taken slightly aback by the comment but remaining resolute in his pursuit of clarity, Walker asked, "When was this?"

"About ten days ago."

"Did you report it?"

"No."

Smiling inwardly and believing that Van der Linden was lying, he asked. "Any reason why not?"

"Because I wasn't sure it had been, at least not initially."

"Go on," Walker said, trying to keep the cynicism from his voice.

"I often let my staff take a bike with them if they work late and need to get home. It's easier for them as they don't need to wait for a bus and better for me as they come in early when it's their day to work."

"Like today?" Conte smirked with irony, looking around at the empty shop.

"My staff don't work every day. It depends on our bookings and how busy we expect to be on any given day."

"So let me get this straight, Nick. You are telling me that this particular motorbike, the Kawasaki Ninja that I'm inquiring about, was stolen from your garage ten days ago?"

"No."

"No? I thought you said…."

"The bike was stolen from the spare ground at the back of the shop. It was parked there where I'd left it for my employee to take with him, when he left work."

"You left it there?"

"Yes."

"But I thought you said you stored it in a garage, two streets back."

"I normally do, but I'd left it on the spare ground as I had used it that morning. I had been to see someone and it didn't make sense to put it in the garage, just for a couple of hours."

Walker rubbed his chin. Something didn't make sense. "Help me out here Nick, as I may be being a little slow at the moment," he said with a pretence that fooled no one. "You said earlier that you didn't know the bike was stolen, but you just said that it *was* stolen ten days ago."

"Yes."

"You'd better explain it to me then."

Van der Linden looked at the two policemen in turn. "It's quite easy Inspector. I left the bike for my employee…"

"Just a minute," Conte said, pencil in hand. "Does this employee have a name?"

"Yes, Charl Prinsloo."

"Is he also Dutch, Mr. Van der Linden?" Conte queried.

"South African, actually."

"Right, can you spell it for me?" Conte asked, writing down the name as Van der Linden did so. Walker looked askew at his Sergeant. The clarification he was seeking from the Dutchman had been interrupted by Conte's interjection.

"Please continue," Walker said, trying to move the conversation along.

"As I was trying to tell you Inspector. I left the bike at the back of the building for Charl to use. When I went home he was still busy with a customer."

"So how did you get home."

"I got a lift."

"And what time was this?"

"About seven. As you can see, we stay open until nine every night except the weekends."

"That still doesn't explain anything, Mr. Van der Linden. I still can't work out how you can pinpoint the day the bike was stolen."

Sighing at what he believed was the stupidity of the policemen, the Dutchman elaborated on what he had already explained. "As I mentioned. I had left the bike for Charl, leaving the keys in my office at the back of the shop." He made a small step towards the black curtain.

"When Charl went to leave that night, the keys and the bike were gone. He thought that one of the other employees had taken them."

"Do all your employees ride then?"

"Yes."

"And?"

"Well, Charl just took one of the other bikes from the garage and went home."

"But wouldn't you have found out that the Kawasaki was stolen the next morning?" Walker asked. "I mean when this Prinsloo character came to work?"

"If that was the case, then maybe, Inspector. The problem here is that Charl wasn't due to come back the following day. He was taking a few days off and going away for the weekend."

"Conveniently?" Walker asked.

"No, *intentionally*."

"Which meant what?"

"That until he came back to work we had no idea that he hadn't taken the bike for the weekend, or that it had been stolen. As I told you not everyone works every day. Some of my employees have regular customers or are asked for by name through referrals. It means the work is lumpy at times and so on occasion there may be just one or two people working. Somedays there are none."

"What do you do then?"

"Well, I'll open the shop for a while and if it stays quiet I'll shut up and go for a ride or something."

"So going back to this specific bike then, you are saying that you only found out about it being stolen a few days ago."

"Yes."

"Did you report it then, once it became obvious to you?"

"No."

"Any reason why not Mr. Van der Linden? It seems odd not to have done so."

Sighing, the Dutchman said, "My girlfriend and I were having some difficulties and I haven't had time to do anything about it."

"What kind of difficulties?" Walker asked.

"They're personal, but for your information we just lost our baby yesterday and the man you just saw me arguing with was responsible. It related to that."

"Mr. Cannon?" Walker said, recalling the name due to him saying that he was an ex-DI.

"Yes, he's a racehorse trainer in Woodstock. He let my girlfriend who is apprenticed to him ride in a race yesterday down in Chepstow. I didn't want her to. It was shocking weather down there and she fell off near the end of the race....she's in a coma in a local hospital currently. Need I say more?"

The two policemen responded empathetically, offering condolences. Walker decided that they had heard enough for now knowing that they could confirm the details of what they had been told, by talking with Charl Prinsloo and perhaps any other employees, if needed. The issue of the fall at Chepstow could also be easily verified, though it had nothing to do with the Sue Gladstone matter that they were investigating..

"I think we have all we need for now, Mr. Van der Linden," Walker said. "Thank you for your time, and I again our sympathies."

"No problem," the Dutchman replied, "I'm glad I could help."

The two Detectives made their way to the shop's door. "Oh, by the way," Walker quipped, half turning and noticing that Van der Linden was about to walk behind the curtain. "I just want to let you know that if necessary we may need to speak with you again."

"Fine," came the reply, "anytime."

Outside the parlour with the door now closed, the two men stood for a few seconds before the cold of the day forced them towards their car parked two hundred metres up the road.

"What do you think, Sir?" Conte asked. "That's a convoluted story if ever I heard one."

"That's right, Sergeant, but it doesn't mean it's not true. Having said that, it is rather convenient though, don't you think?"

"Yes. I'll try and get hold of Prinsloo later and see if he corroborates the chain of events," Conte replied.

"And we need to find that bike," Walker stated. "Let's get the details out to the rest of the country. If someone in the force finds it in their manor, then hopefully they'll tap into the stolen Motorbike Register database and let us know."

CHAPTER 19

Cannon was still annoyed when he parked his car in front of his office. On the way back to the stables after his confrontation with Van der Linden, he made two phone calls. Firstly he had tried to speak with Michelle but she had been tied up in class, the school switchboard telling him that they would pass on the message. They also thanked him for his "nice comments" about Sue Gladstone, who he was told, "was sorely missed".

His second call had been to Cassie. He hadn't spoken to her for a couple of weeks now, or at least it seemed that long to him. She had been between meetings and had been happy to take his call. She gave him an update on the wedding plans. Cannon had let her talk, nodding invisibly as she filled him in on the details that were to be locked in within the next few days. Invitation lists, the design of the cards, colours, even where she was planning to go for her bachelorette weekend. When she mentioned a Bridal shower, he groaned inwardly.

"I've never understood why any of those are necessary," he said, when he finally managed to get a word in.

"Because they are fun, dad, that's why."

"Maybe."

"Oh my God, you sound so old," she teased.

After a few seconds thought, he agreed with her, making her laugh.

"Dad, you know I love you and I appreciate everything you have done for me. A girl couldn't ask for a better father," she said, clearly overcome with happiness.

"Well, we tried. Your mum & I...," he began, but his voice trailed off. A sudden feeling of emptiness overcame him with the thought that he was soon to lose his daughter. The loss of Sally, although years ago, hit him, as if it was only yesterday. A rush of sadness filled his mind. He couldn't speak and she sensed his grief.

"Dad? Dad, are you okay?"

Trying not to reveal his feelings about the past when he was talking about a new future for his daughter, he answered, "Yes, yes, I'm fine. What did Ed have to say about all this?" he added, changing the focus of attention back to her.

"Oh, he's fine with it. He's planning his own bachelor do. Well, he and his best man are."

"So when are we going to see you again? It's been a while."

"We've been hoping to get down to you for ages, as I keep telling Michelle. Unfortunately, Ed is consulting and on call at the hospital so often that we can't seem to coordinate dates, but we will get there as soon as we can."

Cannon acknowledged the problem and let her know that his view was "the sooner, the better." He finished the call with a jumble of emotions. Pleased to have spoken with his daughter. Frustrated that he couldn't get hold of Michelle, and angry with himself to have been caught having an argument in public with Van der Linden. The only saving grace was that with the exception of a slight bruise and a reddening on his chin, there were no more obvious signs of the punch he had received. His shoulder though was still slightly painful and the kick to the abdomen and damage to the skin was fortunately hidden beneath his shirt.

As he climbed out the car a little gingerly, he noticed Telside making his way over to him from the tack room.

"Hi Mike, any word?"

For a second or two Cannon was unsure what Telside was referring to.

"About Angela, the baby..."

"Oh, sorry Rich, no, at least not officially. I haven't tried to call since last night but I had a brief chat with Nick a little while ago and he seemed devastated," he lied, feeling his stomach muscles ache. A sudden thought struck him. Having just spoken with Cassie it gave him an idea. "Perhaps I can get Ed to make some inquiries for me?" he said, "I'll give him a call once I'm settled in my office. Hopefully he can get through the bureaucracy that I can't?"

Telside agreed. "Let's hope so," he said, before moving on to discuss with Cannon matters of a more mundane nature. They were issues related to stable management, feed options, various supply problems and some feedback from Peter Lightman, the stable vet, who Telside had found it necessary to contact while Cannon was in Witney.

Back in Cannon's office Telside explained that one of the horses in the yard, Standup Laurie, a seven-year-old bay gelding had suffered a tendon injury. It had not been apparent to either of them while he and Cannon had been on the heath that morning but had manifested itself later when the horse was being washed down by his groom. Lightman had suggested bandaging the leg along with giving the horse stall rest for a minimum of two weeks with possible therapy thereafter. "The horse could be out of racing until close to the end of the season if its more serious than Lightman thinks," Telside said. "I've let the owner know, and he said that he'll make a decision about the future once the bandages come off in a fortnight and we've had a discussion with him."

Cannon ran a hand through his hair, showing an increased level of frustration. "Shit," he said, "that's not what I needed to hear, Rich. We had hoped to take Laurie down to Sandown in three weeks. There is a three-mile handicap chase that he was ideally suited too."

"I know, Mike. The owner told me that you had mentioned it to him along with the seasons' plans for the horse."

"Obviously he's disappointed?"

"Yes. Very."

"Well that's racing, Rich. It happens more often than we'd like, unfortunately, " Cannon said philosophically, with a sigh. "Any other bad news for me?"

"No, though there is some good."

"Oh yes?"

"I've managed to get Phil Woodhall to ride Brightside Manor tomorrow, down in Wincanton." Phil Woodhall was the leading conditional jockey the previous season. He had outridden his claim very quickly after starting his career but could still ride very light weights.

"That's good news," Cannon said. Then tempering his enthusiasm added, "We both knew that Angela hadn't been available to ride there, but to find as good a Conditional replacement is not a bad outcome. I had entered a 'TBA' about who would ride him when I accepted the horse for the race, just to make sure. How did you manage to get Phil?"

"I just pulled a few strings," Telside said, with a smile. Having been around a long time in the racing game, there were numerous trainers that owed him a few favours still. One of them was Ben Appleby who Woodhall was still apprenticed to. Appleby also had two runners at the Wincanton meeting but had agreed to let his apprentice ride for the stable as he did not have a runner in any of Cannons' races.

"Seeing as I'm managing things as I normally do when you are tied up Mike, I just took the liberty…"

"And I'm so glad you did Rich," Cannon interrupted, a smile eventually crossing his face. His earlier annoyance at things now having temporarily disappeared.

"One other thing."

"Good or Bad?" Cannon queried, hoping for the former but expecting the latter, potentially dispelling his better mood. He instinctively fingered his shoulder and stomach, somehow hiding the pain from his friend.

"Good," Rich answered.

"I'm all ears."

"Giles Mainwaring gave me a call about Summer Kisses, and I let him know how well the horse is going. He's looking forward to riding her tomorrow as he thinks she's his best chance of a winner, despite having five rides for the day."

"Have you had a look at the ante-post market?"

"Yes. She's third favourite at seven to two in the field of eleven, though depending on the weather there may be a few scratchings by the time overnight declarations are confirmed."

"On that basis perhaps the owners could make a few quid?"

"Perhaps, Mike. I think she'll go close, despite it being her first run for the season. She does have a bit of class about her."

"Yes. It's a pity Angela won't be down there to see the race. She has a great affinity for the horse."

"She was never going to go anyway, Mike, as she told us. But I know what you mean."

Cannon gave a sad smile. The irony of Angela intending to see her doctor about her baby's development on the day of the Wincanton races, was now irrelevant given the apparent loss of the child. It was not lost on them. "That's true, Rich," Cannon said, "but at least I'll be there to see the horse run on her behalf."

"Which reminds me," Telside said, suddenly recalling a fact that he had noticed from the form guide for the upcoming meeting. "I see one our former horses is running down there tomorrow."

"Oh yes?"

"Yes. Jacko Lantern, who is now a twelve-year-old. He's running in the race between our two runners."

Cannon turned to his computer which had being sitting idle while they chatted. He opened up a couple of windows on the screen and in the first called up the fields for the Wincanton meeting. "I see since he left us a couple of years back, he's only run a few times and done nothing. His best placing was sixth of ten in a two-and-a-half-mile chase nearly a year ago." He pointed at the screen so that Telside could see.

"Yes, I noticed that when I saw she was running."

"Oh, ok," Cannon replied, forgetting that Telside would have been staying on top of things while his own focus was elsewhere. This was a good example of his thoroughness, for which Cannon was eternally grateful.

"You have to wonder why she's still going around," Telside queried. "Her best is probably behind her. You would have thought that the owners would have sold her off by now, either as an Eventer or a Showjumper, given her poor race form."

"Maybe, Rich. Though as you know, owners can be funny sometimes. It's not always about the cost. It's about dreams. Just a single win can be enough to keep a horse in work."

Telside chuckled in agreement. Over the years he had seen owners transform from being quiet and morse to almost apoplectic with childlike excitement when their horse was first past the post. It was a feeling that both of them knew was the lifeblood of the industry. Without the potential of an owner to find that 'one' horse that would bring that dream to life, there would be no racing and no careers for jockeys, trainers or administrators. The 80,000 people employed in the UK racing industry directly or indirectly produced more than Four Billion pounds worth of economic activity every year. Cannon's stables was just one small part of that.

"I wonder who trains the horse now?" Cannon asked, turning to look at the other window he had opened. It was the BHA website. He typed in the horses' name and found what he was looking for. "Tony Williams, in Roxburgh," he read out aloud. "That's just south of Kelso. It says he had sixteen horses in training, all of them over jumps."

"I haven't come across him before," Telside said. "Where does he usually race?"

"It appears he only started only a few years ago, and he seems to have raced locally for quite a while." Cannon typed on one of the horses listed under the trainers' name and for a minute or so studied the form. He looked at where the horse had raced and what position it had finished in. He then clicked on Jacko Lantern to see where the horse had raced last and who the owner was. He then did the same on another of the trainer's horses, making a mental note of the results. Telside watched Cannons' face in profile, as his boss scanned the screen occasionally typing in another horses' name, before nodding an understanding.

Finally, Cannon said, "I'll be interested to see how Jacko goes tomorrow. Maybe she's learned to enjoy the heavier going by being up there? I suspect she'll think it's like being at home in Scotland, with the recent rains down in Somerset."

"Perhaps," Telside replied, "however I hope it's not too wet down there. We don't want another repeat of what happened to White Noise."

"Agreed, Rich," Cannon responded, just as his mobile phone began to ring. "It's Michelle," he mouthed silently, as he answered the call.

Telside decided it was time to go back to his own office and give Cannon some privacy. He still had arrangements to make regarding the transportation of Summer Kisses and Brightside Manor to the races the next day. The necessary tack needed to be sorted, and the horse float that would be used to take the two animals safely down to the course needed to be checked over to ensure that there were no breakdowns during the three-hour drive. This, in addition to making sure that the staff involved were all going to be available. Late withdrawals due to illness was not uncommon and a back-up plan was always required. It would keep him busy for the rest of the day. As he left the office, he heard Cannon curse.

Amar Hyseni was unhappy with the way payments were being made.

It appeared that his warnings were being ignored. He wasn't sure if it was distance or disdain that was the culprit, but he had had enough. The distribution process was working well. He had evidence of delivery and he was confident that each step in the chain had worked as it should have. The authorities had no idea how things had been set up and he wanted to keep it that way. Individuals who didn't meet their obligations needed to be sent a message. Those that had received such a message, and there were too many of them who had not reacted as expected, needed to be taught a lesson. He picked up the phone in his hotel room and dialled the necessary number. What he wanted done, would be…without question.

Angela was slowly brought out of the induced coma in which she had been placed. Her head and facial injuries, along with her broken right arm, had required MRI, X-Rays and as a result of her pregnancy, an ultrasound. All this had been done while she was unconscious. The hospital had made the decision only after talking to her only known next of kin, her ex-guardian Mrs. Stephanie Powell, who had taken Angela in as a foster child when the girls' father had died a few years earlier. Angela's mother had committed suicide shortly after Angela was born. She had been diagnosed with PPD (Post Partum Depression) shortly after the birth but failed to attend any scheduled checkups for her condition, finally hanging herself while Angela, then ten weeks old, slept. While Steph Powell had no legal responsibility to make any decisions on Angela's behalf, she had become aware of Van der Linden through regular catch ups with Angela. After being advised of the situation by the hospital, she had contacted him having been previously made aware by Angela that he was the father of her child. Stephanie Powell had been practical and not judgemental when faced with the decision she had to make and had acted accordingly.

When Angela was able to understand her surroundings and comprehend her circumstances, the attending doctor let her know of the reasoning behind the decision they had been required to make. The fall from White Noise had resulted in a rupture due to her placenta, though newly formed, having been torn from her uterus. This left the foetus with little chance of survival. By the time she had arrived at the hospital the damage had already been done. The doctors had done what they believed was the best option. Time for any recriminations, if any, would come later. Angela was alive and was told that without the intervention taken, it was likely that she would have died.

It was recommended by the attending doctors that she continued to sleep for as long as possible in order for her body to get over the trauma. They gave her a sedative to calm her so that she would eventually settle down and sleep. As she waited for the drugs to work, various machines beeped and whirred in her room and she heard multiple voices outside her partially opened door. Visitors and patients, nurses and doctors, glided through the corridors and wards beyond. With wires attached to her body and a drip in her arm she contemplated a number of things as consciousness began to fade.

She wondered what Nick would do or say when she was able to tell him about the baby. She wondered how the fall would impact her career and her standing with Cannon. She wondered if she would ever get to ride another horse again.

CHAPTER 20

The gate to the Farmoor Fly Fishing club was locked when Ron Liddell and Sam Green turned off the B4449. It had been an early start for both of them and they hoped that they would be finished around mid-morning. This was a regular trip for the two retirees. It didn't matter too much what the weather was doing as they were ready to fish every single week. Ron jumped out of the 4 x 4 and walked towards the gate, the vehicle's headlights creating an elongated shadow puppet on the ground as it illuminated him. With his club key, he opened the lock that held the heavy chain wrapped around both halves of the metal gate and lifted the catch. This allowed the twin parts of the gate to swing open. After Sam drove the SUV and the attached trailer through the gates, Ron pulled the halves together, made them secure, while leaving them unlocked. He dropped the chain into the trailer, intending to reverse the process when they had finished their mornings fun. Climbing back into the vehicle he complained about the cold wind. Sam let out the clutch and drove them to the car park where they would unload before taking their gear to their usual spot along the bank of Darlow Water.

Fold up chairs, rods, bait, lures and tackle boxes along with spare line and hooks were placed on the ground. They would sit there before being rearranged into the usual positions. The two men chatted, sharing a few jokes and a flask of tea. They were in no hurry.
Fly fishing required the use of both hands and a high level of skill. Totally different to the individual who dropped a line into a canal or the sea and waited for something to happen. The two men had perfected the art of continuously flicking the rods in their hands allowing the lure near the end of the line to dance on the water like an insect.
Ninety minutes later they decided to take a break, having been successful a number of times in catching then recording what they had pulled from the water; Rainbow and Brown trout. They had released each of the fish back into the lake which covered 25 acres, created and nurtured since 1987 from the remains of an old gravel

pit. Returning the catch to the water was what they always did. Theirs was a sport, they were not fishing for food.

Standing underneath a grey and miserable sky in the still strong breeze, Liddell bent to take out a couple of mugs from the weaved picnic basket that his wife had stuffed with sandwiches, pork pies, apples and three flasks of tea. Green was looking out across the expanse of water, its black surface rippling as the wind swirled in hectic circles, pressing the reeds on the far bank and the leaves of multiple trees eastwards. As he watched, a dark shape broke the surface, just for a second, before disappearing again beneath the water. Green guessed that it was a fish, and turned away to see what Liddell was doing.

"Any luck with that tea?" he asked, a smile broadening his bearded face.

"Coming right up," came the reply. It was immediately followed by a groan of pain and a hefty curse as a knee cracked.

"Are you okay, Ron?" Green asked, having heard his companions' expletive.

"Yes, I'll be fine. It's just a bit of old age."

Smiling at the answer, Green turned to face the water again. Taking a deep breath he stretched his arms out wide as if he was embracing the world, saying, "How good is this, hey? How good!"

Liddell passed his friend a mug of hot tea and both men stood side by side enjoying the silence. To both of them, this was their church, their place of inspiration and reflection.

The water's surface was broken again. Both men saw it simultaneously. This time the object stayed above the water line a few seconds, before again slipping silently below the surface and out of sight.

They turned to each other, silent questions creasing their brows. Without hesitation they turned to their individual rods. The object, according to Green, had moved much closer to them from when he had first noticed it. Now it seemed to be less than ten metres away from their position. Within a minute they had rods in their hands and were casting out to where they had last observed the object to be. On the third cast Green felt his line attach to something underwater.

From the tension on the line, he knew that it wasn't a fish, but something much larger. As he started to turn the handle of the reel, he remembered the breaking strain of the line. Having turned the reel less than a complete circle the object broke the surface again. It was now within three meters of the bank and the natural flow of the water was pushing it in their direction.

The two men were too old and too frightened to wade into the water to gather the object, but they knew what it was. They also knew that they had stumbled upon something terrible. Green reached for his mobile. With shaking hands he dialled 999. Given what they had uncovered, they expected that a very long day lay ahead of them.

CHAPTER 21

The drive down to Wincanton was relatively uneventful. Cannon had left his stable yard long after the horse float. With two hours head start, he expected both runners to be settled in their stalls by the time he arrived on the course. As he drove he watched as clouds built on the far horizon before dissipating. This happened several times during the journey. Throughout the trip he drove through differing temperatures and conditions. Mild and dry at one stage, then cold and drizzly and then back again to dry. He finished his trip on a light rain just as he parked the Land Rover in the parking area reserved for Owners and Trainers. He had enjoyed the solitude as it had given him time to think. The arrangement with Silvers and the need to maintain a semblance of normality in his life had necessitated some additional planning. He was hoping to see Jim Franklin during the course of the day having noticed that he was riding in four of the six races on the card, including that of Summer Kisses. The news from Van der Linden that Angela had lost her unborn still concerned Cannon and he felt it appropriate that he should let Franklin know, before it was in the public domain. Cannon having shared the information in trust of her pregnancy, felt it was necessary to provide the update no matter how sad it was. He made his way towards the racecourse office to complete the necessary formalities of his being on course before heading off to see how well his runners had settled in.

Each runner at the meeting was allocated a specific stall by the course management and it was there that owners and trainers could find their horse prior to their event. Normally after each race, a horse would be washed down, loaded onto their transport and returned to their home stables as quickly as possible. This resulted in multiple animals coming and going throughout the course facilities at all times during the day. Before the first race however was always an extremely busy period with nearly all participants of the first two races in particular being readied to run. Horses had to be in the racecourse stable at least 45 minutes before their specific race, as Vet checks, ID checks and other tests needed to be done to ensure that the runners were healthy. The checks for stimulants or drugs would be conducted later, normally post-race, as determined by the Stewards. Cannon walked past the individually numbered stalls where some of the day's runners stood quietly being watered, groomed and readied for their race. He noticed some stalls were still empty but he found the measured cacophony of buckets of water being filled and then drunk from, along with the clanking of bits and bridles as they were hung up or taken down off metal pegs, very reassuring. As he continued along the row he noticed a woman rubbing down a roan-coloured horse that he instantly recognized, Jacko Lantern. The distinctive markings of three white socks and a white fleck on the left ear confirmed it, despite the horse having advanced in age since Cannon had last seen him.

"Hello," he said to the back of a woman with bottle blond hair cut in a pixie style. She was in her early twenties and wore dark blue jeans and a heavy bottle green jacket over a grey jumper. On her feet were what appeared to be hiking boots. As she turned around to see who was speaking, Cannon noticed that she was holding a heavy brush with a black strap across it which totally concealed her hand. It was a grooming tool that she had been rubbing the horse down with, creating a chess-like pattern on the horses' flanks.

"Can I help you?" she asked, wary of who the man was that had begun talking to her.

Cannon noticed that the woman was sweating despite the cold of the day. Her exertions evident by the moisture above her top lip and the beads at her temples. She attempted to wipe them away with the back of the hand that still held the brush. She was pretty. Slim, slightly smaller than average, with wiry arms and legs. She was almost too petite to control five hundred kilograms of thoroughbred, Cannon thought. Her face was stained in several places, a result of the dust that filled the air of the stall. Her green eyes searched his face, looking for an answer.

"Oh, I'm sorry," he said. "My name is Mike Cannon. I have a couple of runners here today." He held out his hand. She untangled her own from the brush and took his fleetingly.

"Rachel Brits," she said. "Are you one of the syndicate?"

"No, I'm not. As I said, I have two runners here today, but I'm not an owner, I'm a trainer."

With a smile of understanding she asked him again how she could help.

"It's nothing really," he replied, "I just wanted to see how the old horse was doing." He gestured towards the quietly standing mare who chewed on the metal bit in her mouth. She seemed completely at ease with what was going on around her. "She was with me a few years ago."

"Right," she said, stretching out the word. Her Scottish brogue was now more evident. She offered nothing else in reply.

For a second he felt embarrassed in the awkward silence, before asking, "How is she doing? It's a long way to come from Scotland."

"How do you know that?" she questioned, her eyes narrowing suspiciously.

Realising that she may be feeling uncomfortable at his questions, he responded quickly, "It's the accent, it's subtle but….," He touched his ear using it as a prop. "Am I right?" he added, trying to recover the situation and dispel any concerns she may have.

"Aye you are."

Nodding towards the horse which stood almost stock still, he asked, "Has she settled down a bit? She used to be quite a handful when she was with me."

Brits patted the horse on the shoulder, receiving a snort and a brief shake of the head in response. "I don't really know," she said. "I've only been with Tony for a month or so."

"Tony Williams, Jacko's trainer?"

"Yes."

"Understood. Is he around?"

"He's here somewhere," she said, looking up and down the stalls, almost apologizing that the man wasn't readily available to him.

"It's not a problem. I was just curious as the horse seems much calmer than he used to be, and I was keen to understand how Tony had managed to do it."

"I'll let him know you were asking," she said, beginning to brush the horse's flanks again. "Maybe he'll come and find you himself."

"That would be good, but only if he can. You can tell him that if I'm not with my horses just up there," he pointed along the passage, "stall numbers thirty-seven and thirty-eight, then I'll be in the O and T bar immediately after my races which are numbers two and four."

"No worries," she smiled.

With a final look at the horse in Rachel Brits' care, which flicked its ears as a belated acknowledgement of recognition of him, Cannon walked off to find his own groom, Colin Wilson, who had the responsibility to look after Summer Kisses and Brightside Manor during the day.

He only had twenty minutes before the first race. Cannon met up with Jim Franklin who was to ride the favourite, Honest as the Day, in the field of nine runners.

Standing at the entrance to the weighing room, Cannon shared with the jockey a couple of thoughts he had gathered since they had last spoken. He asked Franklin if he would be able to catch up with him again after the fourth race, to which the jockey agreed as he wasn't riding in the fifth. Cannon told Franklin that he had an idea and wanted to test his thinking with him. The two men then went their separate ways. Franklin to ride into a disappointing second place behind an outsider called Piggy Tarpulin, trained by local trainer Reg Barnes, and Cannon went off to saddle Summer Kisses.

A slither of sunlight briefly permeated the leaden sky as the field gently clip-clopped around the parade ring in an orderly fashion. Everyone waited for the bell to ring, used on course to advise the jockeys that it was time to mount their rides. The cold wind that continued to keep the temperature down in the low double digits was briefly forgotten by the ever-increasing crowd. With the favourite having been beaten in the first race, punters saw the sun as an omen and piled their money onto the back of Summer Kisses, moving her up to second favourite at two to one. Giles Mainwaring was helped into the saddle by Cannon. Col Wilson waited a few seconds until Mainwaring indicated that he was comfortable, before walking on. The horse appeared nice and relaxed, totally unaware of the weight of expectations foisted upon her by the on-course crowd. Mainwaring reset the length of his stirrups after briefly standing in them to ensure that his saddle was securely fastened around the horse's girth. A slipped saddle over jumps was a recipe for disaster and had been the undoing of many a horse and rider over the years. Senior riders like Mainwaring won races because they looked after the little things.

Cannon watched as the field slowly disentangled from their circling and in single file headed towards the course access gate. It was a good hundred metres away and reached via a chute-like passageway. He had been standing alone, as the owners of Summer Kisses, Harry and Bridget Davids, a pair of married doctors from Lincolnshire, rarely had the opportunity to see the horse run in the flesh due to their workload. They often called Cannon after a race, letting him know if they had had a chance to watch it on television and seeking any feedback he had to offer about the horse. They were keen to hear everything that happened either pre, post or during the race that he felt was appropriate for them to know. The couple, like all owners, loved to win but were always realistic. They were the type of owners who understood the game and believed in Cannon and how he operated. Today's race was a Two Mile, Three Furlong, Class 3 Handicap and Summer Kisses was carrying joint top weight which was why Angela had not been nominated to ride her.

Cannon made his way to a spot on the grandstand where he could watch the race. It always amazed him how a 9-hole golf course could fit on the inside of the racetrack and how the golfers seemed to keep their balls inside the boundary. Wincanton wasn't unique, there were several similar setups around the country, but he had heard that the status quo at Wincanton, would not remain for very much longer. The golf course was to close within the next six months. He had no view either way as to whether it was a good or bad decision, but he was surprised to hear of the closure as he could think of at least five racetracks across the country with a golf course within their boundaries. He was aware of many similar arrangements throughout the globe which seemed to work too.

With eyes searching for his runner, he scoured the field as he sat down in a bright red chair on the Premier stand. It was from there that he could see the finish line. With the stand only a third full, he had found the perfect spot to watch the race and was also able to exit the stand and get to the unsaddling enclosure quickly once the race was over. The field circled around for what seemed an age before the starter called them together and was satisfied that every horse was standing in line ready for the 'off'. While the Starter was procrastinating the weather had changed yet again. The clouds had blocked out the sun and the sky had darkened. Once again rain was threatening but as the tapes flew up for the race to start, the threat was forgotten. The crowd cheered and the battle began. The seventeen fences that the horses needed to clear made the race a test of bravery and of stamina. The ground was wet from the earlier rains, and though not completely saturated, the tight track required the skills of each of the jockeys to be on show.

Cannon followed the all-gold colours of Summer Kisses as Giles Mainwaring sensibly piloted the horse, staying out of trouble by riding midfield and on the outside of the pack. For the first half of the race there was a steady pace set by two of the outsiders. The languid flow of limbs ensuring that safety rather than courage and nerve took precedence. As the still intact field left the straight and headed for their last circuit of the tight track, the race began in earnest. With the two long-time leaders having run their race and beginning to flag, the favourite Boyznightout made a bold move and took the lead. Within a matter of two hundred metres he had swamped the field, moving from the middle of the field to head the others. Jumping serenely he was still leading the field by four lengths with only half mile to run. Behind him there were three casualties, two horses falling, crashing down at separate fences along the back straight and another losing his rider as his saddle slipped. Further back in the race both of the outsiders that had lead the race initially were pulled up, their jockeys sensing that their mounts had given up all that they could.

Summer Kisses was in fourth place a further two lengths behind the third horse. Giles Mainwaring had been biding his time. Underneath him he had a horse full of running and only three fences to clear in the straight. As he began his chase of the leader he gave his horse a whack on the flanks and a dig in the belly with his boots. Summer Kisses responded immediately, lengthening her stride and picking up the bit. Mainwaring felt the power surge through his mount and quickly found himself in third place as he landed over the third last fence still four lengths adrift of the leader. Jumping the penultimate fence alongside the second horse he could hear the on-course commentary and the roar of the crowd. Out of the corner of his eye, he saw, then heard, his rival jockey curse as his horse hit the barrier and the rider cartwheeled before landing on the soft ground with a deafening thud. Without hesitation, Mainwaring shrugged off what he had just heard, concentrating instead on the lead horse and the final jump ahead. Summer Kisses was now two lengths behind the flanks of the favourite who was still travelling well. Mainwaring pushed his hands up and down the neck of his mount urging the horse to rise one last time at the last fence and give his all to try and catch their rival still five metres ahead. As the favourite reached the final fence, the pressure being put on Boyznightout by the chasing Summer Kisses began to tell. Jumping just a few metres ahead of his pursuer, the favourite clattered the obstacle, making the mistake that Mainwaring was hoping for. Landing on the other side of the fence but only a half-length ahead, the favourite stumbled and lost momentum. Summer Kisses was also feeling the effects of the race and the soft ground. Mud spattered and with goggles full of grime from the kick back of those horses that he had followed during the race, Mainwaring managed more by luck than design, to cling on as his mount slid into the lead after landing safely but awkwardly over the jump. With whip in hand, he urged Summer Kisses to the line as the crowd clapped and screamed as the battle down the hill, to the finish line, went all the way. As the two horses passed the post, Cannon smiled. Summer Kisses had prevailed by half a length. The final hundred yards had been a gruelling affair. Each horse and rider had given their all. Neither had been willing to give up and despite a mammoth effort by the favourite, the mistake at the last had cost him the race. With the cheers of the crowd dying down, Cannon made his way towards the winners circle where he met Col Wilson and Giles Mainwaring who waved to the clapping crowd before he dismounted, gently patting the horse on the neck once his feet were back on the ground.

"A bit tight," Cannon said, as he watched Mainwaring unsaddle the horse, while Wilson held Summer Kisses' bridle talking softly to the horse.

"Yes, but she dug deep, and deserved the win. She definitely has the class. The favourite put in a real effort."

Cannon nodded. Despite the fact that Angela exercised Summer Kisses every day, he was grateful to have Mainwaring ride the horse. He doubted whether his young apprentice would have had the strength to lift the horse to the win that everyone on course had witnessed. It wasn't a criticism of anyone, it was just a matter of fact. An experienced jockey could often be the difference between winning and a losing. The game wasn't always about skill. Sometimes race smarts, tactics and strength could be the difference between a win and second place.

"Thanks Giles, a great ride."

"My pleasure, Mike. When she runs again and she's carrying a high weight, I'm happy to be on board if I'm free." With that Mainwaring made his way to the weighing room. Cannon asked Wilson to give the horse as quick trot in front of him, making him do a few turns and circles so that Cannon could check if there were any obvious problems with the horse's action. On face value there were none that Cannon could see. With a smile he told Wilson to take the horse away for a wash and rub down before returning the animal to his stall. As he did so, Summer Kisses was chosen by the stewards for post-race drug testing. A small white lanyard was placed around the neck by a member of the veterinary team. The necessitated the groom to make a detour to the sampling unit where urine and blood samples would be taken. Cannon had no concerns with the decision, he knew that the horse was clean. His main concern was whether Wilson would have enough time to get Brightside Manor ready for his race. He was however concerned about leaving his second runner alone, so he made his way to the stalls to keep a watchful eye on the horse until Wilson was freed up.

As he walked to the particular stall where Brightside Manor was housed, he passed the spot where he had spoken with Rachel Brits. The stall was empty. He was a little surprised as it seemed too early for the horse to be taken to the paddock/parade ring and he couldn't see the horse in the *pre*-parade ring either. Shrugging his shoulders, he continued walking when he heard an announcement on the course tannoy that on veterinary advice, Jacko Lantern had been scratched from the third race. That declaration now made sense as to why the stall had already been vacated. Thankful that both his own horses were fit and well, when he arrived at Brightside Manor's stall, he noticed that the horse appeared to be totally unfazed by the lack of company. It seemed to Cannon that the horse had been so comfortable that it had been sleeping while there was movement and noise continuing all around him. Mouthing a silent note of thanks to no one in particular Cannon began to ready the horse for its race. As he groomed the horse and checked him over for any heat in the legs, he could hear rain tapping on the roof of the building which suddenly increased in intensity, before once again slowing to a stop. Wilson eventually arrived back at the stalls with Summer Kisses, while several other horses made their way back and forth through the stall sheds. Some were heading home, some were to be readied for later races and some were soon to be challenging Brightside Manor for honours.

"You're all wet, Col," Cannon smiled, as the groom shook off beads of water from his hair and coat.

"It was bucketing down, just as I left the drug sampling unit," he replied, "and now it's stopped just as quickly."

"How did it go?"

"It was fine. Just took a bit longer than expected."

"Well, she did well," Cannon stated, "really well." He patted the horse on the neck.

"Yes, she did. She's a real fighter."

"Umm…," Cannon replied, suddenly thinking of Angela, who had such an affinity with Summer Kisses. She was a fighter too. He hoped that she was going to be alright in the long term. He still had no formal confirmation about her situation or about the baby, but if it was true that she had lost it, he felt that it could take months if not years for her to get over it. Cannon let Wilson tie up Summer Kisses. Between them they readied Brightside Manor for his race, listening as they did so to an excited commentator's call of the third race, where a favourite won for the first time that day.

The fourth race was over and some of the punters were already leaving the course. The rain and lack of favourites winning their events, other than in the third race, had impacted their wallets and had made the bookmakers' satchels much fatter than they were, when they had arrived on course. Brightside Manor had run a poor race despite the urging of Phil Woodhall. The champion Conditional jockey reported that the heavier going seemed to have affected the horse's chances. With the rain adding to the already wet ground, it appeared the horse was uncomfortable with the very heavy ground. Had it been just soft, Woodhall believed there would have been a better showing and the horse would have been "much closer" at the finish.

Cannon was disappointed with the run and felt that Angela would have managed a better result. While he did not doubt Woodhall's assessment, he felt the tactics used by the jockey of staying well back from the leaders then trying to catch them on the flat between the last two fences, had cost them a position or two. There was no debate that the winner was superior on the day, but Brightside Manor running fourth only two lengths behind the second horse, and a half length behind the third, was a disappointment. The one positive was that there was no fall or any injury to his charge.

Cannon waited for Jim Franklin just outside the weighing room. Col Wilson had taken Brightside Manor along with Summer Kisses to get them ready to be transported back home. The weather was beginning to get even colder and blusterier. Dark clouds were building in the South-West and the rain, though intermittent, seemed to indicate that there was a heavier downpour likely within the next half hour. Standing under the eaves of the building, Cannon thought of Angela. It was a similar type of day to today, during which she had fallen. Was it only a couple of days ago? He needed to find out how she was doing. He opened his phone and made a decision. He hadn't ever spoken with his soon to be son-in-law before without Cassie being around. Nearly every time they had met with each other previously, it was when Cassie and Ed had met them for lunch somewhere. Occasionally both had been visitors to the stables, but that was few and far between. Cannon had been given Ed's number for emergencies. This wasn't one such event, but Cannon felt it was a worthy enough reason to justify the call.

"You know it's very unusual to do this," Ed Taylor stated rationally, once Cannon had explained the reason for the contact. He then accepted the rebuke from Taylor for Cannon delaying a meeting that his future son-in-law was just about to Chair.

"I know Edward, but all I'm asking is a favour. I don't want all the details. I just want to know if it's true, that she lost the baby."

Taylor sighed. He was a specialist in another field, not Obstetrics, and he felt that such an enquiry would seem odd to those Health Professionals down in Chepstow, who were directly involved in Angela's care. "Look Mike, I'll see what I can do, but I can't guarantee anything. I'll try my best and come back to you once I have something to share."

"I understand," Cannon said, thanking him for trying. "Just text me, if or when, you have any information. There is no need to phone."

Taylor acknowledged the request then quickly ended the call, leaving Cannon to contemplate how he could face Angela again, if indeed she had lost her unborn.

"You okay, Mike?" Jim Franklin said, noting Cannon seemed to be far away, unaware that Franklin had tapped him already on the shoulder.

"Oh, sorry Jim, I didn't see you there. I was just thinking of something."

"No problem." Franklin was dressed in his silks for the next race. Lime green with a yellow sash that ran from his right shoulder to his left hip. On his head was an orange cap. He looked skywards as the clouds began to creep closer to the racecourse. "I'm surprised the Stewards haven't considered abandoning the last two races," he said. "The last one with your runner was pretty slow, and hard going to watch."

"Yes, it was a bit. I suppose the Stewards still think the track is safe enough though."

"Well, they are not riding on it are they?" Franklin said.

Cannon couldn't disagree and said so before asking, "Have you been able to find out anything?"

"Not a lot, Mike unfortunately, though take a look at the horse in my race called Uncle Buck, I heard he might be for sale."

"But it's not a selling race."

"I know, but I heard that the owner wants out. The horse is only an eight-year-old and hasn't done anything for ages. I think this is his first run in nearly two years, other than an aborted run in Germany a few weeks ago. I'm guessing it's a last roll of the dice. According to the jock, Jeff Lloyd, the trainer believes the horse has no chance."

"Thanks Jim, that's useful to know. I appreciate your help anyway and I'll check it out."

"You're welcome," Franklin replied, "and I'll keep my eyes and ears open. I'll let you know if I come across anything else."

Cannon watched Franklin walk out into the steadily increasing rain and make his way to the parade ring. There were no spectators standing at the rails to the ring as the field of seven paraded themselves, guided by their grooms. Most spectators had gone home or were busy staying dry in some of the bars.

In the grandstand a few hardy souls braved the cold to watch the runners make their way to the start. Cannon peered through his binoculars following Franklin and his mount Sir Christopher as they made their way to the start. It was raining heavier now and as the horses cantered to the tapes, huge sods of grass shot up behind them as their hooves sank deeper into the saturated ground. Cannon tried to find Uncle Buck. The race card indicated that the jockey would be wearing a blue and white hooped jacket with a white cap. The colours of Queens Park Rangers. Scouring the field, he was only able to find six runners. None of them was the horse he was looking for. He found it strange given he had definitely seen Jeff Lloyd and Uncle Buck leave the parade ring earlier when he had walked past a course TV screen on his way to the grandstand. Thinking the rain had reduced his ability to see the horses clearly, he scanned the entire track. He began with the straight and then the long course bends, around which the horses would race, until he found the runners in his sights once again. They were still milling around at the start line. He was confused for a second. As it contemplated his confusion, an announcement was made over the course Tannoy system that horse number eight, Uncle Buck, had been scratched from the race. The horse had been found to be lame and had now joined the two other scratchings in the race that had been declared very early that morning. Cannon lowered his binoculars. The announcement answered the question to the puzzle that had been floating around in his mind. Deciding that he had had enough for the day, he began the long walk to his car, braving the rain but intending to make a detour along the way to check that Col Wilson had successfully loaded his two charges onto the horse float. As he made his way passed the back of the Grandstand, he noticed two men walking towards him. For a few seconds his eyes focused beyond them, while his ears took in the start of the on-course commentary that was being broadcast to an ever-decreasing number of spectators.

"Mr Cannon?" the larger of the two men said, stopping in front of him and blocking his path.

"Yes," Cannon answered, suddenly realizing where he had seen the man before. It was the previous day, in the tattoo parlour. They had walked in just as he was about to leave. He tried to recall the man's name.

"DI Sam Walker," the man said. "This is DS Chris Conte. We met yesterday."

"I remember, Inspector. What can I do for you?"

"We'd like you to come with us please."

"I'm sorry?" Cannon queried. "Why? What's happened? Is Michelle okay? Has something happened to Cassie?" A sudden sense of panic careered through him. The police only asked someone to accompany them, for a couple of reasons. Cannon had no reason to suspect anything other than a possible accident involving one his family members.

"Mr. Cannon," Walker continued, "I'm arresting you on suspicion of murder of one Mr. Nick Van der Linden."

"What?" Cannon replied, as Conte gripped him by the arm. Having said it himself so many times before, he ignored Walker as he continued with the obligatory caution.

"You do not have to say anything. But it may harm your defence if you do not mention when questioned something which you later rely on in court. Anything you do say may be given in evidence.

Do you understand what I have just said, Mr. Cannon?"

"Of course I do."

Walker stared at Cannon for a few seconds. It was as if something was troubling the policeman. The two men faced each other, standing in the rain for what seemed an interminable amount of time. While they did so, all around them the voice of the on-course commentator was getting more excited as the fifth race neared its end.

Eventually Walker turned to Conte. "Cuff him," he said.

CHAPTER 22

Nick Van der Linden's body had been taken directly to the pathology lab of Jenny Cribb after the ambulance had collected it from the side of the pond. The two fishermen had been offered counselling if required, but neither accepted. Both had seen bodies during their time in the Royal Navy, the men having served together during the Falklands War in the early 80's. Though it was a long time ago, what they had experienced there had never left them. Even retirees could recall when death came calling.

Angela was upset when she was told the news. and yet in some way she felt relieved. She had feared what Nick may have done, blaming her for losing his baby. Now however, she had lost him as well as his child. Torn between the two she fell back onto her pillow and sobbed, unsure which loss she felt the most.

Her own future was not the only thing that had come crashing down when she had fallen from White Noise, those of others had too.

She knew she should have listened to Cannon.

Another shipment had arrived. Amar Hyseni needed his brother-in-law to work quicker this time. The distribution channel needed to be streamlined again. Demand was increasing, but the ability to meet it was challenging. If Hyseni couldn't move quickly enough, then someone else would probably move in. Other players were always keen to exploit any opportunity to fill a gap when one source showed weakness or became lax. What came in today, needed to be out within seventy-two hours. There were five new arrivals and plenty of supply to go with them. Hyseni had tried to get hold of his surgeon, but there had been no answer. He wasn't sure if it was deliberate or not. He called Ardita and asked for Erjon.

"He's not here," she lied.

Hyseni knew his sister better than she knew herself. He knew when she was protecting her husband.

"Where is he then?"

"I don't know. He said he was taking Dardan to the shops after school. He wants to buy him something for Christmas."

"Ardita, Albania is a secular country but we are non-practicing Muslims, we follow Islam, we don't fucking believe in Christmas!"

She ignored his outburst. He could hear her breathing softly. Finally she responded, and he could tell that she was angry. She knew that he was seen to be a better asset to the family than she was, but she wouldn't take his bullshit. "Look Hyseni, we live in the Netherlands now. Dardan goes to a Dutch school. Erjon and I are bringing him up like his fellow countryman, and that means we *will* celebrate Christmas day *and* Tweede Kerstdag on the twenty sixth, just like every other family here!"

Hyseni was in no mood to argue.

"Okay, okay, I'll ignore the sanctimonious crap for now," he said, his voice filled with sarcasm. "When do you expect him back?"

"I'm not sure," she replied, trying to contain her anger. "He said he was planning on buying the boy an Ajax football strip, but he needed to get the sizing right. He also wants to get Dardan some soccer boots and a new ball, so it may take some time."

Hyseni looked at his watch, he knew that it was already dark outside. Evening was fast approaching and he hadn't had chance to leave the building since arriving at five am. He was tired and becoming angry himself. His anger usually resulted in someone getting hurt or mistakes being made. He couldn't risk the latter and he wasn't in a unique position regarding the former. He sighed loudly. 'Messages' needed to be sent when people crossed him. It was difficult with Erjon and Ardita, the family wasn't always in agreement with him. His own suppliers were not so compassionate. Sometimes he received messages that he did not like. He knew that he was just part of a chain, albeit he had more power than many. When he did receive them he didn't always like what he heard or was told, but business was business and there was little sympathy shown to anyone.

During the day there had been a number of suppliers that he had needed to placate. Some, who he had given promises to previously, now wanted answers. Then there were those in the chain that he had needed to chase himself, to get answers to his own questions. It was never ending. They were involved in the chain because of one thing only; the money. Unfortunately, with the territory, there were men who disappointed him, men who had threatened him and men that he had needed to threaten. Each was a part of his everyday life. Sometimes he felt he was on a knife's edge and at other times he felt that he was on top of the world. Ardita always seemed to bring him down.

"Just tell him to ring me when he gets home," he said, folding his Samsung in half again. "Fuck!" he shouted, frustrated at the way Erjon Abazi was playing him. "Alright you bastard," he said to the empty room. "It's about time you learnt a lesson."

He had been taken into the racecourse office building and made to wait in a small room while Walker contacted Oxford police to let them know of the arrest. The Abingdon police station would be closed by the time they would have driven back north, so they needed the facilities to formalize the indictment. There was also a need for a solicitor to be on hand to advise Cannon of his rights during the interview process. The questioning was expected to take place almost as soon as they got there. While Walker was busy with the arrangements, Cannon used the opportunity given to him, his right to make a phone call, so he immediately phoned Michelle. He told her what had occurred and let her know that he would be taken back up to Oxford where he was to be questioned.

"Are they serious, Mike?" she asked. "Do they really believe that you would have done anything like this?"

"Clearly they do. They wouldn't have arrested me if they didn't believe they had a case, but they are wrong."

"I'll get hold of Cassie and let her know what's going on. I'm sure she can arrange for someone to be at the police station to represent you when you get back here. It will be better than an on-call solicitor."

"I agree and I'd be surprised if she didn't have any contacts," he answered, trying to insert some humour into his voice. He didn't want her to worry too much, he had been here before. Sometimes, he mused, it seemed that something was chasing him.

When in the police force he had experienced many murders, suicides, accidental overdoses and other horrific scenes, and had eventually needed to get away from all the pain that it brought. Sally had been his rock during that time, and she had helped him get through the dark days until cancer had taken her. However, after he met Michelle there were lengthy periods of calm and it seemed that his new profession as a horse trainer had stayed the anguish, but he was wrong. The transient quiet had dissipated over time, and death continued to haunt him.

He had no idea why.

"And can you arrange for someone to collect the car? The spare keys are in my bedside table," he continued. His brief sojourn into his personal history had passed, though not in memorable or particularly satisfactory way. He decided that by talking about such mundane matters, he would lessen her concern. He knew what was coming and it wasn't pleasant, least of all for his loved ones.

"Sure," she answered, still feeling numb and confused about the whole episode.

"And let Rich know that I'll be back in the yard sometime tomorrow. He needs to make sure that the yard operates as normal. I don't want the staff to hear any gossip before I get back, they should just get on with business as usual," he said. "Even if the police charge me, they'll need a magistrate to refuse bail and I doubt that will happen," he added confidently.

When he had finished the call, he was immediately placed into a police car by Walker. Along with Conte and a young constable, who was to drive them back to Oxfordshire, the four men drove out of the racecourse. Cannon looked at his watch as he sat in the back seat with Conte sitting beside him. It was now just after six thirty in the evening. They would only arrive at their destination two hours later.

CHAPTER 23

The drive up to Oxford had been conducted in almost total silence. Cannon had used the time to think about a number of things and whether he need mention any of them when he was eventually questioned.
He was curious as to the basis upon which he was to be charged. He guessed that Walker had suspicions but no evidence, just a hunch, and that in itself was based purely on circumstance. A circumstance that had led him to believe somehow, that Cannon was a killer.
As they continued driving through the rain-filled gloom of the evening, Cannon's mind turned to what had happened at Wincanton. His runners had had mixed fortunes and for that he was grateful. Fortunately the weather had held off long enough for both his runners to compete in reasonable conditions. Unfortunately however, he hadn't had the opportunity to see how Jim Franklin had got on in the fifth race, and he was a little confused by what the jockey had meant about Uncle Buck. The horse had been scratched before the race and had not taken part in it, so Cannon couldn't see any relevance regarding what he and Franklin had discussed previously. He doubted there had been any betting plunges on the horse either, so was he missing something? While he chewed figuratively on what was ahead of him in Oxford, he remembered that he still hadn't heard anything about Angela. He closed his eyes as the hum as the car's engine, and the hypnotic rhythm of the windscreen wipers, slowly worked their way into his head. Drowsiness and fatigue seemed to pull him down towards an uncomfortable sleep. His head lolled slightly as he tried to fight the urge to stay awake. Eventually he lost the battle and the side of his head came to rest against the back door window. When he awoke he wasn't sure how long he had slept for, but in that time, minutes or seconds, the ghosts he tried to avoid had come back again as they usually did in his time of stress. The familiar faces of long buried victims cried for help, begged him for assistance, reached out with their bony fingers and pointed to their wounds before grabbing at his clothing, dragging him down into their graves!

Death Seeks You Out

He woke with a start, his breathing heavy and his body was covered in sweat. Conte was shaking him awake, just as the engine was cut and the heater blowing warm air into the car, turned off. They had arrived.

Cassie had not wasted any time once Michelle had call her. With a network of contacts and after having received advice from a senior partner in her practice, she had been able to arrange for a solicitor from a specialist criminal defence firm to be on hand by the time Cannon and his accusers arrived at the police station. The solicitor, George Chamberlain, had done his research in the limited time available to him, and he had established that Walkers' reputation of jumping to conclusions was true. The solicitor secreted the information in the back of his mind, for later use. With Cannon having been arrested under caution, Chamberlain advised him that he should "let me do the talking" when the police commenced their interview. This would start after the requisite formalities and necessary paperwork had been concluded.

The two men had been given an hour to meet before Walker was expected to question Cannon about the death of Van der Linden. Chamberlain had sought to delay the interview until the morning, but with the limited time available for the police to keep Cannon legally under arrest without charging him, Walker denied the request.

"It's okay with me, Mr. Chamberlain," Cannon had said, "the sooner we get this thing over, the sooner I can go home and the police can get on and find whoever killed the man. And just as importantly, finding out why."

Chamberlain was in his late thirties, of average height with a mop of black hair that covered his forehead and which sat just over the top of his oversized round glasses. The impression it gave was that of a thatched roofed house where the thatching fell just beyond the edge of the eaves. With dark grey eyes and a nubian nose that accentuated his diamond-shaped face and a mouth full of perfect teeth he was both youthful and good looking. He had a habit of constantly wiping his hair away from his forehead and then cleaning his glasses with the insert of his glasses case. Whenever he did this, he stopped talking until he was finished. Cannon wasn't sure if this was for thinking time or just habitual, but whatever it was he found it slightly off putting. After they had discussed the background to the upcoming interview and the tactics to be followed during the session, Chamberlain asked Cannon his most important question.

"So is there any obvious reason for the police to suspect you of this murder?"

"No, but I can guess. Though I suppose we'll find out soon enough," Cannon replied, noticing the door to the interview room starting to open. Walker and Conte entered, Walker carrying a large Starbucks coffee cup, Conte an official police folder. With four men in the room and a small table between each pair, Conte began the process of setting up the recording instrumentation, readying to start the interview. Cannon smiled inwardly when he noticed that there were no cassettes being used anymore. The digital age meant that everything discussed would ultimately be dumped onto a USB stick and shared with him later allowing each party to have an audio-visual copy of the interview.

Walker introduced himself and his Sergeant, his Geordie accent suddenly more prominent, saying "for the tape…."

Cannon watched Conte play with the contents of his folder, while Walker stated the date and time of the interview, noting that even with new technology, an old habit and the use of the word 'tape' along with dates and times was hard to break. Once Walker had finished with his preamble Cannon was asked to provide his name for the record, which he shamelessly did, saying, "for the tape, my name is….."

Chamberlain then followed suit.

"Right, now that we've sorted out the formalities, I'd like to ask you a few questions Mr. Cannon." Walker said, taking the folder from his Sergeant. Cannon noticed that it was quite thin and guessed that most of the paper within it were purely props. He doubted there was much the police had been able to uncover since he and Van der Linden had clashed through to the point when they had arrested him. The timeframe was way too short for any in-depth investigation to have been conducted. He guessed they were working on pure coincidence. He wasn't surprised in a way. He never trusted co-incidences himself. Often they provided the clue that broke a case and he knew that the police were always under pressure to solve crimes, so the sooner they could solve this one, the better it would look on their statistics. More importantly it would send a message to the community that they were on top of things. The optics were always better than the facts. The hierarchy continuously preached this mantra and it left a lot of long termers cold.

Chamberlain encouraged Walker to "fire away."

Taking his time, the Detective asked, "Where were you Mr. Cannon when Mr. Van der Linden was killed?"

Chamberlain tapped Cannon on the knee then advised him that he didn't need to answer the question. Reminding him subtly of their earlier discussion about who would speak during the interview. Cannon nodded but agreed to answer anyway, much to Chamberlains chagrin. He had noticed the trap straight away and wanted to make Walker know that he was aware of it.

"I have no idea when Mr. Van der Linden was killed, so I can't answer that."

Chamberlain smiled. He knew his client was aware of how the police worked, so Cannon's reply solidified his standing within the solicitor's mind. He decided that if Cannon did want to answer a question, then Chamberlain would advise him each time of his right not to do so but would leave the final decision to him.

"How well did you know him?" Walker again.

"He was the partner/boyfriend of my apprentice."

"That is...Angela Fryer?"

The question intimated to Cannon that Walker and his team had at least done some investigation, though again he doubted if it was more than cursory. He got the impression that they were looking for an angle. Something against which to charge him, rather than having anything substantive. "Yes," he answered, noticing Chamberlain had not reacted to his replying to the question.

"And what is your relationship with Ms. Fryer?"

Noting the use of the pronoun relating to Angela, Cannon answered, "As I just mentioned, she was my apprentice."

"Is that all?"

"What do mean?"

"I believe Ms. Fryer was pregnant."

"Yes, she told me. Well she told my assistant initially."

"That's Mr. Telside, correct?"

"Yes."

Chamberlain who had been itching to jump into the conversation, cut across Walker as he was about to continue.

"Look Inspector where is this going? I can't see the relevance of your questions. How does all this relate to the victim and my clients arrest?"

Playing the game that Cannon used to play himself, Walker sat back in his chair with a theatrical sigh. He pretended to look at notes within the folder, then after closing it he placed it on the table and leant forward, looking Cannon in the eyes. "Was the baby yours, Mr. Cannon?"

Almost instantly Cannon gave him what he wanted, an angry response. Walker knew that an angry suspect was like gold. They made mistakes in their answers. They would contradict themselves during interviews. He was hoping Cannon would do likewise.

"What?!" Cannon exclaimed, his voice showing his annoyance at the Detectives temerity. Chamberlain was caught off guard. The outburst was contrary to Cannon's previously controlled demeanour. "That's a ridiculous proposition. Angela is my employee. Nothing else!"

"Really, Mr. Cannon?"

"Really!"

"And you expect me to believe that?"

"You can believe anything you want, but it's a fact."

Walker turned to Conte who had remained silent so far. His job was to watch Cannon's body language and the interaction with Chamberlain. There was no need for him to take notes. The interview would be typed up later by one of the police administrative support team. "I think Sergeant, Mr. Cannon doth protest too much."

The bastardization of the Hamlet quotation was not lost on Chamberlain and he again sort clarity on the line of questioning, accusing Walker of grasping at straws. The Detective decided to be less oblique and more direct.

"Okay Mr. Cannon. Let me ask you this. Why were you at the tattoo parlour the other day? Why did you threaten Mr. Van der Linden?" Chamberlain took a quick sideways peek at his client. This was the first he had heard of any such interaction between the two.

"I wasn't threatening him."

"Really? That's not what we heard," Conte jumped in.

"Well you heard wrong."

Walker smiled again, he then asked a question that was out of left field. "Do you know a lady by the name of Sue Gladstone, Mr. Cannon?"

"Not that I can recall?"

"Are you sure about that?"

Cannon noted the tone and the way Walker had phrased the question. There was something behind it. Cannon racked his brain for an answer. The name rang a bell, but he couldn't quite place it. A lot had happened over the past few days. He responded to the question accordingly, asking, "Why?"

"You tell me."

"As I told you, I don't think I….."

"Then let me refresh your memory Mr. Cannon. Do you remember a horse by the name of …." Walker needed to check his notes this time, "erm Candlelightnight?"

"Yes. I trained the horse for a while."

"Did you know who owned the horse at the time?"

"I can't recall every name, no."

"Well let me remind you. Sue Gladstone was a part owner of that horse."

"And again what is your point, Inspector?" Chamberlain asked, making sure that the policeman had not forgotten that the solicitor was there representing his client.

"Ms. Gladstone was a teacher at the same school were Mr. Cannon's wife currently works. She is also a teacher, correct, Mr. Cannon?"

The reference to Michelle instantly hit Cannon between the eyes. He remembered her being so upset about one of her colleagues being killed, Sue Gladstone! He had been so busy worrying about Angela that the incident had slipped his mind. Walker had continued talking.

"…she was killed a few days ago."

"And you think my client was involved?"

"Well, were you, Mr. Cannon?" Walker questioned.

"No. I hardly knew the woman."

"Okay, then let me put a scenario to you."

"I'm all ears, Inspector," Cannon replied sarcastically, folding his arms across his chest. Conte noticed the defensive nature of the action.

"I think, Mr. Cannon that Angela Fryer was going to have your baby. That your apprentice told her boyfriend that the child wasn't his and he confronted you about it. Which is why you threatened him, wasn't it?"

Cannon remained silent, passive. He knew that a show of anger would work in Walker's favour. He let the man continue. "I think that he was going to tell your wife but after you challenged him he decided to do it indirectly. So he found a mouthpiece and I'm not sure yet if it was by luck or by design, but it was someone who he was able to use to get to your wife. Someone who had access to her, a friend, a fellow teacher....and he let you know didn't he? He told you what he'd done and for that you killed her too."

Walker pointed an accusatory hand towards Cannon, who was trying to process what had been suggested to him. He let Walker continue but wasn't listening to what was being said. The fiction he had been accused of was almost laughable, but there was something within the words that hit a nerve. Once Walker stopped talking, he stared at Cannon waiting for a response but there was none. Chamberlain filled in the silence. "Inspector do you have any evidence to back up this ludicrous claim?"

"We are currently compiling a brief which we will pass on to the CPS in due course and we will share that once we are ready, however I wanted to conduct this interview to give your client an opportunity to come clean. It would be easier for all of us if Mr. Cannon were to confess, but if he doesn't, I'll be laying charges anyway."

"So from what you are telling me, you are holding my client without anything substantive?"

"No, we have witness statements from a number of employees of Mr. Van der Linden who saw Mr. Cannon argue and threaten the man."

"Is that all?"

"We also have a witness who was in the vicinity when Ms. Gladstone was killed."

"And you say my client was responsible."

"I'm saying your client had a motive, and the opportunity."

"What are you talking about?" Cannon queried. "What opportunity?"

"Do you ride a motorbike, Mr. Cannon?"

"Yes I can, but I don't have one."

"But you can ride one?"

"I've just told you that."

"Are you licensed?"

"No."

"Did you know that Mr. Van der Linden had a motorbike?"

"Yes. Angela told me he had several. He taught her to ride I believe, but he was renowned for showing off and riding around town at all hours. His neighbours and many other residents complained regularly about his antics."

"Did she ever tell you where he kept them?"

"No."

"Oh come off it, Mr. Cannon. You knew where to find him at his shop, so it wouldn't be too long a bow to draw, and conclude, that you knew where he stored his motorbikes."

"That's your view, Inspector."

"Yes, it is and I think you stole one of them and used it to run down Ms. Gladstone. So where is that motorbike Mr. Cannon?"

The fact that Walker was asking him to fill in the details as to where a particular bike could be found, meant that they needed it for evidence. It confirmed Cannon's view that the police were guessing. He leaned over and whispered his thoughts into Chamberlain's ear. The solicitor decided to be forthright.

"What proof do you have to all this, Inspector? All I have heard so far is just conjecture." He looked at his watch, it was getting on for eleven pm. "I think we are nearly done here," he said, "so either charge my client now, or we walk!"

Walker ignored the solicitor. "Where were you Mr. Cannon three days ago, on the afternoon of 30 October?"

"I was at home, working."

"Can anyone verify that?"

"I'm not sure. Michelle, my wife, was at the school and the horses were all locked away until the staff came back on site for evening stables."

"So no one would have seen you if you left the premises?"

"We do have CCTV so there would be a recording of anyone coming and going, including me."

"Unless the system was turned off."

"Yes."

"And again, you were alone in the house, the only person?"

"Yes."

"Are we able to see those recordings?"

Cannon hesitated. He would need to speak with Rich as his assistant was in charge of the system. "I can get them to you," he answered, unconvincingly.

Walker looked at Chamberlian then expressed the following. "Mr. Chamberlain, just so you know, I have motive, I have opportunity, all I need now is the weapon." Turning to Chamberlains left, he said persuasively, "Mr. Cannon, what did you do with that motorbike?" He then engaged Cannon with a stare which for many would have resulted in them turning their face away impossible to hold a gaze…any such sign of weakness would have resulted in Cannon being kept in a cell for another 24 hours. Cannon returned the favour, neither blinking nor moving his head. Eventually Walker blinked, reluctantly saying, "You can go Mr. Cannon. Just don't leave the county. I'll be in touch."

CHAPTER 24

It was another miserable day. Cold and still raining, although lighter and intermittent than the downpours of the previous day, allowing Cannon some freedom after his ordeal overnight. He had needed some time and space to address a number of "issues" from the comfort of his office and left the morning exercises to his assistant.

Telside had watched the two lots go through their paces while his boss had also spent the early part of the morning with Michelle before she left for school. After she had departed, Cannon had indicated that he needed to make a number of phone calls, so would Rich look after Angela for a while?

After Cannon had been allowed to leave the police station he had listened to a message that Ed had left for him on his phone while he was offline and being questioned. Angela was to be discharged the following morning and so Cannon had immediately arranged for Col Wilson to collect her. With Nick dead, he was concerned about the effect the news would have on her mental state. It wasn't for him to tell Angela about what had happened, that was the for the police. But, the shock of her boyfriend's death and the loss of her baby, subsequently confirmed in Ed's message, would have floored anyone, let alone such a young woman as Angela. Cannon also knew that Van der Linden was the major breadwinner in their relationship, so without him, he knew that Angela would potentially struggle, financially. He wanted to try and help.

By the time Wilson arrived in Chepstow she had already been given the news. The impact was obvious, she was drawn and moribund. The drive back to Woodstock was conducted in near total silence. Col Wilson could only mouth platitudes which, while sincere, did not seem to penetrate through to her. Angela seemed bereft of everything, she just sat staring ahead, not seeing the rain that had slashed against the windscreen of Cannon's Land Rover that he had collected from Wincanton and then drove to the hospital to pick her up. It had been a long trip for him, but one he was happy to do.

Now Telside and Angela were sitting together in the tack room. She listened without responding to what was said to her. But at least she was now back on familiar ground

"And one more thing," Telside said, watching her face that remained passive, as if it was chiselled from stone, "you'll soon hear that Mike, erm Mr. Cannon to you, is a suspect in Nick's death, and that he was interviewed by the police last night."

Angela stared at him, the words not quite adding up. Her eyes had lost their lustre and appeared dead, the sparkle having gone out.

"We all know that it's nonsense but …."

"When can I ride again?" she asked, as if he hadn't spoken.

Telside looked into her face. He wasn't an expert in anything medical other than when it came to horses, but he was aware of concussion and the impact of a fall. He had less knowledge of PTSD but he knew of its affect. She stared back at him, her skin was pale and sallow. Her hair was still matted from the lack of a brush and beneath her eyes there were dark semi-circles accentuated by raw scratches and bruises on her cheek. Telside took a deep breath. He knew that it would take some time before Cannon would allow her to race again. She would need to be realistic and patient, and her told her so.

"But it's what I want," she said, pleadingly. It was an irrational comment and Telside knew it. He needed her to understand the situation.

"The doctors are of the view that due to your concussion and the loss of the baby, there will need to be at least 2 to 3 months of rest, before you can race ride again."

"Two to three months!" she shouted back at him, "that's ridiculous."

"Well, that's what we've been told, and just for clarity there are two parts to this. One, you need to satisfy the BHA that you are physically fit to ride, and second you need to satisfy the doctors that you have recovered mentally."

She sat quietly for thirty seconds trying to get her mind around what was facing her. Eventually she said, "You know he beat me up don't you?"

As softly as he could, Telside answered, "Yes, we could see. Mike and I were hoping that you would leave him on your own accord, but not like this."

"I would have if I hadn't fallen pregnant. I was hoping to ride out my claim, get my trust monies and it would have given me a start."

"I understand."

"So do you understand Mr. Telside why I need to keep riding? It's my life, I can't do anything else. It's all I ever wanted to do."

Telside nodded, then with a sigh told her what she would be required to do around the yard over the next couple of months, given her desire to see out her apprenticeship.

"I'll need you to work with the horses. Mucking out, feeding, all the usual stuff.. at least until the concussion protocol allows."

"And then?" she asked

"I think we can get you back on a horse, but just slow canters initially. No jumping, galloping or racing." She smiled back at him, pleased at what she heard. "And another thing," he added, "while a couple of months may take you close to the end of the season, just remember how lucky you are. You're alive and you have a future ahead of you. Don't push things too hard. As I told you earlier, Mr. Cannon has a few things on his plate particularly because of being considered a person of interest in relation to Nick's death. His focus will be on sorting that out in the first instance, and he won't need any other distractions, least of all you begging him to ride."

"Why do the police think he was involved?"

"Because they saw him apparently threatening Nick at the tattoo parlour," he said. "The police walked in just as he told Nick to leave you alone. Mr. Cannon, like me, could see how you were affected by the physical abuse you were subjected too."

Angela looked down at her hands, she was beginning to realize how wrong she was in her pursuit of getting back into the saddle. Cannon was looking after her interest and she needed to accept that. It was for the best. The silence between them grew again until Telside asked, "Are you okay?"

"I was just thinking how it was possible that anyone could think of Mr. Cannon being a murderer. Don't the police know that Nick was involved in other things?"

"Like?"

"Drugs and….," she broke off, her eyes now glistening with tears.

Telside stared at her, not knowing what to say. Cannon had mentioned to him in the past that there was something about Van der Linden that appeared 'shonky'. It seemed now that he was right. Not wanting to cast aspersions about her choice in men, Telside decided to remain quiet other than to advise her that the death of her boyfriend was a police matter now, and the process needed to take its course.

She nodded in response. Telside decided to let Cannon know what she had told him as soon as he possibly could.

Cannon had been busy all morning. He had spoken with Chamberlain about whether any charges were to be laid against him at some point, and if so, what options did he have in relation to bail? Once he had finished that conversation, he had a long discussion with Jim Franklin who was in his car on the way to Carlisle where he had five rides for the day. He asked the jockey to keep him informed of anything else he heard about Uncle Buck, the horse that was scratched at Wincanton. It seemed strange that an initial decision had been made to run the horse then for him to be taken out just before the race itself. He was also keen to understand if the horse had been sold or was still in the same owner's hands who had initially wanted to sell him. It was a bold request in some ways that he was making. The normal process was for him to look up the information on the BHA website where the ownership would be displayed. However, Cannon knew that due to paperwork or other reasons, such as new colours being determined for a new owner, the new trainers name and other details required, that data could take a little while to be on-line, sometimes weeks. With someone like Franklin close to the action every day, Cannon suspected that he would hear what was going on behind the scenes well before anything became official on the website. Franklin agreed to keep his ear to the ground and would let him know if he heard anything useful. Cannon wished him luck given the day ahead promised more showers and increasingly colder winds during the afternoon. "Just what I need," Franklin answered, as he terminated the call.

Sitting at his desk he fell back into the daily routine of nominating his horses for upcoming meetings and worked the phones to contact the agents he used to secure specific jockeys to ride for him when and where he required them. He had trouble with a few of them who were either not available or had decided not to ride at certain meetings due to limited opportunities on the day, beyond his own horses, or that the distance to travel to a specific track was too far. Cannon was always bemused by this. The whole point of a jockey was surely 'have saddle, will travel'? Apparently to his dismay that wasn't the case, at least not today. He had to compromise where necessary. Fortunately he was able to secure Phil Woodhall again, as a replacement for Angela, to ride for him in a couple of upcoming races. He was also able to get Giles Mainwaring to ride Summer Kisses at her next outing. With luck he would also be able to get the senior jockey to ride White Noise. The horse had a program that needed to be followed, even if Angela was unable to race ride for a few months. The Champion Hurdle at Cheltenham was still the goal, and the horse needed to run and win in order to satisfy Cannon that he would be competitive there, even if not expected to win such an important race. Once he had completed all the necessary administrative work, he then made a call to John Silvers and told him of his arrest and subsequent release in connection with the murder of Van der Linden. He also mentioned some of his observations at Wincanton and that he had asked for the support of Jim Franklin. Silvers asked him whether he had mentioned to DI Walker that he was working with the police up in Ayr and was advised that he hadn't but would possibly need to do so when appropriate. Silvers agreed. While the police were supposed to work together, at most times there were competition and territorial type battles going on, something Cannon had experienced many times before. He suspected that this was one such example.

"Well for now, let's leave things as they are," Silvers said. "I'll do some digging in the background to see what Walker is up to. If necessary I may have to give him a call, but not just yet. He may be useful to both of us at some point in the future."

"I'm not sure about that John, he seems to have a bit between his teeth, speaking metaphorically I might add. He has no evidence against me in relation to Nick Van der Linden's death, and everything he presented was circumstantial, but for some reason he's finding linkages where there are none."

"Understood," replied Silvers.

Without a lot of confidence as to where things were at between Silvers and Walker, Cannon terminated the conversation. He needed to do a bit more digging himself before he was confident that the police were on the right track and were focusing their energy where they should.

"Did she tell you anything else, Rich?"

"No Mike, just that he was involved with drugs."
"And she didn't elaborate?"
"No. She didn't even know how he was doing it, just that she knew that he was involved."
"And she knows he was involved, how?" Cannon asked.
"Apparently the money he always seemed to have. She said that the tattoo parlour was never going to generate the amount of money he had available, so she questioned him."
"And?"
"Initially he told her that there was nothing going on, but when he bought new motorbikes for them, she asked him where the money came from and after his initial denials, she eventually got an answer."
"How did she do that?"
"The pregnancy. She told him that he needed to be honest with her otherwise she would walk away."
"And he opened up to her, just like that?"
"Seemingly, yes Mike."
"Umm okay," Cannon replied, his mind doing some mental gymnastics. Something seemed a little odd, but he knew that Angela could be particularly persuasive if she needed to be. Cannon and Telside had both observed it in the past, and to some degree she continued to push her case even today while under the restrictions doctors and the racing industry were very clear about.

Cannon thanked Telside for the feedback, noting that he hadn't wanted his friend to take on any additional responsibilities, but under the circumstances it looked like he would need to lean on his friend even more than usual. Telside let Cannon know that he had no issue in helping in whatever way he could and would always do so. It was what friends did for each other.

When Cannon was alone he contemplated once again the real conversation he needed to have with Telside, but it would have to wait. Cannon would have to bite his lip for now. The time would come eventually, perhaps before the end of the season?

Death Seeks You Out

CHAPTER 25

Amar Hyseni had a problem and he needed an answer quickly. Tony Williams had sent him five more and he needed to turn them around as quickly as possible. However, without the money from the agent there were a number of very unhappy suppliers who were beginning to pressure him. In addition Erjon was becoming more of a liability than an asset. It was safe to say that their relationship had become so toxic that Hyseni was concerned that at any minute Erjon would make a dash for freedom, leaving the operation high and dry. Hyseni knew that Erjon would not leave Holland without Ardita or Dardan but he wasn't sure if his brother-in-law had the courage to try and convince them to leave with him. While he contemplated his dilemma of having a hostile family member undermining the operation, he decided that he would start to address the matter by being more hands-on and taking a risk. He planned to spend a few days in the UK, evaluating, finding, then implementing a better solution than existed currently. He wasn't totally happy about it when he spoke to Williams, but the man seemed more nervous than usual.
"Is there something bothering you?" Hyseni asked, observing the man who stared back at him from his phone. The use of WhatsApp allowed him to see the face and the body language of those involved in the operation and whenever he saw changes, either slight or major, then he instinctively knew that there was a need to act. Depending on the change he felt necessary, that could be something small or potentially something drastic. He hadn't spoken directly with Williams for a while now. There had been no need. With the arrangements in place, the supply and demand process had worked as it was meant to. Unfortunately due to someone's greed, the payment side of the equation had now been impacted and Hyseni needed to fix it.
"I'm not sure," Williams answered, "but someone was asking about one of the horses I sent you in the most recent batch."
"What did they want?"
"I don't know," Williams replied sheepishly, "but it was just out of the blue."
"Coincidence perhaps?"
"Maybe, but there is something else."

"What?" Hyseni queried.

"The man who was asking. He has an association with the partner of the distributor who went for a swim recently."

"And you think she may have told this man about the way the system works?"

"Again, I don't know, but it just seems a little too close for comfort."

"Okay, that does seem odd," Hyseni replied. "But it's also important to understand that we can't have *anyone* take advantage of their position in the chain. It only works if everyone plays their part. If anyone tries to skim off the top then they will be made examples of! It was clear that in this case, action was required."

"I understand," Williams answered, a slight croak in his throat, "but whoever was involved didn't do the best of jobs. I heard from one of my staff on the course at Wincanton that the body was found pretty quickly, and the police have already arrested a man."

"Which man?"

"The one I was telling you about. The one asking the questions."

"What's the man's name?"

"He's a racehorse trainer called Mike Cannon."

"Do you know what happened to him?"

"No."

"So he could still be in custody?"

"It's possible, but if he or his solicitor were able to prove that the police had no evidence against him, which is likely, then they would have had to release him by now."

Hyseni took on board everything that had been said so far. "I'll make some enquiries. The family has some good connections in the UK. I'll see what I can find out."

"He's an ex-cop apparently, though that was some years ago."

"Very well. Let's park that for now. What I really need you to be aware of is how quickly we can turn around what you sent me?"

Hyseni could tell that Williams was becoming even more agitated the longer they spoke. The processes had been working well, and the plans especially with regards to expanding the distribution network had been on track, at least until now. The need for a new distributor in the Oxford area was paramount, given that they had been required to shut down one of their avenues, albeit temporarily. This meant taking their eyes off the expansion ball until the hole was filled. If they wanted to keep the lines open to ensure business continuity and other players out of their market, they needed to set up another supply route to market asap.

"I've decided to come over the day after tomorrow. I'll be there for three days only," Hyseni stated as a matter of fact. "We will need to meet and we need to replace our former friend with someone else." While Williams acknowledged what Hyseni was suggesting, Hyseni was also thinking about his own family dilemma. What to do and when to do it with regards to Erjon, and where to find as good a replacement. That problem required serious consideration.

"Fuck!" he whispered to himself. When one problem started it was often followed by others. He now had a number of issues that he needed to clear up. If he didn't act quickly and assert his authority then it was possible that he could become a liability himself, and he knew what the family would do if he started to fail.

"I'll send you some info soon," he said, "via WhatsApp. Once we have resolved the distribution problem, then I want to look into this Mike Cannon character and find out what he knows."

CHAPTER 26

DI Sam Walker was frustrated. He had hoped to obtain some indication of guilt if not a complete confession from Cannon, and having been unsuccessful, the hierarchy now knew about it. He told anyone he could that it was a failure in the system, not a failure on his part. He had every reason to believe that Cannon was involved in murder of Van der Linden. "I can feel it in my waters," he suggested to Conte. Despite his assertion about who was the father of the baby, he knew that DNA testing would be done on the foetus of Angela and from that it would be easy to determine who that person was. If it was proven that it wasn't that of her boyfriend, then Cannon would be in Walkers' sights again, and he would be chasing him for a DNA swab at the earliest opportunity. To try now, without evidence to support his theory, would be a problem.

As he sat in the 'Kings Head and Bell' pub on St. Helens street in Abingdon eating the New House gourmet burger with his Sergeant alongside him, he contemplated their next steps. Conte sat quietly while his boss opined about the length of any investigation and all the hoops that they needed to jump through. Gone were the days of a rubber truncheon in a brown paper bag.

"The problem we have Sergeant, is that the public expect results, but the force leadership doesn't have the courage to challenge the politicians and get us the money and resources we need in order to meet those stupid KPI targets."

Conte agreed by taking a bite from his own burger. While it was still technically lunchtime, most of the customers had finished their meals and had left to go back to work or to go home. The fire in the hearth kept the few remaining drinkers comfortable, several pairs sat around chatting, occasionally laughing at their in-jokes. The policemen had been seated for less than thirty-five minutes, and Walker was already on his third pint of local IPA. Conte was halfway through his second. The two men continued eating quietly, both with their own thoughts, until Walker said, "If it wasn't Cannon, then who?"

Conte looked surprised. Walker had been so sure of himself, but now, without explanation, had he had a change of heart? It didn't make sense and Conte challenged him as to why the sudden departure in thought.

"It's the motorbike that's bothering me," Walker said. "We need to find it. At least Prinsloo did confirm Van der Linden's story that the bike was not in the garage when he went to use it, but what we don't know then, was who took it."

"And it seems that almost anyone who worked at the shop had access," Conte responded.

Walker took another mouthful of his IPA, draining the glass completely. "We need to talk with Cannon again," he said, "there is something I'm missing, something else is going on and there's something he's not telling me."

CHAPTER 27

Michelle and Cassie had spent well over an hour discussing the state of play regarding the wedding. Michelle decided not to talk about the arrest and Cannon's release, other than to thank Cassie for arranging George Chamberlain to act as legal support.
Once they were over that hurdle, there was a lot of laughter which Cannon could hear from his office. He was glad to be out of the loop now. It seemed that the women in his life had finally realized that he was adding little value in relation to the wedding and had taken his advice to just get on with it.
When Michelle had told him that she was going to use Messenger to call Cassie on her iPad, he knew that he needed to move to his office. To hear both of them, each face to face on their devices, talking about wedding gowns, colours and flowers, it was enough to turn any man to jelly.
Due to having no interruptions Cannon was able to use the time quite productively, not least was to provide additional details of his business expenses and income to Cyril Horowitz at Plumberry Accounting. It seemed the ongoing tax enquiry from the HMRC was a never-ending nightmare. An email from Horowitz had requested Cannon to do some additional digging about a couple of horses that he had once had shares in, that he had sold during the previous couple of years. Horowitz was of the view that the Tax query was related to the valuation of a share in the syndicate and the price achieved when the share was sold. During the pandemic there was a lot of buying and selling of horses particularly due to the cancellations of meetings and the loss of prize money on offer. Single owners and small syndicates had found the going very difficult and had cut their losses. It had taken him a while to find what he was looking for, but once he had found the records associated with the sales he was able to scan them, then email them through to Horowitz's' office.
"Let's hope that's it," he said to himself, before turning his mind to what Telside had told him about Van der Linden and his dealing in drugs. Cannon's experience told him that if Nick was part of a chain then where did that start and where did it end? Who supplied and who did he distribute to? How was it done? When was it done, and

why was he killed? He made some notes for himself, then tried to come up with various scenarios to fit in with what he knew, guessing what he didn't. As he worked through things in his mind, there was something else that he had heard previously that had somehow struck a chord, but he couldn't quite recall what it was. He knew that it must be important but he couldn't work out why. As the sounds from the lounge started to settle down into silence, he sensed that the conversation was over and he decided to call it a night. He began shutting down his computer which had been sitting idle after he had finished his race nominations and acceptances for upcoming meetings. He still had high hopes for White Noise amongst others, despite the issue with Angela, and in addition he was particularly pleased with the way Summer Kisses had run and won at Wincanton. The owners, the Davids, had called him during the day but he been too busy to take their call. He had subsequently listened to the voicemail left by Bridget on behalf of herself and Harry and had found an opportunity to talk to them about the race itself and the condition of the mare the day after the race. The thanks from the GP's was effusive and he let them know that he was planning to race her again at Southwell in a few weeks' time. It was to be a Tuesday and he mentioned that that it would be good if they could make it to the track, particularly as the racecourse was within a half hour drive from where they lived. Without committing to anything they mentioned that they would consider it. "The horse seems to do so well without the owners being present," Bridget Davids had said. "Maybe it's not such a good idea to break the routine? Perhaps we will jinx her?"

As a pair of doctors, Cannon found it amusing that there was an element of superstition involved in their approach to seeing their horse run in the flesh, but he knew it was wise not to push things. Where owners were concerned he could probably write a book about their nature, their inadvertent need to tell him how to train, their wishes, desires, celebrations and their quirks. He was glad however, that he had made the offer.

He heard a gentle tap on his office door. "Can I come in?" Michelle asked, carrying a cup of tea for him.

"What about you?" he asked, taking the drink out of her hands and placing it on his desk.

"I've had mine already," she answered, sidling up to him and giving him a kiss on the mouth. "How is it going anyway? You've been here all evening. What are you up to?"

"Not a lot really," he said, aware that she knew that he was lying. "just doing some admin and some research."

"Research? On what?"

"Remember when we talked about the horse Noble Goblet, the horse whose head was found up in Ayrshire?"

"Yes, what about it."

"Well, I've been doing some digging and I'm trying to piece a couple of things together as to how the poor horse ended up as it did."

"Mike," she said, suddenly feeling a little unsecure. "I hope you are not getting involved in something you may regret. Surely the police can handle whatever it is you've uncovered?"

Cannon looked at her face, noticing something he hadn't seen for quite some time, fear. "Look," he said, trying to sound positive, "unfortunately I'm already involved."

"Why?" she asked. "What has the discovery of the head of a horse you once trained, have to do with you? That horse went out of the stable years ago."

"That's exactly the point, Michelle, I don't know. But what is obvious is that there is something behind all this that somehow has links back to me."

Erjon Abazi had had enough. He was sick and tired of doing the dirty work for his brother-in-law and he told him so.

They were in the operating theatre again and with at least five patients to deal with, Erjon knew that it would be a long night. With Amar Hyseni pushing him to finish each operation as quickly as possible, the rows were becoming more heated and each procedure was taking much longer than it should.

"Are you doing this just to spite me?" Hyseni asked, his voice rising again after a previous argument had ended before muting them both.

"No, I'm trying to tell you that Ardita and I don't want anything to do with this anymore."

Hyseni laughed, the sound echoing around the room despite the machines and pumps that kept the patient alive continuing to whirr away in total ignorance of what was being played out around them.

"Well, I'm sorry to have to tell you this, but you have no choice in the matter."

"Yes I do, everyone has a choice."

Hyseni watched as Erjon sliced open the skin of his second patient. A cut down to the shoulder was enough for him to find what he was looking for. The previous patient's operation was quite messy and it had taken a while for Erjon to find the device. Placing the small pill like chip into a silver-plated bowl along with the first, he noted that there were, "two down and three still to go."

Hyseni looked at his watch for a third time. The whole process was going much too slowly. While Abazi's back was turned, readying to move to the patient on the next table, Hyseni grabbed one of several razor-sharp scalpels that were attached magnetically to metal runners on the wall and made a beeline for him. At the last second, Erjon turned around, noticing Hyseni's advance, the scalpel glinting in the lights above. Before he had time to move, Erjon Abazi found himself in a full headlock, the scalpel held a few centimetres from his own neck. Hyseni was the faster and stronger of the two and also had the element of surprise. For a few brief moments, until Hyseni allowed Erjon to free himself from his grip, it seemed that malice would prevail, and the specialist would be dead within a minute. The scalpel had been held with the edge digging into the skin, the carotid artery only millimetres away from being severed. If Hyseni wanted to, he could have killed his brother-in-law where he stood. While he was tempted, he knew that for now he needed him, and it would have been foolish to kill him just yet. That time would come later, Hyseni thought, hoping that the demonstration of power would be enough to convince Abazi not to mess with him.

Hyseni released his grip. Abazi felt his neck, a trickle of blood ran down towards the collar of his shirt, and he noticed the smear of red across his fingers. The warm sticky liquid a reminder of how close Abazi had come to death. Rubbing his hand on the side of his jeans he cursed Hyseni promising him that, "today was the last day."

"You keep saying that, Erjon, but I don't think you have the balls to walk away."

"No?"

"No! And I'll tell you why," Hyseni said.

"Why?"

"Because you are gutless. You only have what you have, your family, your son, because *we* gave them to you."

"What the fuck is that supposed to mean?"

"It means exactly what it says. Without my family, you would still be sitting in that shitty little town of yours, probably a tobacconist like your father. There would be no Ardita and no Dardan, and no money. So, remember this when you try to fuck with me, we made you, and ….we own you!"

The last three words of Hyseni's utterance cut to his very core. Erjon Abazi knew that he had two choices and one of them was to keep his mouth shut, to do what was asked, and to maintain his position within the system. The family had been good to him initially, but as time moved on, he had grown to hate them. He hated them because of what they forced him to do, what they were doing to his wife and son and what they were doing beyond their borders. Abazi knew that he was in a difficult situation and without an executable plan he would be there forever. He had contemplated a number of scenarios and had discussed them with his wife, but despite her initial enthusiasm the idea had waned whenever she thought about Dardan, and where such a move would lead them too. At times it seemed like they were living in a bad dream, desperate to escape but held back by ties that bind, family ties. The very thought created fertile ground for an angry response to Hyseni's boast.

"You don't own any part of me!" Abazi shouted, knowing that he was playing a very dangerous game. The more they argued, the longer the tasks needed to be done tonight would take, and the greater the stress on his brother-in-law. That stress was Abazi's friend. Knowing that there was a tight deadline to complete the operations and that the patients needed to be moved on as quickly as possible, Abazi decided to use the power of time to his advantage. Feeling the blood on his neck again, he said, "I need a break."

"No, you don't," Hyseni replied, "just get on with it."

"I need a break!" was the cry, spoken louder and through gritted teeth. Hyseni knew immediately that he was being played. He knew that Erjon was trying to make a point. A point that had no value other than to increase Hyseni's loathing for his brother-in-law. He decided that he would have to play the game that Erjon had started and believing that he was better than anyone else at it, Hyseni acceded to Abazi's request.

"You have fifteen minutes, after that you will finish the job."

There was no reply, no thank you, no acknowledgement. Erjon

turned his back on his tormentor. Hyseni suddenly grabbed hold of an arm and swinging Erjon around to face him, spat in his face. It was an act of intimidation and one not lost on Erjon. He took a small hand towel from one of the theatre cupboards which also contained bottles of nitrous oxide, packets of syringes, and various swabs and used it to wipe his face.

"I've got to go somewhere tomorrow," Hyseni said, as Abazi continued to clean himself up. "I want this finished quickly and I need everything at the airport in the next 3 hours."

Abazi took his time. It was not the moment to react to the treatment that had been meted out to him. The incident would be added to the list of abuses he had suffered, and payback would come in due course.

With disdain in his voice and disgust on his face, Hyseni said that he would be back in "one hour" and that he expected all the work to have been completed. He then left the operating theatre, leaving a seething Abazi to contemplate the immediacy of the work he was required to complete and to consider his long-term future. He decided to use the time he would have while Hyseni was away, wherever that was, to plan his escape. He knew that it would not be easy, but he was now at the very edge of the chasm, and he needed to jump.

CHAPTER 28

After the two lots had completed their work on the heath Cannon called Silvers, giving him an update about what he'd discovered so far.

"I need to come up to Scotland," Cannon said. "There is a meeting at Kelso in a few days and I'd like to send a couple of my horses up there anyway, plus as we discussed it will give me a chance to test out my theory."

"I suppose so, but Kelso is a long way from Ayr. I doubt I'll be able to be of much help unfortunately."

"I understand," Cannon replied. "It's not as if I'm ignorant of these things. The one thing you can do for me though is work some magic with Lothians and Scottish Borders police and make them aware that I may need their help at some point."

"I'll see what I can do, Mike, but remember while this case is being driven by the Ayrshire Division of Police Scotland, there are boundaries that make it difficult for my team to cross. So, like in England there are many fiefdoms that people try to protect and stepping into another jurisdiction is not always welcome."

Cannon replied that he knew that politics existed everywhere, and all he was really looking for was help if needed. Without committing to anything Silvers agreed to make some calls.

Once he had terminated the conversation, Cannon made his way to the stables looking for Telside. He found his assistant in his office. After they had spent a few minutes discussing the morning's exercise gallops, the continuing pattern of rain and the ongoing challenge of finding the right race for their runners, Cannon explained to Telside the real reason he had sought him out.

"Remember when we talked a few days ago about you needing to take over while I did some work for the police?"

"Yes, I was wondering if you were getting anywhere with it. After Walker took you in for questioning you've been doing what you always do around the yard, so I thought things on that front had gone cold. What he did to you was ridiculous anyway, nothing more than a lazy attempt by him to be seen to be doing something about Nick's death."

"That's true Rich, but I've been talking with the police in Scotland this morning, and it's time now."

"So, what do you intend to do?"

"The first thing is to try and win a few races."

"I'm not with you."

"It's what I said. Life goes on, and we have a new season that's barely started."

"Which means?" Telside asked, trying to understand what Cannon was suggesting.

"Which means that I have a slight change of plan."

"Go on."

"White Noise," Cannon replied. "And the Doc, I want to take them up to Kelso."

Telside remained silent for a few seconds then picked up a small folder that lay on his desk. "Does that mean a change in the bigger picture for these two?" he asked, opening the folder to two specific pages. He placed a finger against each to ensure he didn't lose them as they contained the detailed plans and work schedules for each horse.

"Not really, just a change of place. At least initially."

Telside wasn't totally happy, but relented when Cannon said, "Angela mentioned that the Doc needs more give in the ground than he raced on last time and I think Scotland rather than Southwell will be more to his liking at this time of year."

"And White Noise?"

"Similar, but what I really want to do is get his confidence back under racing conditions. I think getting him onto some soft going over a tough hurdles course will be ideal. In addition it's a left-handed course like Cheltenham."

"As was Chepstow," Telside pointed out.

"True, which is why I want the horse to go around the same way again."

"Who will you get to ride?"

"Giles Mainwaring agreed to ride him previously but that was down here. Being up in Scotland, he may decide it's not worth it. I'll check later."

"Understood, so when do you want to send them up there?"

"Tonight, if possible."

"And when is the meet?"

"The day after tomorrow."

"Have you got anyone in mind up there where you can stable them? It's at least a six-hour drive in the float, so they will only get there in the early hours."

"I know."

"And both the horses will need some exercise during the day tomorrow."

"Which is why I think taking them up tonight will be best."

"If that's the plan, then I'd better let Jack know. He'll probably take young Sam Simmons with him to keep him company."

"Sounds good," Cannon replied. "In the meantime, I'll make some enquiries about accommodation for the horses, and the boys. If I'm lucky the clerk of the course will let us stable our two runners on site."

"That would be good, because the boys will need a break after exercising them tomorrow afternoon."

"Maybe I can get an Airbnb for them. I'll do some digging & come back to you."

Telside had no idea about the Airbnb concept, nor did he care to find out, so decided not to respond to Cannon's suggestion. He let his boss make a few final comments about what he wanted done while he was away, then after Cannon had left to get himself organized for the trip up north, Telside made a few phone calls to get the ball rolling. It would be a busy afternoon, and there were lots of things to organize.

The late morning and early afternoon had been busy enough without the need for any interruptions. Using the BHA website, Cannon had spent most of the time trying to organize jockeys for his runners at Kelso. He also made sure that he had accepted them into their specific race before the necessary cut-off time, thereby allowing them to run at the meeting. Thereafter he discussed the decision to run White Noise with Joel Seeton who told Cannon that as owner, he would have liked to attend the meeting, but given his work schedule, he would have to politely decline.

"I'll be watching on TV though," Seeton had said, "and I'll be hoping for a better outcome this time." The less than subtle jibe from the Northern businessman not lost on the trainer.

Cannon's attempt at arranging accommodation was particularly difficult. He spent an inordinate amount of time making numerous calls which included waiting for information about prices and availability, ultimately getting nowhere. It appeared that many of the hotels in the area were booked out for conferences and other business meetings. Eventually he decided to arrange a cottage for himself and his two staff on Roxburgh street overlooking the river Tweed, just over a mile away from the racecourse itself.

His frustration level was already high when he noticed a car pull into the stable yard and park directly in front of his office. The vehicles running lights shone through his window as the sun headed towards the west and the little amount of light left of the day slowly dwindled. The grey sky which had covered the area had remained without any sign of improvement. Clouds lingered throughout the entirety of the day, hardly moving, or so it seemed,. A dirty, muddy blanket had nestled over the county, making the evening arrive much too quickly. When the doorbell to the house rang, he already knew who had been behind the wheel of the car.

He shook his head imperceptibly, as he let DI Walker and DS Conte into his lounge, showing them where they could sit, but hoping they would be gone by the time Michelle arrived home. She would be at school until five or five-thirty, so he had at least ninety minutes to get through the conversation they obviously wanted. His concern about the two policemen being in the house when Michelle walked in related to the fact that he hadn't yet told her of his plan to go up to Scotland, and he knew that she would be immediately concerned for his safety when he did. The presence of Walker and Conte would potentially exacerbate the issue even more. She would be questioning him about why the police still had suspicions about him and the death of Van der Linden and Sue Gladstone. He had no answer to those questions, at least not yet.

After offering them tea, which they both declined, Cannon sat on one of the couches on the opposite side of the room to where the policemen sat. "Okay, now that's the niceties out of the way, what can I do for you, Inspector Walker?"

"We just have a couple of questions, Mr. Cannon," Walker said casually, making himself comfortable in his chair. "I don't think we will need to take up too much of your time."

The casual nature of the man put Cannon on edge, but he tried not to show it, leaning forward in a gesture of cooperation. "Go on," he prompted.

"The relationship you have with Ms. Fryer. I understand that it soured lately. Is that correct?"

"I'm not sure where you are getting your information from Inspector, but if you mean was Angela upset with me over my refusal to let her ride beyond a month once she told us of her pregnancy, then the answer is yes."

"And did this result in the altercation with Van der Linden?"

"Not directly," Cannon replied. "In fact quite the opposite."

"Explain."

Cannon sighed, he wondered if he was doing the job for them by filling in the missing blanks of their investigation. "Angela had come to work a few days before the fall and I could see that she was limping and had a few bruises on her face."

"And?"

"I confronted her, and she told me that Nick had beaten her up."

"Did she say why?"

"No, but I guessed it related to her concern about his partying, and his riding his motorbike at all hours of the night."

"So you confronted him."

"Yes, the day you walked in on us arguing."

"And what did he say."

"He told me that she had tripped and fallen."

Walker looked at Conte. Both men knew that domestic violence offenders always made that same comment. "What happened after that?"

"Nothing."

"So you never spoke with him again?"

Cannon did not answer immediately. He wasn't sure if he should mention the threat left by the Dutchman on his phone after Angela had fallen off White Noise. He decided not to say anything. He had no proof anyway having deleted the message. Eventually, he answered Walker's question. "No."

The hesitation was not lost on either of the policemen. Walker then asked, "Do you know why anyone would want to kill Mr. Van der Linden."

"No, but Angela said he was involved in dealing drugs. Perhaps that had something to do with it?"

Conte looked up from his note-taking, whispering something to Walker.

"We'll look into that Mr. Cannon, but the Sergeant here just reminded me that you were to provide us some CCTV footage we asked you for, do you have it?"

"Yes I do Inspector," Cannon answered, standing up to make his way to his office. "It's on my desk." Conte followed him along the short passage where Cannon handed over a USB stick which contained the CCTV footage of 30 October that the police had specifically requested. Once they were back in the lounge, Walker said, "One final question, Mr. Cannon."

"Which is?"

"Where is the Kawasaki Ninja motorbike that was used to mow down Sue Gladstone?"

Cannon smiled to himself. "I have no idea Inspector, perhaps you need to ask the killer."

"I thought I was," Walker replied slyly.

The comment did not deserve an answer, so Cannon did not provide one. "Is there anything else?" he asked.

"Not as yet, Mr. Cannon, but I'm sure there will be."

"Then I'll show you out," he answered, trying not to show his anger as he led the two men to the front door.

Cannon watched as the two men drove towards the yard gate before turning right and headed towards Woodstock. Around the yard evening stables would be starting soon. Horses would be fed and groomed, their bedding changed and water buckets filled for the night.

He made his way over to the tack room where he hoped to find Telside. He wanted to confirm arrangements for the trip up to Scotland and to check on the health of White Noise and the Doc. Both horses had seemed fine that morning, but a second look was always beneficial. Cannon had contacted his vet, Peter Lightman, earlier in the day to do some blood tests just to be sure. Cannon was expecting to hear from the man within the hour.

Walker looked out of his side window as Conte drove them back to Abingdon. The sun had already reached the horizon and the fingers of darkness were creeping rapidly across the landscape from the East. It would be totally dark within the next ten minutes. The lights of their car fought against the blackness that lay out ahead of them, occasionally they would be blinded by someone coming in the opposite direction, the high beams stabbing into their eyes before the driver dipped them and they were able to pass each other safely on the narrow road.

"We need to look into this alleged drug business," Walker said, the tone of his voice implying that he wasn't fully convinced of Cannon's assertion. "We know that marijuana was being used in the tattoo parlour, we could smell it when we were there that first time. But, and it's a big but, we haven't any indication that Van der Linden or anyone else who worked there, was involved in anything harder."

"So do you think Cannon was lying?" questioned Conte.

"I'm not sure Sergeant, he may well have just been repeating what he was told."

"By Angela Fryer?"

"Yes."

"So …?"

"So while we are here, let's make a small detour. I've got the address."

CHAPTER 29

The trip to Kelso was long but without incident. Cannon made a number of phone calls during the trip including one to DCI Silvers. He told him of his conversation with Walker and his concern that he was still the main suspect in the death of Van der Linden. Silver tried to ally Cannon's fears and mentioned to him that the 'higher-ups' were aware of what was going on and that they would step in when necessary. The political fallout was not for Cannon to concern himself with.

"Will you be coming to Kelso at some stage?" Cannon had asked, keen to see how much of what he was doing was on his own, and how much support he would have, specifically given Silvers' previous lack of commitment.

"It all depends."

"On what?"

"Whether you are able to find out anymore."

"I can't guarantee anything, remember it's still only a theory."

"I know, but it's beginning to make a bit more sense now."

"Is it?"

"Well from what you have told me so far, it is."

Cannon wasn't completely sure that he was on the right track but his research to date had given him reason for optimism. The next couple of days were key to finding out. He finished the call with Silvers as he passed the town of Pontefract to his left. With a little over half of his journey still to go, he knew that he wouldn't reach his accommodation until after two pm. He called Jack Radcliffe to ask how the horses had endured the trip and what exercise they had undertaken that morning. Cannon had been able to arrange that White Noise and the Doc could work at one of the local trainers facilities in Hume, a five-mile trip from the Kelso racecourse where the horses had been housed overnight. When Cannon had contacted Joel Seeton after speaking to Walker, he knew that Seeton had a number of horses with different trainers and one of them was Les Platt. It was Platt's facilities that he had been able to get access to. A call from the businessman to Platt before Cannon followed up, had paved the way. Cannon had been most effusive and thankful when he was able to get through to the Scotsman who mentioned to him that he also had a couple of runners at the same meeting. Fortunately they were in different races to those that Cannon was contesting. Cannon had never met Platt before but suggested that they have a drink during the course of the day.

"Aye, a whisky or two would be nice," Platt had said, the lack of subtlety not lost on Cannon. It was Platt's way of receiving compensation for the use of his land and the training facilities there.

"I guess it will be hot chocolate for me then," Cannon had laughed. "I believe the weather may be a bit wet?"

"A little bit of Scotch Mist never harmed anyone, Mr. Cannon," Platt had joked.

Cannon knew that Platt was referring to the cocktail, Scotch Mist, made of Whisky over finely crushed ice, while he was referring to the weather phenomenon expected at the race meeting, one of fog and drizzle.

Unfortunately from Radcliffe's feedback, it seemed that White Noise was going to be subject to the same conditions that had undone Angela, but there was nothing he could do about it. After a little more banter, they two men finished their conversation. Cannon was pleased at the positive response and the easy manner of the Scotsman.

Late yesterday afternoon after giving the details of Platts' farm to Radcliffe along with the accommodation details where he and his staff would be staying, he and Telside had watched the horses being loaded into the twin trailer and set off on their long journey. It had then taken him the rest of the evening to convince Michelle that he was in no danger. Thinking back on that conversation as he passed Newcastle with still another ninety minutes' drive ahead of him, he wasn't so sure.

Angela Fryer eventually opened her eyes. It was much later than usual. Usually by now she would have been at the stables readying herself for the second lot….if only. Today was her day off. She had an appointment with her doctor later in the morning to check on how she was doing. Her physical health was one thing but her mental health was another matter. She had been told when she left hospital that there would be ongoing support should she need it. With the foetus she had carried having been cremated by the hospital and Nick's body still at the local coroners morgue she found herself believing that there was no past only the future. What had held her back from riding was no longer a hindrance. It was a strange feeling but one that allowed her to focus. The next few months of not race riding were just a blip in the road, She knew what she wanted from life and she was even more determined to achieve it.

As she lay in bed, she recalled how she had felt only twelve hours earlier.

She had been very uncomfortable. The man sitting opposite her had been very aggressive. The questions he was asking were rapid fire and seemed to be jumping to a conclusion that she knew was wrong.

"What was your relationship with Mike Cannon? Was it more than just as an employee/employer? Did you have an affair with him? Did you tell him that your boyfriend was a drug dealer? Do you think he killed your boyfriend?"

She had burst into tears, resulting in the Detective being asked by his Sergeant to "take it easy." After a few minutes of respite, she had answered all his questions. She wasn't sure whether her responses had been useful but as she went over the conversation again in her mind there was one matter that she still had no answer for.

He hadn't wanted to fly into Edinburgh and would have preferred a lesser profile option, but to do so would have meant a longer drive and he wanted to limit the time he was in the UK. Not being in control of his movements and subject to others taking him to places he was unfamiliar with always made him nervous. Newcastle had been an option but there were fewer flights there and even they required a connection. After taking an EasyJet flight, rather than KLM who he disliked, Hyseni was met by Tony Williams and the two men drove to Roxburgh. During the ninety-minute trip Williams listened while Hyseni spoke. It was obvious to the Scotsman that his visitor was extremely uncomfortable with what had happened over the past few days. The removal of one cog in the wheel no matter how big or small or indeed whether squeaky or silent, impacted the smooth running of the machine. The need to replace it was urgent, vital. There was still a demand for the product and the wheel would continue to turn.

"I've also found out a little more of this man, Cannon," Hyseni said. "It seems that he may be more of a problem than I first thought."

"That's what I was trying to tell you," Williams replied. "When he spoke to one of my girls, he seemed to be very interested in one of the horses."

"And?"

"As I mentioned before. It seemed too much of a coincidence that he just happened to enquire about it, particularly when it was one of those that was about to be sent over to you."

Hyseni rubbed his chin. The more he heard, the more he realized that he needed to solve the problem quickly. Outsiders asking questions was never a good sign.

"What about the girl, the one looking after the horse that day, what did she have to say about this Cannon?"

"Nothing much, but she did question my decision."

"Why?"

"She didn't believe it was the right one. She argued with me that she had travelled all the way down to Somerset for a race and there was nothing wrong with the horse that necessitated its scratching."

"So what did you do?"

"I terminated her employment."

"Was that sensible? An unhappy employee could make trouble," Hyseni answered, thinking of his own brother-in-law.

"If we want to keep doing what we are doing then the answer is yes. I don't want anyone getting too close to any of the horses."

With a tightening of the lips and a brief raising of the eyebrows, Hyseni accepted what Williams had said, then changed the subject.

"When we get to the farm, I need to contact one of our mutual friends in Leeds."

"The one who handles the factory down there?"

"Yes, like the one you use in Ayr."

"To do what?"

"I want him to find us another distributor in Oxford and while he's at it, make some additional enquiries about this Cannon character."

Williams didn't need to ask what 'enquiries' meant. "I have some news that might help you with that," he said.

"What?"

"Cannon has a couple of runners here tomorrow, at the Kelso meeting. I'd be surprised if he wasn't on course to watch them. He usually attends every meeting where he has starters."

"How do you know that?"

"I'm a licensed trainer remember. Despite our arrangements, I still have to be seen to be active in the game or at least keep up the pretense that I do."

Hyseni laughed. He had to agree with Williams that participation was absolutely necessary in order for the scheme to work. "So, we will make a small detour tomorrow and find this Mr. Cannon? Perhaps have a little chat with him?" he queried.

"I have an accepted runner there so I have no problem us going to the course, but I don't think we should get too close to the man and we certainly shouldn't be seen to be too interested in his movements," Williams said. "If anything we should keep our distance and just observe what he's up too. We might learn something that's useful."

Hyseni slapped Williams thigh. "I agree my friend, I agree," he said, looking out at the black sky. Even though they were now out into the country and only a few miles from Williams' farm there was no chance of seeing anything above them, no moon, no stars. Low clouds and an encroaching mist spat drops of rain on the car windows. Welcome to Scotland.

CHAPTER 30

The three of them had woken at five in the morning. Cannon's two staff had left with his car for Les Platts' stables just before six. They were to take White Noise and the Doc to the racecourse after exercising them at an easy canter around a few laps of the all-weather track that Platt had built on his property some years prior. Once the horses were settled in their stalls, Jack Radcliffe would return to pick up his boss, while Sam Simmons would remain at the course.

While he was alone, Cannon made a call to Michelle. She was still feeling the effects of Sue Gladstone's passing, made more difficult by the memorial assembly the school was having that morning to honour the late teacher. The decision to hold the event had been agreed by the school leadership and its board in order for the school community to move on. It would be a while before the coroner allowed a funeral to be held, given the ongoing police investigation, but the Headmistress and teachers wanted to honour their colleague and also bring closure to the students.

"Are you okay?" Cannon asked.

"Yes, I'm fine," Michelle replied unconvincingly, "though I must admit it was lonely here last night."

"Did you speak with Cassie?" he questioned, trying not to dwell on the negative as he understood exactly where she was coming from. It was as if they were so caught up with what they had been dragged into, that over the past 48 to 72 hours they had hardly had any chance to spend any quality time together. His attempt to focus her attention elsewhere was clumsy, but she decided to go with it.

"Yes, and I spoke with Ed as well. It seems that everything has now been decided. They intend to issue the invitations over the weekend."

"How many?" he queried, not really wanting to know the answer. The very thought of the cost of design, printing, and posting the wedding invitations made him shudder, not to mention the cost of the reception and all that went with it.

"Forty," she said, "and they are being sent out electronically. By email."

He was caught off guard. He was expecting two hundred and forty at worst and a hundred at the very least. "Are you sure?" he asked.

"Yes. That's what we have been discussing over the past few months."

"But…"

"Mike, Ed and Cassie want an intimate wedding. They don't want anything over the top. They want the family and a few friends to enjoy the day with them and that's it."

"I'm not sure what to say," he replied, "other than…thank you. I'm guessing you helped them come to that decision?"

"No I didn't. They came to that conclusion themselves. All I did was provide some advice, gave them a few pointers and left it to them."

"So we have a date?"

"Yes, the 29th of June next year."

Cannon smiled to himself. A perfect date as far as he was concerned. The middle of the off-season. The middle of the year. The start of summer and the start of a new life for his daughter. "Perfect," he said.

From her voice down the phone line, Cannon sensed that Michelle was feeling better, apparently having moved on from her earlier comment.

"I hope it goes well later," he said, as they began to conclude their conversation. Michelle needed to leave for school, telling him she was already a few minutes later than usual. He let her go, then immediately called Telside who was standing in the rain watching the second lot of the day as they began their morning schooling and exercise regimes.

"It's raining pretty hard down here, Mike," Telside said, "though we don't have any mist or fog which is a God send. Having said that, it is pretty cold."

"I think we are going to have the same here," Cannon replied, looking through the window of the cottage. He noticed the reflection of the streetlights on the river Tweed, the bank of which was only twenty metres from the front door of the rented house. The water was flowing quickly eastwards. The ripples and eddies of the dark water came and went as the light caught them in a momentary dance before they disappeared from view again. "How are things going anyway?" he asked.

"Apart from the rain, the morning has been okay. We had a small problem with Brightside Manor who was quite unruly with the ground being churned up a bit. As we know he doesn't like it too heavy so I pulled him from the session and we took him back home quickly. I didn't want to risk another injury like we had with Cabin Fever recently. All the others did fine, especially one of the newer horses, Annie Girl. She's done really well today, especially given it's the first time we've asked her to gallop at speed and tackle to fences since she started with us."

Annie Girl was a new addition to the stable a few months prior. A five-year-old mare who was too slow for the flat but had been recommended as a possible long term 'chase prospect. The seller had been introduced to Cannon by an agent, Tim Spector, and Cannon had bought the animal outright, to race it himself. Unfortunately the horse had suffered an injury before arriving into the stable and had been subjected to treatment and box rest until recently. After ten weeks of the horse being cooped up, Telside was cautious but rather excited by what he had observed and he advised Cannon accordingly. "It's still too soon to be sure, but given today was her first real outing, she appears to be very brave and as her fitness improves she may well be one to watch."

"High praise indeed, Rich, she must have done very well then."

"Her exercise rider, Bill Torrens, was really excited by her action and her attitude, even at this early stage."

"Good to hear, Rich," Cannon said, before concluding the call, hopeful that his day would be as successful as that of Telside's. While he waited to be collected by Radcliffe, he made use of the time, connecting his laptop via the free Wi-Fi connection available in the cottage and continuing his research. It was likely to be useful if his theory was right. An hour later he called DCI Silvers to provide an update, concluding the call just as Jack Radcliffe arrived to take him to the track.

CHAPTER 31

Les Platt was what one would call a jolly fellow, someone larger than life. Easily likeable, he was in his late fifties. A man who was rotund with a beard that wasn't yet white, but he could certainly pass as Father Christmas if only his hair had played the same game. His bald pate was covered with a Tam 'o Shanter and he kept out the cold and damp with a heavy green parka. Cannon noticed the drinkers nose and the broken veins in the man's cheeks where the beard had not yet covered. Of a similar height to Cannon, Platt held out his hand as the two men met for the first time in the stables where their runners were being kept and where they would be readied later for their individual races. The facilities were more than adequate but Cannon was surprised at their charm. He had never raced at Kelso before and the small blocks of wooden boxes were quite unusual.

"Welcome to Britain's friendliest racecourse," Platt said, as the two men shook hands, "and welcome to our famous weather," he added, his broad smile and broad accent adding an extra appeal to the man's likeability. Cannon offered his sincere thanks at Platts' hospitality in allowing his charges to be exercised at the Scotsman's facilities, which was greeted with a "no problem at all," reply, and a more than passing reference to Joel Seeton, their "mutual owner."

"Perhaps we can have that drink that I owe you, just before the start of the first?" Cannon offered. "Mine are in race three and five and yours are in two and six."

"I see you have done your homework, Mike," Platt replied. Cannon noticed Platt's use of his Christian name. That was a good sign, he thought.

"Well, I came up here with the hope of getting close to a win," he joked. He didn't need to expand on his motivation for the long trip, that was between him and Silvers.

"Good on yer, lad," Platt smiled. "I'll see you shortly for that drink then. I've got work to do myself so I'll meet you in the Owners Pavillion Marquee at midday?"

Cannon nodded an affirmation before watching Platt walk off to check on his two runners. Checking his watch he knew that he had just over seventy-five minutes to look in on his own horses and to try and find Tony Williams' runner and meet the man himself. If he was right then he knew what would happen during the course of the day and what would happen to Williams' horse, Dark Chocolate, in the fourth race.

"Does it ever stop raining in this place?" Hyseni asked, as he and Tony Williams walked into the racecourse. A soft rain had started to fall from the low clouds that shrouded the eastern part of the UK from Aberdeen down to Hull. It was just after eleven am. Williams didn't answer, just adjusted his collar to keep his neck dry. Without a hat his dark locks were slowly becoming plastered to his head, water dripped onto his shoulders and down his chin. He was a powerfully built man, the opposite to the quintessential, caricature of a Scottish landowner. At one metre eighty-five, his wide shoulders and muscled legs were hidden beneath dark blue jeans and a heavy grey duffle coat. Hyseni wore a light raincoat that Williams had lent him. He was feeling the cold wind that whipped across the track and he suggested that they find a place to stand that was out of the breeze.
"I need to go and let the Stewards know I'm here and then I want to quickly see the horse," Williams said. "Just before the third race I'll do what is necessary so that will give us time between now and then to see what Cannon is up to. I'll meet you in the bar in the Tweedie stand in twenty minutes. We can go from there."
Hyseni was pleased to be able to get out of the rain, and though he didn't know the place, the signage and design of the small course meant that facilities were easy to find. Within minutes he had his first coffee. He would decide later if he would break his own alcohol ban.

Cannon stood against the wall of the stable block, the overhang kept most of the drizzle from falling onto him. He had a partial view of the individual box where Williams' horse was located, having sneaked a look at the meeting information board when he registered as being on course with the stewards. Unfortunately he did not have clear line of sight from where White Noise and the Doc were housed, so he needed to appear active while others moved around with their tack of saddles, racing colours, blinkers, winkers, nose rolls and other items they would be using to prepare their runners for the first race. With a set of reins in his hands he surreptitiously kept his focus on the box, waiting to see if anyone joined the young girl who he had noticed was busy grooming the horse inside. Cannon had no idea what Tony Williams looked like. He had tried to find a profile of the man using various on-line resources. Google, Linked-In, Facebook and others but none of them included a photo or any kind of picture. Even the website Williams used to promote himself as a racehorse trainer was void of any likeness. Cannon knew that this was unusual and it was one of several things that collectively were beginning to cement his view about what was going on. Cannon at one point had thought to ask Silvers to find a photograph of Williams, from the licensing or passport authorities, but had eventually decided against it. Apart from the time things could take, there was always the questions to be answered of why the request, for what reason and for whom? Cannon was helping Silvers in an unofficial capacity even if those in more senior positions to the Detective were aware of what Silvers had requested Cannon to do. The last thing anyone wanted was for a clever lawyer to get involved and cry privacy breach or unlawful sharing of personal information, which could result in the investigation being unsuccessful or even compromised.

Cannon had established that the horse, Dark Chocolate, was owned solely by Williams, which was a common trait he had uncovered during his investigation to date. Another similarity was that Williams had bought the horse recently. If Cannon was right, then he knew what would come next. As he glanced towards the box where Dark Chocolate was standing, a man in a grey coat walked up to the horse box, spoke to the person inside over the top half of the barn door, then quickly stepped inside before closing both sections completely. Cannon guessed that this was Tony Williams, but he wanted to be sure. He pretended to be busy working on the reins while maintaining his focus on where he believed Williams remained, within the horse box. After a few anxious minutes and a couple of glances at his watch, Cannon saw the stable door open and the man he was interested in, walk out and make his way towards the Tweedie stand. Cannon immediately jogged to White Noise's box and dropped off the reins with Radcliffe, telling him that he would be back after the second race. Continuing at pace, he made his way to Dark Chocolates' box, slowing down to a walk as he reached it.

Inside was a young woman who was busy grooming the horse,

including polishing the horses hooves, which Cannon thought was unnecessary given the weather conditions and the likely going of the racetrack itself. She had her head down as she worked, but she was facing the door. He tapped on the open top half. She looked up at the noise. Cannon noticed a name tag on a lanyard around her neck.

"Hi Emily," he said, hoping that he had read the identity tag correctly as it started to flap around her body as the wind swirled into the box, blowing up some of the sand and straw that was scattered on the floor.

"Oh hello," she answered, thinking that it was someone she knew, before suddenly realizing that it was a stranger.

"I'm sorry to bother you, but I wondered if you had seen Mr. Williams at all? I'm a member of the syndicate who wants to buy into this horse," he lied, pointing towards the animal under her care, "and I need to speak with Mr. Williams about it. Are you able to help me?"

Emily was no more than eighteen years old. She was obviously a local girl, the height of the average jockey, with reddish blond hair under a *TW Racing* cap, light green eyes with a pale skin and a button nose. She was wearing a *TW Racing* bottle green jacket over a jersey and T-shirt, black jeans and a pair of hiking boots. She seemed similar looking to Rachel Brits who Cannon had met at Wincanton.

"You have just missed him," she replied, her Scots brogue harsh to the ear but at least still understandable. "He left about 5 minutes ago."

"OK," he answered, "Thanks, I'll see if I can find him."

"No problem," she smiled, before reverting to her grooming.

Cannon quickly moved away from the boxes. He had what he needed. Now he had to be careful with what he did with the information. He decided to take a chance and take a quick walk underneath the stand and then circle back to the owners marquee where Platt would be waiting for him. He had fifteen minutes before they were due to catch up.

As he walked quickly through the spectators, much fewer than he had expected, he suddenly felt exposed. The sparseness of the crowd would make staying out of sight very difficult and he guessed that the weather had kept people away from the track, along with the fact that it wasn't a weekend meeting. Cannon was only mildly wet when he reached the entrance door to the area underneath the Tweedie stand. He entered and took a quick look around. His eye caught the back of a grey coat and he recognized the face he had seen entering then leaving the box which housed the horse, Dark Chocolate. It was Tony Williams. Cannon noticed that he was talking with another man as they both walked towards the exit on the opposite side of the building. Cannon decided to follow them for a few minutes, keeping a sensible distance behind. He had no idea who the other man was, but it clear to him that they were deep in conversation and that the other man appeared to be unfamiliar with racecourses. Walking in the soft rain the two men glided past the bookmakers ring, the tote booths and the parade ring which was slowly coming to life with runners for the first race and yet the stranger hardly seemed to notice anything that was going on around him. Finally they made their way towards the Owners marquee, the same place where Cannon was to meet Platt. He wasn't sure if it was serendipitous, but it certainly fortunate.

The Scotsman was waiting for him, sitting at a table by himself, two small whisky glasses already empty, stood like soldiers on the table.

"Can I get you another?" Cannon asked, pointing towards the bar. "I do owe you, you know."

"That would be fine," Platt answered, letting him know his preferred tipple. "An Isle of Skye," he said, referencing the local whisky. Cannon strode the ten yards to the bar purposefully. He wanted to keep an eye on Williams and his friend, but also needed to ensure that he didn't lose focus on his upcoming races. Having acquired himself a tea and Platt his scotch, Cannon sat down in a position where he could continue his surveillance. At one point the other man glanced in his direction, and Cannon noticed the man's eyes. During his years in the police he had come across multiples of thugs, wife beaters, murderers, thieves and other degenerates who gave him the same feeling when he looked into their eyes – a sense of evil. This man was similar. Even in a few milli-seconds, Cannon felt it. He shuddered. If he was right, this investigation would not end well. For some strange reason he suddenly thought of Michelle.

CHAPTER 32

Les Platt had thanked Cannon for the whisky and had promised him a bed for the night should it be required. With both likely to be busy for the rest of the day, Cannon indicated that he would give the Scotsman a call if he decided to take up the offer. In his mind it would depend on what happened over the next few hours. If things went differently to expectations, then he was likely to be heading home after the fifth race, however he knew that Platt would still be around until after the sixth, the last race of the day. He would talk to him then if necessary. Cannon smiled to himself wondering how many drinks Platt would get through by the end of proceedings. His observation was that the trainer seemed to handle things well, irrespective of his alcohol intake, and who was he to judge anyway?

The second race was won by a local trainer, Bill Madeley. His horse, Touch of Sun, romped home by thirty lengths. Of the seven starters only four finished, the others being pulled up at various stages during the event. Fortunately there were no falls or injuries, but the ground was getting softer and heavier as the day wore on and the drizzle continued, turning to rain at times.

"I suggest you try and keep near the front," Cannon mentioned to Giles Mainwaring who had agreed to ride both his horses at the meeting. "With the track beginning to cut up a little you don't want to get him stuck in the middle of a mud bath, even if he likes to get his toe into the ground."

The jockey smiled. He had already competed in the first two races, with a second place in the first race and fourth in the second. As an experienced pilot of horses he was always fascinated when trainers gave instructions. Even the best of them couldn't help themselves, he thought. He listened politely knowing that what happened in the race depended on the horse's will to win, its bravery and how fit it was for that specific event. Everything else played out as it would. There were so many variables to contend with even over the short distance of a two-mile Handicap Hurdle race. The race had been chosen to give White Noise more confidence, and in time to challenge for honours at Cheltenham. The plan was to continue to race him during the season, and if he qualified, he would run during the festival in March, still some four months away. However, if he didn't, Cannon's plan was to target the race the following year and he had the support of the owner, which was always a positive. The horse had huge potential, but what use was that if it wasn't realized?

Legging the jockey up into the saddle, which was already wet and slippery, Cannon let Jack Radcliffe lead the horse away from him and continue walking around the parade ring with the rest of the field. Cannon watched for a few seconds, noting that Joel Seeton's colours of red with a white band from left shoulder to the right hip, blue sleeves and a blue cap were already showing signs of being impacted by the rain. Mainwaring, however, didn't seem to worry as the thin jacket stuck to his slim body. Turning to make his way to the Grandstand, Cannon noticed Williams and his shadow staring at him. The two men were standing alone behind a raised stonewall platform under a shared umbrella, roughly ten metres from the outer fence of the parade ring. It was obvious that they were taking a keen interest in him, as much as he was of them. Pretending not to have noticed he made his way towards the Grandstand, where he intended to watch the race. The two men followed him staying twenty metres behind, then just as he reached the bottom steps of the stand, they veered off and turned back, making their way towards the horse boxes. Cannon looked at his watch, the runners for his race were still making their way to the start. With ten minutes to go and forty minutes until race four, he was waiting for an announcement. With two minutes to go before the off, it came.

"Please note that in race four, horse number three, Dark Chocolate, has been scratched on the advice of the vet. Once again, horse number three in race four is now scratched. Bookmakers please draw a line and punters please note there will be a deduction in all winning bets."

It was what he had been waiting for. The question he now needed to get an answer to was why. He would need to act quickly once White Noise's race was over.

Hyseni waited for Williams to make his way to the car. He had seen enough and on their way back to Roxburgh, he would make the necessary call. His observation was that Cannon knew that something was going on, so before he became too much of a problem, he would have to be dealt with. The two men had discussed Cannon's background as well as him being the employer of the young girl, the partner of their former associate in that part of the country. Hyseni had agreed with Williams that it was more than just a coincidence, which was why he was about to take steps to address the problem. As he closed the car door on the rain, a distant voice of tin echoed over the racecourse and the parking lot, signalling the start of the third race.

Giles Mainwaring anticipated the starter pushing the button to lift the starting tapes by milliseconds and found himself immediately in front of the nine other runners. White Noise took off full of running, his action comfortable despite the heavy going and the now steady rain. The eight flights ahead of him over the approximately two-mile course were mere bumps in the road as he maintained a steady gallop to win the race by eleven lengths. Being out in front throughout and circumnavigating the entire circuit twice with barely a challenge the entire way, brought a smile to Cannon's face. It was exactly what he had hoped for, and Seeton's message to his phone, as the horse crossed the line, added positively to his mood.

"A perfect ride," he said to Mainwaring as the jockey jumped off the horse in the winners stall. A few brave punters who were standing in the rain and who must have backed the horse, clapped as the jockey removed the saddle. Cannon noticed that the jockeys colours were still relatively mud free, the result of racing upfront. Those of the second and third placegetters were caked with dirt.
"Thanks," Mainwaring replied, "at least that's one favourite home today."
"And so he should have," Jack Radcliffe noted, as he took the reins and led the horse around before taking him away back to his box for a wash and a rub down. Cannon agreed. It was a great result. He let Mainwaring go to weigh out, promising to let him ride White Noise at his next outing and confirming that he would see him again in the parade ring for the ride on the Doc in race five.
With the back of Mainwaring receding, Cannon looked around to see if could see any sign of Williams or the other man. He had no luck so

decided to make his way to where Dark Chocolate had been housed. When he arrived, the stall was as he expected; empty.

He made his way to the Stewards rooms as he needed to ask them a discrete question.

Diogenes the Cynic, affectionally known as Doc, gave Giles Mainwaring a difficult ride. Contrasting with how well White Noise had run, the Doc had shown that each racehorse had a different personality and some could be stubborn. During his three mile chase the Doc appeared to lose interest at times and though the field of four runners chopped and changed leaders during the race, Mainwaring found himself in front as the two remaining runners in the race arrived at the last fence. With the rain still falling steadily the race had become a slog. The Doc was enjoying the ground and was just a little fitter than his rivals. With his mount barely clearing the last and out on his feet Mainwaring used the persuader to keep the horse's mind on the job, crossing the line five lengths ahead of the only other runner to finish.

"A little different to the earlier race," Cannon said, as he again congratulated him on his ride.

"Bloody right," Mainwaring said. "I'm knackered after all that," he added with a grin that highlighted his perfect teeth which contrasted with his panda eyes on a mud-spattered face. "I'm glad it's my last ride for the day, the track is starting to cut up really badly."

For a moment Cannon froze, the words of his jockey had hit a nerve. A lightbulb suddenly switched on in his head. Was that the missing piece to his theory? Could it be that simple?

He thanked his jockey once more, then turned to Radcliffe who would again take the horse to be washed and readied for the long trip home. Sam Simmons was already taking care of White Noise and the two grooms would be driving back to Woodstock as soon as they could.

"Drive safely on the way home, Jack," he said, "I'll be back tomorrow. I've just got a few things I need to sort out with Les, so I'll be staying overnight at his place."

"No worries, boss," Radcliffe replied, "it's been worth the trip hasn't it?"

Death Seeks You Out

"Absolutely."

With a handshake they each went their separate ways. Cannon needed to speak with Platt urgently. He found the man at his runners box. The immediate area around them was extremely quiet. Most of the earlier race participants had left the racecourse already or were in the process of being loaded up into their travelling boxes. With only five runners in the last race what had once been a hive of activity was now muted. Only the rain seemed to have consolidated, the people had dispersed for the warmth of home or a local pub.

"A good day for yer," Platt said, a smile on his face. "Are you buying?"

"Happy to put something on the table," Cannon replied before asking Platt if his offer to stay the night was still valid.

"Of course, man, no problem at all. I could use the company."

Cannon knew from their earlier conversation that Platt was a widower and lived alone. He had his racing staff and a housekeeper, but his evenings were his own. Apologizing to his host Cannon asked, "If it's alright with you, I need to make a small diversion before I get to your place so it may mean I'll only get there a bit later. Perhaps around eight? I'll bring a bottle of Scotland's finest with me though."

Platt grinned. "Sure, do what you need to, Mike. I'll leave the door unlocked just in case I fall asleep, but don't forget I like the Kingsbarns Doocot."

The two men laughed together at the reference to one of the best Lowlands Whisky around, which Cannon promised he would try and find. They then exchanged mobile phone numbers before Cannon wished Platt well with his horse, Gladiator, in the last race of the day. It was now ten past three and the final race was due to start in twenty minutes. The sky was still tipping its contents onto the course and across the surrounding countryside. The low cloud caressed the tops of the nearby hills and night wasn't too far away.

Cannon made his way to his car. When he finally settled into his seat he was wet from the knee down. His boots felt uncomfortable so he took them off and placed them in the footwell of the passenger seat, deciding to drive in stockinged feet. Starting the engine he turned on the heater at full blast switching the mode for the air to blow below the dashboard and onto the floor. With luck his feet and his boots would be dry by the time he reached Roxburgh. Before he put the car into gear he called up Silvers' number and filled him in on what he had been able to establish so far. He then called Michelle, but the phone did not ring, going instead straight to voicemail. He was initially confused until he remembered the memorial service for Sue Gladstone that the school was holding that afternoon. He left a message.

As they drove the short six-mile trip to Roxburgh, Hyseni told Williams that he had made arrangements for someone to send a message to Cannon. "It won't be a local but someone else," he said, not adding any more colour to the inference. "However, tomorrow afternoon I want you to take me down there."
"What, down to Oxford?"
"Yes."
"But its…"
"Yes, I know. A long way."
"Six hours plus."
"Well even better. I can use the time to make a few calls," Hyseni replied. "I can't use public transport while I'm in the country as I don't want my name being picked up by the authorities. If you hadn't been such a long way from London, I would have caught the Eurostar and gone to Oxford directly from there. "
"To do what?"
"To organize a new distributor."
Williams knew what Hyseni was referring to and decided to stay quiet. He had been given an instruction rather than a request and he would be foolish not to comply. After an uncomfortable but short silence between them, they arrived back at Williams' farm. The headlights of the car shone ahead of them, brushing the road and a line of trees as dusk closed in. The fading light was exacerbated by the continuing rain, but the floodlights that illuminated a group of buildings up ahead of them created a strange silhouette against the coming night. They drove up a short driveway to park behind a wall that hid the racing stables from the road, and noticed a horsebox being unloaded. A young woman, still wearing her ID tag from the racecourse led Dark Chocolate, the mare she had been prepping before Williams scratched the horse, down the ramp of the trailer.

"I want to see what happens next," Hyseni said, pointing through his window towards the young girl who began to walk towards a large barn which from the light shining from within appeared to hold other horses as well. Hyseni could see a curious head or two looking over internal barn doors.
"You mean...eventually?" Williams asked.
"Yes. I assume you have a few."
"I do, but that's not one of them," Williams pointed towards the disappearing backs of both horse and groom as they entered the barn building. "That one is coming your way first. I just need to arrange the paperwork and nominations for Duindigt and Cologne."
Hyseni seemed unfazed, "Okay....when then?"
"I've arranged a truck for nine pm. The location is a fifteen-minute drive from here. The crew who do the job start at ten pm and are left unsupervised from midnight. If you really want to...."
"Yes, I really do!" Hyseni interrupted, his voice rising. It was the first time that Williams had experienced any outburst of anger from the man sitting next to him. They were supposed to be colleagues and partners, but as they remained seated in the car, the engine still running and the windscreen wipers flapping across the glass, Williams wasn't so sure. Sighing inwardly, he accepted that he had no choice in the matter.
"Okay, we'll leave sometime after ten," he announced.

Cannon used his phone to navigate to Williams' farm. Along the way he called Silvers again and left a message on Silvers' voicemail, letting the policeman know of his whereabouts and his intentions. He would have preferred a one-to-one conversation just in case something went wrong, but that was not to be.
He parked his car a quarter of a mile from the entrance to the farm in a lay-by that seemed to have been used last by the Romans. The area was overgrown in many places, with weeds poking through the gravel road base and thick tree branches hanging so low that any car that went underneath them would come out with heavy scratches on the roof as well as the rest of the car's body. Cannon had stopped just prior to the overhang, braking suddenly when he saw the dangerous fingers of the trees reaching out for their next victim. Turning off the engine, the darkness and silence that surrounded the car suddenly

engulfed it. The lack of traffic on the road created a sense of standing, quite literally, in the middle of nowhere. The farm itself was hidden by the contour of the land and a hedge that ran alongside the road. To his left, somewhere over a hill that loomed up beside him, the tip of which he could just make out, were the lights of Williams' farmhouse and his stables. With the rain still falling steadily, he put on his still damp boots then opened the car door and jumped out quickly, thankful for his coat and cap that he had brought with him from home and which kept his body dry. He placed his racing binoculars into an inside coat pocket and slowly climbed over the dark and sodden hedge. He didn't think that Williams would have any security cameras monitoring a fallow field, especially one so far from the house, but he couldn't be sure. A quick use of the torch on his phone revealed no sign of anything but he still needed to be cautious. Not sure what to expect, he made his way up the hill before seeing Williams' house for the first time. It was situated some distance below. The racing facilities were roughly two hundred metres away from the building. From the top of the hill, Cannon noticed that the house and the stables were all lit up like Christmas trees. In the gloom that surrounded them, they appeared like islands in a dark sea. He scanned the area quickly but couldn't see anyone moving around so decided to move closer. He didn't have any specific plan, but he had a theory. The question was how to prove it. The opportunity to do so was still out of his hands.

CHAPTER 33

Michelle took the call after her mobile phone rang more times than she would have liked. It was the same number each time, one which she did not recognize. She had finally relented, answering it after the sixth attempt. She was exhausted and was sitting on a couch in the lounge staring at the TV news but not taking much of it in, when the phone had rang for the first time. She had decided to ignore it until she noticed that there were no voicemails being left each time the call ended. It was then that she realized that it was possible that someone may have been calling on behalf of her husband or even on behalf of Cassie. It was this thought that finally made her answer. It had been a difficult day already, especially with the memorial service for Sue Gladstone having taken place, and while she had listened to Cannon's message when she got home, she was hopeful that he would call again before she went to bed. She muted the TV. The persistent caller was Angela Fryer.

"I'm sorry to bother you so late," she said, her voice teary and apologetic, "but I need to speak with someone and I…" The rest of her words seemed lost in a jumble of sound. Michelle was unable to make out what was being said as the young apprentice broke down. Trying to get her to calm down, Michelle offered words of comfort but was unsure whether anything was getting through. With long pauses between them, she waited until Angela regained her composure. Eventually the line went quiet, leaving an opportunity for her to speak.

"Can you tell me what it's about?" Michelle asked.

"I could, but I would much prefer to talk about it face to face. It's rather personal and it's why I called."

Michelle wasn't sure what could be so personal that would involve her but as a teacher who had many pupils over the years with 'personal problems' the subject could be almost anything. Given the recent events, she was sympathetic to the young girl's appeal and she suggested that the pair meet the next day.

"I assume you will be here as usual tomorrow?" she asked, aware that the young jockey was not allowed to ride but was working in the stables.

"Yes, I'll be there around seven thirty."

This was much later than Angela used to be at the yard when riding, which was closer to six, but as she was limited to working on specific duties, as needed by Rich, she had no reason to be available so early anymore.

"Unfortunately, as I'm sure you will understand, I'll be on my way to school by then," Michelle answered. "How about coming here before evening stables? Say around six? I'll be home by then. You can have dinner with me if you are up to it?"

Having made the offer, Michelle realized that it may not be such a sensible idea. An apprentice jockey, like all others, needed to watch their weight and when they weren't riding regularly could easily add unnecessary pounds due to eating differently from their norm.

"That would be nice," Angela replied, sounding better for the compassion shown by Michelle.

"Mike might even be back by then, though it's a long drive from Kelso He left me a message that he will be staying there at least until tomorrow afternoon."

Without commenting further, Angela thanked Michelle for her time and ended the call. Looking at the screen on her mobile, Michelle wondered what was behind the request to discuss a personal matter that she had just agreed to.

As the TV flickered its silent picture she felt a shiver down her spine unsure whether it was a premonition of some sort, or something else. She turned off the TV, checked the locks on the front and back doors and headed to the bedroom. As she reached it, the phone in Cannons' office began to ring. In the silence of the house, it gave her a fright and she let out a cry of surprise. After picking up the phone, she answered with a greeting. "Hello," she said, "Can I help you?"

There was no reply, so she asked the same question again before sensing that it was scam call. Then she noticed that the usual few seconds wait before a click sounded and the inevitable voice came on the line to tell her that it was the tax office calling or that a parcel delivery was being delayed had passed without anything happening. There was just an empty silence. Then, barely, just for a second or two, she could hear someone breathing.

"Hello?" she repeated again, but without receiving any response. Then as she strained to hear anything at all, the line cut out. "Good riddance," she thought, replacing the phone onto its cradle.

She went to bed twenty minutes later annoyed that a wrong number had scared her as much as it did. She missed not having Cannon lying beside her and knew that she would have a restless night without him.

CHAPTER 34

Cannon moved closer to the house. He tried to check his watch but the rain ran into his eyes making it difficult to see despite the peak of his cap, and he was concerned about checking the screen on his phone. His battery was beginning to run low as he had used it throughout day and he had not been able to charge it much in his car, as the journey from the racecourse had been so short.

Keeping low to the ground he bent double and managed to find himself at a corner of the house. With his back to the wall he was able to look over his left shoulder and peer along the front of the building. Squares of light from various rooms could be seen on the concrete footbath that encircled most of the property, some illuminating the grass that slid up the hill from where he had come. To his left, roughly forty metres away was the barn building that housed the stalls where horses were stabled. From what he could make out they were big enough to house far more than the sixteen horses that were registered in work to Williams as a trainer. With the doors of the barn open Cannon was able to see at least twenty stalls before he lost count as his visual perspective was lost. Noting that there were three barns of similar size, he concluded that the operation was much larger than he had originally anticipated. Standing in the shadows, his focus elsewhere he suddenly noticed a sound behind him. He was about to turn around, ready to face being discovered, when he realized what the sound was. A popping and chattering from a generator that had come to life. He hadn't noticed it initially as it was covered under a wooden box standing close to the wall of the house. It must have been on a timer and was something Cannon had come across many times himself. He guessed that like most farms, solar panels and generators were in use where possible so that the farm could be off grid. With the sun having gone down some time ago, the generator was likely kicking in as the solar battery began winding down. This noise was the sound that had scared him. Hoping his heart rate would slow and the beating in his chest subside, he continued to observe what he could from his vantage point. He thought about sneaking his way around the building and trying to look into the illuminated windows but his concern was being caught. His rationale for being at the farm was to prove his theory, not to get involved in an arrest or a bust, that was the police's job. He had done that in the past and he had no intention of repeating it. Rubbing away the rain that spat into his face, he noticed a light that had suddenly appeared from over the hill, in the direction that he himself had come. Within seconds the light had split into two eyes. The beams of a truck lit up the driveway that led to the house and terminated at the stables. The sound of the diesel engine came closer and louder as the truck trundled along, stopping thirty feet away from the first of the three barns. As he watched, Cannon noticed the front door of the house open and Williams and the other man who had been watching him at the races, suddenly appear. They were dressed for the conditions. They shook hands with one of the two men who had exited from the cab of the truck. While he could see gestures being made, Cannon could not hear what was being said. He looked around to see if he could get closer but realized it would be impossible to do so. Frustrated at where he found himself, he decided to make his way back the way he had come. The light from the house could not reach beyond the first couple of yards of the grasses that covered the hill. He made his way into the darkness then stayed in the shadows, creeping around in an arc to try and get closer to where the now four men stood together. He thought he saw Williams pointing to the back of the truck then noticed more lights coming from his right. Down the road came another two vehicles, similar to the first. All three of them were dark in colour. He couldn't make out whether they were black, blue or green but he recalled the girl at Kelso, Emily, was wearing a bottle green jacket. It was the same type that was worn at the races at Wincanton by the girl whose name he couldn't remember. He guessed that they were all trucks that belonged to Williams and likely had the name of his racing stables on them somewhere. But why three he asked himself? The answer became clearer the longer he watched, and he was staggered at the size of the operation.

"Those in barn A are for your truck," Williams said to driver of the first vehicle that had trundled down the road. He pointed in the direction of the closest building, "And you know where to take them don't you?."

The man nodded, and along with another who had climbed down

from the truck's cab, walked towards the glowing lights of the barn, where a number of other men were waiting. Cannon remained low and squat, moving slightly closer to where Williams was standing. It was as far as he dared go, stopping right on the fringe of the lit area, remaining in the shadows. The rain continued to fall and he felt his jeans becoming heavier, though he was thankful that his feet were still relatively dry. He watched as the unknown man standing with Williams shouted in a language he didn't understand. The man was waving an arm around like a windmill. A universal sign to speed things along.
"You!" he heard Williams shout to the drivers of the second and third trucks, respectively. "Those for the boat, they are in barn B. Those for processing, take them from your truck into barn C. Let us know when you are done." With that, Williams and the other man went back into the house leaving the operation to the others. Cannon then watched for another twenty minutes or so as the three trucks were loaded or emptied as instructed. It was clear that this was a very sophisticated endeavour and had been in place for quite some time, given how smoothly it seemed to function. As he watched the comings and goings of various horses, he noticed with horror that one of the animals being put onto the first truck was the horse he had seen at the races just a few hours ago, Dark Chocolate! He recognized the shape of the small white blaze on the horse's head and the single white sock on its off-side foreleg. The first truck quickly filled and Cannon found himself in a dilemma. He had been working on a theory, one that he had shared with Silvers and now he wasn't sure if he was right or wrong. Having heard the instructions given by Williams, he knew that he had to make a decision, and quickly, as the first truck would likely leave soon. His instincts kicked in and he moved back, further into the darkness, away from the light and into the grass. Keeping low he staggered up the hill hoping that the lights burning below wouldn't create a silhouette of himself as he reached the top of the hill. With a quick look back over his shoulder, he noticed Williams pointing at something as the first truck's engine started up. As Cannon crested the top of the hill he failed to notice a rock that protruded out of the ground and he tripped, falling down the rugged slope towards the hedge below, gathering speed then crashing into it feet first. His legs felt the brunt of the impact, as the small privet and yew branches scraped along the fabric of his jeans,

piercing them in places leaving bloody scratches, scars and tears. The pain came a few seconds later from the flesh that had been torn. "Fuck!" he exclaimed, as he rose to his feet and gingerly climbed over the offending barrier. He limped towards his car and slammed the door against the continuing rain the moment he was inside. He felt like a drowned rat. During his fall he had lost his cap, leaving it somewhere on the hill. His coat was wet, mud-caked in places, particularly on the elbows, but as he briefly sat back in his car seat to take stock of his legs he began to feel a pain in his ribs. It was a subtle ache but as he went to undo the coat buttons, ready to remove it, he lifted an arm and felt the pain increase dramatically. He knew immediately that he had cracked a rib, maybe more than one. The culprit was his binoculars, that were remarkably still in his inside coat pocket. He guessed that he must have landed on them as he tumbled over and over down the hill. Ignoring the pain, he removed the coat then reached for his phone just as the lights of the first truck began to stroke the dark and silent road on which he was parked. A brief look at his mobile's screen showed him that it was after ten. Through the rain spattered windscreen he could see the beams of light getting bigger and brighter as they came closer to the end of the driveway and the open gate of Williams' farm. He threw his mobile back onto the passenger seat, started his car, leaving his lights off and waited. Within a few seconds the truck showed itself, turning left onto the road and began to drive away from him. With his car air conditioner and heater now set on the highest setting, Cannon turned onto the road and keeping a safe distance behind the truck, followed it to its destination. He wasn't surprised when they got there.

CHAPTER 35

Cannon had driven past the entrance and the long drive down to the abattoir, stopping in the empty and desolate grounds of the old Eckford church two hundred metres further down the road. With the engine still running he was able to make a call despite the signal on his mobile being so weak. He left a message giving the details of what he had seen, where he was and what he was planning to do next. He felt sick and not because of the pain in his leg and chest. The facility alongside the Teviot river at Kalemouth made perfect sense. It was close to Williams' farm, it was remote and it had just the place to get rid of any evidence, the river itself.

Putting his car into gear, he headed back the way he had come. He now knew that his instinct was right, but he didn't have any official proof yet to back it up. From what he had seen, the answer was in the barns. He needed to get into them somehow. Cannon hoped that the facade that Williams had created in relation to his farm and his training facilities were less like Fort Knox and more in line with that of most trainers, secure areas with general accessibility. He hadn't seen any 'Beware of the Dog' signs on any of the farm fences and he hadn't encountered any either nor had he noticed any CCTV stickers on windows when he had watched the house from his hiding place. The lack of such notices however didn't inspire him with confidence as not everyone advertised their security systems, something he was well aware of in relation to his own yard.

Pulling his car back into the same lay-by he had parked in earlier, Cannon rubbed his legs. The pain from his fall had subsided slightly but his ribs had gotten worse. Outside the rain had slowed a little and was now more of a light drizzle. He shivered involuntarily, the temperature outside would be of significant contrast to that he enjoyed inside the car. He felt it as soon as he decided that it was time to climb out.

"How much should we have this time?" Williams asked.
"From this lot, we should have thirty kilograms."
"So just over a million pounds."

"More at street level," Hyseni replied. "We just need to get it out. Where is your vet?"

"He's on his way," Williams replied.

Cannon had navigated the hill again, taking care on his way down towards the house so as not to fall. It was now close to midnight. Keeping to the shadows he watched as the activity around the two remaining trucks started to slow down, though not before another vehicle, a Land Rover like his own, had arrived and came to a stop in front of barn C. A man with a bag jumped out and was greeted by Williams. In turn, Williams introduced him to the third man. Cannon was dying to know who the stranger was, but he easily recognized the new arrival. It was obvious that the man was a vet. Cannon had seen the type of bag he was carrying, many times. It was one that contained the tools of the trade. After the vet and the stranger had shook hands, Cannon noticed the former turn towards the hill, gesticulating something, but he had no idea what it meant. It could be anything, he thought, ultimately deciding that it was an irrelevance to him. He watched as the three men went into the barn just as the engine of the second truck fired up. The driver of the truck reversed the vehicle a few yards before conducting a three-point turn and then headed towards the farm gate.

"For the boat," Cannon recalled Williams saying. As the noise of the truck slowly ebbed away, the immediate area surrounding the last vehicle and in front of the house became eerily quiet. All the activity had shifted in the direction of what was called barn C. The horses that had arrived in the second truck had all been transferred there. The handlers and the others were now all inside. Cannon wrote a quick text to Silvers on his mobile, hoping that the policeman would get the message and do what was necessary. Crouching down and moving quickly he managed to cross to the truck, staying on the side where the light did not reach. Standing in the darkness he felt his heart beating and his breathing felt laboured. He wasn't as fit as he used to be, he thought unhelpfully. Stopping to hear if there was anyone in the immediate vicinity, he sensed movement on the other side of the truck. He lowered himself, noting a pair of legs and boots but he could see nothing else from the underside of the vehicle. Holding his breath he watched as a cigarette end was dropped into a puddle, a whisp of smoke rose from it before dying in the drizzle. A few words were muttered but he couldn't make out the language. The man appeared to be talking to himself. Suddenly there was movement, the vehicle rocked slightly as the smoker climbed back into the cab. Cannon was afraid that he might be seen in the passenger side mirror so he moved around to the back of the truck then made a dash towards the third barn where a single door was wide open. Light from inside spilled onto the gravel driveway. Next to the entrance into the barn, to the right, was a large garage type door that Cannon had noticed was the same in all three barns. These doors had been used as entry and exit points for all the horses that had recently arrived or had been removed, like those on the first truck. Dark Chocolate had come out of barn A and had been taken away from there unknowing that it would be his last ride.

The sound of the soft rain that continued to fall prevented Cannon from hearing anything other than a few snorts and whinnies coming from inside the barn. The voices of the three men inside that he was interested to listen in on were muffled. They were too far away from the door entrance. He strained to hear what was being said but couldn't make anything out at all. Deciding to take a chance, he leant forward in order to peer inside. As he did so, something smashed into him from behind. It felt like a baseball bat being hammered into his back, right between the shoulder blades. The pain in his ribs was forgotten as he fell forward cracking his head on the door jamb. Sounds faded and darkness engulfed him.

The ten new arrivals were compliant. It had taken over an hour to get every one of them into a state where they could be worked on. Xylazine was the preferred drug of choice and it had worked well. When Abazi had worked on them before shipment he had needed to use Ketamine and Diazepam to anesthetize them, but that wasn't necessary at this stage of the process. Tied up in their individual stalls the vet was easily able to extract the small packages of 300g each. Three kilograms inside each animal was not enough to cause them too much discomfort. Horses were known to defecate fairly regularly due to their diet but using a simple undetectable technique perfected by his brother-in-law, Hyseni had been able to establish a route to market that was both reliable and lucrative.

As Williams weighed the packets and the vet cleaned his long-sleeved gloves in a large white ceramic sink there was sudden commotion behind them. A thud, a cry, then a man fell through the open door some fifteen metres behind them. As the man's unconscious body hit the ground the driver from the remaining truck stood at the opening, a cricket bat in his hand. In broken English he said, "I found this man, here, standing in the gap, I think he was spying on you."

CHAPTER 36

Cannon had no idea how long he was unconscious for. When he started to open his eyes his first reaction was to vomit. His head ached and felt like it was too heavy for his shoulders. He dry heaved, surprised that his mouth was unfettered by anything. As he became aware of his surroundings, he began to feel the cold and the numbness in his hands and feet. He was alone, his arms bound to his body and his legs tied to those of a chair. Way above him, unusually high, was strip lighting, a singularly long globe emitting a phosphorus like white light. He could hear machinery somewhere, and a strange smell stunned his nostrils after the occasional dull thud was followed by the squeal of what sounded like metal on bone. He knew instantly what it was. Glancing around he saw that the room he was in was no more than the size of a prison cell. Two metres wide, Three metres long but with the high ceiling. He stared again at the lighting above him and noticed a crane-like claw, a 'hand', attached to a heavy draw chain that snaked along a beam before attaching itself to a hook about a metre-and-a-half off the ground. The hook was situated alongside a single door, the only way into or out of the windowless room. He had seen many such contraptions before. They were used to lift heavy things off the floor, either to move them around or to hang from it. With nowhere to move items to in the small space, Cannon assumed its use was the latter....hanging.

He shivered at the pernicious temperature inside the room. His head ached and his ribs screamed in pain. His chest seemed like it was going to explode, exacerbated by the damage inflicted on him when he was hit from behind on his shoulders and back. His legs felt weak and he felt extremely tired. His surroundings seemed to envelope him, the room making him feel claustrophobic and he almost fainted. Slowly the pain began to subside and he tried to apply some logic to his circumstances. Realising that he was wearing slightly damp jeans and drying muddy boots, but without his coat, he guessed that the drying process meant that he had only been inside the room for a couple of hours. He used the state of his clothing to give him an idea of how much time had passed since he had peered through the barn doorway. It was just a guess but he suspected that it was not yet dawn.

He could not see his hands and wrists but he sensed that whoever had tied him up had removed his smart watch. It was obvious that those holding him were clever enough to remove all methods of contact and it was then that he realized that he had no access to a phone. His mobile had been inside one of his coat pockets. He needed to think.

Where was he? What were his captors intending to do with him? With a sense of desperation he called out, unsure who might enter the room. He had no choice. In order to get out, he needed to know what he was up against. Having tried a number of times to free himself from the ropes that bound him but without success, the only option was to somehow get his captors to untie him and when they did, take whatever opportunity showed itself.

"Hey!" he shouted, "Hey!"

He waited to hear if there was any response. After a minute, the silence of the room consumed him again. The sounds he had heard earlier coming from outside continued unbated.

"Hey!," he screamed louder, "is there anybody there?!"

Again he waited for a response. Again there was nothing.

"Hey, you out there! Hey, can you hear me?!"

He continued to shout as loud as he could until his chest began to hurt again. He had hoped that at some stage he would get a reaction. Eventually, after a few minutes, he heard a key being pushed into the door lock. While he waited for someone to enter, he was conscious of the key turning, then the light in the room suddenly went out. He was in complete darkness. The door opened slowly and he saw somebody in a brief silhouette before a bright light from a torch of some kind was shone directly into his face. Cannon turned away and closed his eyes as the light followed him. The brightness burnt into his eyes when he turned his head back towards the source to try and get a glimpse of his captor.

"Who are you?" Cannon asked. "And why am I here?"

The question sounded insipid given what had happened only a short while ago. His actions had gotten him into a dangerous situation and he needed to react quickly. Any response, no matter how limited, or any information he could gather about his circumstances, would be valuable. Anything could help when faced with life or death. The

individual behind the beam of light that shone into Cannons' face did not reply. In the immediate quiet, the sounds that Cannon had heard earlier were now much more distinct, and the smell much more pronounced.
It was the stench of death.
"Is that you Williams?" Cannon asked, trying to illicit any type of response at all from the still silent figure. There was no reply, just the sound of breathing. Suddenly the figure turned around, walked out and slammed the door closed. Cannon heard the lock turn then waited for the light to come back on. It didn't.

"What should we do with him?" Williams asked. He was scared that he would be drawn into something that he didn't want to be part of. He had never killed anyone and he didn't want to start now.
Hyseni looked at him sideways, a glint of sadism in his eyes. They were standing together watching three men, all dressed in dark clothing and wearing dark aprons made of mesh, known as chainmail PPE, who were busy with their work.
A bolt to the head saw the animal killed before chains were wrapped around its legs. The carcass was then lifted and moved along a steel beam to another area, ready for slaughtering. Head separated first just above the shoulder, then the rest cut off in stages. Legs first, then the body quartered. It was horrific. Blood, entrails and faeces mixed on the concrete floor. The workers, immune to the process seemed to work efficiently. It was unusual for them to have any observers. Their work was normally done without spectators and with less care. They used the river when they needed to, whenever there was a problem such as the machinery breaking down and they could not complete total dissection. When things did go wrong, which happened on occasion, the dumping of the various pieces in the nearby waterway was their backup. Mostly however, it was just the heads that were a challenge. The skulls were difficult to work with but the rest of the carcass, excluding the tail and hooves, was easily turned into meat ready to be supplied to the dog food companies.
The three men, all from Serbia, were workers who had compatriots working at similar facilities across the country. They were illegals, smuggled into the country by associates of Hyseni and were cheap

labour for the owner of the abattoir who turned a blind eye to those that worked the late shift or stayed on after hours. It was their job to ensure that when the morning shift came in, nothing was to be found of what they had been busy with. No residue whatsoever.

The response from Hyseni had unsettled Williams. He had already seen enough, more than he needed to. Being the facilitator of the process, the front man rather than the operator, he usually stayed away from this part. He knew what went on but he didn't want to see it. He never became attached to any horse but he didn't enjoy seeing what became of them. He looked at his watch. It was nearly three in the morning.

"I'd better get back to the farm," he said, "some of the staff will be coming in soon."

"What for?" Hyseni said.

"Look, Amar, you may not fully realize this, but to keep up the pretence I need people to think that I am running a racing stable. In reality I do and this whole operation only works because of that."

"Your point being?"

"If we make mistakes, we get caught."

"And you think we have?" Hyseni asked, pointing in the direction of the room where Cannon was being held.

"Yes, I do. It's obvious that somehow something went wrong and our 'friend' in there worked it out."

"So?"

"So, I need to ensure that we don't make things any worse by giving any of the workers in my stables a reason to be suspicious. Also you need to make sure that those that have become a threat," he indicated the room where Cannon was being held, "are dealt with."

Desperate to leave the building as quickly as he could, Williams took a step towards an exit door then stopped and faced Hyseni again, trying to maintain a sense of inner control that he did not feel.

"When you have finished here, call me and I'll pick you up to take you down South as agreed," he said.

With a smile, Hyseni patted Williams on the shoulder then glibly replied, "Mr. Williams, you do your work and I'll do mine."

Silently relieved at the comment, Williams turned away. Hyseni held him back for a second. "Just so you know. When I leave I have arranged for one of these men here to take me to Lempitlaw Airfield."

Williams knew where the place was, roughly nine miles away. Hyseni continued with his explanation. "While you were busy earlier, I made a few phone calls. I have a UK sim card in another phone and I have organized a charter plane to take me to a place called Ventfield Farm Airfield a few kilometres from Oxford."

"But I thought you wanted me to drive you there?" Williams answered, silently pleased at not having to make the long trip anymore.

"I've changed my mind," Hyseni answered, "I need to move quickly and I have arranged to meet someone there later today, someone who I have already been in contact with. I have also asked them to do a couple of jobs for me first, and then afterwards help me find another distributor in the area. Someone more trustworthy than the previous individual," he added unnecessarily, staring right into Williams' soul. For a few seconds the two men locked eyes. Hyseni smiled. Williams blinked first, turned away and made for the exit. What happened to Cannon was of no concern to him.

Erjon Abazi knew that this was the only chance he had. With his brother-in-law out of the country for a few days, he and Ardita had made the decision to flee. Keeping their plans to themselves and only letting Dardan know that they were going on a 'secret journey' at the very last minute, they hurried to the airport being purposefully late. Hyseni had left just a few hours earlier. Erjon believed they had forty-eight hours to make their escape.

The route was convoluted but had been deliberate. Even the way they had acquired the tickets. Bought on-line with two flights from each airport in the chain, one which they would use and another which would leave without them and would make tracing them very difficult. They had no doubt that if someone really tried, they would eventually find the country that the three of them would ultimately arrive at, but when they did, would they still be there?

The cost of all the flight bookings was horrendous, but what price could one put on freedom? They bought two tickets for each of them from Amsterdam, one to Rome and one to Porto. Then two more tickets each from Rome and likewise two more from Porto. Those four flights of which none would be taken were repeated again from

Singapore, Auckland, Los Angeles and Perth. Of those additional eight flights bought for each of them, again none would be used. They wanted to stay right under Hyseni's nose. They planned to drive from London to Luton then catch a flight to Reykjavik. While he was in the UK they knew that he wouldn't expect them to be anywhere else other than in Holland.

From Iceland, using Air Canada, they would ultimately end up in Dallas, well away from the traditional areas where Albanians lived in the US; the Northeast and Midwest. It was where they wanted to settle. Erjon also believed that in time his surgical skills, his qualifications, would eventually allow him to get a job in a medical facility, should he need to. However with the money he and Ardita had put away over the years, they had no concerns in the short term about access to funds.

A new life beckoned, the visas they had secretly applied for had arrived a few months prior. Their departure was just a matter of timing. They would not be back.

CHAPTER 37

"Still no sign of that motorbike?" Walker asked, an undertone of angst in his voice.

"No, Sir," PC Timmly replied, staring at his computer screen.

Walker pursed his lips. He was annoyed that things appeared to have stalled. Leads had dried up and the report received overnight from the pathology lab had confirmed that Angela Fryers' baby was indeed that of Nick Van der Linden. DNA analysis had been undertaken and the result was unambiguous. Walker asked Conte to join him in his office.

"I'm getting a lot of heat from upstairs," he said, once the two men were seated. "It seems the Headmaster of the school where Sue Gladstone taught has been onto the Chief Superintendent and complained about our progress in catching her killer. The entire school seems to be on edge."

"Surely the old man knows where we are at with the investigation?" Conte responded, referring to Jason Pritchard, the top cop and head of the LPA, the Local Policing Area.

"I'm sure he does, but you know how it goes. He's not a detailed person, he'll just be aware that progress is slow."

"So?"

"My guess is that he would have told her that we are doing our best, and all available resources are focused on the job."

"Which is a laugh in itself," Conte replied.

"Of course it is but remember it's all about the optics. You need to make it seem that you are doing something, even if you are not. It's politics, plain and simple. You don't get to his level without being able to schmooze people, and once you have done that, you can shit all over everyone else."

"Which is what happened?"

"Yes, first thing this morning."

Conte scrunched his face. He knew that Walker had met with a number of senior officers at their weekly meeting earlier in the day. He guessed that it would have been a lively affair. "So what now, Sir?" he asked.

"We need to look at this differently."

"Go on."

"Well, given we haven't found that bike yet, and it's the only one we can't account for, it's obvious to me that the Dutchman was involved with its disappearance somehow. I'm not sure if we'll ever find it, but from the little information we got from Angela Fryer about Van Der Linden and his business, I think we need to take another look into who is running the drug trade around here?"

"How do you mean?"

"Well if Van der Linden was a bigger player than we first thought, and his tattoo parlour was just a front, then we need to find out who was supplying him. Perhaps then we can find the link to the motorbike. Perhaps someone even took it off his hands."

"Can't we get any help from the NCA?"

Walker laughed. "Do you know how much paperwork you need to complete to get anyone in the NCA interested in our investigation?"

"No."

"Too bloody much, Sergeant. Those buggers are busy with drug busts on the high seas and at container ports. Pushers like our Van der Linden are just the small fry."

"As far as we know."

"Well based on what we could establish from the girlfriend, yes."

"And that she was telling us all she knew." Conte replied, scratching his head, a thought turning over in his mind. He wondered if Walker was being too hasty in where he was going with the investigation. He had observed his boss arrest Mike Cannon with a zeal that was almost obsessive. The decision that Walker had taken to do so and the conclusions he had drawn without evidence had confirmed the reputation that always seemed to precede him. Walker's arrest first policy was old policing. His modus operandi of obtaining a confession to fit the narrative rather than getting the evidence to fit the crime was a residue of the past. Conte sensed that his boss was about to do the same again. Heat from above could only be tolerated for so long before people jumped to get away from it. "So what now?" he asked, reluctantly.

"I want to speak with the girl again. If she knew her boyfriend was a dealer then she must know where he got his supply from and how he distributed it."

"But she told us she had no idea."

"So she did, Sergeant, but I don't believe her."

"You may well be right, Sir," Conte replied, hardly convinced, "but if

she is telling the truth, then what?"
"We'll double cross that bridge when we get to it," Walker replied, "but I'm sure she knows more than she is telling."

The light in the room came on without warning, blinding him for a few seconds. Cannon waited. When the door to his cell finally opened, the noise outside had softened but the smell was all pervasive. The stranger slowly crossed the threshold, walking with a swagger that indicated that he was in control and had power over Cannons' destiny. Outside the room, Cannon could hear men talking but in a language he still couldn't place. The sound of spraying water from heavy hosepipes assailed his ears and he knew what was happening. A clean up of the detritus from the butchering of the horses was in the final stages.

The man stopped in front of the chair, staring into Cannons' eyes.

"I could put one of those bolts they use, right here," he said, touching Cannon on the forehead with his forefinger. Unable to move his body Cannon tried to turn his head away but the stranger grabbed his chin, squeezing his face so that his lips pursed and his cheeks felt like they were almost touching. Struggling, Cannon shook his head vigorously trying to loosen the man's grip, but as he did so the ribs in his chest told him that it was a bad idea. The stranger eventually let go, producing a large butchers knife hidden underneath his shirt in the small of his back. He put the blade a few millimetres below Cannon's left eye. The threat was obvious.

"Or perhaps I can take out one of these. Or maybe both?" the man continued, his Eastern European accent now more obvious. "What do you think?"

Silence was Cannon's only response, knowing that to antagonize the man in the confines of the room would be suicide. He needed time to think and space to move, this wasn't it.

"How much do you know?" the man asked.

"What about?"

"Don't fuck with me!" the man shouted, taking the knife and deliberately nicking Cannon on the cheek.

A trickle of blood ran down Cannons' face and slid down his chin. The bright crimson liquid then dripped onto his chest and onto the ropes that bound his arms.

"Or what?" Cannon said, trying to hide his fear. He was in no place to be cocky but the arrogance of the stranger gave Cannon an idea. If he was right, the man's ego would get the better of him. He would reveal himself, boast about how clever he was, say more than he should. Cannon had negotiated with many men over the years, particularly in domestic disputes, but in his latter days in the Force, he had worked on freeing hostages in bank robberies gone wrong. While those days were a long time ago, the ability to negotiate had never left him. It was a skill that he used during the racing season. He worked with jockeys almost every day and many of them had huge egos. With some jockeys he needed to convince them to race the way he thought best for the horse and to use the tactics that he believed was right under the circumstances. Some listened to him and won, some didn't and won. Sometimes he was completely unsuccessful in his attempts. He hoped that this wasn't one such time.

"Or what?" the man echoed, maliciously. "Perhaps you would like to lose an eye? Or maybe an ear?"

With the knife against his left earlobe, Cannon waited for the pain to come as his flesh was sliced. He closed his eyes but nothing happened. The stranger laughed again, enjoying the moment. As he did so, one of the men from outside came to the door opening, pointing to the ceiling. "*Zoteri* Hyseni," he said, "we need to go. The airplane."

"Two minutes, then we kill this man," the stranger replied. "Get the gun ready."

Cannon knew what was meant. The earlier comment about the captive bolt used on the horses was not a joke. Cannon struggled against the ropes but his actions made the stranger laugh.

"It is of no use Mr. Cannon," he said, laughing at his prisoner's surprise reaction. "Yes, I know who you are."

"Via Nick Van der Linden?"

"Amongst others. You have a reputation with some people in the racing game too."

While it would be of little use to him now, at least one part of his theory was confirmed, even if the stranger didn't realize it. Van der Linden *was* involved far more than others may have suspected.

"Irrespective of how you worked things out or how much you know," the stranger went on, "it doesn't matter anymore."

As Cannon stared into the stranger's face, the man who had been asked to get the gun a minute earlier showed himself again. "We must do this thing now, Mr. Hyseni. Quickly. We must go. The gun is ready."

"So, Mr. Hyseni is it?" Cannon said, trying to stall for time. "From somewhere in eastern Europe."

"Irrelevant now."

"I was a policeman once. Came across many migrants in that time. The accent is obvious, the family name seals it."

"Shut up!"

"Hyseni? Where's that from, Serbia? Bosnia?"

"Shut up!" Hyseni repeated, jabbing the knife towards Cannon's chest. Turning to the other man who was still at the door, he told him to cut away the ropes on Cannons' legs, but to leave the bindings around the arms. The man filed past Hyseni and tried to undo the ropes around Cannons' legs, but in his haste, struggled to do so. Cannon's earlier attempts to free himself had actually tightened the knots.

"Get out of the way," Hyseni said, pushing the man aside, using his knife to cut through the bonds. As the last strands split, Cannon leapt up catching the others off guard, kicking Hyseni in the chest and sending him sprawling, the knife from his hand dropping onto the floor. The third man seemed shell shocked and stood his ground as Cannon barged into him with a shoulder, knocking the man against the wall. A loud crack rent the air as the man's head hit the concrete rendering him temporarily unconscious. Cannon ran through the door, pulling it closed with his foot. Outside, a second man stood with his back to the doorway, the pneumatic stun gun in his hand, ready for use. The butt of the gun was attached to a long pipe which connected to a compressor. This provided the power to fire the bolt into an animals brain. Cannon diverted left and scrambled to find an exit. The man with the stun gun, dropped it to the floor and gave chase. Cannon jinked his way through some steel tables and past several oversized saws that were on reticulating arms above each bench. With his arms still pinned to his side it was only a matter of time before they would catch him. He couldn't see a way out but he did notice a number of red stop and green start buttons on the walls near each table. With nothing to lose he rammed a shoulder against the first green button he reached, then did the same against a second. With his breathing laboured from the pain in his ribs and the exertion from running, the chasing man caught up with him, knocking Cannon against the wall. The man tried to punch Cannon, but as he went to do so, a sound started above them. A whine, then a whizzing noise began to fill the air. Cannon noticed that Hyseni was now twenty feet away picking up the bolt gun, his anger showing on his face and his intention obvious. Kicking out at the man who had caught up to him, Cannon noticed both the saws above them were slowly lowering themselves towards the tables, gathering speed as they rotated. He guessed that they would automatically stop at some point, at a height useable by those who normally butchered the carcasses.

"Bring him here!" Hyseni shouted, above the now increasing noise from the two spinning blades. There was no instruction to Cannon's pursuer to hit the stop button. In his haste, Hyseni had made a mistake. It was his second. He made a third just as quickly. The ropes around Cannon's arms had started to loosen. When he had barged his way out of the room, the flexing of his shoulders and chest along with the impact with the wall had lessened their hold. Cannon shrugged off an attempt by the man to drag him towards Hyseni, instead freeing his own arms from the cord, letting most of it slide to the floor. The speed of his movement was unexpected and he caught the man unawares. He quickly wrapped some of the rope still within his grasp around the man's neck and started choking him, the tension crushing a windpipe. Cannon used the man as a shield.

Hyseni was unfazed. Pointing the bolt gun towards them, he pressed the trigger. Cannon instantly dropped to the floor dragging the other man down with him. The bolt struck Cannons' captive in the chest, piercing the sternum and lodging itself to the right of the man's heart. Death was instant.

Hyseni looked to reload the gun shouting at the first man, who had scrambled his way out of the room where Cannon had been held, to find another bolt. Seeing his compatriot lying on the floor a few feet away from them with a bolt sticking out of the chest, the man screamed at Hyseni. They were words that Cannon neither heard nor understood. The blades above the tables were no more than two metres away from them and continued to spin viciously. Pushing the screaming man away and still intent on finding another bolt, Hyseni briefly took his eyes off Cannon and the other man, making his fourth mistake. Cannon charged towards him, Hyseni still holding the gun, took a step back and slipped on the pipe that snaked on the floor behind him. As he did so, Cannon grabbed his other arm and using all the centrifugal force he could, swung Hyseni in a giant arc. Hyseni twisted as he began to glide sideways, letting go of the bolt gun just as his torso slammed into one of the speeding saw blades. Cannon and the other man watched as first the left arm, then the chest were sliced open just like a fish being gutted. A scream had little time to escape from Hyseni's lips before the saw decapitated him. Cannon turned away at the sight, the other man vomited before making for a door and charging through it. The sound of the saws continued to reverberate their deadly tune, the noise seemed much more aggressive and louder now that there was no one else around. Cannon slumped against the wall, his mind numb. He was exhausted but the adrenaline pumping around his body kept him awake forcing him to sit on the cold cement, while the horror he had witnessed, the blood and tissue lay all around him. Afraid that the other men would come back, possibly with Williams and others, he dragged himself up, using the wall as a crutch. Slowly he staggered over to the red stop buttons and slammed a palm against each. Relieved at the sight of the saw blades slowing down he scoured the immediate area, looking for his jacket and phone but there was no sign of either. He averted his eyes from the mangled body of Hyseni as much as he could, finally assuming that what he was looking for was back at Williams' farm. Realising that his car was also parked where he had left it, a sense of frustration came over him. He needed to get to a phone somehow. Finding his way out, he was hit by a cold breeze that chilled him to the bone. It had begun to rain again, a steady curtain of water adding to his misery and he was soaked within a minute. There was no one around and the parking area was devoid of any vehicles. Still dark, there were a few spotlights that lit up various buildings including another two sheds similar to the one he had just exited. He stumbled to every door in each of the buildings. It took him nearly 15 minutes. All of them were locked. Despite the rain, he knew that he needed to get to the main road where he hoped he could flag someone down, ideally a passing car or a truck.

He began to walk along the single driveway that disappeared into the distance. As he left the abattoir behind him, flashes of the last two hours replayed themselves in his mind. They were like the ghosts of his past that came to haunt him when he slept. Sometimes they were silent for weeks or months, sometimes they came nightly. What he had just experienced, he knew, would be added to that recurrent trend. He hated their visits. He would hate this new ghost just as much. Trying to focus one step at a time on feet that were numb, he was thankful that his eyes were now accustomed to the dark. He noticed that he couldn't feel his hands due to the cold. With his head facing downward to protect himself from the rain, he sensed a light coming towards him. He moved to the side of the road, dropping down onto a grass verge. A car was heading in his direction, its lights on full beam. He looked around. There was no way he could outrun it and there was no fence or tree to climb over or even hide behind. Around him were open fields, some with grass, others fallow. Within seconds the lights caught him, raindrops piercing the beams. The car began to slow, coming to a stop ten metres in front of him.

The call via the third party had been received overnight. Two requests had been made of him, the most difficult of them required some planning. The first however was his bread and butter, introducing sellers to buyers, and he had already arranged for a contact of his to meet at a secret location not far from the airfield. There were always those who wanted to make lots of money and his contact had several people interested in doing business. It was a tick in the box. The first request would be completed by day's end.

He would be meeting the plane shortly though he had initially struggled to find the location of the airfield, eventually establishing that it was a private strip out in the sticks near a place called Horton-cum-Studley. Such a remote place was exactly how he expected things to operate and he smiled at the caution shown.

With regards to the second request, the man followed the girl as far as he dared. When she drove up the narrow lane to reach the yard, he kept a safe distance in his own vehicle. It was still not yet light and the roads that had felt the ire of the rain lashing down upon them over the previous twenty-four hours were still littered with deep puddles of water that stretched across them in some places. In the ditches that hugged the asphalt lying between the road and the stonewalls of numerous farms, water gushed at pace creating streams like black snakes that squirmed and twisted as if hungry for a victim.

Thankfully the rain had ceased for now though there was no chance of any sun when it finally decided to rise above the eastern horizon. He saw the car start to indicate before turning left into a stable yard. As he passed the entrance he tried to see if the girl had alighted from the vehicle already but the micro-second that he had to check was lost. His view became obscured by the wall and trees on the right-hand side of the entrance gate. Unconcerned at this stage, he had what he needed. Even a simple deduction about an individual's daily habits was enough for him to make plans.

The second request and the one he would enjoy the most required the elimination of the girl

CHAPTER 38

Walker had planned to question Angela Fryer again. He and Conte had expected to leave around ten. They would drive directly to Cannon's yard where they knew she would be. It would be surprise visit as he did not want to give her any advance warning, intentionally hoping to keep her off guard, not allowing her to get her thoughts in sync with what she had told them previously. Walker was still convinced that Angela was a party to Van der Linden's drug dealing even though she had previously denied it. Just as she had denied knowing where her late boyfriend's metallic blue Kawasaki Ninja motorbike was hidden. By catching her unawares he hoped that she would make a mistake.

The unexpected call came through just after eight. It was still dark outside. A strong breeze from the west had helped the sky to feel less heavy. Clouds still threatened but were expected to thin out slightly, potentially reducing the chance of rain, though he doubted it. Walker had just sat down, a large takeaway coffee cup sat on his desk and he was about to reach for the Gladstone file when the phone began to ring. Picking up the receiver, he mumbled a "Yes?" into the mouthpiece.

"DC Walker?" the voice questioned.

"Yes," he replied insolently, at the voice that was disturbing his review of the case file that he had just started opening.

"This is George Froome, Director of Threat Leadership at the NCA."

Unimpressed and unsure why he was receiving such a phone call, Walker used his best Northeast accent in reply, "Oh aye, how can I help you?"

"I have some information for you which I think might be useful."

"Go on."

"I understand that you are looking into the death of a certain drug dealer in your neck of the woods?"

"What of it?"

A little exasperated at the tone of Walker's reply, Froome said, "Do you want my help or not, DI Walker?"

"Depends what it is."

"Well, I'll be succinct. After that, you can do with the information as you wish."

"I'm all ears."

"Good to know, Detective. Let's hope your brain is just as engaged."

Ignoring the insult, especially one from a more senior officer, Walker waited for Froome to continue.

"My colleague from our Intelligence section, has advised me of a certain flight from Scotland that is expected to arrive at an airfield near you within the next couple of hours. On it is a man called Amar Hyseni. He is a significant player in the importation of drugs into the UK. We are unsure how he has been doing this but our Intelligence folk have had a tip off that he is looking for another distributor in your area after the killing of a previous middle-man."

"One Nick Van der Linden?"

"If you say so."

"So you're suggesting that Van der Linden was a bigger player than we were to believe?"

"I'll leave that to you to decide."

Walker smiled to himself. He *was* right! Angela Fryer *was* the key.

"And this Hyseni?"

"If you do things right, he's yours."

"Meaning?"

"That if you arrest him, there is enough evidence to put him away for a very long time….and at the same time a significant drug network will have been smashed."

"Why are you telling me this…George? Isn't this your area?"

"Usually, yes. But I'm doing this as a favour to a colleague in Scotland. He knows that you are looking into Van der Linden's murder and the death of a school-teacher…."

"Hang on," Walker interrupted, "how does he know all this?"

"Look Inspector, all you need to know is that there has been an investigation going on for some time now, right across the country. Evidence has been collected and it will be led in due course, so rest assured…"

"What evidence? Where from?" Walker interrupted for the second time, annoying Froome considerably.

"As I said before, get out to the Ventfield Farm airfield and arrest Hyseni."

"Where the fuck is that?"

Froome provided him the details, letting Walker feel like a complete idiot. After Walker had repeated what he had been told, Froome immediately dropped off the line.

"Fucking hell," Walker said, curious and frustrated, banging down the phone handset onto its cradle. "Sergeant!" he shouted.

"Yes, Sir?" Conte answered, as he stuck his head through the open door.

"We've just got a lead on who may have killed Van der Linden. We need to get out to a fucking airstrip on the other side of Headington and quickly. Get some back up, we may need it."

Cannon was blinded by the car's headlights. Cold, wet, exhausted and fearful, he heard the splashes as someone stepped through several puddles, followed by the crunch of boots on stones that littered the edge of the road, between the tarmac and the grass where he sat.

A hand touched his shoulder and he flinched.

"Are you alright?" the voice asked.

Cannon looked up. Staring back was a face that was hidden in the beams of light that emanated from the car behind him, its engine still running. Recognizing the voice, Cannon smiled. "DCI Silvers am I happy to see you," he said, then began to laugh with sheer relief.

Silvers stuck out a hand, helping Cannon to his feet. "You look like a drowned rat," he said, turning back towards the car and signalling for help. The driver's door opened and Silvers shouted for the man to assist him to get Cannon to the car. "And bring me a blanket or a jacket or something, this man is drenched and may be suffering from hypothermia. And while you are at it, ask one of the others to call for an ambulance".

Responding in the affirmative the driver went to the rear of the car and opened the boot, finding a pair of blue police overalls and a camping blanket that was usually used in stakeouts.

Cannon thought Silvers' statement about his condition was over the top but didn't argue with the sentiment. Stumbling with support from Silvers, Cannon noticed that there were two other vehicles behind the first. It seemed the cavalry had come prepared. Once inside the car he removed his footwear then struggled out of his clothes. With the pain in his ribs causing him to stop and take a breath a couple of times he eventually managed to rid himself of his wet clothes, replacing them with the overalls. As he buttoned them up he pointed towards the abattoir buildings. Dawn had not yet broken but the buildings were visible, still lit up by the spotlights, just as he had left them. "There's a bit of a mess, down there," he said.

Silvers nudged the driver of the car. "Drive down there and stop at the bottom. I want the team to seal off the place off until I get back."

"Yes, Sir," the driver replied.

The convoy of three vehicles moved down to the buildings, stopping in front of the door that Cannon had exited from.

"I'll be back in a minute," Silvers said. He jumped out of the car and into the rain. Cannon watched him through the rear window, issuing instructions to a group of five men from the other two cars. With an unheard voice, hand gestures, arms like windmills, Cannon could see what Silvers wanted done while he was away. No one other than Forensics to enter any building, a cordon to be put around all of them and when an ambulance did arrive it needed to wait for him until he was back on scene. Once he was finished and back inside the car, Silvers told the driver to "step on it." The driver responded eagerly.

As they turned onto the main road heading towards Kelso, Silvers said, "It was just as well that you let me know where you were going, Mike. I nearly lost you."

Cannon was confused. "I didn't know that I'd end up here. The last time I messaged you, I was at Williams' farm."

"But you did tell us about this place, remember?"

Thinking for a second, Cannon recalled that during his reconnaissance he had driven past the entrance to the abattoir and had provided the information to Silvers.

"One thing I don't know though," he said, "is how you got here so quickly. Ayr is a bloody long way from here."

"That's true, but I've been in Melrose all along, ever since you agreed to come up here. It's about twenty-five minutes from Kelso."

"Bloody hell," Cannon replied.

"I'm sorry, Mike, but I needed to stay on the periphery and give you space. Without your help we wouldn't have been able to crack this case."

With a heavy sigh Cannon sat back into his seat. He was relieved that his ordeal was over. He wanted to get home as soon as he could, suggesting to Silvers that his wounds were superficial.

"We'll let the doctors determine that," the policeman replied. "Then later today, once I've returned from having a look at what happened back there," he pointed with his thumb in the direction that they had come from, "and you are ready, you can tell me all about it."

CHAPTER 39

The man waited in his car. He had parked it alongside the small hut that stood by the side of the grass landing strip. The structure was little more than a five metre by four by three tin shed. He looked at his watch. The plane was late. After rubbing away the condensation with his hand, he stared upwards through the misty windscreen and then through his own side window. The only thing visible were low grew clouds, moving quickly, perhaps a hundred metres above the ground. He wound down his window slightly, hoping to hear the engines of a plane close by. Nothing!
Feeling annoyed but also wary that something may have gone wrong he looked at his watch for a second time in as many minutes. He would give it five more then he would leave. Finding another distributor wasn't his job anyway. His first obligation was to *help* the man on the plane with introductions, no more, no less. He knew the passenger was called Hyseni but had no need to know anything else about him. Apart from collecting Hyseni, he was also required to act as muscle, as protection and to ensure that the visitor left the country knowing that there was solid business to be done with whoever Hyseni came to an agreement with. His other purpose, and the one that he would enjoy the most, was the elimination of the girl.
It had been easy for him to take out the boyfriend. He had pretended to be a customer wanting some action after a late-night appointment at the tattoo parlour. The man had convinced Van der Linden that all he wanted was to score, and to score big. They had arranged to meet in the garage used to house the shop's motorbikes. The Dutchman was always keen to sell more product. Doing so allowed him to cream more off the top. He regularly claimed that he was being short-changed on weight and on quality by his suppliers, and often refused to pay the full price for what was supplied to him. He had become greedy and eventually his behaviour became unacceptable. He believed that he was too far removed from the source and that the market was large enough for the big boys to leave him alone. Unfortunately they were not. He had made a fatal mistake. He thought that his new customer who had used the right name as an introduction could only be good for business. Van der Linden soon found out that it wasn't.

The man waiting inside the car had used a knife with a twenty-centimetre blade that he hidden inside his jacket sleeve. When Van der Linden had turned his back on him, a single thrust through the back and into the heart had been enough. A bullet to the head was done for good measure. Disposal of the body had been just as easy.
Starting to get impatient and no longer willing to wait he was just about to start the car when he heard a plane approaching. He was unable to tell from which direction the sound was coming, as the cloud cover seemed to be creating a distortion; the Doppler effect. He looked left and right then back again, just as the plane sank below the curtain of cloud touching down onto the grass runway a few seconds later. The man silently commended the pilot for his skill of landing the plane on a runway that had no navigation lights. As the Cessna 172 Skyhawk slowed to a stop and began turning around and making its way to the shed, the man climbed out of the car. As he watched the small craft glide towards him, its whining engine quietly masked the three cars that turned off the Straight Mile Road and sped through the gates that led into the field where the airstrip stood. The three vehicles slithered across the grassy paddock stopping in a well-practiced cordon, almost encircling the man's car. Noticing them at the last minute, the man had no time to run. Car doors opened and shouts of "Police", "Get Down," "On your knees," "Hands on your head" rang out, as six police officers, some from the Tactical Wing appropriately armed, took their positions. For a second the man wasn't sure if he should try and shoot his way out of trouble. The odds were against him anyway and as far as he knew, the police had no idea who he was. They certainly wouldn't be aware of his involvement in the killing of Van der Linden. That had been done without any witnesses. As far as he was concerned he was just a hired taxi, asked to meet a passenger on a plane. Where he was to take the passenger would be a discussion for later, if at all. The reason he was carrying a gun however would be much more difficult to justify.
The plane stopped ten metres in front of him, the engines were cut. The man knelt down, his hands in the air. He pretended to look confused, a picture of innocence. Facing the numerous policemen, he watched as one of them who appeared to be the senior officer, begin walking towards him.
Showing a warrant card, the policeman identified himself as DI Sam Walker.

"What are you doing here?" Walker asked, curiously, keeping the man on his knees, his hands now on top of his head.
"I've been asked to collect someone."
"Who?"
"A passenger," the man replied, blandly.
"Do you know his name?"
"No."
Walker could tell the man was lying. He looked towards the aircraft that now stood silently. The pilot was climbing out of his seat and down onto the grass.
"What's going on?" the pilot asked, looking confused at the sight of the armed police. Walker pointed at the plane. "Anyone else?" he asked.
"No, no one turned up. I waited for a while then as there was no sign, I left. Been paid upfront so not my problem," he said.
"Fuck," Walker said under his breath, thinking that he had been sent on a wild goose chase. Looking at the man on the ground in front of him, he asked, "What's your name?"
"Charlie Smith."
Walker knew that the name was bullshit. "Sergeant," he called, "frisk Mr. *Smith* here, let's see what he has on him."
Conte helped the man up from the ground and within seconds the gun was found, a Beretta 92 semi-automatic. Conte held it up with two fingers for Walker to see.
"Arrest him," Walker said, smiling.
At least their efforts weren't in vain or a total waste of time, he thought. The arrest of a taxi driver with a gun, someone waiting to pick up a drug lord at a remote airfield was something! You didn't see that every day. Silently, he thanked George Froome and the NCA.
"Take him away," he said, "we can have a little chat down at the station."
"And what about me?" the pilot asked. The man had remained still, leaning against the plane's fuselage and watching what was unfolding in front of him.
"My men will get your details, and we'll be in touch," Walker said, thinking that other than how the pilot had been paid, and by whom, there was likely very little information the man would be able to provide them that would be of any use. Walker guessed that Froome already knew the answers anyway. He didn't think that the pilot was

involved with Hyseni, concluding that the man was simply providing a genuine charter service. His experience told him that anyone involved in drug running would have known who his passenger was, especially someone as involved as Hyseni and if the passenger didn't arrive as expected then the pilot would have tried to find out why. Flying off without the expected 'cargo' would not have been a good idea, particularly if the flight had taken off and gone to the original destination. Such a trip would have been unnecessary and potentially risky even if someone was waiting to meet it. Private charter planes were often small independent one-man businesses, even jockeys used them at times. The services were often discrete, no names being asked for except an understanding that time was money and that the planes had to be paid for. Accordingly they needed to be in the air as much as possible, generating income. If passengers didn't arrive when they should, even if they had paid for the trip, pilots didn't wait for them any longer than was absolutely necessary. Walker waved the man away and headed towards his car.

The pilot called out a thank you still bemused by what he had just experienced, then watched as two of three groups of police climbed back into their cars and drove away. The two police officers left behind, took photographs with their mobile phones of the small aircraft, paying particular attention to the tail number and establishing from the pilot the call sign he used to identify the plane during flight. Once the remaining policemen had all the details they required including the pilot's personal details and a contact number, they also drove away leaving the car of the man they had arrested standing forlornly in the now empty field.

"I guess they'll come and take it away," the pilot said to himself as he climbed back into his cockpit and checked his diary before writing the details of his latest flight into the airplanes logbook. He noted that he had another customer to collect and was required to take them to Barton Aerodrome near Manchester. "I'd better get a move on," he said, starting the engines and checking his instruments.

CHAPTER 40

Cannon's release from hospital was quick. His departure for home was less so. With his ribs strapped and his wounds treated he had spent the entire afternoon and early evening with Silvers taking him through what had happened at the abattoir.

The debrief was long but Cannon was prepared for it. Having been involved in many such discussions he knew the process and the rationale behind it. When he been allowed to leave the hospital, he had been taken to the Kelso police station where he had been able to contact Michelle. With no phone of his own he had relied on the police's generosity. It had taken a while for her to answer the strange landline number she had noticed on her mobile phone's screen, initially thinking that it was nuisance call, but eventually they had connected. He had explained that he would only be home the following day, but that he was okay, fit enough to drive and safe. Remarkably, despite being stripped of his coat and his mobile, the police found that his car keys were still inside his jeans pocket. They had come across them when they removed the bundle of his wet clothes from the back seat of the police car used to take him to the hospital. Silvers had instructed one of his men to collect the vehicle, which they found was still where Cannon had left it.

Sitting inside the interview room with a face that felt full of scratches, cuts and nicks, his ribs ached while he sipped the hot mug of tea that Silvers had arranged for him. Two other police officers had joined the debrief at Silvers' request. A recording of their meeting would be used to transcribe his commentary into a written statement.

Cannon explained in detail what had happened at the abattoir after he had recovered consciousness there. He advised them that he had no idea where those who had escaped the building had gone to.

"We've been able to resolve that," Silvers said. "Seemingly the death of one of their colleagues was enough to frighten them all into handing themselves into the police at Hawick. Apparently they were illegals hired to work in the abattoir and to do what you have already described."

"And not only here either?" Cannon questioned.

"No, it seems that there are a number of sites where the same

arrangement is in play. Leeds, Worcester and not forgetting Ayr."
"Just as I thought," Cannon said.
"Yes, you did a great job Mike, we wouldn't have been able to do this without you."
"And Williams, what's happened to him?"
"He's also been arrested and he's been very cooperative."
"How?"
"Well the killing of people was probably a bit too much. Seems he didn't mind the horses, but …"
"Which seems contradictory doesn't it," Cannon interrupted, "given he's supposed to be a horse trainer."
"Probably a greedy one at that, but he does have some humanity in him."
"By not being involved in my murder?"
"Yes, but he's also opened up a lot since we arrested him." Silvers said. "He's been trying to strike a deal, to save his skin. He gave us some details about a flight that his visitor, his boss, Hyseni, was going to take…to your neck of the woods actually."
"To do what?" Cannon queried.
"It seems that Hyseni was to meet with someone down there to discuss them becoming a new distributor. Apparently Hyseni had arranged for …"
"Nick Van der Linden to be killed," Cannon interrupted.
"Yes, and it seems the same hitman was to kill your apprentice."
"Bloody hell!"
"You can say that again," Silvers said. "Thank Christ Williams lost his nerve. We passed the information on to the NCA and I believe they did the same to your 'friend' DI Walker…as a favour to me. Let's hope he has acted on it."
"I hope so too. It would certainly get him off my back," Cannon replied.
"Absolutely."
Relieved at what he was hearing, he took a sip of tea then said, "You know that this wasn't only about drugs don't you?"
"What do you mean?" Silvers answered, quizzically. He looked at the others in the room. They too seemed surprised.
Cannon guessed that what he was about to say would shock Silvers From the collective reaction, it was clear that Williams had not confessed to everything. Taking his time, Cannon explained what he

had uncovered..

"It was the scratchings that gave it away."

"The scratchings?"

"Yes. When I was at Wincanton and I looked in on the horse that I used to train, a horse called Jacko Lantern."

"What about it?" Silvers asked.

"Well two things stood out. One, the horse was way past her best, and could never have competed in the race she was down for. Secondly the girl grooming her, Rachel Brits, she had only been working for Williams for a short while and had very little knowledge of the horses' capabilities. It seems that this was deliberate, his M.O."

"You lost me," Silvers said, looking at the other two men in the room who had stayed silent so far. Both shrugged their shoulders as if to say, "me too!"

"When I got back home I checked up on the horse, where it had run in recent years and who had owned it since I last had her in my yard. I did the same thing again, later. Jim Franklin one of the senior jockeys who sometimes rides for me, mentioned something about another horse called Uncle Buck when we were at the Wincanton meeting. I looked into its races as well. It seemed to have gone across to Germany to race but never did. That was the clue."

"Germany?"

"Those horses were never going to race. They were a ruse. Williams did exactly the same with another horse called Dark Chocolate which he nominated to run here this week at Kelso."

"Which was why you came up here?"

"Yes, and I guess I got lucky. I just happened to be at the right place at the right time," Cannon continued. "The three trucks that I saw at Williams' farm yesterday evening helped proved my theory."

Silvers was finding the explanation a little confusing. His two colleagues agreed. He asked Cannon to explain what he meant, recalling that the investigation had originally started after he had contacted Cannon for help after the discovery of the head of the horse known as Noble Goblet in a field near Kilmarnock. At that time the only thing they knew was that someone was illegally dumping the bodies of thoroughbred racehorses.

"Okay, let me take you through it," Cannon said.

"That would be useful," chimed in the elder of the other two police officers in the room.

"Firstly let's talk about the three trucks. One was used to take horses to the abattoir. These were horses that I believe had been used as drug mules, then nominated later by Williams as if they were to race somewhere, but never would. The nomination idea was used as a pretence. It was designed to make it look like Williams was running a proper training and racing establishment."

"The scratchings," Silvers noted.

"Yes. As I mentioned, I checked their racing history. Many of them were nominated to race in Europe, but never showed. They were taken across to the continent, operated on, drugs inserted inside them, then shipped back over here, ready to be processed."

"Hang on, Mr. Cannon, if I may," the third police officer said. "How did you come to that conclusion?"

Cannon smiled. In his past life as a cop, he had always enjoyed the process of questioning things. The tying up of a suspect in verbal knots during an investigative interview was a skill that he had been able to use successfully many times. It seemed that he was having the same effect on the three men that were sharing the room with him.

Carrying on with his explanation, he said, "When I looked into all the recent scratchings that Williams had declared, every one of them was a mare. As I have mentioned already, each of them had been sent to Europe but none ever raced. This was extremely unusual as you'd imagine." He paused for affect, then added, "I assume you gentleman know about the anatomy of the male and female horse?"

In reply to his question, he received only shakes of heads.

"A female horse has a uterus, just like a human female, though obviously different in design. So, without going into too much detail what I can say to you is that the animals sent abroad, were sent there solely to be operated on and drugs inserted inside them, just like humans occasionally do. The uterus was the box where the drugs were hidden. Once the drugs were in place, the animal was then shipped back to the UK."

"And then what?" the second officer asked, leaning forward in his chair, placing his elbows on the table and his hands under his chin.

"Simple. The drugs were removed and the horse was killed, in the abattoir."

"But wouldn't someone working with horses be aware of this? Didn't you say you spoke with the groom of your old horse? Jacko Lantern, wasn't it?"

"Yes, and that horse was scratched as well. For the same reason that I mentioned previously, it was all a sham, a pretence. You see Williams was trying to make it look like the horses he had to scratch from races were both female *and* male. To only scratch female horses would have raised a red flag. By doing what he did it would appear to the authorities on track, the Stewards, that something had happened to the horse as they often do in racing. Horses occasionally arrive at a racecourse with a temperature or are found to be lame. He used this uncertainty to his advantage. Oh, and regarding your question about the groom, it seems that Williams moved them on very quickly, giving them little time to get used to the horses under their care and know their true racing capability."

"Another part of the ruse," Silvers said.

"Yes, but that's only part of it. That wasn't the only game in town."

"Go on?"

"As I've already stated, there were three trucks there last night. Each of them was to be used for a different reason." Cannon stared into the faces of each man in turn. He could sense their anticipation, hanging on his every word. "One of the horses I saw going onto the first truck was a horse called Dark Chocolate. It was scratched at yesterday's meeting. Being put onto that very same truck was another horse, one I mentioned earlier, Uncle Buck. Uncle Buck was a gelding, a male. He had been put up for sale and somehow Williams got hold of him."

"Which meant what?"

"That there was something else going on."

"How do mean?" Silvers asked.

"Jim Franklin, the jockey I told you about, well he let me know a few days ago that the horse had been bought by Williams on behalf of a third party for one hundred and twenty thousand pounds."

"Isn't that cheap for a racehorse?" the second officer asked? "I've heard they can cost millions."

"Not for a horse with little ability and supposedly competing in the jumping game. Ten grand at the most would be what the horse was worth….if that," Cannon replied, realizing as he spoke that policing and horse racing knowledge didn't always mix.

"So what are you saying, Mike?".

"That the purchase of Uncle Buck, and I'd guess most others that Williams was involved with, was all about money laundering."

"What?"

"Yes, think about it. All the money made through their drug network has to be washed somehow. Buying a racehorse that you are never going to run but intend to use it as a drug mule, quite literally, makes perfect sense to me, particularly if you are 'paying' an inflated price for the animal. In fact if you have a friendly agent to help you with the transaction, that's even better. You can use that agent as a way to send the cleaned money overseas…it works perfectly. Nowadays to transfer money through any number of banks to any number of countries, especially those in tax havens is easy if you know how."

"But doesn't the seller get the cash for the purchase?

"No."

"So how does paying over the odds help anyone?"

"It works like this. Williams would have been invoiced by an agent for the purchase of a horse, such as Uncle Buck, at a price far in excess of what the original seller was asking for it. It's the agent who actually buys the horse from the seller. The agent purchases the animal at X pounds, then 'sells' the same animal to Williams at an inflated amount. The actual price the agent would have paid to the seller would be minimal. Williams then 'settles' his account with the agent using the cash collected from the drugs they brought into the country using the female horses. The agent takes a commission from the 'purchase' price and ships the rest of the money to wherever Williams wants it to go. They do this repeatedly. It's a vicious circle, but highly effective."

"And you were able to tie this together based on the three trucks that you saw last night?" the second officer asked, still struggling to understand how simple yet how clever the whole scheme was.

"Yes, they were the key, particularly when I saw Uncle Buck being loaded. As I already explained, truck one was going to the abattoir. These were horses that had been processed already. They were no longer useful. Of the other two trucks, one contained the new arrivals, horses that had been previously shipped out, nominated in races on the continent somewhere but never participated in. They were the carriers having been operated on and having the drugs inserted within them. When they arrived at Williams' farm the drugs were to be recovered and either the horse would be used again later to carry more drugs or they would be just become dog meat, like those on the first truck."

"And the other truck, the third?"

"They were the newly purchased horses. The ones that were paid for at inflated prices. They were being shipped out to be operated on, sent by boat I'd guess, as if they were going to race in Germany, Holland, France or somewhere else. Once they had the drugs inside of them, they would have been shipped back, and the entire cycle would have been repeated."

"So, some in, some out, some killed, then do the same again, is that what you mean?" Silvers asked.

"Ostensibly yes."

"And these agents you referred to do you think that Nick Van der Linden, was one."

"Probably," Cannon replied, "though I don't know for sure. It wouldn't surprise me if he was, as he always had more money than his tattoo business would have been able to generate."

As he said the words, he suddenly thought of the request from the HMRC for the thousands of pounds that they were claiming he owed them. He would need to phone Horowitz again as soon as he got home. It gave him an idea. "Perhaps look into Williams' tax records as well. I'm sure you will find some anomalies there too. He won't be able to hide everything."

CHAPTER 41

DI Walker was pleased with himself at the arrest they had made. The ballistics of the gun seized from the man at the landing strip were being checked against the bullet used on Van der Linden. Despite the body having been found in the water, the slug had remained lodged in the Dutchman's brain and had been easily extracted.

"A callous and unnecessary action," Jenny Cribb had said when she had examined the body. "He was already dead before the shooting."

Walker was certain that the man they had in custody was the killer. His impatience and propensity to jump to conclusions still bothered his team and despite further work needing to be done before they could lay charges against the man, Walker advised them that his waters were telling him that he was right about the suspect.

Now all he had to do was close off the Gladstone case. He contemplated the evidence that they had accumulated so far. He decided that there was no other solution. There was no motorbike, Cannon was off the hook and Van der Linden was dead. As far as he was concerned, the case was closed. You couldn't charge a dead man. Karma had come for Van der Linden after he ran down Sue Gladstone and that was that.

He concluded that their job was done.

He picked up the phone and made the call.

Cannon arrived home just as the second lot were being unsaddled in the yard. The rest of the staff were busy with the general cleanup of the horse boxes from overnight and the settling down of those horses from the first lot. A feed and a washdown for those whose exercise and training had been completed earlier, was already underway. The morning light was almost nonexistent, thick cloud cover still hovered overhead and the cobblestones and cement at the base of each stable glistened from the steady drizzle that had fallen overnight. The bright spotlights that lit up the yard reflected in some of the puddles that rippled and shook as a breeze from the west skimmed across them. Fortunately the rain had stopped for now but was expected to start again at some point during the day. Woodstock was warmer than Kelso but the horses still gave off steam from their exertions and he was happy to see it. He was glad to be back.

Having left Scotland at three in the morning, the drive down south had taken him the best part of six hours. Fortunately, with the exception of a few trucks that barrelled along the motorway, the road was quiet, at least until halfway.

After the meeting with Silvers and the other two officers had finished, Cannon and the DCI had decided to grab a bite to eat together at The Cobbles on Bowmont Street. The pub was a short walk from the Cross Keys hotel where Cannon had been able to get a room for the night. He had originally expected to leave for home immediately after the meeting but Silvers had suggested to him that given his recent experiences, a good meal and some bed rest was a more sensible thing to do, rather than to rush things. Reluctantly Cannon had agreed, though he planned to sleep for a few hours only. Getting home was his priority as he still had other matters to resolve, not least of which was to have his conversation with Rich. After dinner he had contacted Michelle again using his hotel room landline. They had shared a brief call and he had let her know that he was sore but comfortable. He had agreed to give her a complete rundown about what had happened when he eventually got home. Before turning off the light he had checked his watch, it was 9:45. He had hoped to call Rich earlier but had forgotten and now it was too late. He knew that his friend would be asleep. He would catch up with him once he was back in Woodstock.

Michelle ran out to greet him, giving him a huge hug which caused him to wince. He hadn't mentioned the damage to his ribs or anything else about his injuries and when she looked into his face, she held a hand to her mouth, shocked at how swollen it was. She took a step back and pointed at his clothes.

"A new set, courtesy of the Ayrshire police" he offered, "well perhaps not so new, but from a good Op-Shop at least," he said, smiling at his own joke. "It's the best that they could do for me under the circumstances."

"My God, Mike," she said, taking him by the arm and leading him into the house, "come and sit down in the lounge. I'll make you some tea in a minute and then you can tell me everything."

She noticed that he had a slight limp and asked him about it. He shrugged it off as nothing serious. Reluctantly, though doubtfully, she accepted it as such.

"I took the day off as I wanted to be here with you," she said, as she walked to the kitchen. "The school was okay with it, now that poor Sue Gladstone has been farewelled."

"Thank you," he called in response. "I suppose things are slowly getting back to normal then?"

"Hardly, but the Headmaster has started advertising for a replacement already."

"That's good to hear. Hopefully it will mean that you'll get some hours back for yourself."

"I hope so. It's been hell this last week or two."

"I'm sure," he answered. He expected her to continue talking but she stayed silent, clearly busy. Sitting quietly, he closed his eyes and let his head slump onto the back of the couch. He could hear cups and spoons clinking together and water boiling in the kettle. When she brought the cups into the room he opened his eyes, rubbed them gently, then sat forward. He was about to reach for the drink that she was holding out to him, when a sudden thought struck him. It was something she had said. It was the answer.

"I need to speak to Rich as soon as I can," he said.

Michelle answered him indignantly, letting him know in no uncertain terms that he had hardly sat down and insisted that he tell her everything that had happened to him, before he did anything else.

"Rich will come in to see you at some point this morning, just as he always does," she said. "Let him do what he needs to do around the stables first, before you start chasing him."

"Okay," he conceded reluctantly, too tired to argue.

"By the way, he's done a great job as usual since you went up there," she added. "When I got home from school the other night he called and told me the results from the Kelso meeting. Everyone was so pleased."

"I hope the staff had a few quid on them?"

"He didn't say, but he did tell me that the horses had arrived home safely and had eaten up well. It seems that they have both pulled up okay from their respective races."

"Those boys are great," he agreed, referring to Radcliffe and Simmons. "We are very lucky to have them."

"Talking of being lucky, and I hope it didn't get down to that Mike," she said, her voice expressing her concern, "but you said last night that you would tell me everything that happened to you up there once you got back. So…. Now's your chance."

It took him longer than he expected and when he had finished, his ribs were hurting more than ever. She interrupted him with questions whenever she felt that he had left something out. At certain times he did, particularly the gruesome details of Hyseni's death and that of the abattoir worker. He used the words 'shot' and 'collided with a machine' leaving her to draw her own conclusions as to what type of gun and what type of machine he was referring to. As he shared with her, he felt that he was reliving the ordeal and he saw the ghosts of the dead in his mind's eye. He knew at some point in the future, like many others from his past, they would come to visit him again.

"So, it's all over now?" she asked.

"Yes, other than the trial of Williams and those who worked for him."

"You said that this thing, this mule business was all over the country?"

"In specific towns, yes."

"And Nick Van der Linden was a big part of it."

"Yes, more than anyone realized."

"Poor Angela," she said, sympathetically. "That girl has been through hell."

"True."

"Oh, I almost forgot," she said, tapping a hand to her head, indicating her sudden recollection of what she needed to tell him. "That detective…DI Walker, he called last night and told me that Sue's case had been closed. The police believe that it was Nick who killed her. He said that the evidence they had was only circumstantial because they haven't found the motorbike despite an extensive search for it. They've tried locally and have been through the DVLA records but come up empty. He said that they think Nick dumped it or destroyed it somehow, but as he's dead, they won't be taking it any further. The coroner will probably declare death by person or persons unknown, despite the police's suspicions."

He was about to reply when the phone in his office started to ring.

He stood up, wincing slightly still feeling slightly unsteady on his feet. "No rest for the wicked," he said, making his way towards the hallway and his office, "and that's without a bloody mobile too!" He called jokingly, pulling out the lining of his 'new' trouser pockets, to show her that he had no mobile phone on him.

Picking up the handset on the sixth ring, Cannon answered with a bland, "Hello."

"Mr. Cannon?" the caller questioned, "Cyril Horowitz from Plumberry Accounting."

"Oh right. I was just thinking about calling you."

"Well, no need, Mr. Cannon. I'm glad I got in first," the Accountant said, chuckling to himself, "and I have some good news for you."

"I could do with some, Cyril. I've had a difficult couple of days."

"I'm sorry to hear that, Mr. Cannon. I hope that what I'm about to tell you goes some way to improving things for you."

Cannon stayed quiet, letting Horowitz have the floor.

"It relates to the issue with the tax man," Horowitz explained, "As we discussed previously, the assessment you received recently had to be incorrect. Well, indeed it was and I was able to prove it. I'm happy to say that the HMRC has accepted the matter as their error and have agreed to rescind the request for payment."

"That's good to hear. So what happened?"

"Without going into too much detail the problem related to how the HMRC assessed some of your activities. For instance a significant deduction on the return that we did for you was wrongly dismissed by them. They misunderstood the details of a syndicate that you were in and assessed you as if you were the trainer of the horse that the syndicate owned. In fact as we know, you had no direct involvement with the horse, other than simply being a syndicate member. Therefore they taxed you on the winnings made through the syndicate, incorrectly. Those winnings are actually tax free. In addition, on the dispersal sale of the horse, when the syndicate ended, no capital gains tax was to apply. Again they wrongly assessed this. Finally, there was a VAT error as well. VAT on the purchase of a racehorse that you own outright, one Annie Girl I believe, is actually recoverable. They missed that too. There were a few more, less troublesome matters as well, but we were able to sort them out for you. I hope that answers your question?."

Cannon didn't know what to say. The complexities of the tax system he left to his Accountants.

"So I suppose you'd like to know the net of all this?" Horowitz asked.

"Yes, as long as it's not too large a bill, I suppose I'll live with it."
"I'm sure you will Mr. Cannon, however the net, net, of all the changes means that you are due a refund."
"A refund?"
"Yes."
"How much?" Anything back from the tax man was always welcome. Rare but welcome.
"Seven thousand, six hundred and forty-two pounds and eleven pence."
"That's amazing Mr. Horowitz. Fantastic. You've made my day."
"Glad to be of service, and I just want to add one thing."
"Yes?" Cannon said, expecting a 'but'.
"The figure I quoted you is net of our charges, which were five hundred and sixty-five pounds."
Using a bit of mental arithmetic Cannon realized that the turnaround Horowitz had achieved was almost ninety-two thousand pounds, if the actual tax refund before fees was over eight thousand. It definitely had made his day.
"I will send you the revised assessment by email shortly," Horowitz advised.
"Thank you."
"Is there anything else I can help you with Mr. Cannon?"
"No, I think you've done plenty well Cyril. I really do appreciate it.
"That's my pleasure and thank you for using Plumberry Accounting."
The conversation ended and Cannon sat back in his chair thankful that at least one of his problems was solved. Now though he had to address the most difficult problem of all and it was one that he had been loath to do, putting it off several times, either by design or due to circumstance.
From the quiet of his office, he heard voices. Rich and Michelle. Telside had obviously come into the house while he had been talking with Horowitz and concentrating on the call.
He went to the door and motioned down the hallway, letting them know that he was free to talk. Telside shared a quick laugh with Michelle then walked down to the office. Cannon asked him to close the door.
"Must be serious, Mike," he said, before asking him how he was feeling.
"To be honest Rich, I'm not sure how I'm feeling. In some ways I

feel okay physically, except for my ribs, but mentally….! One positive thing though, my head and face doesn't hurt as much as it did, it just looks worse than it feels."

"Well I can't tell you how happy I am to see you. Michelle was filling me in on some of what happened."

"I'm happy to be back too," he replied. "The horses went well up there as you know, but the rest of the trip was a nightmare, something I wouldn't like to experience ever again."

Although Cannon sounded weary, Telside answered him honestly, "Perhaps!" he remarked, a sad smile crossing his face.

By way of a reply, Cannon nodded, "Maybe you're right Rich, and that's why I want to talk to you."

Telside was already prepared for the conversation. He had seen how his boss had tried to introduce the subject several times in recent weeks and had already weighed up all his options in advance of it happening.

"Go on, Mike. Say you want to say."

Gathering his thoughts together, Cannon took a few seconds before answering. "I've been worried about you Rich. Ever since your by-pass I've been wondering when it would be time for you to put your feet up. Perhaps that time is now?" he asked.

"And what would I do then, Mike?"

"I don't know. Travel with your missus. Read books, play some bowls. I suppose you could enjoy more free time and do whatever you want to do with it."

"That's not very convincing, Mike," Telside replied, "and anyway, tell me, what would you do without me?"

"I haven't given it much thought to be honest. I wanted to get your view first before I did anything."

Telside chuckled to himself, saying something that Cannon had no answer for. "All I know is horses. It's been my life longer than I can remember. Since you and I got together, we have gone from my mentoring you, right the way through to a friendship that to me is unbreakable…especially at my age," he joked. "During that time we have relied on each other, in so many ways. Me on you, when I was ill and you on me, when you've been away."

"That's indisputable, Rich."

"And I'd guess, as I said earlier, that it's likely to happen again."

Cannon was going to interrupt him but decided to let his friend continue speaking.

"I'm not ready to hang up my boots, Mike. In fact I don't think I ever will be. Horses, this place, our relationship, is what keeps me going. I hope you understand that?"

Cannon noted the quiet pathos reflected within Telside's words. He only had one response. "I do, Rich," he said, "I get it. I never really wanted to have this chat, but I also didn't want you to think that I was taking advantage of you, especially given recent events."

Telside smiled, then held out his hand. "Thank you Mike," he said, "for listening, and for being who you are."

The two men shook hands. Cannon was glad that the conversation was over. They could get back to normal now, with nothing standing between them. It also meant that he could focus on the final piece of the puzzle that had been niggling at him for days. He decided to fill Telside in on what he was thinking, adding "I'd like your help with something, Rich, perhaps a bit of advice too."

CHAPTER 42

They had decided that it was best to talk to her that evening. She would be busy before then with evening stables as she still wasn't allowed to ride. Despite the ban she was diligently doing all the other jobs that were requested of her. It was all they could ask. The timing they had agreed upon was perfect as it gave him the opportunity of using the afternoon to send Silvers some of the detail that he had collated about Williams and the way his operation worked. He had been able to show how the man had been constantly adding or removing horses into or out of his portfolio, keeping a consistent figure of sixteen horses supposedly in work, when in fact that number was an ever-revolving door, through which multiple horses traversed. Cannon was also able to provide the price paid for each horse, having found a source on the web where every official racehorse sale was recorded. What he didn't know however was how much Williams' agents invoiced the trainer, for each horse bought. He hoped that sometime soon, the HMRC would be on the case, and good forensic accounting would quickly be able to get a much better picture of the millions of pounds of dirty money that had been cleaned through the scheme. Despite this gap, Cannon knew that he was right about the way things operated. He was even able to show Silvers how few runs the geldings Williams had acquired, actually made, and where they finished in each of their races….those that did run, never finished anywhere near the front. This proved how Williams had tried to keep up the pretence of being a genuine trainer, just as Cannon had highlighted. The clincher that confirmed his theory however was the detail behind the number of mares that Williams had bought and how most of them were sent to the continent to race but were always scratched before even reaching a racecourse. He had also been able to get hold of records from the APHA who were supposed to monitor the movement of horses into Europe and beyond, and whose officials were required to check a horse's passport whenever they came into or left the UK. He found out with concern, that the agency had admitted some years earlier, that they could not check every one of the movements, and if a microchip could not be found in a horse's neck when presented for transiting across borders, they would be guided by the photograph on the passport. If it was the same, then they would let the animal through. Cannon wasn't sure if Hyseni or his co-conspirators ever managed to find a way to beat the system in this way, but he told Silvers to have a Vet look at the mares that were still at Williams' farm and have them checked to confirm or otherwise, if any had had their chip removed. If they had, he explained that it was likely that some of the horses being brought into the country may not be the same horse that went out of the country in the first instance. A ringer could have been used. His conclusion was that some of the horses that Williams sent into Europe would have died when having drugs inserted inside them. The process was not easy and would have been uncomfortable and dangerous to the animal. So, if they needed it, a horse passport and a missing microchip was too good an angle for Williams to ignore. The ringer horse coming into the country was to be slaughtered after being processed at Williams' farm anyway. Like those sent to the abattoirs in the other parts of the country, the ringer would have done its job and would not be needed any longer than absolutely necessary. The evidence, the poor animal, would be quickly disposed of. How the animal's heads were being destroyed or gotten rid of, he couldn't articulate completely, but the use of the river or deep water was a possibility, especially given the closeness of the abattoir in Kelso to the rivers Tweed and Teviot. Recalling what had happened to Noble Goblet it was possible that some workers may have panicked, concerned at what they were getting involved in. It was also possible that they made their own decisions and tried to bury heads in nearby fields rather than dispose of them some other way. He guessed that mistakes could have been made by the workers too, either that or they showed dissent to their masters and ignored the rules. Either way, such a mistake had started this entire thing off.

After finishing his report which he emailed to Silvers just after five pm, he had received a phone call, within minutes, from the detective.
"I've just seen your document, Mike. Pretty extensive, thank you."
"I hope it helps."
"It does, and no doubt it will corroborate what our friend Williams has to say for himself. He's singing like a bird."
"Good to hear, John."
"Oh, by the way, we found your coat and your phone. I'll courier

them down to you. With luck they'll get to you the day after tomorrow."

"Thanks."

"No, Mike, I should be thanking you. I dragged you into this and you nearly got killed. I didn't ever intend to put you in danger."

"I know, but it can happen," Cannon replied. "Thank God we all got out of it relatively unscathed."

"Agreed. One more thing though before you go. I've got Interpol involved to look into Hyseni and his operation in Europe. I'm not sure how long it will take but I may need you to act as a witness when Williams comes to trial."

"Happy to help."

"I knew you would. Anyway, I have to go. Take care….and thanks again."

Cannon and Michelle had been able to have some dinner together.
He shared with her what had kept him busy all afternoon.
When he had finished telling her about his chat with Silvers he remembered that he had forgotten to tell her about his call with Horowitz. Ready to take a bite of some chicken, she stopped, holding the fork a few centimetres away from her mouth. She hesitated then placed the fork back onto her plate. Cannon noticed her reaction. He smiled before popping part of a roast potato into his own mouth.

"So what did her say?" she asked, knowing how concerned he was about the tax he had been asked to pay.

"Nothing really," he teased.

"Nothing? What about the…"

"The debt we owe?"

"Yes, where are we going to get that amount of money from?"

He smiled at her. "We don't."

"We don't?" she repeated.

"No, it was all a mistake."

He explained to her what he had been told and mentioned the refund. As he did so, he saw her smile. He knew that he had made a mistake.

"Perfect timing," she said. "I wanted to talk to you about Cassie's wedding dress."

Within seconds he had tuned out, hardly hearing what she was saying to him. He nodded when he had to and shook his head when

required, ultimately ending the conversation with....
"Whatever you and Cassie decide, is fine by me love."

CHAPTER 43

Sunset had come and gone and the beginnings of a crisp winters night had well and truly settled in. The yard was still lit up with spotlights and the sky seemed lighter, less menacing, having lost most of its cloud cover. A breeze had come up and the heavy front that had been all pervasive over recent days had begun to drift off to the east.

The ground was still very wet but as the rain had stopped for most of the afternoon the grass and stone that separated the stable blocks glinted in the lighting where small pools of water still lay.

They were sitting in Cannons' office. Telside had already completed the final nighttime checks of the stables after asking Cannon if he could do so alone. He wasn't trying to prove anything to his boss, given their conversation earlier, there was no need for that, he just wanted Cannon to rest, and to spend some time with Michelle. Cannon had been grateful for the offer and had told him so. As they chatted briefly about the work done by the various horses that morning and the upcoming race meetings that they had nominated for, they heard the house doorbell ring and Michelle answer it. A few words were said and then footsteps could be heard coming down the hall. A tiny hand knocked on the open door.

"Come in," Cannon said, pointing to the same chair she had sat on many times previously. "How are you?" he asked.

Angela Fryer seemed a little intimidated. She knew that Telside always left for home after evening stables and Cannon himself would normally do a final check for the night, yet here was the old man sitting with Cannon in the office. She wondered why. Telside had told her during the afternoon that his boss wanted to speak with her, but she didn't expect to see them both.

"I'm feeling fine," she answered, trying to hide her nervousness. "Getting stronger every day."

"Strong enough to ride?"

"I think so," she replied, beginning to relax, her body language now more positive. "Is that why you wanted to see me? To let me start doing work again, with the horses I mean."

Cannon looked at Telside who remained stoic, his face set like stone, expressing an element of sadness.

"No, it's about something else."

"What do you mean?" she answered, reverting back to feeling uncomfortable.

"The death of Sue Gladstone."

"I'm sorry?"

"The teacher killed near Boddington Lane."

"What about her?"

"It was you wasn't it?" Cannon said, feeling a tinge of sympathy the moment he made the accusation. "It was you on that motorbike."

For a second, her voice caught in her throat. She looked at the two men, fear showing in her eyes. "No!" she answered finally. "It wasn't me."

Cannon shook his head. "Listen Angela, the police know that it was an accident. They told me that they spoke with you about the missing bike and you told them you didn't know anything about it."

"That's right, I didn't, I don't."

"Really?" Cannon replied, cynically.

"Yes."

Cannon sighed. He had wanted this to be easier. "It's not true though, is it?" he said.

"Sorry?" she queried.

"You not being involved."

"Why do you say that? What makes you think that I was?"

"Nick told me so," Cannon lied. Hoping that his bluff would work.

"What? How?" she said. "When?"

"While you were in hospital after the fall at Chepstow. He left me a message telling me that he would kill me if you died, particular after he found out that you had lost the baby. He said that he loved you and would take the rap for you if the police ever discovered the motorbike, which he knew you had used that day."

"So why didn't you tell the police then?" she challenged, feeling emboldened.

"I had already deleted the message as I thought that he was lying. I had assumed that he was the rider of the bike, but then I remembered something."

"What?" she queried, looking across to Telside for some moral support.

"The day after the motorbike accident, you had a limp and bruises on your leg and your face. You said that it was as a result of a domestic dispute with Nick and that he had hit you."

"It was, and he did." she exclaimed.

"No, it wasn't solely his fists that had caused those injuries, it was also as a result of the crash wasn't it?! You tried to deter me from asking more questions about your injuries, making me think that it was Nick's fault that you were limping, but I knew there must have been something else."

Cannon stopped himself for a second. He wasn't finished with his questions but he knew that he was right with his assertions. Only a few hours earlier he had done to Michelle, exactly what Angela had done to him. He had told his wife that his injuries from what had happened in Scotland were "nothing serious." This was what Angela had said to him when she too was limping the day before her fall at Chepstow. When Michelle had questioned him, Cannon had tried to distract her using the very same expression. He had been trying to tell her not to worry about him, but in reality that was personal subterfuge, a lie and he shouldn't have done it. It was in that instant of quiet remorse that he remembered where he had heard the comment before. It was in that instant that he knew that he had been lied to, and it was then that everything fell into place…

Angela began to cry heavily. While she did so, Cannon was unsure if she was still listening to him, but he continued with his commentary anyway. "The reason the police couldn't find the motorbike is because Nick got rid of it for you, didn't he? Strangely, he was protecting you from them. I think that he *did* love you in his own way."

She looked up at him with tears in eyes which ran down her cheeks and pooled under her chin. Her mouth was set in a grimace of pain. She wailed with grief. Telside moved uncomfortably on his chair.

"I think you argued about the bike," Cannon continued, "perhaps telling him that you wanted to go to the police and report the accident, but he wouldn't have it would he? That's when he hit you, adding insult to your injuries."

"Yes," she said, so softly that both men struggled to hear her. "He didn't want the police around as he believed that they would ask too many questions. He wanted to keep them away. We fought because he said that he didn't want his kid to be born in jail."

"So the easiest thing was to get rid of the bike. He was really trying to help you."

"Yes."

"By pretending that it was stolen."

"Yes."

"But we both know that it wasn't, was it? You see you also told me that he taught you to ride that bike. When I checked with some of the staff they told me that the person who was supposed to take it, Charl Prinsloo, wasn't actually in that day. They said that they had heard you discuss taking the bike with Nick."

"So what do you want me to do?" she asked.

"Do you know what he did with the bike?"

"No, and when the police came and asked me about it, I told them that I had no idea. I didn't then and I still don't. Mr. Cannon, please… I want you to know that what happened was an accident…I swear to you."

Cannon stared at her, his facial expression one of sympathy. He sighed again before sitting back in his chair. Inadvertently he put a hand through his hair, a stabbing pain in his ribs stopped him doing it again.

He contemplated the dilemma they were facing.

"What do you think, Rich?" he asked. The older man shrugged. He knew what should be done but raised an eyebrow letting Cannon know that whatever he decided to do, Telside would support him.

"We need to clear this up with the police," Cannon said, realizing that his long-held principles about right and wrong trumped his sympathy for his young apprentice. He had cautioned her several times about getting involved with Nick and while it had been her choice to make, she needed to accept the consequences of that decision, no matter how understanding he was of her plight. He looked at Telside, "As I said earlier, the police have concluded that Sue Gladstone's death was an accident and that Nick was responsible for it, but now that we know that it Angela was involved then there are a couple of things that they will likely consider after we inform them."

"Like what?" she questioned, fearful of where her confession could lead.

"Well, in the first instance, whether they charge you or not," Cannon replied. "There are a number of issues they will need to look at, including you not stopping to render assistance at the sight of the accident."

"But I didn't know that I had hit anybody at the time. The lights of the car that came from Boddington Lane briefly blinded me, and I thought that I'd hit a fallen tree or something like that. It was only later when the incident was reported and that the police were looking for a motorbike rider that had been on that specific road, at that specific time, that I realized it must have been me. I told Nick about it there and then."

"Well the police may consider his threats as mitigating circumstances and that's why we need to get this sorted out asap. I don't think you, nor I or Rich, could live with ourselves, now that we know what we know, and do nothing about it."

"Not to mention keeping Michelle in the dark," Telside said.

"Exactly," Cannon replied.

Angela was starting to cry again. She had no idea where this could lead. Her future in the racing game relied on integrity. If the authorities took the view that she was untrustworthy, could she end up being banned from racing? For how long? Months? Years? For life? And what would the police's position be? She felt her world was crashing in on her.

"The other thing the police will look at," Cannon continued, "is whether they think you lied to them about the accident because you were under duress from Nick, or whether they think you did so deliberately, intending to pervert the course of justice. You should know that a hit and run normally results in a six-month jail term if you were found guilty."

"Oh my God!" she wailed, "please Mr. Cannon, please, please can you help me?"

Seeing her in the condition she was, and sensing that she had learnt her lesson, Cannon took sympathy on her. He knew that at heart she was a good kid. She worked hard, she was committed to her job and though she had made some life mistakes, he recalled that he and Rich had taken her on as an apprentice, because of the qualities they had both seen in her. She *was* honest. She was kind to the horses she rode and he had no doubt that she would get through whatever punishment she would be subjected to, if indeed she was charged with anything. Ultimately he believed that she would become a better person for it.

"I'll see what I can do," he said, "now go home. I'll make a call to DI Walker in the morning and let's see what he wants to do once I've given him the rundown."

Angela rubbed her eyes, clearing the tears. She ran her hands over her cheeks removing some of the dark trails that had drifted down to her chin. Cannon smiled at her. Her tired face slowly returned to normal, the lines under her eyes and down her cheeks gradually disappearing. She looked to Telside who nodded as if to say, "things will turn out fine." Standing up, she moved forward, her arms spread out wide, making as if to hug Cannon who was still sitting down in his chair, but she stopped a metre in front of him, her face turning red with embarrassment.

"I'm sorry," she said, "I couldn't help myself."

"I understand," Cannon replied. "I understand."

With those words running through her mind, she moved to the office door, opened it and mouthed a "thank you" to them both, then made her way along the passage to the front door of the house.

Telside smiled, the craggy features of his face no longer set in stone. "I think you made the best decision, Mike. We can both act as a character witness for her if she needs, but the police need to be the final arbiters of what to do next."

Cannon responded with a gentle movement of his head, before saying, "You're right Rich. We'll do all that we can to help because I wouldn't like to lose her, even for a short time. Unfortunately it's not up to us."

Placing his hands on his knees, and beginning to get out of his own chair, Telside said, "Well I'd better be off. I'll see you in the morning. Oh, and by the way, thanks for our earlier chat, you don't know how much it meant to me."

"I didn't think you'd do anything else, Rich, but I'm thankful anyway that you made the decision you did. I really am."

"Me too, Mike, me too."

"Goodnight my friend. It's been a big day, get yourself home. I'll see you nice and early tomorrow morning."

He waited until they were lying in bed. It was just over an hour after Telside had left. He told her about the conversation they had had with Angela, and the decision they had taken with regards to the police.

She was upset to hear about Angela being the person involved in Sue Gladstones' death and initially doubted that she would ever be able to look at her in the same light again. However, when he explained what he believed had happened that day and that Van der Linden had prevented Angela from going to the police and reporting the accident, her position changed slightly.

"Do you think she is genuinely remorseful?" she asked him.

He stared at the bedroom ceiling before turning to face her. "Yes I think she is."

"So what do you think Walters will do?"

"I'm not sure."

He turned onto his back. Silence lay between them again. A minute or two passed and he thought that she had fallen asleep.

"What should I tell the school?" she said quietly.

"I don't think you should say anything. Let the truth come out when it will. If the police decide to take matters further, then it will soon become evident, and the school will know," he replied. "As far as you are concerned I know you can't forget what I've told you, but at the same time. Neither you nor I were involved in this."

"I know that Mike, but she was a colleague at school, a friend even."

"And once a syndicate member of a horse I trained," he reminded her.

"Yes."

"And that's just it Michelle. Things happen. Good and bad. Sometimes to us and sometimes to people we know. I'm just grateful that somehow we got through a pretty difficult time recently. Things can only get better from here."

"I hope so," she said.

They both turned off their bedside table lamps. She snuggled into him, placing her arm across his chest.

"Ouch," he said, as his ribs took the weight.

"Are you okay?" she asked.

"Yes, I'm fine."

"Good, then about the wedding," she said, "I got some news…."

CHAPTER 44

DI Walker listened to his story. Conte sat in on the meeting, taking notes as they sat in one of the meeting rooms at Abingdon police station. Cannon had laid out everything he knew and despite him being the original prime suspect in both the death of Van der Linden and Sue Gladstone he held no grudge with his accuser.

When he had finished, Walker took his time to respond.

"You know Mr. Cannon that there is some conjecture in all this."

"Yes."

"That Ms. Fryer could quite easily deny everything you have told us when we get to interview her again."

"She could, but I don't think she will."

"How can you be so sure?" Walker asked.

"Let me put it this way, Inspector. What has she got to lose by being honest?"

"Her liberty, for a while…and her career."

"Assuming she is convicted."

"True, but with her confession, it would make it so much easier to achieve. The DPP would be more than happy for us to prosecute the case, of that I'm sure."

"And what about the mitigations? The attempt to do the right thing? The beatings she received for trying."

"Well, no doubt a court would take that into account."

Cannon felt a little annoyed with Walker's attitude but tried not to show it. He had met many such men before; when he was in the force and after he resigned from it. Sometimes their position of authority or sheer bloody mindedness clouded their judgement, and they focused on themselves and not on what was sensible for the community or body they were supposed to serve. While had didn't condone Angela's actions, he couldn't bring himself to see her future destroyed. He decided to play another card. "I tell you what, Inspector," he said, "as I understand things you already have the killer of Van der Linden in custody, don't you?"

"Yes we do, and we have a least one of the weapons used in his murder," he added, unnecessarily.

"And you now have all the information about the death of Sue

Gladstone."

"Yes. If what you have told me is the truth."

"So given Van der Linden was dead, what had you concluded during your investigation of Ms. Gladstone's death before I came in here this morning.?"

Walker looked across at Conte who had suddenly stopped writing in his notebook. Cannon noticed the exchange and waited for the detective to answer his question.

"I had decided to close the case to be honest. Without the motorbike we could only assume that Nick had lied to us, that he had ridden it himself that day, knocked Ms. Gladstone down and then somehow gotten rid of it. That conclusion however was based on circumstantial evidence but given the few leads we had we decided not to spend any more time on it."

"So that was it. Two crimes solved?"

"Yes."

"So do you want to open one of them up again? A case that may result in no conviction at all?" Cannon asked.

Walker rubbed his chin. He knew that he could be wasting his time, something he had little of, if he decided to pursue another line of inquiry to the Gladstone case. He had other fish to fry, the higher ups having already congratulated him on the results *he* and his team had achieved, but now wanted more. Crime stopped for no man. Walker was sympathetic to Gladstone's passing, no one deserved to die as she did, even if it was an accident. "I think we'll let sleeping dogs lie," he said, eventually. "The file is closed and nothing we do will bring Sue Gladstone back."

"Very pragmatic of you, Inspector."

"There is one thing though, Mr. Cannon."

"Which is?"

"I need you to talk with Ms. Fryer again. Tell her that she needs to be careful with her decisions going forward, and if you can, get her to understand how lucky she is to be indentured to someone like you. Many other people in the same position would have cut her adrift and left her to fight her own battles."

"Agreed Inspector, but I suppose I'm not like many others."

"Indeed you are not, Mike. Indeed you are not."

He let her know what the police had decided to do. The relief she felt was so intense that she broke down in tears, falling into his arms, sobbing uncontrollably for several minutes. Once she had calmed down, he told her that she would be able to start riding work again in a couple of days. Once she was fit, he would put her up to race. He told her that he expected her to start in a race very early in the new year, and that he wanted her to ride White Noise whenever the horse was handicapped with low weights. He explained that in the short term he would still need a more experienced jockey to ride the horse whenever he was given heavier weights to carry, like in some of the feature races when level weights were required....but in time she would become his first choice to ride the gelding.

The Champion Hurdle at Cheltenham was still the target.

EPILOGUE

Angela was well on her way to ride out her claim by the end of the season, only seven wins away from the 50 she needed. Her return to riding and her hunger for it showed and she won a number of races that propelled her to being a star of the future. She won three more times on White Noise but his last run before the Cheltenham meeting March was a disappointment. The horse injured himself and was pulled up when second favourite to a horse that went on to run third in the Champion Hurdle a few weeks later. Cannon was extremely disappointed at the outcome, but took a philosophical view as did Joel Seeton, the owner. Cannon told him that he knew the horse still had improvement in him, and despite the injury had done extremely well during the season. "Any horse that has five wins in seven races, can only be considered a success," he said, when he spoke with Seeton on the phone immediately after the race in which the horse was injured. "The vet doesn't think it is too serious, but it's enough to take him out of training for a while."
"Well there is always next year," Seeton said.
"Which is exactly where my head is at," Cannon replied. "We'll give him the best treatment we can, let him have the summer off and bring him back stronger and better, next season."
"And we'll try again for the Hurdle?" Seeton asked.
"Yes, absolutely, and this time we won't be making up the field. We'll be going out there to make a statement," he answered, positively.

Cassie and Edward Taylors' wedding occurred at the end of the season. A decision was made to hold it in late May. The original date of the 29th of June was amended due to being unable to find a suitable location for that day. It seemed that many of the venues the couple had looked at were either booked out or were too big for the type of reception they wanted. They had decided they wanted a place that gave them a feeling of intimacy and closeness with their immediate family and good friends. Fortunately the weather played ball. It was a warmish day, with little breeze and plenty of sun, which made them forget the wet and miserable winter months the country had endured.

The wedding ceremony took place at St. Giles' church, Oxford, on the Woodstock Road, not far from the stables, which was a Godsend for everyone involved. Cassie was able to dress for the ceremony at the yard, having spent the night there along with her two bridesmaids. Cannon proudly gave her away after taking the short trip to the church in a grey Bentley decked out with white ribbons on the bonnet. Cannon smiled throughout most of the day, including during the speeches made at the reception at Foxcombe Hall in Abingdon, a five-mile journey from the church and ironically just a short distance from the Abingdon police station.

When the festivities were over, the photographs taken, the guests gone and the newlyweds on their way to the Caribbean on their honeymoon, Cannon and Michelle made their way back home and sat together sharing a few laughs as they sat down, both with a cup of tea.

"What a beautiful wedding," she said, kicking off her shoes and curling up onto the couch opposite him.

"Yes, they were very lucky with the weather, and the venue was great," he replied.

Sighing, she said, "I think they'll be very happy together."

"I'm sure they will."

She stared at him for a few seconds. He didn't notice as he had closed his eyes, the days experience finally tiring him. He wasn't used to being awake so close to midnight anymore. She smiled, not wanting the day to end, then said, "Oh, those flowers in the church were lovely too. It really made the place look nice, don't you think?"

He opened his eyes slowly, "I suppose we can thank the taxman for that," he said, "or Plumberry's."

"Well whoever it was, they did look really lovely."

"Just like you do, my darling."

"Flattery, Mr. Cannon will get you everywhere," she joked.

"Good," he said, "let's go to bed."

ABOUT THE AUTHOR

Other books in the Mike Cannon series:

- *Death on the Course*
- *After the Fire*
- *Death always Follows*
- *Death by Stealth*
- *Death never Forgets*

Books in the DI Brierly series

- *Killing Mr. D (under pseudonym – Saul Friedmann)*
- *Damaged (under own name but writing as Saul Friedmann)*

A former Accountant with a lifelong love of horseracing. He has lived on three continents and has been passionate about the sport wherever he resided. Having grown up in England he was educated in South Africa where he played soccer professionally. Moving to Australia, he expanded his love for racing by becoming a syndicate member in several racehorses.

In addition, he began a hobby that quickly became extremely successful, that of making award-winning red wine with a close friend.

In mid-2014 he moved with his employer to England for just over four years, during which time he became a member of the British Racing Club (BRC).

He has now moved back to Australia, where he continues to write, and also presents a regular music show on local community radio.

He shares his life with his beautiful wife Rebecca.

He has two sons, one who lives in the UK and one who lives in Australia. This is his sixth novel in the Mike Cannon series.

Printed in Great Britain
by Amazon